More Exuberant Praise for
Shadows and Elephants

"**A generous and lively novel.** Hower's knowledgeable enchantment with an enchanted India illuminates this exploration of the peculiar mental and emotional life of the notorious Madame Blavatsky as she seeks enlightenment in a land that in no way takes her seriously. "
—Joy Williams, Author of *The Quick and the Dead*

"**Edward Hower's *Shadows and Elephants* is one of the most engrossing novels I've read in the past few years**, and is certainly the most engaging—and entertaining—novel I've read in quite some time. Given the present rise in spiritual concerns, connected as they are with questions about the sterility of materialistic culture, Hower's superb fictional evocation of the world of Madame Blavatsky and Colonel Henry Olcott has a special pertinency today. In describing them and their milieu, he manages a rare combination of comic irony and sympathetic understanding: the wry attitude which a tolerant Deity might feel, upon examining the record to date of the human race. Hilarious as the novel frequently is, it also takes us into the deeper regions of the psyche. *Shadows and Elephants* grows in emotional intensity as it proceeds, and provides a resolution that strikes me as so inspired I'm almost inclined to believe that unseen spirits moved the author."
—James McConkey, Professor of English, Cornell University

"In *Shadows and Elephants*, I got that genuine imaginative uplift that only good fiction can give."
—Lamar Herrin, Winner, Associated Writing Program Award for the Novel

Shadows and Elephants

Also by Edward Hower

Queen of the Silver Dollar
Night Train Blues
Wolf Tickets
The New Life Hotel
The Pomegranate Princess and Other Tales from India

Shadows
and
Elephants

Edward Hower

Leapfrog Press

Published in 2002 in the United States by
The Leapfrog Press
P.O. Box 1495
95 Commercial Street
Wellfleet, MA 02667-1495, USA
www.leapfrogpress.com

Printed in Canada

Distributed in the United States by
Consortium Book Sales and Distribution
St. Paul, Minnesota 55114

First Edition

The characters and events in this book are fictitious. Any similarity to actual
persons, living or dead, is coincidental and not intended by the author.

Library of Congress Cataloging-in-Publication Data

Hower, Edward.
    Shadows and elephants : a novel / by Edward Hower.--1st ed.
       p. cm.
    ISBN 0-9679520-3-4 (alk. paper)
1. United States--History--Civil War, 1861-1865--Veterans--Fiction.
2. Women mediums--Fiction. 3. Spiritualists--Fiction. 4. Journalists--Fiction. 5.
New York (N.Y.)--Fiction. 6. Bombay (India)--Fiction.
7. Sri Lanka--Fiction. I. Title.

 PS3558.O914 S53 2002
 813'.54—dc21

                                                        2001038082

10 9 8 7 6 5 4 3 2 1

For Alison

Part One

America

1

Ben strode among the spiritualists, watching and listening, his pipe puffing impatiently, but he heard only the same old gossip about ghosts. Like an agnostic at a church picnic, he was poised for flight. The seekers at the plank tables were a sober-sided crowd, the men in gray suits, the women in faded dresses, and instead of astral visitors, they might have been expecting a wagon-load of relatives to come rattling down the road from the next village.

Then, at the far end of the farmhouse yard, Ben saw a patch of color flicker like a sunspot, a woman in a long gypsy skirt and a blue velvet blouse that twinkled with jeweled pins. Over her head she held a blue umbrella as if she were expecting turbulent weather. Her figure was delightfully operatic; her round face was fringed by fleecy brown hair. As Ben drew nearer, she took some tobacco and paper from an antique leather pouch. Her fingers moved so quickly that he couldn't detect the stages in the process; without glancing down, she rolled a cigarette with one hand. Then she raised her eyes directly at him, as if she'd always known he'd be there. He reached into his jacket pocket for his matches.

"Permit me, please."

Gazing up, she touched her cigarette to the flame. Her eyes were astonishing: enormous, heavy-lidded, and blue as radiant blue marbles. "Thank you," she said.

Ben hadn't seen American women smoking in public, but he knew that it was the custom among aristocratic ladies in Europe. This woman's rings and pins were of sparkly glass, though—costume jewelry, all of it—and her cuffs were badly frayed. Yet she looked cultured, intelligent. She was in her mid thirties, Ben judged, a few years younger than he was.

"Madame." He tipped his hat. "What's brought you here to-day?"

"I read in a newspaper about the séances." A smile crossed her face. "But I hesitated to come. I was afraid that Captain Benjamin Blackburn might drag me into his next article."

She pulled a copy of the *New York Daily Graphic* from her cloth handbag. On its front page, a box announced that Ben was to cover one of the "spook shows" that had been attracting flocks of spiritualists to this upstate village all summer. His articles, the paper reported, had already been compiled in a best-selling book, *Shadows of the Other World*. The sketch showed him as a tall, barrel-chested man with side-whiskers, pince-nez, and a well-tailored tan suit. His hair was swept back from his forehead as if he were charging into a high wind. His eyes held an expression of intense longing that he'd never seen before, until this woman held up the picture to him.

"You needn't worry, Madame," Ben said, "As you've seen, I'm Ben Blackburn, at your service. I won't write about you unless you allow it."

"I am glad finally to meet you. My name is Irena Milanova." She gazed up at him. "I think, Captain, you would like to sit down?"

He did, taking out his notebook. Soon, with her permission, he was scribbling down her story. She was Russian; having resided in many countries, she had recently settled in New York City. She wouldn't say where in the city she lived, or how she supported herself there.

"And may I ask," Ben said, "what you think of American spiritualism?"

She leaned forward, lightly touching his arm. "Flapdoodle," she said.

He smiled. "How so?"

"I suspect that many mediums here—how do you say it?—gild the lily." Holding her palms together, she parted her fingertips, making a graceful flower in the air. "I can tell this is so, because I have witnessed true communications with the other world." She folded the lily back onto her lap. "Often in India, which is the most spiritual of countries, I observed powerful ascended Masters at work. But I fear that people in America take spiritual events as mere entertainment!"

"Exactly!" Ben stared at her.

Irena released a long silver plume of smoke from her lips. "I can observe that you are in some despair about this yourself."

"It's true." Ben sighed. "You must be clairvoyant."

She smiled. "I have been called many things."

With his sons grown, his marriage dissolved years ago, and his prosperous law practice dwindling though his lack of interest, Ben finally had a chance to indulge his life-long passion for spiritual science. The old occult tomes he read were brilliant stuff, and if he could have interviewed their authors, he would have enjoyed becoming their modern-day prophet. But in America in 1874, the practitioners of ancient wisdom often seemed no more enlightened than circus barkers.

"You are a 'famed investigator,' according to your newspaper." Madame Milanova's voice was soft, like the velvet of her blouse, but darker. "You successfully discover corruption among mediums and conjurers. And yet. . . ."

Ben gazed out across the fields at the distant hills that were turning hazy purple with autumn. "And yet I long to find something more, something real."

She watched him, her eyes glowing blue. "You know, I never expected to meet anyone here who understands this kind of struggle so well."

"I was beginning to doubt that I would, either."

"Perhaps, at long last, I may acquire . . ." Her hand moved in the air as if seeking the right word. ". . . a chum!" She closed her thumb and fingertips together.

Ben beamed. He'd had many cronies but never had a "chum", someone he could share his radical ideas with. Now he listened as torrents of words gushed forth from Madame Milanova: descriptions of Indian fakirs and Byzantine dervishes; quotations from the Hindu and Buddhist texts on every subject. Ben put down his pencil—taking notes would be like trying to record the sound of a river as it surged past him, revealing glimpses of treasures snatched from banks of the fabled lands it passed through.

Suddenly a woman clanked a cowbell from the doorway across the yard. The program was about to begin. Irena pointed her furled umbrella toward the farmhouse door. "Shall we make our entrance, *Mon Capitain?*"

Ben rose, sighing. "I doubt if anything miraculous is going to happen."

"Don't be too sure," she said, and took his arm.

Feet thundered on the floorboards overhead as Ben and Irena climbed the stairs. They entered a long room where rows of wooden benches faced a homemade plank stage. Dyed black sheets were draped over the windows, giving the air a murky tint. Ben found two seats in the front row. The farm owner's wife played a parlor organ near the stage. When everyone had sat down, singing commenced.

> *Speeding through the air, ever in the night,*
> *Come the Angel Band from their homes of light!*

A clergyman with fuzzy white chin-whiskers stepped forward. "Let us welcome the unseen visitors who are hovering near," he intoned, raising his face to the rafter. "I know they are as eager to materialize as their friends below are to greet them." The friends below said quiet amens.

Ben watched some children set out tables, chairs, crockery, and musical instruments on the platform for the expected guests. Sitting forward, his chin in his hands, he suddenly recalled the rural theater where, at age eighteen, he'd played in *The Tempest* for twenty Saturdays– the wizard Prospero, in majestic robes and turban. Orphaned that year, he had three sisters to support, and this was to be his last theatrical performance. He wrote newspaper articles by lamplight, studied to pass his bar examination, and by day struggled to keep the farm going. His success had come rapidly. Decorated during early battles in the war, he'd been appointed by General Grant to investigate fraud among suppliers to the Union Army. Later, President Johnson had asked him to lead the inquiry into the assassination of Abraham Lincoln. But then, his task completed, he left Washington abruptly, refusing to explain why he was giving up a brilliant future in politics. His life in Gilded Age New York looked successful enough to satisfy most men. But not Ben; how empty it appeared now, compared to his earlier artistic triumph.

Two white curtains closed across the front of the stage, and all but one of the lamps were blown out. The audience hushed. The near darkness grew agitated with the fluttering of ladies' fans. The air was heavy with the smell of lamp oil and sweat. Nothing happened.

"I abhor a vacuum," Irena whispered to Ben.

"I know what you mean," he said.

Suddenly a faint glow appeared behind the curtain, becoming brighter like a moon rising behind a cloud. Into the glow stepped a dark-skinned woman in braids and a tasseled buckskin dress. "I am Tanta, a princess of the Iroquois Nation!" She spoke in a quavery voice. "I was murdered near this village a century ago, but I have returned. . . ." Ben watched her move to the beat of an unseen tom-tom. Her long dancing shadow flickered against the curtain. Now her ankles, her calves, even . . . here some ladies twittered, gentlemen quickened their breaths . . . even her naked knees became visible below her swirling skirt. One by one she pulled silk scarves from her bodice and tossed them into the air; the audience sighed as the cloths fluttered down in a circle around her like a flock of trained birds.

Tanta was a "gatekeeper spirit," as she put it, able to invite spirits to possess her and speak through her lips to members of the audience. Tanta's eyes went white, her pupils all but vanishing as she gazed upwards to channel voices from the next world. She brought messages to parents from children who had died, their voices piping about the glades and glens of Summerland—the Afterworld—where they now gamboled cheerfully. Ben heard husbands killed in the Civil War speak lovingly to their widows. Women sent messages of hope to relatives left behind on the Earthly Plain.

"A lady . . . Mary . . . she wishes to speak to someone!" Tanta whispered from the stage.

Ben clenched his fists at his sides. For years he'd tried to contact a woman called Mary, but he'd never heard anything resembling her sad voice from the lips of spirit mediums. Recently he'd given up his attempts. As it was, he saw her suspended often enough in the darkness of his dreams.

Someone behind him asked for the message from "Mary"—a common enough name—and again the voice Ben heard was alien to him. Finally, looking wan, Tanta wafted from the platform. Lamps were lit behind the curtain, making a pale white glow in which shadowy figures were silhouetted. Ben heard music—an unseen figure was strumming a mandolin. As Irena lean closer to him, he inhaled the strange, incense-like scent of her perfume. It seemed to clear his head of shadows.

The curtains parted with a whoosh, and a squadron of frontiersmen spirits in coonskin caps marched onto the stage, carrying muskets on their shoulders. Two apparitions dressed as swarthy Gypsy girls followed with tambourines. A dozen more astral beings clothed in gauzy white garments arranged themselves on a raft and gave a stirring rendition of the popular song "Storms at Sea." An orchestra of concertinas and brightly tinkling dinner bells accompanied it. Waves of light undulated across the stage. Several spirits in gossamer nighties danced through the breakers. The Gypsies went into a frenzied crescendo of crashing tambourines.

The lamplight faded. Spirits swished off into the shadows, and the curtains whipped shut again. The organist played louder than before as if trying to drown out noises, or footsteps Ben suspected, and he pictured a procession of actors behind the curtain clambering out a second story window and down a ladder. The farm owner, a hulking man in a black suit, stepped onto the stage.

"Friends," he announced, "our spirit guests have all returned to the Astral Plain—"

"Oh, no, they haven't!" Irena rose from her seat, pointing to a bulge in the curtain. "I espy a fraudulent foot!"

The bulge vanished, but not before she had rushed forward and grabbed hold of something just below the bottom of the curtain. It kicked her hard in the knee, but she didn't let go. Ben heard gasps and shouts from the audience. The light flickered wildly. Unseen things toppled and skidded. Through all the commotion, Irena kept her grip on the foot's bulging shape. Now both curtains were flapping like topsails in a hurricane. Out of the shadows above them an ectoplasymically white hand rose, gripping a mandolin. The instrument glided forward until it was floating directly over Irena's head.

"Watch out!" Ben lunged from his seat. The mandolin retreated into the shadows. Irena fell back against him—a soft but powerful sensation—and he had to hold her around the waist to keep her from falling.

The room went black. Ben heard women crying out in the audience, children wailing. He lit a match, and in a moment other little flames flared up around the room. The curtains had collapsed to the platform. All across the boards, tables and chairs lay with their legs in the air. Shards of broken china were strewn everywhere. The round-bellied mandolin lay sprawled on its side like a headless armadillo, its long neck broken, its wire nerves tangled.

Ben saw several people give Irena angry looks. A man spat an arc of tobacco juice onto the floor at her feet. She drew closer to Ben. Jumping onto a bench, he raised his arms in the air. "Everyone . . . stand back! Calm down!" His voice boomed above the noise. "The lady's intentions were the best. There's no cause for alarm."

The people turned toward him as he gazed solemnly around the room. Grumbling and whispering ceased. Finally he broadcast a warm smile. "Young man. . . ." He gestured toward a boy in a cloth cap. "Can you take charge of a work brigade; get some fellows to straighten up the furniture?"

"Yes, sir!" The boy saluted.

"And you ladies?" He turned toward three teenagers, who quickly began to pick up the broken crockery. Glancing down, he saw a little girl standing close to Irena, her hair falling to her shoulders in long black waves. "Would you like to help?" he asked her.

She nodded and wiped her eyes. "Will they ever come back?" she asked, pointing to the empty stage.

Irena shot him a look; one he would remember all his life.

"We'll see," he said. Suddenly he felt like an accomplice. But how could he fail to be delighted with the girl's smile, and Irena's?

Ben stepped out the farmhouse door into the fresh air, feeling as if the earth had been transformed while he'd been far, far away. The yard was silent and empty; the sky had turned blue-black. A harvest moon rose onto the shoulder of the hills to gaze across the fields, illuminating Irena's face in its orange glow. Ben waited with her for the wagon that was to take some of the visitors to the train station. He himself had hired a one-seater gig; he'd left it in a nearby barn for the day.

"Well, thanks to you, I won't have to file the same old story," he said.

"I'm glad you were inspired." She smiled. "But now I must leave you." Still limping from the pain in her knee where she'd been kicked, she stepped toward the road. A team and wagon were waiting there for passengers to the local train station.

"Madame Milanova. Here's my card," Ben said, handing her one from his case. He waited for her card in return.

Instead, she extended her hand. "Good night, Captain Blackburn," she said. "And thank you for rescuing me so eloquently."

"A pleasure. Who'd have thought there were so many hazards in the spirit world?" Holding her hand—graceful, soft, and plump it was—he wondered if he should follow the European custom and kiss it. Something about her invited it. But something didn't. "How will I contact you?" he asked.

"If it is to be . . . you will find a way." Her hand slipped unkissed from his grip.

Then she was gone, hurrying across the grass.

Ben strolled back to the farmhouse yard and sat at a table. Lighting his pipe, he watched a swirl of smoke rise like a dervish and dance away on the breeze. A sound of voices came from the road: men and women climbing into the wagon. He heard Irena's laughter as she squeezed in. Wheels creaked; the clopping of horses' hooves gradually grew fainter. Up, up, the wagon rolled along the crest of the black hill in the lunar light. A dust cloud billowed behind it like a veil of sparks. Ben sat back, facing the strange orange moon, puffing dervishes into the air.

2

When Irena read Captain Blackburn's piece about her in the next evening's *Daily Graphic*, she could forget the squalor of the boarding house she shared with twenty other Russian immigrants and ignore the view of ash heaps from her window. If she opened it, she let in the winds that screeched up the narrow alley like transparent dragons. But if she shut it, she suffocated in her own fireplace smoke and her dark, smoky thoughts.

The girl from down the hall looked over her shoulder as she read. Her name was Sarah, a slim, red-haired nine-year old whose smile tilted at one corner, making a dimple. Her braids bobbed as she bounced on the balls of her feet. "That's you!" Sarah pointed to the artist's sketch.

Irena laughed. "The artist had only the Captain's descriptions to go on." She stared at the exotic woman on the page. "Good heavens, that must be the way Ben sees me!"

"My mother thinks the Captain likes you a lot." Sarah leaned closer, her cheek resting against Irena's shoulder. "She says our bad days are about to end!"

Now that she'd been profiled in the press, Irena could sell her own articles to American newspapers as she occasionally did to ones in Moscow. She started with an article about the Great Brotherhood of Masters who preserved ancient wisdom in subterranean libraries of remote Himalayan temples; she described them so vividly that she seemed to have visited them herself.

When the article appeared in print, it incited a war of words among New York's many experts in the field of spiritual science.

Each time she was attacked, she shot back a passionate defense. Now journalists from every paper wanted to interview her. They left messages with the *Graphic's* editors, but her replies (taken to the office by Sarah) never included her address. She refused to tell Ben where she lived, too, though she corresponded with him almost daily via the newspaper office. More articles about her Indian mentors—the fatherly, gray-bearded Master Moreya and the roguish black-bearded Master Kut-huri—appeared in print. Like the great sages of Atlantis and Alexandria, they communicated with a few mortal adepts, such as herself, via astral currents, which were known in the West as telepathic energy. "Moreya," she wrote to Ben, "may be looking for an apprentice, a *chela*. I have suggested you as a candidate."

"I'm eager to hear from him," Ben wrote back. Meanwhile he turned out more articles.

The Great Controversy
by
Captain Benjamin Blackburn

In farmhouses and tenements, in churches and parlors all across the country, a great revival of spiritualism is taking place. I'm often asked, why? I believe it's a reaction against the disturbing ideas of materialist scientists like Charles Darwin. According to them, human life originated in an ape-filled jungle that was governed not by divine laws but by a creed called "evolution." I have met intellectually enlightened men who are in favor of this new theory. But I've also found others who say that it removes all hope for spiritual solutions to man's problems. Whose word can one trust? Most public figures today are zealots for either religion or science. Few are visionary enough to see that, in our exciting new age, the two fields of endeavor will inevitably be synthesized into one. I'm certain that physicists will soon discover ways to transmit wireless messages around the globe via astral currents. And one day experts will invent a device that can summon the voices—perhaps even the visual images!—of persons whose corporal selves are no longer among us. The movement cries out for a man of unimpeachable integrity to investigate its findings and validate its claims. . . .

To Irena, it was clear that the Captain has already decided who that man would be. She concurred.

If only she were better able to help him! Her health was bad, her financial prospects even worse. Since her arrival in America a year ago, she'd worked along with Sarah and her sickly mother, Natasha, in a basement factory on the Bowerie where she was paid eleven cents an hour to make decorative silk flowers out of cut-up silk gowns—the sort of lavish dresses she had reluctantly worn to balls as an adolescent. But since being kicked in the knee at the spook show, she'd been unable to work. Along with Sarah and her mother, whom she'd been helping, she was faced with eviction. Again she turned to journalism, creating herself yet another time for a new audience.

A Baptism of Fire
by
Madame Irena Milanova

Readers will recall the true tales I have told of astral beings I have met on my journeys. But never before have I revealed the story of my very first encounter with the Other World.

On the day of my christening in 1845, an ascended Master named Moreya entered the ancient stone chapel on my family's estate near Kiev. There, for the first time, He heard my voice: not the sound of an ordinary child, He told me years later, but "a yowl tremulous with yearning for more than material comfort." Rising, my cry burned through the frozen air, and a tree full of ravens exploded like ink into the white sky.

Moreya searched the pews for me. He was a swarthy man with glowing eyes and a salt-and-pepper beard. His superiors had sent Him to Russia from an assignment in India; He still wore a white turban, long flowing robe, and camel-hide slippers. He was, of course, invisible except to children and a few elderly household servants.

The odors of incense and piety made Moreya's nostrils twitch. Black-robed priests scuttled by. A consumptive organ exhaled chords. Banks of candles gave off a yellow glare but no warmth. Near the baptismal font stood gentlemen wearing frock coats, shiny boots, monocles, mustaches. Ladies in furs and bulky dresses shivered in the gloom. Child relatives, confined by tight Sunday outfits, whined and tormented their nurses.

Also present was a host of *diakka*, or astral beings. A gaggle of apprentice angels admired their likenesses in the stained glass windows. Trolls and needle-nosed fairies played among the shadows that groped up the walls. And near the font stood a *domovoy*, a little hairy man who lived behind the kitchen stove in the family's mansion. Ordinarily such beings are content with souring the milk and scorching the pots, but this one looked as if he had a more drastic action in mind. Behind his whiskers, his eyes burned with a strange restlessness.

Suddenly voices hushed. All faces turned toward the chapel's center aisle. The child, Irena, was coming. I rode in the arms of my nurse, kicking and thrashing. Many of the people had been expecting a mere babe, but various family illnesses had forced postponements of the christening, and I was now a plump, curly-headed, round-faced little girl of four. It was obvious from my struggling that I was already far too independent to want anyone to carry me, especially to a destination I hadn't chosen myself. Moreya was enchanted with me. What an adorable creature, He thought. Such beautiful, bright round blue eyes! But I had been stuffed into a long, lacy dress that He could tell constrained me beyond endurance. The nurse passed me to a white-haired priest, a sinewy old bird whose grip seemed to me even tighter than my clothing. I began to yowl again. To Moreya's occultly trained ears, my shrieks were glorious melodies. They sliced through the organ's groans like bold scimitar strokes; they scratched wild calligraphy into the frosted windows. My face glowed red like a radiant sunrise, and not at all like a baby pig, as Moreya heard one elderly countess whisper. He nearly cuffed the crone.

The priest, his bony hand clamped over my mouth, moved slowly toward the altar where the glow from hundreds of flickering tapers caused the air to vibrate as if in a state of ecstasy. Then, as used to be the custom in the Russian church, the cleric performed an ancient ritual to cast out the evil eye from a consecrated place. He spat into the air. The moment the saliva shot from his lips, there was an astral commotion. Fairies stampeded down the aisle. Angels fluttered against the windows like trapped moths. A pair of trolls who had been copulating behind a stack of hymnals fled through the nearest doorway. But the *domovoy*, shielding his eyes, held his ground.

To me, the priestly effluvia that splashed against my cheek felt like a spray of acid. My screams clawed at the cleric's face and caused the racks of candle flames to ripple like a golden wheat field blasted by a storm. Gasping for breath, I stared forlornly about in search of someone to rescue me. But who? My father was far away on military business, as usual. My mother, a slender nineteen-year-old girl, was gazing dreamily through a window. I had not yet spotted Moreya.

The priest set me down in an empty pew as he greeted the baptismal sponsors. At first I looked as if I might bolt. Then I turned my face toward the *domovoy* and exchanged glances with him. I eased myself off the pew, toddled across the floor, and sat near the altar on the cold, flat stone. From there, I could reach out and pluck a taper from the bottom row of the rack. For a few moments I held it in my lap, as if gazing deeply into the source of the flame's energy. Then, as the *domovoy* slipped out a side exit, I raised the candle high over my head.

Several guests began to notice me now. I must have seemed to them a cherubic statue. More people turned toward me, smiles breaking across their faces. My visage remained somber, my arm swaying slowly in the air as if I were waving a fiery wand. Then, as I became the center of attention for almost the entire church, my features relaxed into an expression of beatific glee.

Among the few people who hadn't yet noticed me was the white-haired priest, who had his back to me and was still greeting relatives. As he bowed and smiled, he moved backwards toward the altar, one step, then another, then another. Intent as I was upon absorbing the adoration of my first big audience, I did not see him until he had backed right into my swaying candle. The flame took a big bite from the hem of his robe.

From the pews, the faces of the children grew animated as the pretty yellow blaze blew sideways, sharing its flames with other dark-robed men. Thrilling screams echoed everywhere. Adults scattered. Billows of smoke flapped in the air like gigantic black wings. One of the youngest of the priests, perhaps unaware that his lower parts were smoking, snatched me up. Then, his eyes filling with panic, he tottered beside the font as the turmoil swirled around him. I pummeled his chest with my tiny fists.

Masters do not normally intervene directly in mortals' karma, as my readers know, but Moreya could not just stand by and let me be roasted in the arms of that priest. So He whispered in the man's ear: "Drop her, you fool!"

Splash! I landed on my bottom in the baptismal font.

Someone threw a cloak over the priest as he collapsed in flames to the floor. Children were yanked toward the door. Men barked orders. Women wailed. The scent of scorched clerics wafted through the air.

Sitting in the font, my plump legs kicking, I gurgled prettily. Eventually, when all the fires had been extinguished, another priest fished me out of the little stone tub. As I rose dripping from the water, I reached out both hands and gave a little cry. A chuckle, some said later. An ominous cackle, the priest insisted.

But, I assure my readers, it was merely a cry of recognition: I had seen Moreya's face for the first time.

"Will you be my guardian?" I whispered to the Master. "Will you stay with me always?"

"Always," He replied.

And He did. From that day on. I became a labor of love for Him, He told me in later years, a challenge that would test the limits of His vast and fabulous powers.

The money she earned for the article didn't last long. As sick as she was, she went back to the factory. Then limping home down Madison Street with Sarah, who also worked in the factory, Irena stared up at the web of telegraph lines strung across the gap between buildings. A drizzle floated down, making the wires drip as if weeping from an overload of sorrowful messages. She was used to thinking of herself as a benign spider tugging on gossamer threads to help pilgrims toward the center of the universal network of spiritual wisdom. But today she felt like a mere fly about to be strangled in the web of poverty that connected every tenement in the city. Wagons rumbled over the wet cobblestones. A filthy rag picker lunged past with his enormous bag on his shoulder like a Father Christmas of the Damned. The smells of horse droppings and roasting potatoes mingled strangely in the air. Sarah paused to stare into the doorway of a livery stable, where three newsboys slept curled around each other like cats among the hay bales. Did the poor girl fear that she, too, would soon be a homeless orphan? Irena held her hand.

"Look!" the girl said, gazing up. Dangling over the storefronts hung big painted likenesses of the wares being sold: a wooden shoe as big as a rowboat, a hat the size of an upside-down cauldron, a tin corset that imprisoned the invisible torso of a giantess. And over the door of an exterminator—where Sarah was pointing—hung a dog-sized gray rat made of wood. "One of those ran across my bed last night," she said.

Irena shuddered, recalling the vermin in the filthy hotels of Europe and Asia where she'd lived. She jabbed the top of her umbrella at the wooden rat, but it just swung back and forth, its greasy leather tail brushing against the blue silk with a hideous sound. Suddenly she scooped up Sarah in her arms. "We can't go on," she cried. "I have to change our fortune!"

Alone in her room, she locked the door and sat at her desk with her mixture of Turkish tobacco and Moroccan hashish. As in the past, she saw Moreya's kind, dark eyes flash from the clouds of smoke. Often, as his spirit possessed her, she had seen ink smears form into bright artistic diagrams of airships swooping in astral trajectories; she had watched confused word-knots untangle and flow effortlessly forth in graceful sentences of luminous truth. Tonight, though, the words were simpler:

CAPTAIN BENJAMIN BLACKBURN—MASTER MOREYA GREETS YOU.
SISTER IRENA HAS CONVINCED ME TO SELECT YOU AS MY APPRENTICE.
GO TO HER NOW. . . .

3

Though he'd visited New York's Lower East Side before, Ben was appalled that a woman like Irena had to live in such dreary surroundings. Odorous piles of manure shared the gutters with coal-ash barrels. Wagonmen carried slabs of bacon into the basement-level shops along the rows of tenements. Ben watched an old woman snatch a greenish slab of bread from a heap of garbage and press it to her mouth. When some boys sitting on a stoop hooted at Ben's fine clothes—his brown suit, long greatcoat, and beaver hat—he strode into their midst and left them all holding coins, waving to him as he walked on through the crowd.

He had to bang loudly on the door to #15 Madison Street before the little red-haired girl, Sarah, opened it to let him in. Smiling, he tipped his hat to her. "That's a lovely ribbon you've got," he said to Sarah. "The green matches your eyes."

"Madame Irena gave it to me." Sarah touched her hair. "She said for you to come with me."

The girl led him up a narrow staircase where the smell of stale cabbage hung in the air. As she raised her small fist to knock on Irena's door, it opened, and a tubby little man pushed past Ben with an empty metal cage under his arm. Sarah fled.

An amber glow spilled out of Irena's room. Stepping inside, Ben suddenly felt addled with exhaustion; for thirty hours, as Moreya's letter had commanded, he had eaten nothing. Irena reclined on her bed in a nest of bedclothes and red velvet cushions that might have been auctioned off by an opera house. Surrounded by swirls of strange-scented cigarette smoke, she wore a long, black, fur-trimmed overcoat over her nightgown. In the flickering light from the grate, her face was pale and round as a weary moon's, but Ben was moved by the warmth of her damp blue eyes.

Smiling, she reached out her hand. "Thank you for coming, my dear chum," she said.

"How could I refuse?" He took her hand in his, sitting in the armchair beside her bed. "Are you feeling any better?"

"In less pain now than before you came. My first doctor said I was almost ready to 'kick the bucket'," She smiled. "My leg was so dark and swollen I thought he would want to chop it off, but I told him, 'Mortification and sugar plums, I won't have it! Imagine my father's daughter on a wooden leg!'" She was interrupted by a whimpering noise. On her lap lay a small black puppy.

"Good Lord! What's that dog doing here?" Ben asked.

"He was brought by the second doctor, the man who just left. Do not worry so! My little friend is draining off the poison, a living poultice." She hugged the dog tight to her belly. It let out a yelp.

"Must be an experimental treatment," Ben said. When Irena handed him her tobacco pouch, he filled his pipe and lit it. Something deep in his chest began to glow like a live coal. "I haven't seen you in several weeks, Irena," he said, "yet I feel we're resuming a conversation that was interrupted only a minute ago."

"I too have that impression. But I am embarrassed that Moreya ordered you to visit me in this foul place. I have not always lived this way."

"I've assumed that you're a lady."

"Yes, I am more than I appear. And sometimes less, I am afraid." Irena half closed her eyes. "My mother thought me less . . . shall I tell you?"

"All right. Do you want me to write it down?"

"No, no. This evening is only for the two of us."

Evening? It had been late afternoon when he'd arrived, Ben thought. Probably Irena had lost track of time, with the thick curtains drawn, the lamplight flickering. He pulled his armchair closer to her. On the cluttered table beside Irena's bed were silver-framed oval photographs: a mustachioed man in a military uniform, a slim young woman with long, yellow tresses.

"My father...my mother," Irena said, pointing to them. Her mother, she said, had been a famous writer of romantic novels; much too busy to be encumbered with a difficult daughter. Irena adored her father, a distant relative of the Czar and a general in his army, but she rarely saw him. Lonely and forlorn, she fled the family's cold mansion to take refuge in the cottages of the family's serfs. Crossroads were haunted by invisible demons, they said; but over her bed angels spread their wings in luminous canopies. "In the forest at night, gauzy silver mosses hung from the tree boughs," Irena whispered. Her hand rose slowly from the bed-clothes. "If I reached out to touch them, they would dissolve with a faint crackling sound, like moonbeams."

"Ah." Ben closed his eyes. As he inhaled the fragrant pipe smoke, he felt the inside of his nostrils expanding pleasantly. For all her dishevelment, Irena was beginning to glow beautifully.

Occasionally, she said, her parents tried to confine her to the nursery with her English governess. They gave her frilly, vapid-faced dolls—to be models of what she should become, she suspected. "I buried them in the flower garden, at night," she said. Often she wandered unattended among her grandfather's occult books in the mansion's library. It became her haven; the smell of old paper calmed her. Her favorite picture there was a reproduction of Gurov's *Ascension of the Virgin.* Wearing layers of colorful robes, a lovely, round-faced woman was suspended on a chair as she rose into a silvery sky; from among the clouds, bearded patriarchs supervised her flight, and below, gathered at the edge of a sea, adoring crowds gazed up at her. "I was not at all a religious child, though," Irena said. "I was an unholy terror at times." A peasant boy on her family's estate, she said, heard Irena's cousins call her bad names and thought that he could, too. As she tried to read beside a river, Irena begged him to stop. Finally, reduced to tears, she threatened to call a *roussalka*—one of the water sprites that lived beside Russian streams. "She is going to strangle you with her green hair!" Irena screamed, making her eyes huge. The poor boy cried out in terror and ran blindly along the river bank out of view. Later that afternoon, she saw peasants drag his sodden corpse from the water. She wept inconsolably.

Irena fled to her grandfather's library, searching in the great, musty books for she knew not what. And then she saw him—the tall man with the kindly eyes, the gray beard, the white robe and turban—and heard his voice for the first time since her baptism. "You never meant to harm that child, or anyone else," he said, "You are absolved of all blame, now and forever."

"That was...Moreya?" Ben asked.

"Himself." Irena sat up. "He told me I must promise to use my spiritual powers only to help people in their struggles against the rich and powerful, never for selfish purposes. And I did promise."

Irena turned her gaze slowly toward Ben; he thought he saw a mischievous glint in her eyes. "But now that I had discovered I could call forth these spirit beings, I was like a child with a magic lamp," she said. "How could I keep from rubbing it?"

Ben finished his pipe. Irena dozed off as peacefully as the puppy that lay against her thigh. Ben, too, slept, for how long he couldn't have said. When he blinked open his eyes, the room, so stiflingly hot before, was as chilly as if a sun had set in his absence. The walls seemed closer; the ceiling seemed curved. *Like a dungeon*, he thought. But apparently he'd spoken aloud, for Irena stirred in her bed.

"I think that you feel endungeoned at times," she said, lighting a cigarette. "Memory is your jailer."

Ben felt tears welling up in his eyes. "Like you, I remember things...." Again he felt her blue gaze penetrating the clouds of smoke; he floated into the gaze, buoyed up, no longer sinking.

"I see a dark corridor." Irena pressed her fingertips to her forehead. "I see a cell . . . a woman who believed fervently in a cause. . . ."

"Yes," he said. The woman, illuminated like an image in a magic lantern show, was vivid now. Her dark straight hair fell over her cheeks. "She was called Mary. She's come into my dreams many times, especially during this past year."

"Visits from the astral plane," Irena whispered. "Restless spirits who have died unnatural deaths and can find no permanent resting places. This has been written about from ancient times."

" I see Mary staring at me from her cell . . . our cell." Ben wiped his forehead with his sleeve. "When she was alive, I was in charge of her interrogation, after President Lincoln's murder. I promised her her life . . . if she'd tell me everything she knew about the conspiracy. She'd let the assassin, Booth, stay at her boarding house in Washington. But Mary Surratt was never one of the plotters."

"She trusted you with her secrets about them, though." Irena whispered. "Did you love her?"

"It wasn't quite like that. But a strange, powerful feeling develops between prisoner and interrogator. I've never known anything like it. She feared me, yet she wept with loneliness if I was late visiting her. I dreaded seeing her, but I couldn't sit still at home, or at the office . . . or anywhere except in her cell with her. In a way . . . yes, I did love her. But only once . . . well, she flung herself at me, and I held her close." Ben looked down at his hands; he remembered her soft cotton dress against his fingers.

"And then she told you everything."

"Yes." Ben's pipe bowl glowed painfully hot in his palm. Evidently he'd lit it again. "Later, I presented her testimony to the judges. I knew they'd find her guilty, no matter what I reported. But I told her I was sure they'd spare her the death penalty."

He remembered a steaming hot afternoon in the Washington Arsenal courtyard. A plank scaffold had been erected with nooses swinging from the crossbar. The condemned prisoners climbed the wooden stairs—thirteen steps, by tradition—to the platform. A man fastened a cord around Mary's long skirt at the ankles to keep it from flying up. "I was ordered to witness the hanging," Ben said, his voice sunk low. Tears stung his eyes. "I heard Mary pleading with the hangman, 'Don't let me fall!'"

And now Ben saw again the man pulling the black hood over her head. The noose was lowered, drawing the hood tight. Soldiers on the wall had been shouting the details to their friends outside, but they stopped. The courtyard went still. General Hancock clapped once. The sound ricocheted between the high brick walls. Twice. Three times. And with a dreadful clatter all the trap doors sprang open at once.

"Mary fell—"

"Terrible." Irena reached out and rested her fingers on his arm. "Barbaric."

Ben buried his face in his hands. How long he sat hunched over like that, he didn't know. When finally he opened his eyes, Irena was lying back on her cushions, watching him.

"I, too, am haunted sometimes," she said in a whisper. "Spirits drive me mercilessly. The astral plane is not only a place of musical gypsies and dancing Indian maidens."

"I've never told anyone all of this," he said.

"I will not betray you," she said. "And you will never betray me."

"Never," Ben murmured.

"Now we will rest." She let out a long stream of smoke and fixed him again in her gaze. "You . . . will . . . sleep. . . ."

He heard the bedclothes whisper. The puppy gave a whimper and went silent. The floor beneath his chair seemed to slant downward. Slowly he drifted off along its slope.

And when he next opened his eyes, the lamp was extinguished and the curtains were outlined by bright morning light. Rips in the fabric cast thin bright stripes across the carpet. Irena was sitting up in bed stroking the puppy. Its tail made a fast whump-whump-whump sound against her belly.

"Welcome back," she said, smiling.

Ben rubbed his eyes. "Are you . . . are you feeling better?"

"Yes, look!" The pup wriggled as she nudged it off her lap. She pushed down the bedclothes to reveal a few inches of flesh below her knee. It was lovely and pink. "You see how my little friend has poulticed me," she said.

"Extraordinary!" Ben said, and she covered herself again.

"But this house is too cramped, dirty, unhealthy." She sighed. "If I stay here, I fear the illness will return!"

Ben rose and pulled open the curtains. Now he could see just how small and shabby it was, with its stained plaster walls and ragged bedclothes and threadbare carpet. Outside, a mountain of ashes and garbage leaned ominously against the house. "You mustn't stay," he said. "You need a real doctor."

Irena sighed. "I am very sorry, but I have to confess. I cannot even pay the rent here." She shut her eyes. Tears shone on her cheeks. "I have nowhere."

He sat on the edge of her bed and took her hand. As she leaned her head against his shoulder, he felt the rhythm of her breathing. "My dear Irena, please, will you let me help?"

"Moreya chose you for a *chela* because you are a kind man, a man of action." Her eyes blinked open. "If it were my decision only, I would refuse. But the Master has told me. You are part of my destiny."

Ben smiled. "Good, then let's start packing your things today!"

He told her knew of a comfortable lady's residence house where she could stay. And Sarah? Yes, he'd help her and her mother, too. For now he had enough money from his law practice and book royalties. Together he and Irena filled several trunks with her enormous collection of books.

Then he left the room as she packed personal things. The black poultice puppy ran ahead of him down the stairs. As Ben descended into the basement kitchen, a gust of fresh air from an open door blew into his face. He hugged his arms tight across his chest as if suddenly awakening, chilled and alarmed.

"What have I done?" he said aloud, his voice echoing in the stairwell. The sound faded into silence.

The strange little dog gazed up at him and wagged its tail. Then it ran off, its feet skidding over the stone floor. Ben watched it vanish through the kitchen door into a tiny courtyard. Pushing the door open wider, he peered outside. He expected to see the pup running around on the yard's red brick floor. The walls rose up from the bricks on all four sides, with no exit. But the space was empty. The dog was nowhere to be seen.

4

The landladies Ben found for Irena couldn't put up with her
strange hours, and eventually he moved her into a three-story
brownstone on 47th Street that he'd recently rented for himself.
She accepted his generosity, making it clear, of course, that she
was a spiritual, not a sexual seeker. He agreed, stating that he already had a lady friend to satisfy his secular cravings. Irena
would help him with his spiritual ones. There'd be room for Sarah, too, as well as her mother, Natasha, and a marmalade cat
named Charles. If Philistines wanted to make a scandal out of
Irena's living arrangements, let them! She'd find a way of using
her notoriety for higher purposes.

She and Ben happily scavenged Broadway second-hand shops
to furnish their new home. In one bedroom Irena installed a brass
bed with velvet cushions and red quilts. Ben took a separate bedroom with a canvas cot that reminded him of his soldiering days.
The downstairs sitting room, parlor, and study became a cozy
orientalist haven. A six-armed Hindu goddess gazed out from
among potted palms as if from an overgrown Indian temple. A
brass Buddha meditated on the piano. From dried leaves and bits
of mirror, the chums constructed a wall-collage of an elephant
contemplating a pool of water. A stuffed owl (she named it "the
Captain") perched over a doorway; a mechanical toucan
squawked (in Russian, Ben said) from the mantel. A purple
overstuffed sofa looked as if it had flown in through a window on
its carved, dragon-wing arms. In the foyer Irena and Ben installed
an enormous oil painting of Tibetan monasteries draped in silvery

moonlight. Visitors dubbed the place "The Lamasery." And visitors there were. Irena encouraged Ben to fill the place with a steady stream of his influential friends—newspapermen and artists, scholars and Spiritualists. Sarah, wearing a new green jumper, gazed at men dressed mostly in fine dark suits and some in white Arab robes; there was even an Indian prince in a knee-length gold jacket and a turban the color of raspberry sherbet. Many wore huge mustaches that looked useful for steering faces with. Ladies sailed by in rustling gowns and broad-brimmed, plumed hats. One wore a man's suit, another a hoop skirt, another a sari. Irena was the most glorious of all. Her pendants dangled, her brooches glittered, her rings flashed—all glass, still, though now she could have afforded better. Sohe wore a black and yellow striped skirt that had once belonged to a fortune teller and a shirt of turquoise blue. Ben looked splendid, too, as he leaned over to shake hands with Sarah. He looked ready to lead a cavalry charge in his military boots and long cutaway jacket, except that his trousers were a smart tan check like the kind journalists wore. He might have been riding a horse into battle, waving a sword-sized nib pen.

Among the guests were the dapper Thomas Edison, inventor of a machine he called a "phonograph"; the somber-faced Andrew Jackson Davis, the famous Poughkeepsie Seer, who often lectured on Swedenbourg's discourses with angels; and Felix Green, the mustachioed theatrical producer who swept through the rooms with a bevy of young actresses. Among them was Ben's mistress, a dark-haired young woman named Zia, who was starring as Ophelia in a new production of *Hamlet* in which the ending had been changed so that she could marry the hero in a musical finale. The ramrod-straight General Abner Doubleday, who'd been credited with inventing the game of baseball, swapped war stories with Ben and other veterans. The woman in a huge velvet hat was the notorious Victoria Woodhull, who had had grown rich giving Commodore Vanderbilt investment tips that she received from the spirit world, once nearly causing a Wall Street panic. The first person of her sex to ever run for president, she was often attended by woman suffragists gathering signatures for their petitions. Ben always signed them. No stranger to radical causes, he was often asked to repeat the rousing courtroom speeches he'd made in defense of these brave women. Sometimes he'd lighten the mood by donning a bowler hat and reciting Irish monologues to Irena's piano accompaniment. This was when she first dubbed him "Maloney" and he called her "Mulligan," private names that no one else ever used.

Irena's old-world colleagues were drawn to the Lamasery as well, many of them players in what people were calling "The Great Game" between the Russians and the British in Asia. Irena's Moscow editor, who was also a member of the Russian Intelligence Service, encouraged her to keep in touch with his agents, who included prominent Masons, Rosicrucians, and local representatives of Swami Saraswathi Dayananda, a leading anti-colonialist Indian leader.

As "empress" of New York's leading Spiritualist salon, Irena was the subject of newspaper articles as well as the author of many pieces herself. Puffing on her famous cigarettes, she gave interviews day and night. Her childhood? She'd been persecuted for her occult beliefs even then, she said; her parents had hired a succession of pious tutors who punished her for reading "pagan" books. "Punished?" asked a journalist, but she turned away, her lips pressed tight together. Here she was remembering the divinity student who had yanked up her dress, spanked her bare buttocks hard, and impaled her with his fingers until she shrieked for mercy. Her voice had echoed throughout the vast house: flapping like a panicked bird against the walls of the corridors, fluttering past the empty bedrooms of her parents, diving headlong down the staircase into the hall where it was smothered by the dark velvet curtains. That evening, when she tried to tell her mother what the tutor had done, her mother's slap had sent her sprawling to the carpet. Never again did Irena mention the incident to anyone, not even to Ben.

"My adolescence?" She repeated a journalist's question, turning back with a quick smile on her lips. "I kept on reading." She revealed that she'd been especially inspired by Edward Bulwer-Lytton's immortal novel *Zanoni*, whose heroine, Viola, loved an immortal stranger who led her into the light of pure wisdom. But when Irena turned seventeen, her parents found a forty-year-old general for her to marry. A few days after the wedding, she fled from him . . . intact, she insisted.

Then she left Russia to take work as a bareback rider in a circus that traveled through the Balkans. This may have seemed an extraordinary job for the daughter of an aristocratic family, she said, but she wasn't suited to the usual occupations open to a young woman on her own: children's governess, lady's maid, or gentleman's mistress. She was too nervous to supervise children, too proud to serve any lady, and too willful to be a slave to any man. Besides, she loved galloping round village squares with her cape flapping in the breeze, a bright scarf streaming from her clenched teeth. For the next two decades, she traveled through India, Europe, and the Middle East in search of enlightenment. (She mentioned nothing about her tragic love affairs and clandestine political involvements, or about a spiritual endeavor that had ended in scandal: she and a colleague—who now ran a boarding house in Ceylon—had been accused by Turkish authorities of smuggling Byzantine icons.) This period of her life she simply referred to as her "veiled years."

Irena wouldn't give speeches to large audiences, but as she had in Europe, she accepted invitations to preside over small gatherings of wealthy matrons. In parlors on New York's Gramercy Park, she directed the faithful to hold hands in a circle to create powerful energy fields. Soon the guests heard the rappings on the table made by unseen presences. Ladies asked questions for the spirits to answer; Irena wrote them on a slate, turned it face down in the dark, and when the gaslights flared up, she flipped the slate over to reveal answers written by a just-departed astral visitor. Wherever she was invited, astral bells tinkled from shadowy corners, sending shivers down the fleshy backs of her hostesses. Her reputation was in orbit.

One night at the Lamasery, Irena met a woman named Mrs. Elaine Hardinge Britten, a former actress who was packing houses from Boston to San Francisco with her animated lectures on Spiritualism. Though no younger than Irena, Mrs. Britten was a great American beauty, as slim and fair as Irena was round and dark. Pale hair swirled high on her head and cascaded down her back. As she swept through the Lamasery, her gauzy white gown fluttered around her like an entourage of fairies. She had, apparently, just completed a book dictated to her by an eighteenth century American mystic. Mrs. Britten's large teeth gleamed when she smiled. "May I show you something, my dears?" The company in the room gathered closer to look at the announcement of her new book, *Love Magic*. "It will give Spiritualism a great boost!" she declared.

"Seven dollars!" Ben said. "Good heavens, who'd pay that much for a book?"

"Sign us up for two, Ben," Irena said. "We have to help out our fellow authors."

"Don't tell me you're producing a book too, Madame Milanova?"

"Of course I am. But so many spirit mentors have been working with me. . . ." She fanned herself with the flyer. "Such wisdom cannot be scribbled down overnight." Now her brain was roiling: why write articles when she could produce a book *revealed to her by the Masters?* "The truth," she suddenly announced. "is that American Spiritualism is finished!"

"Finished?" Ladies cocked their heads. Gentlemen's cigars froze in mid-air.

"Yes, my friends," she said. "It has turned into a refuge for false prophesy and free love."

A few eyebrows rose at the mention of "free love." Many guests knew that the Captain had a mistress, and everyone knew he was "keeping" Irena, too, though in a reportedly *mariage blanc*. "Free love" was a phrase bandied about to describe utopian experiments such as Oneida, in the "burnt-over district" of Western New York, where John Humphrey Noyes had attracted moral concern (as well as some envy) about the "temporary marriages" enjoyed by his colony's members. They engaged not only in joyous amours but patented such profitable inventions as the garter belt and (somehow this seemed equally wanton) a washing machine that involved mechanical rubber boots stomping about on stilts in a tub of soap suds. The Mormons, who claimed to have received a charter from an angel in Palmyra, New York, were now practicing polygamy in the Utah territory. Many American spiritual enterprises were becoming suspect.

"All genuine occult knowledge," Irena intoned, gazing at her wall-collage where the elephant perpetually approached the watering hole, "is now coming from the East!"

And just at that moment, a stroke of amazing synchronicity occurred: Irena's old friend Countess Lydia Pachkoff arrived fresh from an expedition in the Syrian desert. Like Irena, Lydia was a Russian aristocrat who'd fallen in love with adventure and written many lively travel articles. Now thirty-six, she was a striking woman, with flaming red hair, high cheekbones, and flashing dark eyes. The guests fell silent as she and Irena began to swap tales.

"Do you recall our caravan of Indian nomads?" Lydia asked, lighting a small cigar.

"Nomads . . . really!" said Elaine Hardinge Britten, chasing away the smoke with a peacock fan.

Irena sat beside Lydia on the overstuffed divan. "And the great ruins of Arsum."

"Ah, yes. 1869 it was. We built a fire in the sand. You threw incense into the flames, and you spoke powerful spells." Lydia rippled her fingers in the air. "A cloud of vapor arose."

"And the vapor took on the shape of a bent old man."

"And the old man said. . . ." Lydia's voice sank to a whisper. "'I am Hiero . . . Ascended Master . . . keeper of ancient rites!'"

"I asked him to show us the site as it had been, centuries before. . . ." Irena opened her hands before her, palms up. "And a vast white city filled the plain, as far as the eye could see!"

"With temples and golden statues!"

"Canals and bazaars!"

"Great avenues filled with horsemen and chariots!" Lydia smiled.

Irena's hands fell to her lap. "Then . . . it was all gone . . . vanished!"

"There were only the empty desert sands around us."

"And the howling of jackals in the moonlight," Irena finished.

With a sigh Lydia rested her head on Irena's shoulder, her hair spreading like red rays down her friend's bosom. When at last Lydia raised her face, her cheeks were damp and she required the use of several gentlemen's handkerchiefs. "How much we have learned in India," she said, tapping her cigar. "How little they know of it here in America. You must write it, Irena."

"Yes." Irena reached out her hand toward Ben. "Will you help me do this, my great chum?"

Ben took her hand. "I will!"

The guests let out their breaths. The applause was tumultuous.

And soon everyone was seated in the parlor hotly discussing the formation of a new organization to study the wisdom of the East. Ben proposed that it be called the Alexandrian Society—after the first century Greek-Egyptian association of scholars who had investigated the secret knowledge of the ancients. The company agreed, and a membership list was drawn up. Irena gazed admiringly at Ben in his new salt-and-pepper beard. "I nominate Captain Blackburn for President!" she exclaimed. A few members urged Irena herself to consider accepting the presidency, but she protested that she'd never so much as kept a household ledger in her life. So Ben was unanimously elected President, and Irena became Corresponding Secretary, a position more suited to her literary talents.

"Henceforth," General Doubleday announced, "the two of you shall be known as . . . *The Founders.*"

Applause thundered through the room, leaving Irena breathless. And though her body held down a divan in a crowded New York parlor, she felt her astral self ascend into even more exalted realms. Recalling her favorite painting from childhood—Gurov's *Ascension*—she heard music stir the air like the notes of an Aeolian wind harp. Rising, rising, she beheld the faces of the masters among the fluffy, white clouds. Moreya and Kut-huri, her rival guardians, shone amid the heroic turbaned visages. And from their burning eyes, ribbons of light flowed toward her, winding themselves around her like cloaks of shimmering gold.

5

For a year, Ben helped Irena with her great opus of ancient wisdom, *The Astral Veil*. As the chums worked far into the night at their huge double desk, the Lamasery's study resembled a smoky wizard's cave. A hearth fire blazed out of the shadows; stuffed owls and snakes dozed in bookshelf niches. Jill, a canary, cheeped in its cage. Irena scribbled furiously, breaking pen nibs, splattering ink. Ben rewrote her sentences in clear English and checked through books stacked in precarious cairns all over the floor. He was amazed by her talent for declaiming long passages, as if reading them aloud from volumes held open for her by unseen hands. Moreya, the idealist, contributed scholarly wisdom; Kut-huri, the egotist, produced imaginative ideas.

The book came to nearly a thousand pages. Irena fretted about its critical reception, but on publication day she sailed majestically into the Lamasery. Acknowledging the members' applause, she thanked Ben for his invaluable contributions to the book. Standing before the fireplace, he read the reviews aloud. Many were good, such as *The Spiritual Clarion's*: "At a time when the materialism of science is becoming as arrogant as the dogmatism of the church, much courage is required to launch such a brilliant assault on both their houses!" Cheers, applause. *The Springfield Herald*, however, called the book "a large dish of discarded rubbish." Hisses, boos. *The New York Times* declined to review *The Astral Veil*, stating, "We have a holy terror of Madame Milanova." Resounding laughter. "One more—from *The Graphic*," Ben announced, neglecting to mention that he'd written the review himself.

"'The Astral Veil is an inspiration to us all to join the great quest for universal truth and international brotherhood.'"

Despite steady sales from both Irena's and Ben's books, The Alexandrian Society was having trouble paying its bills. Ben gave more public lectures. He launched a plan to merge the Society with a huge Hindu organization in Bombay run by a swami named Saraswathi Dayananda, but a reply from India was slow in coming. Meanwhile, the Founders had to keep up appearances: holding soirées, sponsoring lectures, being seen at the opera. At the Music Academy downtown, they attended the American premiere of Il Vascello Fantasma, a work by a young German composer named Richard Wagner. Ben wore a new top hat, frock coat, and dark woolen trousers, an outfit which attracted the glances of young ladies and matrons alike. The premiere was a gala occasion, with President and Mrs. Grant in attendance, but the audience was also fascinated by Madame Milanova as she glided regally about on Ben's arm. The press reported on her costume: "Plumes leaping like exclamation points from her velvet hat, a blue satin dress dripping with fur trimmings: a more out-of-fashion ensemble could not be imagined, yet the women in the audience possessed with half her age and beauty were outshone, as if by a moon casting its vibrant glow across the starry firmament."

When the opera finally started, Ben was put off by all the screaming, but he enjoyed the storms at sea made by an invisible mechanical device that caused a wooden ship to rock while cardboard waves splashed up its sides. And all in rhythm with the booming of kettledrums and moaning of bass fiddles! Irena seemed enraptured by the captain, a bearded Dutchman who complained to a large blonde woman about being refused a harbor to dock in. Surely, Ben considered, such a refusal was in violation of international maritime laws. He deduced the reason: the harbor authorities must have suspected the sailors of carrying contagious diseases. His evidence: their unhealthy pale faces and feverish eyes, and the tattered condition of the sails, which the poor fellows must have been too weak to take proper care of. Why wasn't a medical crew brought out in a longboat? That would stop the interminable screaming. Irena, who understood Italian, whispered to him that the captain—the "Flying Dutchman"—was under a spell that kept him roaming the globe until a woman saved him. The sailors were actually . . . well, something like materialized astral beings. Ben paid more attention, now, even picturing himself as the drama's driven, wandering sea captain.

Between acts, Ben stepped outside for some fresh air and spotted the President among his Pinkerton agents, having a smoke by the street door. He walked over to renew his acquaintance.

"What d'you think of the show?" he asked Mr. Grant.

"Noisy, ain't it?" the President replied.

"I think I'm getting the gist of the thing." Ben lit up his own cigar. "It's about a man saved by a good woman."

The President chuckled. "I read in the papers that you've got some Russian lady who's redeeming your own soul. Or maybe who's stealing it, I forget which."

"Some of both, probably." Ben laughed.

Mr. Grant pulled a silver flask from his inside pocket. "Drink to redemption?"

"Don't mind if I do." Ben said, and did.

That night, Ben was to meet Zia, his mistress, but when he reached her flat downtown, he found her gone. A note told him she'd gone on the road with *Hamlet* accompanied by her "fiancé," director Felix Green. Ben trudged all the way back to the Lamasery mournfully recalling Zia's lively dark eyes, her smile, her curls . . . until, curiously, her face began to fade. Dawn broke over the city, pink and golden. Ben watched a drayman ladle milk from the can in his wagon into the pitchers that women held out as they stood at the curb. Ice coated the laundry lines strung between tenements like sparkling cobwebs .

It was nine o'clock when Ben reached the Lamasery and threw open the parlor curtains to let in the sunlight. Hearing a splashing sound from the bathroom, he approached the door. It was ajar. "Don't tell me you heated the water yourself, Mulligan," he called.

"There was no one else to do it," she shouted from the tub. "Were you out tomcatting again?"

"Pussy found another Tom." Ben expected to hear triumphant laughter, but instead, Irena's voice was soothing.

"Poor Maloney," she said.

What was *this?* Ben moved closer to the bathroom door to hear a cascade of water: Irena rising.

"Have you considered," Irena asked, "now that you are fully accepted by the Brotherhood—that you can put all fleshy desires behind you?"

Ben frowned. "You know, Moreya may be a master, but he's also a man. I don't think he'd want me to stop being one, myself." Ben saw Irena's shadow moving in the crack of light. She was drying herself. He could actually hear the fluffy towel rubbing against different parts of her body—a very pleasant sound.

"I suppose you would be of little use to the Society if you were a eunuch." Her movement stopped. The curved shadow of her hip appeared on the wall just inside the door. "Well, in that case—" She began toweling again, the shadow wobbling furiously. "Another thought occurred to me, but I cannot say it."

"I just thought of it, too." Ben rested his hand against the doorframe. "Were you thinking that I ought to imbibe both physical and spiritual inspiration from, as it were, the same fountain?"

"Something like that. Perhaps not in such poetic terms."

Ben chuckled. Slowly he pushed open the door. She could close it at any moment, if she chose to. But she stood her ground on the tiles. He stepped into the light, and there he found a rounded, sweet-smelling bundle—Irena—wrapped in towels from ankles to neck. A hand appeared from the wrapping. He took it in his and drew her toward him. Her face was damp and radiant. At first her lips were taut, but they softened, and for a few moments, it was she who was thirstily drinking from his fountain, pushing so eagerly against him he nearly fell back against the wall.

"Come," he whispered, pulling her by the hand.

In her room, she flung herself onto her bed quilts while Ben stirred the coals in the grate. When he had a warm fire crackling, he removed his clothes and joined her.

"Are you cold?" he asked, feeling her shiver as he held her in her arms.

"N . . . no—"

He kissed her again, feeling more tightness in her lips than thirst. With some difficulty he peeled layers of towels from her until she lay magnificently flushed and naked beside him. "I never dreamed how lovely you'd be," he murmured, kissing a soft round breast. "I thought of you differently. . . ."

"I wanted you to." She made an oofing sound as he pressed closer.

He stroked her back, her marvelous graceful buttocks, her legs. She still hadn't moved an inch in his direction, so he continued caressing, gently kissing. Hoping to hear moans, he heard only pained breathing. Was this passion or worry? When he finally lay between her thighs, he found her tight with terror, and he couldn't enter her.

"Please!" she cried, scrambling from beneath him. She lay on her side, knees drawn up against her belly. "Oh, Ben, I am sorry!"

"Dear Irena, never mind." Feeling her shiver again, he covered her with a quilt.

She turned to him, her face streaked with tears. "I feared that this would happen. It often has."

He stroked her hair until she lay her head on his chest. "You know," he said, "maybe this wasn't the best idea. But good things can come from it."

"It must be a sign that our intimacy will be greater than merely physical." She wiped her eyes "My fear of your . . . male nature is gone."

"And your feminine appeal doesn't distract me as it did."

"I think we can enjoy a better kind of chum-ship in the future."

"I'm enjoying it right now."

"Are you?" She raised her face to look into his eyes. He smiled at her. "I am glad," she said, and rested her cheek against his chest again. "Karma."

Ben lay very still, lest any movement alarm her into rolling away from him. The low flames in the grate cast flickery shadows on the wall. Firelight was reflected in the vases around the room like golden eyes glowing. He took slow breaths, enjoying the clean

smell of Irena's skin and the scent of smoke from the cedar logs.
She felt warm beside him, on the verge of sleep.

"I was remembering," he said, "when I was a boy. My sister
and I ran away from the farm people we boarded with. We hid in
a barn—deep in a haystack. It was like a nest—sweet smelling,
warm."

"Mmm." Irena smiled, closing her eyes.

"We snuggled in close for the night. I remember how we
breathed in unison. . . ."

"Lovely," Irena murmured.

"We laughed and yawned and whispered secrets," Ben continued. "You know, until tonight, I haven't felt that peaceful in
about thirty years."

Feeling Irena squeeze his hand beneath the quilt, he finally
closed his eyes.

Ben was as surprised as anyone in New York when he learned
that Irena had accepted an assignment from a Philadelphia newspaper, *The Inquirer*, to report on the activities of the controversial
medium Jenny Holmes. He repeatedly pointed out to her she
didn't need the notoriety that such a risky assignment might
bring. Irena refused to change her mind.

Mrs. Holmes was a willowy Main Line socialite whose séances
always beat out the local competition because she had as her
spirit guest a famous eighteenth century beauty named Katy
King. Recently, however, Katy's genuineness had been challenged
in a literary journal named *The Atlantic Monthly*. In response to
the challenge, the eminent philosopher Robert Dale Owen wrote
an article for the magazine proclaiming Katy's authentic spiritual
attributes. Looking exquisite in her gauzy gown, Katy had often
allowed the old gentleman to stroke her blonde tresses while she
sat on his knee. She even let him give her jewelry to take back
with her to the astral world.

Then a newspaper article reported that the charming spirit was
sometimes unavailable during the evenings when she was called
to emerge from the ether. On these occasions, Mrs. Holmes admit-
ted, she hired a young actress named Eliza White to appear in

Katy's place. When Mr. Owen learned this, Miss White confessed all; to avoid arrest, she returned the old man's gifts. He immediately mailed off to *The Atlantic Monthly* a retraction of the article he'd written that had validated Katy. But it was received too late; the magazine was already in the shops. The public humiliation was too much for Mr. Owen to bear. He went mad, and had to be confined to an asylum.

Armed with the latest spirit-testing techniques, Irena set off for Philadelphia. There, she joined an audience of prominent persons who watched as Mrs. Holmes was tucked into a canvas sack. Only the lady's head protruded from it. Ropes were tied securely around her until she looked like a large ball of yarn. She was carried into the medium's cabinet and fastened to a heavy chair with a chain. Parlor lights were dimmed. Voices hushed.

Then, as if seeping up through the carpet, a luminous young woman appeared just outside the cabinet. It was Katy! The audience burst into applause. As she swayed in place, arms raised high, the glow of an oil lamp shone through her diaphanous robes and silhouetted her graceful body. She seemed to be clothed in nothing but astral sighs. Finally she faded back into the darkness of the medium's cabinet. Holding a lantern, Irena flung open its door. Katy was not concealed anywhere; she'd returned to the astral plane! Only Mrs. Holmes remained, still trussed up to her chin and pop-eyed with discomfort.

"Jenny Holmes's innocence is displayed!" Irena proclaimed in the next day's edition of *The Inquirer*. This should have been a great victory for her. But her three-page essay about the séance was cut to a quarter column on page eight. On the first page was a more somber article. A black headline announced that the beloved Robert Dale Owen had died in the madhouse of a broken heart.

The scandal of this sad death soured the public on Katy in particular and on spiritualism in general. Irena's reputation, having risen so fast, began to slide precipitously. Ben noticed that attendance at his Alexandrian Society meetings was falling off. The Lamasery was empty of guests for weeks at a time. With diminishing demand for his lectures, Ben threw his energy into writing more articles, but fewer and fewer publications accepted them. Seated at his desk in the Lamasery study, he stared out the window as a parade of Republicans convened in the street. A tuba's brass bell glinted in the sunlight; men in red, white, and blue uniforms milled about with their instruments. "Bread and circuses!" he muttered.

In no better a mood, Irena entered the alcove. "Jenny Holmes again!" She dropped a newspaper onto Ben's blotter. "I am sick of reading about that gilded humbug!"

Ben glanced at the paper. "Damn it, you just wrote an article calling her 'a true spiritual practitioner!'"

"The cause must be defended again and again." Irena sat across from him on her side of the desk. "Now Jenny Holmes demands a character reference from you for publication in *The Inquirer.*"

"Why me?"

"You're considered a man of great integrity."

"Spook shows aren't our cause nowadays! We've got serious principles!" Ben mopped his brow. The band began oom-pah-pah-ing in the street below, and the canary in its overhead cage responded with some loud twittering. "Mulligan, you mystify me at times!"

"I mystify many people. Visionaries always do." Sitting across from him at the desk, Irena handed him a piece of cream-colored stationery. "Now please, read this."

Pacing the study, Ben read Jenny Holmes' request. She said she'd come into possession of letters written many years ago by a British woman named Emma Coulomb who claimed that she and Irena had been involved in some "scheme" involving Byzantine icons. Mrs. Holmes was generously offering to send the British woman's letters on to Irena—"to keep them from public scrutiny," she said. But she would only do so in return for a character reference from the eminent Captain.

"It's blackmail!" Ben threw down the papers. The canary fluttered. "I refuse to compromise our integrity!"

Irena folder her hands on her blotter. "It is time," she said slowly, "for you to understand certain things about leading a great movement. People want spectacles." She pointed at the band outside in the street. "And spiritual people crave spiritual miracles. At times, a movement's leadership must provide such miracles." As Ben opened his mouth to protest, she raised her hand. "Listen to me! You speak of principles. The principle of spirituality, it is still a true one, is it not? The principle that human souls are reincarnated—that they exist for a time on the astral plane,willing to communicate with people on this physical plane in order to give them hope of the brotherhood of all mankind—you do not dispute this, do you, Ben?"

"No—"

"Do you not agree that people desperately need to hope for something better than the hardships of this material world, for something transforming and redeeming and luminous?"

"I know that—certainly."

"Once you have given people such hopes, would you snatch them away again? Would you add your voice to those of the Philistines who mock the hope-givers?" She leaned toward him, her eyes dampening. "And Maloney, would you hand those villains the ammunition they need to persecute me?"

He reached out to rest his hand on Irena's arm. "Of course not!"

"It is not just a personal issue," she said, placing her hand on his. "Any attack on my reputation—those scurrilous letters Jenny Holmes has—is an attack on our organization's integrity. And on your own as well. You and I are the Founders, linked forever in the public mind. Think of the Society, and all the good work it will do for humanity!"

"But damn it, I've always assumed Alexandrianism was dedicated to the truth!"

"A *higher* truth! A truth greater than the vulgar scandal-mongering of journalists." Irena brushed old tobacco crumbs from her bosom as if they were flecks of dried newsprint. "Every illustrious movement has set-backs, they are sent to make us stronger," she continued. "Look outside. One day, throngs will be marching for Alexandrianism! Meanwhile, old chum, you must take this opportunity to protect our Society's good name."

Ben breathed through gritted teeth. "All right," he said finally, "I'll write the reference this time."

As if on cue, a great cheer rose from beneath the window. The band had pushed off, its kettle drums thumping.

"The Masters chose wisely when they chose you." Irena smiled.

Ben glared down at the pen on the desk. "But so help me, if I ever have to do this sort of thing again. . . ." His voice rose in a questioning tone; the only response he received was from the songbird, which flapped its wings furiously against the bars of its cage.

6

I fester in a hiatus! Irena wrote in her journal. She wasn't just re-
ferring to her ailing leg, but to her mind as well. With no book to
work on, she missed visitations from astral scholars and all-night
writing sessions with Ben. Fewer journalists visited the Lamasery.
The Jenny Holmes fiasco had led to editorials charging that Spiritualism and Alexandrianism (as if they belonged in the same
nest—grackles and nightingales!) were worn-out creeds. She
could see that Ben was restless, too. At breakfast he complained of
alarming astral visits from Mary Surratt. During the evenings he
charged across a room, snorted and pawed the carpet and thundered off again. And he'd been seen riding about Central Park in
the carriage of the perfidious Elaine Hardinge Britten. During one
of Elaine's dinner parties, Irena stole a peek at her boudoir. She
could imagine the lady's pearly teeth smiling from their glass on
the bureau as Ben bounced about on the bed with their owner.
The room reeked of floury face powder; her sheets looked sticky
white. Irena pictured the bedclothes gathered around Elaine's
body as lightly as a shell of meringue, her famous high bosoms
wobbling like twin molds of vanilla pudding.

Can my career in America be waning? Irena wrote.

The Alexandrian Society still had some influence in New York,
though. After reading about cremation in India, Ben publicly ad-
vocated the custom in "The Dangers of Live Burial," a pamphlet
that attracted several thousand readers. Many people still remembered tales of wounded Civil War soldiers who, mistakenly interred

in pine boxes, had to claw their way out of their tombs in moonlit graveyards.

One reader found his way to the doorstep of the Lamasery to praise the author. "Allow me to present myself, my esteemed Sir," he said to Ben, clicking his heels and bowing. The smartness of this gesture contrasted with the decrepitude of his costume—his frayed trousers and coat were a size too large, as if he'd recently shrunk inside them. The silk of his waistcoat was a pastel design of gravy stains, and he gave off a mixed odor of old fish and cologne. But the letter he produced attested to his good name: Baron Ludwig Von Palme, a former officer in the Royal Bavarian Cavalry. "I am long a student of the occult," he said, tipping his top hat as Irena appeared in the doorway beside Ben. "When I read of your learnéd society, I know that I must meet its brilliant founders."

Ben invited the Baron in. As they all had tea in the study, Irena gave him some suspicious looks. Where had she seen him before? She questioned him in French. It seemed that she and Von Palme had visited many of the same watering holes on the Continent. It wouldn't do to be too critical of him, she thought, for who could tell what he might know about her past? He had some delightful gossip to share about people they'd known, and soon the two were laughing and wolfing down sandwiches. The Baron settled back in an armchair, his fingers idly combing the few gray hairs that streaked his bald dome like errant cobwebs. From time to time, he gave off a deep cough that racked his body. Irena could see that the poor man was in bad health. He confided that a sum of money due to him had inexplicably been delayed in the mails, and he was reduced to lodging in a wretched boarding house. Irena's heart went out to him. That evening, he moved in with his trunk to the empty room on the third floor.

Over the following weeks, the distinguished guest was initiated into the Society. Though he contributed surprisingly little to discussions of occult matters, he charmed the members with his accent and gracious European manners. But his health didn't improve. He spent his days lying on his bed sipping medicinal brandy. Irena called in a doctor, who told her that the Baron was suffering from an advanced stage of nephritis. He was, in fact, on his deathbed.

"I have such a horror of live burial!" Von Palme whispered to Ben. "So many body-snatchers there are these days!"

Ben agreed: medical students digging up cadavers for dissection were a terrible menace. "And burial's unhealthy for the populace," he went on. "The poisonous gasses given off by corpses in overcrowded graveyards. . . ." He saw the Baron's face go pale. "I assure you, no offense intended—"

"Please . . . have my remains cremated!" Von Palme raised himself from his pillow, his rheumy eyes pleading. "If you will do this, I will deed all my properties to your great Society."

"Poor old Baron," Irena said later. "I don't blame him for wanting to go up in flames."

"Me, neither," Ben said. "I'm going to see what I can do for him." He began drawing up a will for Von Palme, who revealed that his assets included gilt-edged stock certificates, a Colorado silver mine, and two castles in Bavaria. All deeds and particulars, he said, would be found in his trunk.

A few days later, the Baron's soul departed to the astral plane. Irena shut herself in her study, too sad to help Ben write the obituary. Ben, determined to keep his promise to his friend, announced in the press that the Baron's body would be consumed by fire in the first cremation ceremony ever to be held in the United States. Before the event, which he'd arranged to take place in Pennsylvania, the Alexandrian Society would hold a solemn Rite of Transition for the deceased at the Masonic Temple at Twenty-third Street and Sixth Avenue in Manhattan. Reporters asked about this Rite, but Irena, knowing how intriguing a mystery could be, refused to divulge any details. So the press made up its own.

Mme Milanova, authoress of *The Astral Veil*, will don a golden girdle and play upon an eight-stringed balalaika. Grand Hierophant Blackburn, in a leopard-skin robe, will march beside an Indian sarcophagus drawn by four oxen. Slaves will pour libations of New Jersey cider. Beating on tom-toms,

Alexandrian officers will sing an ancient Theban dirge:
Isis and Nepthys, beginning and end,
One more victim to Hades we send,
Pay for the fare, and let us not tarry,
Cross o'er the Styx on the Roosevelt Street ferry!

No such bizarre ritual took place, of course. The casket arrived at the Masonic temple in an open carriage attended by ladies and gentlemen of the Alexandrian Society wearing dignified mourning clothes. Thomas Edison wore a frock coat, striped trousers, and spats. General Doubleday was in full dress uniform. Elaine Hardinge Britten, carrying an ostrich feather fan, was—according to the next day's papers—"radiant in a high-necked white gown with a vest and skirt-front of ecru silk taffeta overlaid with lace."

Ben had sent out a hundred tasteful invitations on black paper with silver writing, but mobs of uninvited guests were attracted by the newspaper publicity. Men in caps and overalls jostled the bier and knocked off the top hats of the pallbearers. As Irena ascended the marble steps in her black blouse and skirt, someone stepped on her corns, eliciting a terrible Russian epithet from her. More than two thousand persons crowded into the hall, showing no respect for the deceased. Among them, Irena noticed fanatical Christians waving signs that denounced the ceremony as blasphemous.

Ben, wearing a plain black robe, delivered a eulogy for the deceased. "Our friend, this noble cavalryman, resides now with the Great Astral Light to await his next Posting upon the Earthly Plane—"

"That's paganism!" shouted a placard-waving Christian. The noisy crowd surged forward.

Irena glanced worriedly at Ben. Sweat was trickling down his forehead, and his pince-nez slipped sideways on his nose. Calling forth all his dignity, he strode to the bier, rested his hand upon it, and turned his face slowly upward. *We are in the presence of Death!* he intoned.

A hush fell over the hall. Ben continued his eulogy. But after fifty minutes of his booming oratory, the crowd grew restive again. A policeman collared the placard-waving Christian. People began to murmur and hiss. "That man is a bleary-eyed bigot, he is!" Irena suddenly shouted, as the offender was led away. A wave of laughter passed through the audience. The mood became more jovial, but the crowd was edging forward again, waiting for more spectacle.

Ben turned to Elaine Britten. As if infused with light by his glance, she rose on tiptoe and glided up to the podium, blondely angelic in her lacy white gown. Irena glowered at her from the back of the dais. Mrs. Britten's voice rippled through the air in silver flute-like notes. Quoting from her book, *Love Magic*, which she happened to have brought with her, she described choirs of spirit visitors whom she'd spotted fluttering above the Masonic temple's roof. She concluded by scattering handfuls of rose petals onto the bier. Top hats were held over hearts. The crowd quietly made its way to the street.

The press, however, called the event a "near riot" and a "barbarian rite." But Ben kept his promise to the deceased—the cremation took place the next day in a small Pennsylvania town. Only one journalist was there. His headline announced:

BROILED BARON: VON PALME DECENTLY DONE

"Never mind the newspapers. We have the Baron's inheritance!" Irena announced. She and Ben climbed the stairs to the room of their deceased guest. Spotting his old wooden trunk, she held Ben's arm tight. "Think of it! We can build an international headquarters . . . in the Tropics, perhaps! An estate with formal gardens and shaded meditation groves. Thousands will come!"

"How about a New Alexandrian library?" Ben said. "And a Great Hall of the World's Faiths, with bas-relief figures of Buddha, Krishna, and all the Masters!"

Irena nodded. "And marble statues of the Founders. . . ."

Kneeling, Ben slowly lifted the trunk's lid. Irena leaned over it. A sour odor rose to her nostrils. Evidently the Baron had been stuffing his soiled clothes inside rather than washing them. Ben held up a rumpled white shirt, one of his own that he'd lent the Baron. Ben's name-stitching had been picked out from the collar.

"Keep digging!" Irena beat her fists against her sides.

Beneath more laundry, she spotted some papers, but they turned out to be unpaid bills from hoteliers and tailors. Where were the stock certificates, the deeds for Bavarian castles? A few documents did turn up, but they merely attested that the Baron's family property had been auctioned off years before to pay creditors.

Surrounded by old clothes and paper, Ben stared down into the empty trunk. "Our legacy," he said, "consists of castles in air."

Irena's response was the Russian word she'd uttered at the funeral when her corns had been assaulted. As she stepped away from the trunk, she noticed the bed's yellow-stained mattress, and felt a twinge of sadness that tempered her rage. The man had been incontinent, as well as broke. "Poor old scoundrel," she said. "A true artist, in a way, he kept up the grift to the very end."

Ben sighed. "We never really knew him."

Irena stared into the trunk. Suddenly its hideous emptiness taunted her like a cruel echo. "Some great judge of character you turned out to be!" she muttered to Ben.

"Judge of character? After the way you defended Jenny Holmes!"

"I had no choice! She was going to destroy me!"

"You get good will built up—then for some damned reason you sabotage it—"

"*No!*" Irena shut her eyes tight, her tears dripping down her cheeks. Finally she felt Ben's hand rest gently on her shoulder.

"Mulligan, we mustn't fight," he said.

"You are the one who wanted the great funerary rite. You even got Elaine to coo at the crowds—"

"Shhh. . . ." Ben held her closer, stroking her hair. "I won't abandon you for anyone else."

Irena wrapped her arms around Ben until she could feel his heartbeat against her breast. "Oh, Ben, our Society could be finished in America now!"

"We'll survive. We just let ourselves get puffed up with dreams of the Baron's riches."

"I never really cared about being rich. Either did you. We probably never will."

"I know. But the idea of stocks and castles—they made us fight with each other." Ben shut the trunk's lid. "It's as the Buddha says—preoccupying oneself with material things causes suffering."

"We do have a mountain of bills..."

"There are worse problems."

"You are so damned—" She was about to say "spiritual!" but couldn't quite bring herself to do it. "You are supposed to be the practical one, Maloney!" she finished.

"Hasn't Moreya always said, 'Karma will provide?'"

Irena rolled her eyes. "Yea gods! Moreya and I have created a monster!" Then, taking Ben's arm, she couldn't keep from chuckling. "How absurd we are sometimes, you and I!"

Ben smiled. "Speak for yourself, my dear."

"Oh, I will," Irena said. "I will!"

Worried about Irena's restlessness, Ben visited a pet shop and brought home Pip, a mate for Jill the canary, who stopped thrashing about her cage. Irena left its door open so the happy couple could fly about the room. They nested high in the brass chandelier, making a nest out of hair tugged from stuffed chairs. "Soon we'll be grandparents to an egg," Irena told Ben. She checked regularly on the birds, leaving out saucers of fresh water for them to splash in. But feathered surrogate children weren't enough to keep her mind busy. Fortunately, though, an event occurred—as if out of the blue—to stir up the Lamasery nest. Swami Saraswathi Dayananda, of Bombay, India, contacted the President/Founder of the American Alexandrian Society.

"He proposes forming one great organization with us." Ben said, showing her the swami's letter. "He wants us to actually move to India!"

"He would sponsor us, help us to get well established," Irena said. "I know him well."

Ben cocked his head. "Did you have something to do with all this?"

"I may have communicated something to the Swami via astral currents." Irena smiled.

"Or via Western Union." Ben went to his office to draw up legal papers, which he sent to Swami Dayananda. The documents formally joined the Alexandrian Society of America with the swami's

Arya Samaj organization of Bombay. Thus, with the stroke of a pen, the Society's membership was increased from thirty-nine souls to three thousand.

From deep inside her cell, Ben wrote in his journal, *Mary Surratt said goodbye to me. She lifted off the heavy noose she'd been wearing around her neck for so long; a dark scar remained on her skin. Her long black hair shifted, leaving one eye visible. Her face shone like hot glass; her eye flickered like a lantern flame. The cell door swung wide open. She stood back in the shadows, fixing me with her scorching stare, her arm raised, waving. . . ."*

Long after midnight, Ben paced the floor of the Lamasery. A heavy black miasma settled over him. The bookshelves looked like high stone walls. The statues seemed like petrified dwarfs struck dumb before they could finish speaking. The stuffed creatures looked frozen in motion: animals about to leap, birds about to fly. A doleful scene. Yet in the golden days, before the scandals and fiascos, the Lamasery had been such an enchanted place! He'd managed to keep the Society alive, but the effort had made him tense and cautious. *Cautious!* he wrote, *If I stay here much longer, I'll become like the décor, a stuffed Captain like the owl over the parlor door, gone out on a limb, but no further.* Then he wrote: *If I go, will I leave Mary behind forever? Is she trying to tell me to be free of her?*

"She is!" he declared, and threw down his pen.

With the same determination and energy with which he once made New York the birthplace of Alexandrianism, Ben set about planning to transfer the Society's headquarters from New York to India. "To explore, to seek, to discover—what greater purpose can one's life have?" Ben wrote in the newsletter he sent to the Society's members, notifying them of his decision. To set up ventures that would sustain the Society in Bombay, Ben obtained appointments from several companies as export agent for their products, which included agricultural implements, patented apple-coring machines, and Swiss cuckoo clocks. He wrote to the

Secretary of State in Washington requesting an appointment as honorary consul. Though the appointment didn't come through, he did receive a letter signed by President Hayes empowering him to promote cultural relations between the United States and India.

Irena filed the necessary papers to apply for American citizenship. Since Russia was England's rival in India, she feared that India's British colonial government might harass a Czar's subject, and she wanted the protection of American consulates. Because she was the first Russian-born woman in history to become an American citizen, she once again attracted the attention of the press.

"You wonder that I am anxious to leave my adopted land so soon? Have some cakes, boys," she said to the reporters, pushing a plate across her desk toward them. Ben took one, too. "I love America," she went on. "I don't mind if the newspapers here say I am a heathen, an adventuress, a felon. But Captain Blackburn and I have a great mission to fulfill."

"We shall journey throughout India in search of holy sages and sacred sorcerers, ancient texts and antique temples," Ben said,

"We shall give vital encouragement to India's cultural revival movement."

"And have experiences by which we will learn first-hand the wisdom of the East."

"Spiritual pioneers?" a journalist asked.

"Exactly," Ben said. "And you'll be getting our dispatches regularly."

"So do not worry." Irena raised her teacup to the press. "You have not heard the last of us!"

In a new, joint journal, Ben and Irena wrote entries chronicling their preparations to begin their new adventure.

BB: November 20: *Collected subscriptions from the members: we have enough for passage!*

IM: November 22: *The thought of returning to India excites me so—how good it will be to speak again with truly enlightened beings—here in NY the landlord demands overdue rent—*

BB: November 25: *Irena in a frazzle pestering me about the canaries Pip and Jill. . . . There's no egg after all, only an empty nest in the chandelier. . . . I donated the canaries to my club, narrowly averting a cataclysmic rift in Russo-American relations. . . .*

IM: November 27: *The cat, Charles, is gone missing, the ungrateful wretch—Sarah is distraught, and Ben says we cannot leave without finding him—*

BB: November 30: *Irena looking for the cat all morning. . . . . Lamasery a railway station of visitors that she continually invites to dinner. . . .*

IM: December 1: *I started selling things, got $20 for a broken chair, shame on me—*

BB: December 4: *A cable arrived from one Hurrychand Chintamon, secretary of the Arya Samaj . . . he promises to meet us in Bombay, take charge of all particulars for us, obviously a fine man. . . .*

IM: December 5: *Ben is slow as a sloth on crutches about travel arrangements, but I persevere—sold a table to the merchant on the corner—*

BB: December 6: *Irena will never finish packing all her scrapbooks and tomes. . . . Dinner party this evening: Edison, Lady Loring, Vikram Narayan, Rev. Plankton, Natasha and Sarah from upstairs, and actor named Jim O'Leary who told fortunes with cards, predicted a shipwreck for travelers!. . . . This is all Irena needs in her current state. . . .*

IM: December 8: *Ben bristling with nerves these days, a walking cactus—Landlord demanded $205 back rent—I fainted on the floor, very graceful, haven't lost my touch—sent him on his way with $90—Charles the cat is back, what a relief!—*

BB: December 10: *Irena sold the landlord's window blinds to someone for fifty cents! The landlord is apoplectic about it . . . I paid him, and sent Irena for a long walk in the Central Park . . . she's like a buffalo who's swallowed a beehive. . . .*

IM: December 12: *Had two teeth extracted, Ben was per-turbed about the dentist bill—I asked him, would he prefer me to go to a bicycle repairman in India, lie down under a neem tree and have the man yank out my molars with rusty pliers?—*

BB: December 14: *Wrote a letter to Colombo promising Ceylonese Buddhists a visiting Alexandrian delegation next year as they requested. . . .*

IM: December 15: *I had 24 photos made of my noble visage, some to distribute to the loyal here, some to take for Indi-ans—Ben finally shipped 2 trunks for himself, 3 for me—*

BB: December 16: *The Auctioneer's flag hung over the door-way of the Lamasery today, nearly everything sold. . . . I'm sometimes sad, but how much lighter I feel these days! . . . Irena fled to the Battery to meet a Master, unable to bear seeing the apartment's contents depart, poor old girl. . . .*

IM: December 17: *At the Battery I met Katkov's agent, who gave me a secret list of sages, swamis, Maharajahhs, and Indian nationalists to contact for the cause in India—*

BB: December 18: *She sold my spare spectacles!. . . . Where am I to find an oculist open on a Sunday? . . .*

IM: December 19: *I packed my last suitcase—I am at peace in my soul—*

BB: December 19: *The damned cat is gone again, in the rain. . . .*

IM: December 20: *I wonder, will anyone come to our farewell party?—*

On the evening of December 21, the Lamasery, once the great-est salon in New York, looked like an empty warehouse. The floorboards were carpetless, no curtains hung on the windows or pictures on the walls, and a chilly gray mist drifted in through a broken pane of glass. The Founders got a rousing send-off none-theless. General Doubleday wore his uniform for the occasion. Zia, now Mrs. Felix Green, came back for old times' sake, looking pretty in a full skirt and pink ruffled blouse. Jim O'Leary, the ac-tor, accompanied her. The Reverend Plankton was all in black as usual but, helping himself to Mr. O'Leary's flask, became very jolly and blessed the company—in a non-sectarian way, so as not to rile Irena. . . . Sarah's mother, Natasha, looked willowy, much improved in health now that Ben and Irena had found her a good job. Sarah was adorable in green, her hair pinned up like a lady, but not too grown up to cuddle her old friend the cat, Charles, who finally returned sleek and plump from a hunting expedition.

Irena read some palms. Ben stood on a trunk and sang some Irish songs to keep things cheerful while Irena and Natasha huddled together in overcoats against the cold. Valises were all there were to sit on, since the furniture was gone. Irena and Ben served tea in the remaining three cups; the guests took turns drinking from them and eating cookies off pieces of cardboard. Mr. Edison arrived to explain the workings of his phonographic machine, and the guests gathered around it to make a historic recording on tinfoil:

Irena: We shall miss our faithful friends in America.
General Doubleday: May every encounter end in glorious Alexandrian Victory!
Mr. O'Leary: Keep your powder dry, Captain, and your peck—
Zia: Don't you dare say that, Jimmy!
Reverend Plankton: The nation—is this thing on?
Mr. Edison: Lean closer to the speaking tube.
Reverend Plankton: Our nation will always remember the Alexandrians' contribution to its spiritual enlightenment—
Irena: Flapdoodle!
Mr. Edison: The scientific world awaits your discoveries.
Natasha: Oh, Irena—Ben—Sarah and I will miss you so!
Sarah: I hope you find lots of swamis!
Ben: We'll do our very best. (Ahem) Now, my good friends, on behalf of the Society, I'd like to leave you with a few words on this great occasion. . . . What's that cat doing?
Sarah: Charles wants to say goodbye.
Mr. O'Leary: Let's hear it from Charles!
Natasha: Hold him up.
Sarah: Is he really mine, now?

Irena: He certainly is, dear—
Charles: Meeeow. . . .
All: Hurrah!

Later that night, a steamship glided out of New York harbor through silvery moonlit. A foghorn gave out a long farewell blast. Irena stood at the rail with her blue umbrella raised. As Ben stepped beside her, she took his arm.

The chums cast not a glance back at the city. Their eyes were on the horizon.

Part Two

Northern India

7

Just before dawn on April 16, 1879, Irena finished her last ship-
board letter to Sarah and her mother: "I hope that one day you
will come to visit me in my magnificent new home!" she wrote.
She was being optimistic about India—which had yet to materialize outside her stateroom window—and more prescient about Sarah than she knew.

Hours later, the Founders' ship steamed into Bombay harbor.
Standing on deck, Irena watched the black night dissolve. The
sky turned silver-pink, like a silken theatrical ceiling, above the
city. Clouds of fog billowed on the water: velvet curtains parting
to reveal a panorama of quays, avenues, temple domes, graceful
palaces. A magnificent stage, she thought, where she was to play
out the drama she had been preparing for all her life.

Beside her at the rail, Ben gazed out at the palm trees, minarets, bullock-drawn carts. Rivulets of sweat streamed down his
red face; his pince-nez was fogged over in the heat; but his enthusiasm—like Irena's—remained undampened. They searched the
docks for a delegation from the Arya Samaj. Irena expected men
in robes and turbans, women in colorful sarees and sparkling
bangles, all holding garlands of flowers to drape around the necks
of the pilgrims from America. An open carriage would be delightful, but even better would be an elephant, its forehead painted
auspiciously with purple and orange designs, a silver howdah
strapped to its back to seat the visitors....

"*Ex Oriente, lux!* Behold the light from the East!" Ben pointed
to the sun hovering above the molten water like a hot coal

wrapped in gauze. He'd outfitted himself at Aden in a pale cotton suit and broad-brimmed hat, looked as comfortable as a white man could look in this climate.

"I see it," Irena wiped the sweat from her face. "And *feel* it." Her small blue umbrella offered little protection from the glare, but she kept it slowly twirling over her head as if it might drill a hole through the gelatinous heat and let in a shaft of cool air. She was still wearing her layers of dark clothes; her hair stood out in heat-curled wires from her scalp. Fifteen years earlier, she'd arrived in India over the mountain passes from Afghanistan and stayed six months in the cool Himalayas. She'd held fascinating discourses with holy men, including a younger Swami Saraswathi Dayananda, and for the first time in her life, had been surrounded by people who regarded her mystical yearnings not as a signs of freakishness but as evidence of spiritual advancement. Somewhere, out there in the mist and heat, she would find another haven waiting.

Meanwhile, a lack of breeze kept the pilot boats from approaching the steamer. The ship's crew began hoisting crates up on deck from the hold. She heard the caw of a crow—a hopeful sign, she said—like Noah's dove. Just then a crash caused her to whirl round. A crate lay up-ended on the deck where it had toppled. Snapping sounds came from within the box, like metal birds trying to tweet.

"My clocks!" Ben moaned.

"India is a timeless place," Irena consoled him.

She wondered if the crow had been somehow responsible for the crash—a *diakka* in disguise. Had it called out to the cuckoo birds, making them believe they could fly? As Ben rushed off to see about the clocks, she watched the reed sail of the first pilot boat cutting through the fog. Dayananda wasn't on it. Or the next boat. Or the next. Where was he? Irena sat in the last boat between Ben and some nearly naked paddlers. Soon her heart began to reverberate like a tom-tom as she made out the palm-lined streets, the terra-cotta houses, the temples with their gaily-colored flags. A hum of voices radiated out from the quays.

Ben must have felt their vibrations, too; he leaned forward on his seat, wide-eyed as a boy at his first magic-lantern show, and as the prow crunched against shore, he leapt out, his boots splashing on the steps. The other passengers, some British gentlemen and Indian merchants, cast curious glances at him and Irena as they stepped onto the wharf. The docks swarmed with people. But Dayananda was nowhere to be seen. British men shook hands with compatriots; Indians bowed to each other with palms pressed together at chest level and murmured *"Namaste"* in greetings. Wicker cases were lifted onto coolies' heads. Crates rolled away on rumbling bullock carts. Gradually the crowd thinned.

Finally, only Ben and Irena were left standing in the glare beside their trunks and the crate of smashed clocks. The sun had slipped out of its gauze wrapper; now it seemed to float like an incandescent jellyfish only a few yards above the dock, its red-hot tentacles singeing the top of Irena's head. She twirled her umbrella faster. Smiling gamely, Ben watched it as if it were a spinning prayer wheel. He began pacing.

"I cabled Chintamon our exact arrival time!" he said. Mr. Chintamon was an officer in the Arya Samaj/Alexandrian Society who had promised to meet them.

"He will come." Irena sat on a trunk.

"Of course he will!" Ben said. His new suit was already drenched; his whiskers glittered with beads of sweat.

Finally a procession of strange-looking carriages rolled up. The first was pulled by a slat-sided horse that seemed to shrink, head drooping, as soon as its reins were slackened. A stout, bespectacled man in a white *dhoti* and linen jacket leapt from the vehicle and rushed along the quay. "Hullo, Hullo!" he called, skidding to a halt, his hands clasped at his chest. "Hurrychund Chintamon, at your service!"

"Hello!" Ben made a lunge for his host and grabbed his hand. The Indian shrank back, his eyes shut tight. Irena averted her own eyes, knowing that Brahmins hate to be touched by anyone outside their caste. Ben gave the man a few hearty American slaps on the back before releasing him. "Thanks for coming to meet us!"

Mr. Chintamon brushed himself off vigorously. "The pleasure is mine."

"*Namaste,*" Irena pressed her palms together. "I bring you respectful greetings from the members of the American Alexandrian Society."

Mr. Chintamon looked around the empty quay. "But where are they? I am expecting a dozen eminent Americans—General Doubleday, Mr. Thomas Edison, Miss Victoria Woodhull. . . ."

"They were unable to get away at present," Irena said. "They send heartfelt regrets."

"I also have heartfelt regrets," Mr. Chintamon said, staring at all the carriages he'd hired. He waved all but the first two away.

"Many Westerners will follow," Irena said. "We are merely the first—the *avant garde*—in a vast procession of wisdom-seekers."

"We are now one vast family," Chintamon said, managing a smile. "The members have all enjoyed Madame's book of Astral Veils. Also the journalistic clippings about famous phenomena—the bells, the materialized sketches, et cetera. I hope you will honor us with some of them."

"Us?" Irena spotted no one in the carriage but a driver. "I don't see the Swami," she said.

"He is eagerly expecting you very soon." Chintamon gave a shout, and from nowhere several coolies came running to load the second carriage—a tonga, it was called, Irena remembered. She and Ben sat facing backwards on a hard wooden seat scarcely wide enough for one person. Their host sat beside the driver facing the horse's flanks. After many strokes of a whip, the poor beast lurched forward.

"You misrepresented the size of the delegation to Chintamon!" Ben whispered.

"I only said the others *might* come." Irena glanced away. "I suppose to someone whose English is not good—"

"His English is nearly perfect."

"Well, *he* promised that *Dayananda* would be here!" She pouted. "Dear Ben, you don't want to fight on our first day here, do you?"

"No." Ben sighed. "But please, no more exaggerations!"

Smiling, Irena took his hand. She sat back to observe the city that was to be her home. The tall green-trimmed mosques, the whitewashed Hindu temples, the imposing terra-cotta-colored civic buildings—all enchanted her. She inhaled the magical scents of India: the sun-tinted dust, the clouds of pungent spices, the sky full of smoke from thousands of tiny cook fires. She flowed—or bumped—along the great rivers of humanity, passing dark Maharashtrans and turbaned Punjabis and mustachioed Rajputs. There were Chinese shopkeepers and Malay goods-haulers and a few incongruous white-suited Europeans. Moslem women covered head to toe in black *burqas* glided by like moving shadows; saree-clad Hindu women swayed gracefully in and out of the crowds. The clamor of Eastern languages surrounded her like an orchestra of plucked and whistled instruments.

Beside her, Ben strained to take in the parade of vehicles: plodding bullock carts, faster-moving pony carts, a palanquin borne by trotting barelegged men. He looked up to see a flock of birds flutter across the sky. "What are they?" he asked. "Those green ones settling in the great feather-duster trees?"

Irena laughed. "Wild parrots!"

"Splendid!" Ben leaned back to watch the birds swooping among the tall, graceful palms.

Eventually the tonga left the city's bustling center and rattled down a dusty lane into a courtyard. The air went still. As Irena stepped down, the earth beneath her feet seemed to tilt precariously, and she was glad to have Ben's arm to hold. Months ago she'd written Chintamon with instructions to rent a modest bungalow in the Hindu quarter. But since her letter evidently led him to expect a large Alexandrian delegation, he'd provided a tall, three-storied house. Awnings protruded from above the windows like green visors. The verandahs were resplendent with potted geraniums and papyrus plumes.

"Welcome to your new headquarters!" Chintamon smiled, his cheeks puffing out. Inside, Irena saw servants raising clouds of dust with short-handled brooms. The furniture was sparse: one bed—a four-footed platform with a thin *dhurry* for a mattress—no chairs, only pillows on the floor, and no desks or tables. "Everything is coming!" their host assured them, shouting at the bare-chested servants.

All that week and the next, they filled the house with heavy European furniture, none of it matching. In the front yard Irena sat writing and smoking under a neem tree; she remembered the importance of staying quiet during tropical afternoons. It made her tired to watch Ben bustle around overseeing the placement of desks, bureaus, beds. Between shipments, he often paced the verandah, dressed in his new suit as if expecting throngs of Alexandrians to arrive at any moment. But the yard remained empty except when boys herded a few goats across it or servants laid down in the shade of a bush to nap. Every day Ben rode in a pony trap to the headquarters of the Arya Samaj; every day he found its door locked with an enormous padlock. A watchman told him that Dayananda and his officers were away on a pilgrimage.

One evening, Irena watched him set off on a walk up the lane. In half an hour, he returned at the head of a dusty parade of ragged, keening beggars. "I ran out of coins!" he told her, slipping inside the gate. His jacket was mussed from being clutched and yanked. The tragic look in his eyes reflected the misery of all Asia. "There's a camp of these people by the main road. They're living in shacks made of old boards. They're practically naked. No one seems to have any food!"

"They are refugees from the famines on the indigo plantations." Irena said. Men and women turned their plaintive faces toward her; their dry lips stretched back to display black and missing teeth. Some pointed to their bellies and moaned. "The British tax them so that they have to stop raising the food crops which made them self-sufficient. The poor souls have to plant single cash crops, like indigo, to pay the taxes. Then when the international indigo market drops, they starve."

"And they're put off the land with nothing?" Ben asked.

"Yes. It is horrible!" Irena took a big handful of coins from her handbag and gave the money to him to distribute.

"I used to hate the Brits for secretly supporting the Confederacy, but that was just . . . theoretical, compared to this!" Ben pointed to a naked infant clasped in the arms of a ragged teenage girl. The baby's head looked like a parchment-covered skull; flies walked over his caked eyelashes. "We've got to find ways to feed these people!"

"If we let twenty through the gate today, there will be two hundred tomorrow." Irena gazed sorrowfully at the baby. "The Masters have ordered me: first make the Alexandrian Society solvent, then help the Arya Samaj to drive out the Britishers who are draining India. Then the Indians themselves can use the railways and plantations the English made for themselves."

"All right." Ben sighed, patting the head of a child pushing up against his side. "There was a German who wrote about Indians taking over the railways and so forth. London correspondent for the *New York Tribune*. . . ." Ben handed out his last coins and watched the beggars shuffle off down the lane. Once they were gone, he collapsed into a wicker chair next to Irena's beneath the neem tree. Now the only sound in the yard was the hum of insects and the servants' voices in the house. "That German fellow . . . I think his name was Marx," Ben said, mopping his brow.

"He wrote a book, too. I tried to read it." Irena yawned. "Too much materialist flapdoodle."

"I remember reading the *Trib* in the Lamasery. . . ." Ben looked down at the ground.

"Do you miss the Lamasery, Ben?"

"I don't know. I'm disoriented here. Funny expression: '*dis-Orient-ed*.'" His smile was a bit crooked. He searched his pockets for his pipe, but couldn't seem to find it. After a while, he just sat there sweating amid the strange sounds of India, his hands hanging awkwardly at his sides. "I expected to be busy organizing things, setting up projects, but how am I to meet people without some liaison?"

"We have been here scarcely a fortnight, Maloney. In India, everything takes longer." Irena leaned toward him across her armrest.. "The waiting is part of the Masters' plan for us," she explained. But she could see from the lines around Ben's eyes that this was as little consolation to him as it was to her.

Chintamon came almost every day promising that a delegation from the Arya Samaj was about to arrive, but for all his smiles and silken words, he didn't convince Irena. She sent off cables and waited for replies. Meanwhile, she needed something to cheer Ben with. One day karma provided: from the lane she heard the staccato beat of a drum. She called Ben from the house, and they followed the sound to some mud huts clustered beside the lane.

"That's called a *damaru*. All the conjurors carry them," She pointed to the little hourglass shaped drum that a turbaned man with an enormous mustache carried. The man squatted before a hut, his hands flying, and drumbeats agitated the air. Drawn by the rhythm, people began to cluster around him. Irena sank into a squatting position like the Indian women around her; Ben, observing the men, sat on his haunches as best he could. The magician spread a woven jute mat onto the ground and with his hands drew a circle in the air. "The net of Indra, god of magic." Irena whispered. "He's pulling us into it."

"*Yantra mantra jula-jula-tantra!*" the man moaned.

"What's he saying?" Ben whispered.

"It's *jadubhasa*, the secret language of the magician caste. Now you will see true Eastern *prapti*, the ability to cause materializations!"

Ben's face was rapt, his eyes wide. This was the sort of evidence of Eastern paranormal powers he'd come to India to collect. The magician held up a seed and an empty basket. Then he dropped the seed and clamped the basket upside down over it. Irena recalled how she'd marveled the first time she'd seen this done in Delhi, or was it Damascus? "In ancient times," she told Ben, "this performer would have been invited to the courts of Maharajahhs and revered as a high priest."

"*Gilli gilli!*" the man intoned, his mouth opening wide. Slowly he raised the basket. And there, beneath it, was a tiny mango tree growing out of the sand!

"*Aah!*" exclaimed the spectators.

"Extraordinary!" Ben applauded vigorously; at the same time, he leaned forward to get a good look at the magician's sleeves.

Now the spectators' faces grew tense. The magician led a small girl into the enchanted circle. Her lips seemed to quiver in terror. Irena steeled herself—she'd seen this sort of demonstration before, but it always made her cringe. Snarling, the magician threw a dirty burlap cloth over the child and forced her down to the ground. The audience stared in horror as she thrashed pitifully.

"We can't allow this!" Ben said.

Irena dug her fingertips into his wrist. "Be still! If you interfere, there will be an uproar. The Society will be finished here!" She watched the magician pick up a rusty sword.

"*Yantra mantra!*" the man moaned. Suddenly he thrust the sword point first into the mound of burlap. Again and again he plunged it down. The child's screams brought tears to Irena's eyes. Finally the magician pulled away the cloth. The girl lay motionless, her limbs splayed out in a posture of death. A hideous wound encircled her neck. Blood dripped from the raw flesh into the dust, staining it dark red. The crowd shrank back, groaning. Now the magician's face was contorted with grief. His huge dark eyes gazed at the onlookers, reflecting their pain, and his words flew from his lips with an awful urgency.

"If we throw coins, he can use them to bribe the spirits into restoring the child's life," Irena whispered. Ben reached deep into his pocket and threw some money onto the mat.

The magician let out a blood-curdling cry. Moving his lips fervently, he covered the child completely with the burlap again. The spectators silently repeated the incantation. "*HO!*" he shouted, and whipped away the cloth. The little girl sat up, rubbing her eyes. The wound was gone from her neck; only a few smears of blood remained on her delicate brown skin. She smiled at the man, then at the audience. The air filled with cheers. Irena heard Ben's hoarse voice among them. Color was returning to his face.

Her grip on his arm relaxed. "True Eastern magic can be a dark force," she said as they walked back down the lane. "There is more to it than little mango trees."

"Strange—I saw what I saw, but my mind won't fully accept it." Ben's voice wobbled. "Could such a ritual truly have the power of life and death?"

"It has been occurring since ancient times." She gave him a somber look. "You must beware, Ben, never get too close to these powers without an experienced guide!"

One afternoon, the Founders took a trap into the city and

walked through the narrow alleys of the bazaar. Irena still preferred to wear the clothing she'd brought with her, but Ben
wanted to buy some lightweight Indian-style outfits. The merchants called out to him from their shadowy canvas grottos and
held up bolts of white silk. Scorning such expensive material, he
didn't stop until he'd found a shop that sold homespun cotton
cloth. Tailors measured him and sewed garments as he waited.
They helped him into the clothes. When he looked in a mirror, he
saw a totally new, Eastern version of himself—a pink-skinned
graybeard in a long white *kurta* shirt and loose trousers, a cloth
cap and sandals.

"Don't you think I look a little strange?" he asked.

"Not at all," Irena said. His new outfits would accomplish two
useful things, she reckoned. They would make him look outland-
ish to the British—literally beyond the pale. And they would en-
dear him to the Indians. "You look distinguished," she told him.

And indeed, when Chintamon saw Ben stepping down from the
trap back at their house, he clasped his hands with pleasure. "A
Yankee pandit!" he exulted.

"Thank you." Ben smiled. "I'm ready to greet the entire Arya
Samaj!"

But Dayananda still didn't come.

One day an impish-looking adolescent walked into the house
and sat down on the carpet in Irena's room. "An emissary from
the Swami?" Ben asked.

"The Master Kut-huri has sent me a servant," Irena explained.
"This is Babula!"

The boy leapt up from the floor and salaamed to Ben with an
exaggerated hands-together, elbows-out gesture. He wore a pink
turban and matching silk pants; his *kurta* shirt was of bright yellow. His eyes seemed to be lined with kohl, the pupils dilated.

"Well, hello there!" Ben shook the boy's hand vigorously.

Babula gazed at his palm when Ben let go of it. "*Wull hol-loo
they-err!*" the boy imitated Ben's English. Glancing at Irena, he
giggled. She spoke sharply to him in Arabic, and he scurried to
the corner.

"The kid'll have to learn to stop salaaming, now that he's working for democratic Americans." Ben said. "But I don't know if we can afford to keep him." He hadn't sold many of the mechanical apple-corers he'd brought, due to an unexpected shortage of apples in India. His agricultural implements weren't sharp enough to penetrate the hard, local soil. Only the cuckoo clocks were selling well, those that weren't broken. The Alexandrian Society was getting by on Ben's dwindling savings account.

But Irena kept Babula on. Katkov, her Moscow editor, had arranged for the boy to find Irena in Bombay. Babula was a Pathan who had recently worked for an Afghani arms smuggler paid by the Russian Intelligence Service. Knowing Ben's reluctance to involve the Alexandrian Society in politics, Irena never spoke to him about the important information-gathering work she was sure Moscow would begin assigning her any day now.

"We will need the boy to help us prepare for very important visitors," she said to Ben.

And toward dusk that very day visitors did arrive: four elderly Brahmins wearing white *dhotis* and carrying black umbrellas. Watching them climb down from a large tonga in the yard, Irena's heart sank: Dayananda wasn't among them. But the scholars said they were in constant communication with the swami and would personally convey to him the Americans' greetings. Irena knew that if their report about her and Ben impressed Dayananda, he would provide them an Indian sponsor everywhere they went. But if the scholars weren't impressed . . . well, she couldn't bear to think about that.

Ben recovered from his disappointment quickly. By now, he'd learned to make the clasped-hands gesture of greeting and to say *Namaste;* the problem was getting him to stop doing it, once the visitors had been made comfortable on pillows in the sitting room. Irena shouted for Babula, who screamed at the household servants; eventually tea and cakes were produced. Ben showed around a copy of *Shadows of the Other World.* The sages, who all spoke English, admired its text and ghostly illustrations. Irena explained that, according to what Master Kut-huri had revealed to her, such spirit materializations were produced when the soul departed from a dead man, leaving behind an astral shell, which for a time retained the appearance and senses of the deceased, the "spook" of the séance parlor. She then linked this phenomena to several similar ones described in ancient Indian lore, and launched into a discourse about some Sutras she had been studying recently.

The visitors, not used to listening to a woman sitting like an equal among the men, glanced suspiciously at her. Gradually they positioned themselves on the pillows so that they were clustered around Ben. Irena was relegated to a spot on the periphery of the circle. Ben continued speaking to the visitors, but he didn't need psychic intuition to tell him that Irena, her hooded eyes glowering lethally, wasn't sharing his enjoyment of the discussion. He changed the topic to spirit phenomena, speaking of her contributions to this field of inquiry.

"Is it true that Madame can produce such phenomena that have been described in our ancient holy texts? We would be grateful to see one," said one of the sages, a small wizened man with tufts of white hair spouting from his ears. "Not as a test, please be assured," said the man, "but merely as a gesture of good will."

She half-closed her eyes and touched her forehead with her fingertips. The men waited. Outdoors, a peacock squawked; a peddler shouted his wares from the lane. Irena opened her eyes and dropped her hand to her lap. "The Masters are nearby," she said in a low, whispery voice. "They are looking for a special way to welcome you here."

Ben resumed talking. Babula hovered about, listening carefully as he poured tea, and then took himself off to the sewing room. Now the discussions very much included Irena. The sages listened avidly as she spoke of occult matters that they could never have imagined any woman, much less a Western one, could understand. They kept bringing the subject back to magic; Irena continued to deflect it away. Finally she suddenly rose from the circle and walked with a slow floating movement toward a teakwood sideboard. The men went silent as they watched her arms rise into the air. Like a bird soaring instinctively toward a nest, her hand dove behind the sideboard and reappeared with a large, white handkerchief.

"An astral gift!" she declared. Bowing, she presented it to the oldest of Hindus. "Please observe the stitching on the border."

"P. Ganesha," the gentleman read, his eyes growing wide. "My very own name!"

A collective sigh went up. The scholar showed his treasure to his colleagues. They smiled and murmured. Ben, too, looked heartened. Before the pandits left, each of them received a personally embroidered handkerchief. Irena stood beside Ben on the verandah, watching the visitors approach their tonga beneath the neem tree in the yard. One by one they folded their black umbrellas and climbed up. The horse stepped forward; the big wooden wheels creaked and turned.

Irena waved to her visitors. "I would have given them a handkerchief for Dayananda. . . ."

"But you want him to come in person to get one." Ben smiled.

"It seems you're getting to know my methods."

Ben nodded. "A few of them, Mulligan."

"Well, let us fervently hope that this one has worked." She avoided his anxious glance. "If it has not," she concluded, "we may as well join the throng of wandering mendicants in this country."

8

They say that for the white man in India, the first monsoon is the
hardest, and the one that washed over Bombay in July of 1879
nearly sucked Ben into a black whirlpool he couldn't swim out of.
Unlike the British, Ben had no cronies at the club or the regimen-
tal mess or the polo grounds to commiserate with. There was no
lady's sewing circle or church committee where he could send
Irena to be consoled. They had only each other, and had to tough
it out—appearing vulnerable threatened to weaken the partnership that both depended on for survival in this new land.

So on his worst days Ben shut himself in his study to wait out
the deluge. Such a source of joy to the local people, who rushed
outdoors as if for a public holiday, the pouring rains stirred the
outdoors into what looked to Ben like a watery brown slough of
despond. The rain sent a floating dog carcass to nuzzle the verandah step. The rain flushed out a crab-sized cockroach that he
beat with a sandal as it scuttled across his desk, splattering its
damp gore on his blotter. Rain clattered in a *minié*-ball barrage
against the roof. Rain hissed at every window. Rain fell past the
doors in gray sheets that confined him like the walls of the dungeon where he'd interrogated Mary Surratt. He hadn't left her
back in America, after all. No, he heard her voice in the rain,
whispering, whispering, "You promised me my life! I trusted
you!" Shutting his eyes tight, he pictured her trembling her in her
cell. Its door was still open, as in his last dream, but she remained
pressed against the back wall. Now he listened to the rain turn the
house into a floating prison ship, destined to take him wandering

into storm after storm forever.

Ben remembered hiding in the hayloft during heavy rains; he'd pressed his sister's mahogany darning egg between his palms for comfort. Now he trudged to the local market, his Indian clothing soaked, his hair dripping water down his face, to buy an ostrich egg, the closest thing he could find to his childhood talisman. At night he sat in his study, rubbing it carefully in both hands, fearful that if he pressed it too tightly it would crack.

What am I doing here? He wrote in his journal, underlining the question once, twice, thrice, five, ten times, until there was no more space on the page. *Inactivity wraps its scaly leaden tail around my ankles; inertia sucks me empty of resolve.*

Since the four sages arrived two months ago and left with handkerchiefs, he noted, only a few visitors had come—and none of them were Dayananda.

Also, his sons never responded to his letters. He stared at his boys' pictures and wept.

Also, the Society was nearly out of funds! Chintamon came to the house in his *dhoti* and jacket and solar *topee* and demanded 3000 rupees rent—for the house, the furniture, the pony trap, even the tonga from the port. But the original agreement was that everything was to be a donation from the Arya Samaj! Ben protested. And what about the 1000 rupees (equivalent) he'd sent Chintamon from New York? Gone for "operating expenses!" Chintamon said. Ben roared at him. Chintamon fled. But he'd be back.

Ben railed at Irena: "How could Dayananda—a living Master!—have sent a thief to welcome us?" She didn't know. "Does Dayananda even exist?" He demanded, pacing in his study. The stagnant air felt like a murky liquid in which he was barely treading water

"Do you want to go back to America?" She bit her lip.

"To what? My law practice? It's finished. My family? Scattered. I've cut myself off from everything I had!" He picked up a wooden image of Ganesh, the tubby elephant-headed god, from his desk. Its bemused face suddenly looked like an absurd child's mask. "I've been here for months and accomplished nothing!" A chorus of rain hissed from all the windows. "All I can do is . . . is yell at this pot-bellied *elephant!*"

Irena carefully took the image from his hand. "Lord Ganesh is a Master, too," she said. "The patron of scholars like you. He wrote all the volumes of the *Mahabharata* without lifting his pen from the paper. He is also the god of new beginnings. Just let him guide you. . . ."

The god beamed his millenniums-old smile at Ben. "Yes, yes," Ben muttered. Irena's words kept him composed for several hours, but they weren't enough to get him through the night.

At about eleven o'clock he found a bottle of brandy in the attic and drank it. He also found an old revolver in a bureau drawer and took it back to his study to examine it. The next thing knew, he heard a crash—his French windows flying open—and Irena came lunging through them, trying to wrestle the gun from his hands. She was in her lumpy old bathrobe; he was bandy-kneed in his nightshirt. They grunted and swore. The gun clunked to the floor without discharging. Snatching it up, Irena threw it out the window into the garden. There, inexplicably, it exploded in a wet rosebush, spraying red petals all over the verandah.

"What are you doing in here?" Ben shouted, sitting down hard on his camp bed.

"I saw you in the lamplight!" she panted, collapsing beside him. "You were pointing the gun at your forehead!"

He stared at the hand that had held the pistol. "Really?"

"Do you think I came flying into your bedroom out of sudden lust?" Irena wiped her face with the lapel of her bathrobe. He eyes were damp and red rimmed. "I suppose you *could* thank me."

"Thank you," Ben sighed.

"I was about to bring something to cheer you." She showed him a note written in gold ink on black paper.

Keep Faith Noble Chela—I Will Appear To You Soon.

He read. He knew he should take heart from the message, but it cheered him about as much as the elephant-god's smile. When Irena read the message aloud, though, her voice was so intense that he nearly believed the message as fervently as she obviously did.

"Thank you, old chum," he said, with more conviction this time.

"The rain is stopped, Maloney." She rested her head against his shoulder.

He listened. The urgent hissing had ceased; only calm dripping sounds came from the windows— like slow tears of relief. A cool breeze blew into the room. For a moment, he had a powerful impulse to collapse sideways with Irena onto a bed like a boy falling into a haystack, to bury himself with her, to weep and laugh and pluck straw from her hair. But she was struggling to her feet now, holding out the golden-scripted letter to him.

"Keep this," she said quietly.

He felt the stiff paper between his fingers. "Tell Moreya I'm grateful, Mulligan," he said.

It was the right thing to say. She beamed a smile at him as she turned to leave. Only then did he notice that she was barefoot. The sight of her toes, naked as white snails on the dirty cement floor, brought a small cry to his throat.

Ben stayed awake till dawn. Most of the rose petals had blown off the verandah; only a few red spots remained stuck to the stone to remind Ben that last night's events had really taken place. He found the pistol, unloaded it, and buried it deep in the mud. Then he returned to his study and began drafting letters. He could no longer wait for Dayananda's help. He'd organize the Alexandrian Society in India himself, as he had in New York.

Ben called the Society's Bombay headquarters "The Crow's Nest" because of the way its top story rose above the surrounding rooftops and looked down over the water half a mile away. He climbed to a little balcony beneath the roof to watch the sun rise over the Warli Bridge. *Bom Bahia* ("good bay")—the old Portuguese name for the port—was alive with sailing ships cutting across the shining pink water like knife blades through a swathe of silk. Smoke from neighborhood cook fires brought him the scents of frying chilies. In the yard, a woman milked a buffalo beneath a palm tree. Beside a stream down the lane, a laundryman sang *ghazals* in a high, sweet voice and slapped wet clothes against a stone, each slap echoing against the pastel-tinted sides of the houses. Ben took his mat to the balcony and sat cross-legged in meditation, breathing rhythmically before statues of a smiling Ganesh and a serene Buddha. Then he rose, refreshed, and went to his study to begin a new day's work.

Scarcely lifting his pen from paper all morning, Ben drew up plans for the first official meeting of the Bombay Alexandrian Society/Arya Samaj. He sent out press releases to newspapers, invitations to religious organizations, announcements to the new Bombay university.

On the day of the meeting, nearly a hundred pandits turned out to view the exotic Americans. The old and the young were there, the light-skinned and the swarthy, the rotund and reedy. Men wore long robes, scull caps, colored turbans; their faces were fuzzy with flowing gray chin-bushes and sweeping black mustaches. The Arya Samaj was represented by several sages, but Dayananda was not among them.

After Babula and the other servants had supplied everyone with Indian pastries and tea, Ben gave a short welcoming address. His old confidence was back as he strode about the room, making the *Namaste* gesture with clasped hands, discussing the weighty books he'd been reading. Among the guests were gurus who'd actually meditated in Himalayan caves, gone on pilgrimages to important centers of spiritual power, entered ecstatic trance states to view the faces of deities. Ben's reverence for them showed on his ruddy face; the eyes sparkled behind his pince-nez, his voice boomed, his whiskers seemed at times to vibrate with enthusiasm. The visitors found Ben impressive. Here was a white man who honored Indians by dressing in their homespun clothes—a sight they'd never seen before. He wasn't British; he came from that wild, anomalous continent of cowboys and frontiersmen who'd once chased colonialists from their own land. He had no wish to convert Indians to Western ideas; instead he spoke with great respect about Asian culture and religion. Big, blustery, guileless, effusive, he made people smile with amazement when he approached.

One professor from the local university came: Dr. Bertram Gordon, a British historian. He was accompanied by his wife, Daisy. Smiling, the lady extended her hand to Ben.

"I've long been eager to meet the author of *Shadows of the Other World!*" she said.

Ben flushed. "Thank you—but wherever did you find it?"

"The American consulate in London." Mrs. Gordon's voice had a musical lilt to it. Her face was fringed by light brown curls that danced when she cocked her head to get a better focus on Ben. She looked about thirty-five, with big lively green eyes behind a pair of round spectacles. Ben noted that she was pleasantly round all over—her bosom, her flanks, her plump cheeks. Most British women he'd met were more angular.

"I see you're in native garb," she said, touching his sleeve. "How exciting!"

"Very comfortable, in fact," Ben said, glancing down at her graceful white fingers on his wrist.

"At a fancy dress ball at Government House, some of the English ladies actually wore sarees. I wanted to, but alas, my husband forbade it. For you to live here in the Hindu quarter—" She glanced around at the brightly colored wall hangings and pillows. "Well, it must be quite an adventure!"

"I like it," Ben said. "If I want to learn from Indians, I need to live among them."

"I dare say you'll learn more than my husband. He didn't want to come here." She gestured toward Irena. "He doesn't care for mediums."

"Mediums? We've put all that sort of thing behind us," Ben said.

"'We'? Are you married, Captain Blackburn?"

"No!" He laughed. "The partnership is entirely platonic."

"Ah." Mrs. Gordon smiled again, and he got a whiff of her lilac perfume.

For the next half-hour, she prompted him to tell her about his investigations of paranormal phenomena in America and India. She gobbled up his stories like someone who'd been eating bland food for so long she'd nearly forgotten what spices taste like. Ben could tell that Daisy Gordon's husband hadn't the means to appreciate a robust woman like her. He had a thin chest and sparse wispy hair. When he eventually rejoined Mrs. Gordon and she introduced him, his handshake, Ben noticed, was limp.

"We saw that trick in Egypt," Professor Gordon said, pointing toward a corner where Irena was holding up a name-embroidered handkerchief before an astonished group of Indians. "All the wizards there can do it. I must say, though, Madame Milanova's knowledge of the *Bhagavad Gita* is quite extraordinary. Unusual mind she's got, for all her frank language."

"I adore frankness," Mrs. Gordon said. "Won't you introduce us, Ben?"

He did. Irena, sparking with costume jewelry, sat on an old plush armchair as if it were a throne. She nodded at Mrs. Gordon, her eyes narrowing for a moment. Then, turning back to the Indian men surrounding her, she launched into a story about Mr. Lytton, the present British viceroy who was famous for his splendid clothes and huge formal parties.

"He is known as 'The Great Ornamental,'" Irena said, blowing a steam of cigarette smoke into the air. "While thousands of natives are starving to death in the South, his imperial self travels not only with a French chef but an Italian pastry-maker." The Indians, embarrassed for the professor and his wife, glanced nervously about, but Irena steamed right on like a runaway locomotive. "Ye gods, I'd have expected better behavior from the son of England's most visionary novelist!"

"I note the debt you acknowledge to Mr. Bulwer-Lytton in your own work, Madame," one of the Hindus remarked in a hopeful voice.

"Artists have their own nationality, regardless of where they happen to get born. Scholars, too," she added, nodding to Professor Gordon. "And their lovely wives and any others of their breed brave enough to come down here among us mystics."

"Enjoying your own Italian pastry, are you?" Professor Gordon gestured toward the plate of *ramgulams* beside Irena.

Irena laughed and patted her stomach. "I always enjoy my pastries, but these are from the local market. Do try one!"

The guests held their breath, knowing how fearful the British were of Indian food not prepared by their own cooks. Professor Gordon tried to paralyze his wife with a frown. But she popped one of the sweet sticky spheres into her mouth. "Yum!" she declared, beads of honey sticking to the corners of her lips. Her husband turned away.

Ben inclined his head into Mrs. Gordon's lilac aura. "You, too, enjoy adventures."

"I hope to," she said, and before she left that afternoon, she slipped him her calling card.

The house continued to fill with visitors during the following weeks, and the Founders were asked out, as well. Lavish lunches were served them in the homes of Zoroastrian merchants. Hindu scholars invited them to their book-walled rooms for discourses on the *Vedas*. Ben and Irena were given tours of mosques and mirrored Jain temples. Sikh priests called for them in two-wheeled *gharis*, which Irena described as "Indic chariots" in the newspaper articles she sent off to Moscow. Up and down the hills Ben and Irena rolled in all manner of open vehicles. "What a spectacle we must present," Ben remarked, pointing at a stampede of children raising dust behind them on the road.

When Professor and Daisy Gordon sent an invitation to visit an island in the Bombay harbor, Irena tossed it aside, but Ben picked it up again. "We don't have to alienate all the British," he said. "A few of them are getting sympathetic to our ideas."

Irena sniffed. "So I have noticed." But she agreed to visit the island.

Mrs. Gordon, her little girls, and their ayah arrived in an open carriage; sadly, the professor was not feeling up to the excursion today. First, Mrs. Gordon showed Ben and Irena the grandeurs of Bombay's Victorian architecture: the Rajabhai clock tower, the Town Hall, the Mechanics Institute, all the lofty Indo-Saracenic buildings with their *faux*-minarets, Ali Baba gateways, cenotaphs sprouting like aerie mushrooms from castellated rooftops. Ben had to admit he was damned impressed with all the "civic cathedrals." He bought Mrs. Gordon's children clay animals from a street vendor, and Irena, warming to the company, told them stories about Russian fairies that made them shriek with delight.

Off they all went in a bunder boat to visit Elephanta Island. The harbor sparkled like a blue carpet strewn with diamonds in the sun. As they sailed farther from the city, the Malabar Hill behind it rose like a purplish ghost-mountain. Ben was fascinated by the primitive but ingenious little stove on which the boatmen cooked their rice, and he got the crew to explain its construction while he took notes.

As soon as the boat landed, the Gordon children raced up a footpath with their ayah. Everyone else bounced up the hill in boxy open palanquins on the shoulders of sweating coolies. When the path became so steep Ben feared he might break his bearers' backs, Ben insisted on climbing on foot. At the top, Irena set up her portable easel and began to sketch the crowds of worshipers circumambulating a stone temple. Ben watched Indians wrap garlands of flowers around the necks of giant gods hewn from rock walls. He gaped at emaciated holy men sitting in painful postures—knees twisted up over heads, feet behind backs—like giant mantises. Along with the other pilgrims, he splashed himself with holy water that had been used to bathe the stone gods.

After lunch, he walked deep into one of the caves with Daisy Gordon. The walls gave off a damp coolness. The sunlight vanished—indeed the entire world, as they'd known it, seemed to recede far behind them in the cavern's shadowy depths.

"I know how Ariadne felt in the Minotaur's lair," Daisy whispered.

"And I Theseus," Ben said.

"Oh, are you going to rescue me?" She asked, smiling.

"Anything's possible in this amazing land," he replied.

When they reached the end of the passage, no Minotaur awaited them, but something even more ancient and awesome did: a six-foot tall stone *lingam*, or erect phallus, representing the Hindu god Shiva. It was black, utterly frank, undeniably there, and it struck them speechless. Half closing his eyes, Ben felt the ground tremble with the power of rocks shifting miles deep below his feet. The sensation rose up his legs, stirred his loins; he felt as if only a moment had passed since the great stone god had pushed its way up from the earth's core and had broken through the cave's floor, its red-hot glow hardening into this black primal shape.

"*Oh*—" A breath caught in Daisy's throat.

He inhaled a whiff of her scent—lilac mixed with raw sweat—as she swayed against him. His arm went around her waist; the stone deity seemed to command him to hold her, its voice coming in reverberations that hovered in the air like the echoes of a struck gong. Time slipped away; they could have been standing in the cave's cool shadows for minutes or aeons. Then they found themselves walking slowly back along the narrow corridor toward the glow of the sunlight. In the shade of overhanging rock at the cave's mouth, they stopped to gaze at one another. Daisy's eyes flooded over. With her thumb and forefinger she lifted her glasses. Ben gently wiped the tears from her lashes with his handkerchief. Her damp eyes shone up at him.

He pulled her close. "Daisy—"

"The tears feel good. I don't know why!" She blinked hard.

"Did the place frighten you?"

"Yes, but . . . it was marvelous. Something from a dream." She pressed his hand against her cheek. "There was a . . . a *presence* there. Did you sense it, too?"

"Yes. And I think we may feel it again." Ben stroked her hair. She leaned forward, resting her face against his chest.

Hearing voices, they walked together from the shadows into the glare of the outer world. There they separated: Daisy to find her children, Ben to explain Alexandriainism to Indians who stopped to introduce themselves. Every now and then he looked for Daisy in the crowd, and saw that she was searching for him, too. The synchronicity seemed miraculous; it made them both break into smiles.

A day after Ben had given an informal talk at the home of a wealthy merchant family, he and Irena answered a rapping on the door to find a tall, thin adolescent standing outside in the rain. He wore a white rubber waterproof and a cap with flaps. The afternoon rain streamed from the end of his long nose; his eyelashes blinked like wet hummingbird wings. He introduced himself as Davidar Krishna.

"Oh, Sir. I heard you speak yesterday! And I was never so inspired in my life! I had to come—" The melodious, reedy voice choked off. Davidar's huge eyes, so deep in shadow they looked bruised, were fixed on the wall in the foyer as if he'd seen a ghost. Which he had, in a way. "That man . . . that man. . . ," he stammered.

What he'd seen was a large sketch of Moreya that Irena had drawn. Davidar, suddenly recognizing the subject, half-swooned to his knees. "Master!" he exclaimed. "You are *here!*"

Ben held him up by the arm. "Are you all right, boy?"

"Who on earth are you?" Irena stood in the foyer, a cigarette smoking between her fingers.

"Sorry, sorry, Madame—" Davidar tried to scramble to his feet, but his shoes slipped on the puddle he'd made. Irena and Ben had to lift him by the elbows and drag him to a chair in the sitting room. After Irena had placed a cup of hot tea in his hand, Davidar explained that he was a Brahmin who had completed his university studies, though he was only nineteen.

"As a child," he explained in perfect, formal English, "I once become so ill that my parents thought surely I would die. But late one night, a bearded, turbaned stranger appeared to me in my bedroom. 'You must gain strength and live,' the man intoned to me. 'for I have great things in mind for you.'" He recovered, and dedicated his life to gaining strength so that if the astral personage appeared to him again, he'd be prepared. This story amazed Ben, but not Irena, who said she knew that in India such Masters are often met on physical and astral planes alike.

"My body looks slight, but my mental powers are highly developed," Davidar said. "When I learned of Madame's spirit phenomena and heard the Captain's eloquent address, I knew that I must investigate this Alexandriainism. Now that I have seen the Master's picture here, I know it is my karma to be a part of your great mission!" He sat back, his eyelashes quivering. "If only you will have me!"

"You are welcome, my boy," Irena said before Ben could speak.

"But what about your family?" Ben asked.

Davidar said he was glad to leave his home, where he'd been forced to marry a girl of fifteen who was making base carnal demands on him that threatened to distract him from his spiritual studies. "But I have never once succumbed to her wiles!" he declared proudly.

"Perhaps you should try them," Ben said. "And then see if you want to dedicate yourself to our work—"

"Nonsense!" Irena snapped.

Ben frowned at her. "Damn it, Irena, what right have we got to change his life so radically?" Here he went silent, for the boy's eyes were flooding with tears.

"Oh please, sir, don't send me back!" Davidar pleaded.

Ben glanced at Irena, who was gazing at him with the blue-eyed intensity he remembered from their very first meeting.

"All right," Ben relented, smiling, and turned to Davidar. "For a while—but only till you make things up with your voracious wife."

So Davidar came to live at the "Crows Nest." He soon proved himself indispensable, typing, taking dictation, translating documents to and from Hindustani, Marathi, and Urdu. He became the managing editor of *The Alexandrianist*, a magazine Ben and Irena started to raise funds for the society; he wrote articles about mahatmas, or Hindu Masters who had guided the affairs of men since ancient times. On Irena's suggestion, he began a correspondence with Sarah in New York; her mother was ailing so badly, the girl needed a friend, Irena told Ben. He agreed. Since Davidar's arrival, he and Irena hadn't argued about anything; the three of them worked together in harmony for ten, twelve, fifteen hours each day. Ben had little money to pay Davidar, but the boy seemed happy enough to work for room and board.

"Before meeting you and Madame," he said, "my future looked meaningless. I was to join my father's business, with no prospects but acquiring gross material wealth."

Ben could sympathize with Davidar's aversion to the materialist life, but as funds ran low, he became increasingly worried

about a lack of materialist wealth in the Alexandrian treasury.
This problem was exacerbated when, without consulting him,
Irena hired a sharp-nosed, middle-aged Englishwoman, Emma
Coulomb, and her French husband, Alexis, as housekeepers.
Wasn't this the very same woman who had threatened to expose
Jenny Holmes with old letters, Ben asked? Why on earth did
Irena want to involve herself with such a person? But Irena in-
sisted that Emma was a very old and dear friend who was down
on her luck and could not be refused a refuge.

Originally from London's East End, Emma had worked in
Egypt as a governess, but had abandoned her profession to set up
as a medium in France. She and Irena had founded the French
Miracle Club several years before, holding séances for wealthy
European ladies. The organization had been disbanded after several members accused the mediums—one or both of them was
never clear—of cheating them in a scheme having to do with some
ancient Pharoanic jewelry. Emma had fled to Ceylon, where she'd
married. The boarding house she ran there lost money, and at age
forty, she'd cabled Irena in Bombay, begging for employment in
Bombay.

Emma's red-bearded husband, Alexis, was a Marseilles seaman
who'd been shipwrecked off the coast of Ceylon. He'd been working as a handyman for Colombo merchants when Emma found
him sitting outside a sailors' tavern. Now sixty, he was a secretive
man whose carpentry skills allowed him to make things that fell
apart several months after they were finished, requiring him to
return again and again to repair them. Irena, who normally
couldn't tolerate the use of alcohol, put up with Alexis's drinking
for reasons Ben couldn't fathom.

"It's time we turned our minds to more spiritual matters,"
Irena announced one day, after Ben had complained once again
about the Coulombs' rudeness. "Kut-huri has ordered me to
make a trip across Bombay, and you must come, too." Irena
smiled. "You deserve a reward for all your patience!"

"Kut-huri!" Ben immediately rose from his chair. "You mean,
I'm actually going to meet him?"

"Anything," Irena said, "is possible."

Babula raced ahead of her into the lane and in seconds, it seemed, appeared with an open carriage. Ben noted that Babula didn't ride back in the carriage to the house, but trotted in front of the horse; thus, he'd have had no time to inform the driver about any route. As Ben climbed into the vehicle, he thought it curious that Irena gave no directions to the driver, either. The old man, curiously dressed in antique robes and curly-toed slippers, seemed to know exactly where to go.

After a morning rain, the freshly washed city shone in hazy rays of sunlight. Tree branches echoed with the screeches of parrots. The scent of hot, damp vegetation hovered everywhere. Up one lane and down another the carriage rolled, its wheels crunching in the dirt and gravel. Finally it creaked to a halt before a bungalow surrounded by plumed coconut palms. The house was shimmering white, almost too radiant for Ben to look at directly, as if it had just arrived on the site a few moments before from the astral plane and was throbbing with its own source of light.

"Wait here." Irena fixed Ben with a stare.

"Of course—"

"Do not . . . follow . . . me," she said, slowly raising her palm into the air. Without another word, she walked off through a lavish rose garden toward the house. Ben settled back in his seat to watch the flowers ripple in the sunlight. Their sweet scent surrounded him; he could feel the soft pollen against his skin. Sometimes a breeze blew the roses toward the house in rolling waves; sometimes they all went still at once, holding their breaths as if trying to overhear conversations inside the house. Now Ben could hear low voices, too—Irena's rich contralto and a man's rumbling bass. Suddenly he sat up, squinting hard. On the verandah appeared a tall man clad in white from the top of his turban to the hem of his long robe.

His beard was black like those on the printed portraits Ben had seen of the Masters; his eyes burned when he stared at Irena, yet as his lips moved, his voice was too hushed for Ben to hear. Now the man handed Irena a bouquet of roses. Then he turned slowly and vanished with a kind of gliding motion into the house. The door closed noiselessly. Irena returned up the path.

"These are for you." She handed up the bouquet to Ben. "Gulab Singh sends them with his complements. He says that your seeking of spiritual wisdom here is bound to succeed."

"I'm glad." Ben held the flowers tight, "But who *is* he?"

"Gulab Singh is a Living Master, an *avatar* of Kut-huri."

"An *avatar*—a corporal representative?"

"Exactly," Irena smiled, an expression that gave off nearly as much radiance as the house. Except now the bungalow behind her, for all its whiteness, seemed to be faintly fading. Ben wiped the sweat from his forehead and eyes, blinking hard, staring into the flowers.

"*What's this?*" he asked suddenly, waking the driver from his nap.

"Take a look if you like."

Embedded in the roses was a black envelope made of heavy paper. His fingers trembled as he tore it open. There was no message inside, but something more wondrous—a long piece of white paper with filigreed designs around the edges and printed letters in red ink and a flamboyant black signature at the bottom. "A bank draft, Mulligan!" He waved it in the air. "Six thousand rupees—we're solvent again!"

"Ah!" Irena smiled. She didn't look astonished.

"The check's made out to the Alexandrian Society, from someone called 'H.R.H. The Maharajah of Watika.'"

"A friend of Gulab Singh," Irena said, nodding. "I was told the Maharajah wants us to visit him."

"Then we shall!" Ben gripped Irena's arm. Karma had provided; harmony was restored.

Back at Headquarters, Irena announced that she had an experiment to propose. "I will bet you ten rupees that you cannot find Gulab Singh's place again," she said, her eyes sparkling. "You can take Babula with you. But . . . look at me Ben. . . ." She stared into his eyes. "You will NOT . . . see . . . the . . . house!"

For a moment, Ben felt a rush of dizziness. Then he laughed. "You're throwing away money!" he said, but he took the bet. Babula raced off to find another carriage. He and Ben directed the new reinsman to drive on what they were sure was the exact same route. But Ben found no whitewashed bungalow surrounded by roses. They got so lost on the winding roads that Babula nearly wept. Ben discovered that the boy knew some English after all. "Madame will laugh, I not finding house for you," he moaned. Several times Ben was sure he was in the right place, but where the house should have been he saw only boulders, bushes, and coconut palms blowing in the breeze, their fronds rubbing together to make an eerie sound like rain falling through sunlight.

Finally, Ben headed back. When he and Babula arrived at the house, Irena was dozing in her cane chair beneath the neem tree. She slowly raised her hooded eyelids. "You owe me ten rupees, Ben."

"How do you know what happened?" he asked.

"Now I will reveal all," she said.

"What do you mean?" Ben frowned, wiping his forehead.

"Listen, old chum, and I promise that you will not regret taking the bet. It was a priceless part of your *chela*ship." Like all centers of spiritual power inhabited by Masters, she explained, Gulab Singh's dwelling was protected against intruding strangers by a shield of *maya*—illusion. In this case the shield was made up of trees, boulders, and bushes, all erected by astral servitors before the second carriage trip.

"But on the first trip, I was allowed to see the Master and his house. . . ," Ben said.

"I was instructed to show them to you," Irena said. "But I was told little else in advance."

"That was why no instructions were given to the driver."

"Yes, you have understood well." Irena smiled at him.

Ben nodded. "You know, the second trip, it was very like post-hypnotic suggestion." He sat in the chair beside Irena, his forehead shining with sweat, his spectacles glinting. "I've read of this principle used in hypnotism experiments in France. Subjects get prevented from seeing things that are blocked by visual barriers which—in the strictly physical sense—don't exist!"

"So you think I bamboozelated you?" Irena asked.

"Not at all. It's a powerful convergence of psychometric and spiritual energy. Charcot and Liebault would be amazed to hear about what happened today."

Irena lit a cigarette. "You know, Maloney, this is a reason we have come to Asia, to find evidences of phenomena like this one. Mayavic engirdlement has been known in India for centuries."

"*Mayavic engirdlement.* I should write a paper on it!"

Ben stayed up writing in his study for seven nights. His paper came to forty pages. Then he spent five more nights translating the paper into French. The next morning, bleary-eyed but exhilarated, he rushed off to cable brief abstracts of the article to the Royal Academy in London and the *Institute Neurologique* in Paris. The cables were costly, but Ben had no doubt that his discovery's importance warranted the expense. After several weeks of anxious waiting, though, he received cables back from professors in London and Paris informing him that they had no interest in reading his paper.

"Scrofulous crustaceans in academic robes!" Irena exploded. "It is a brilliant, important paper those fools turned down!"

"Those people wouldn't know a significant scientific innovation if it reared up and bit them on their asses," Ben raged.

Irena sighed. "You may as well get used to this sort of thing, old chum. It is the fate of all visionaries to be mocked during their lifetimes."

Ben squeezed her shoulder, acknowledging her attempt to console him, but in fact her words inspired an awful question: was it his fate to be mocked for his advanced ideas?

For days, he tried to shrug off the rejections, but a dark slough of despond bubbled around him again. A gathering of pandits and other guests, including Daisy, took place at the "Crows Nest" as scheduled, but Ben retreated to his study. Daisy found him brooding there, and asked what the matter was.

"*Hypocrisy and custom make their minds / the fanes of many a worship, now outworn,*" he muttered, quoting Shelly's *Prometheus Unbound.*

Daisy read the cables from London and Paris. "What dreadful news. I'm so sorry, Ben."

He told her of his search for Gulab Singh's house and the validation of the Mayavic Engirdlement Principle that the experiment so clearly demonstrated. As he spoke, she sat in an armchair gazing at him attentively from behind her wire-rimmed spectacles. She wore a long purple dress today, the top buttons open against the heat; its gauzy material radiated a feathery light into the otherwise somber room.

"That's certainly a . . . well, it's a fascinating story," she said. "I'm no scientist, of course, but . . . when you say that no one was given directions to the Master's house—couldn't the driver have been instructed beforehand, say on the previous day?"

Ben shook his head. "The driver was chosen at random by Babula. Except it wasn't at true random, if you take into account the principle of karmic predestination."

"I see. . . ." Here Daisy's voice trailed off. She rose from her chair and lay her hand along his cheek above his beard. "You're such an intense man, Captain Blackburn. So inquisitive and strong-willed."

"Thank you!" Her fingers felt cool against his flushed skin. "But won't you call me Ben?"

"All right. And I'm Daisy." She sighed. "You know, sometimes one needs lightness, gentleness. Like you were with me, in the cave. You've no idea how I've longed to be touched in that way again."

"I've though of it, too!" Ben slowly encircled her waist with his arm. He brushed his lips against her cheek—so cool and smooth, so beautifully lilac-scented. Her eyelashes fluttered and closed. As Ben and Daisy kissed, their spectacles clinked together like glass bells.

Gently he pressed his lips into the hollow of her shoulder, feeling her fingers explore the back of his neck. He pulled her closer, delighted at the way her knees parted as she pressed herself against him. He opened a button of her dress and kissed her pale flesh, releasing a sigh like a dove flown from her bosom.

"We mustn't—this place is so full of holy men!" She laughed. "But I love the feel of your beard—" Her breast swelled out of its bodice, a lovely soft white globe quivering in his palm. He caressed her pink nipple with his tongue, and more bird-sounds fluttered into the warm air. "Ben, the presence—it's like in the cave!"

"Yes." He raised his face. "We must find a place to meet!"

"Soon!" She stood up straight, causing the miraculous globe to vanish back into her dress.

"Your husband. . . ?"

"Believe me, he'll be glad that I'm occupied. He hasn't the slightest interest in this sort of thing." Sitting in Ben's desk chair, she smiled. "But d'you know what he is interested in? Science!"

Ben wiped his fogged spectacles with his handkerchief. "The Mayavic Engirdlement Principle?"

"Oh, all sorts of spiritually scientific principles, I'm sure. Listen, dear Ben, why don't you give me your abstract, and I'll have him show it to his Indian colleagues at the Bombay University. I'm sure he can get them to invite you to speak."

"Well, yes . . . that'd be very useful. You're sweet to do this, Daisy . . . a wonderful woman." Ben sighed. "But before anything happens . . . I have to be honest. There's no question of abandoning my partnership with Irena. And I'll need to travel a great deal in my work."

"There's no question of my leaving my family," Daisy said. "But I love to travel, myself. I'm sure we'll meet up in many places."

Ben smiled. "Then I'm sure of it, too."

Ben had always been ashamed of his lack of formal education, and though he had several years of occult studies behind him, he wasn't sure if he could deliver a lecture before a *bona fide* academic audience. The generous reception he received from the welcoming committee at Bombay University's lecture hall did little to calm his nerves, for as yet he'd shown them nothing to prove himself worthy of such hospitality. Over a thousand people awaited him. Most of them were Indians, including Davidar, though he spotted Daisy in the front row, and Professor Gordon, his sponsor, was among the dignitaries waiting on the stage for him. Irena sat in the first row of chairs, radiant in a long skirt and embroidered cotton blouse, her head partially covered in a swathe of red

Kanchipuram silk. Everyone rose as Ben strode up onto the stage: a Jain monk who was naked to the waist, some Hindu scholars in *dhotis* and long jackets, a shaven-headed Buddhist monk, several Islamic clerics in robes and cloth caps. Ben wore one of his Indian outfits of white homespun cotton with a pair of sandals.

Following a flowery introduction, Ben took a deep breath and moved to the podium. At first, he stuck to an outline based on Irena's book, but he kept repeating, "What is Alexandriainism?"—almost as if he himself were groping for the answer. Finally he departed from his text, launching out on his own.

"First, we Alexandrians dedicate ourselves to the study of the great faiths of Asia from which Western thought has taken such vital inspiration," he said. He heard applause, and his voice grew more resonant; his words traveled in trajectories that echoed off the back wall. "Second—we dedicate ourselves to the study of the unseen forces of the universe. . . ." Here Ben slowly parted his hands in the air. "Mesmerism, celestial gravity, astral projection, psychometry, Mayavic Engirdlement—all to be used for the progress of humankind!" As this sentence rolled toward its climax, heads nodded as if the entire audience were following the progress of a great ship riding steady waves toward its harbor. "And the third great purpose of the Alexandrian Society—which you all are invited to join today—is to break down every barrier between faiths, between political beliefs, between nationalities and races—in short, to form the nucleus of the Universal Brotherhood of Man. . . ."

On and on he went, past the half-hour he'd planned, past sixty minutes. Though many listeners were mopping their brows, no one made for the exits. "The Society's aim for India," he thundered, "is to fortify Asia's great faiths against the onslaughts of Western missionary colonialism!" He paused. "And soon, every Indian mother shall recount to the child at her knee the glories of her land's Golden Age!"

A roar went up from the hall that shook the windows. Never before had a white man spoken so admiringly of India, so disparagingly of India's foreign masters. The walls seemed to bulge outward from the pressure of the sound. A foot-stomping began, it was so loud that Irena had to clamp her hands over her ears. Garlands were looped around Ben's neck until his beard, his chin, his nose vanished beneath them and he looked like a man buried up to his eyes in a garden. Students rushed onto the stage. Davidar fought his way through them to hold Ben's arm to keep him from being toppled over.

"*Zindabad Blackburn!* Long live Alexandrianism!" a chant went up. And it didn't subside until Davidar ushered Ben, a walking flowerbed with only the gray top of his head showing, off the platform into an anteroom. There, gasping for breath, Ben was allowed to sit down. Davidar removed the garlands. Ben's *kurta* shirt was soaked through with sweat and stained bright colors from the sweet-scented petals. When Davidar handed him a tall glass of water, he drained it in three long gulps.

"Do you have anything to add to your address?" a young man asked, identifying himself as a reporter from the *Bombay Gazette.* Journalists from the *Amrita Bazaar Patrika, Calcutta Herald, Madras Evening Standard* also identified themselves, pressing close around Ben.

"My work . . . in India . . . has just begun," he croaked, but could say no more, his voice was so exhausted. He pointed toward Irena, who had just walked in, her clothes rumpled from the crowds, her red headscarf slipped down diagonally across her chest like a runner-up's sash. Ben expected the journalists to rush up to her, as they usually did, but today they ignored her and continued to hover about him. Two of them were excitedly sketching him in their notebooks.

A small, cool hand squeezed his fingers. Daisy was beaming at him. "You are magnificent," she whispered, leaning close to his ear. He felt her breath against his skin. A smile broke across his face.

Davidar stood nearby in his immaculate white clothes, his dark eyes glowing as if he'd just stepped close to a burning bush. "Captain. . . ." He pressed his palm to his chest. "I thank you. All India thanks you. You are one of *us* now!"

"My boy. . . ." Ben swallowed hard. "Everything became clear. I can't just be here to learn from India. I have to travel the land— I have to speak—to *share* what I discover. . . ."

Professors and students pushed closer around Ben. By the time the crowd finally thinned out, he could hardly stand. Irena was collapsed forlornly into a chair, her feet sprawling out on the floor.

"I thought I was going to go up in a state of spontaneous combustion in that cauldron of an auditorium," she gasped, wiping her flushed face with a handkerchief.

Ben touched the remaining garlands at his chest. The floor around him was a great splash of yellow petals. "Mulligan, I have to tell you something. I've . . . I've found my mission here!"

"Oh, have you?" She clenched her handkerchief in her fist.

He walked to the window and gazed out across the expanse of grass and palm trees. Clouds marbled the vast blue sky. As they approached the horizon they converged into a long white ripple like the wake of an invisible galleon sailing high above the land. Ben could almost make out its ghostly masts and pennons. It seemed to beckon him.

"Today, it was as if the Masters—or some powerful force—were speaking through me," he said in a hushed voice. "I feel I've discovered on my own . . . how to act in harmony with a great purpose."

"On your *own?*" Irena narrowed her eyes. "Beware, old chum...."

But he scarcely heard her voice, so intent was he on following the flight of that enchanted galleon.

9

My Dearest Sarah, Irena wrote in September of 1879, *I was delighted to hear from you before I left Bombay. Happy 13ᵗʰ Birthday! I have sent you some translations of Indian folk tales. When I was your age I read them, too, and also the novels my mother wrote. They were about sad wives of military officers who ran off with dashing dragoons. I am afraid my mother died young without meeting her own dragoon. I am sorry your schoolmates are so beastly to you. You were quite right to hit that boy who called you a heathen. One must always defend oneself vigorously from persecution. I struck many of my tutors, myself, from a very young age. Having private tutors, I never learned to mix with other pupils. If I had, I might not have had to learn everything in life the hard way. So perhaps you should not hit all your tormentors, just the cruelest ones, and find ways to make strategic alliances with the others so as to surround yourself with protectors. But I have no business advising you how to be a child since I was never really one myself.*

Irena wrote to Sarah's ailing mother, Natasha, as well, including descriptions of her journey across northern India with Ben, Davidar, and Babula. She reported that after Ben's triumph in Bombay, he received invitations to speak in towns and cities everywhere. Now officials, priests, rajahs, and Maharajahhs were eager to join the Society. They provided transport and lodging for the Alexandrians wherever they went. At each stop, Ben cabled Swami Dayananda at the various addresses he was given at local branches of the Arya Samaj; from time to time, replies came back and meetings were promised. But so far, the Swami had not materialized.

Meanwhile, the party moved on from town to town via carriage, train, bullock cart, and the occasional caparisoned elephant. Since Irena didn't like to speak before large groups, she kept busy collecting evidence of links between ancient Eastern magic and modern Western spiritual science. She frequented ruined temples, listening to their mysterious echoes, searching their cool shadows for signs of astral activity. Ben, too, wandered around in temples, his green canvas bag full of notebooks swinging from his shoulder, and with Davidar's help interviewed priests about spiritual matters. At one desert temple, a group exorcism was in progress, and Ben heard as much about local folk gods and goddesses, witches and demons, as he did about the great philosophies of India. Later, at guesthouses or encampments, he composed scholarly lectures while Irena wrote travel articles and stories (sometimes they were hard to tell apart) for Russian newspapers.

During her previous brief stay in India, she'd never left the mountains; now the great open roadways of the plains were as thrilling to her as any Himalayan vistas. Behind clip-clopping horses she rode in a *tika ghari*, an open four-wheeled carriage bearing the seal of the rajah who had sent it ahead for the Alexandrians. Wagons pulled by majestic, sleepy-eyed camels rumbled along beside the carriage. Clusters of women in red and gold sarees, men in white *dhotis* and orange turbans, herds of goats, wandering holy cattle—all streamed by amid billowing clouds of dust. A gypsy's shaggy brown bear reared up, clanking its chains, and danced to delight the ragged children. Irena inhaled the scents of wood smoke and spices from roadside kitchens. She watched a row of bare-chested men suddenly bend forward in unison and rise like a rippling wave, bowing to Mecca. She loved being surrounded by the sounds of wooden wheels creaking, drivers grunting, whips snapping—an orchestra perpetually warming up, ever promising the opening crescendo of a vast symphony.

While she viewed the spectacle around her, Indians viewed her with curiosity, as well. And not only Indians—a lone English sergeant in civilian clothing was following on horseback. Each time the Alexandrian party stopped to explore, he shuffled clumsily behind on foot at a distance. Irena called him "Sergeant Bumble," though his real name—according to Babula, who made inquiries in the towns—was Angus McGregor. His face was burnt red from the sun, his blonde mustache drooped, and he looked none too happy with his assignment. Irena occasionally gave him a gay wave when she saw him hiding behind a temple pillar or market stall.

Though she complained to Ben about the spy, she was rather pleased to be considered important enough by the British colonial government to warrant surveillance. It encouraged her belief that she was being useful to the Russian Intelligence Service (though it hadn't actually given her any assignments as yet.) Her editor, Mikal Katkov, who was an officer in the secret service, wrote her that she was much too flamboyant a figure to be a good agent; she should just concentrate on meeting her writing deadlines. Irena toned down her activities for the time being, and continued to send off "intelligence reports," sometimes in a coded language of her own devising. She scrupulously avoided talking about politics to Ben or Davidar. It wouldn't do for her activities to create some sort of international incident, making the job of other Russian players in the Great Game more difficult.

A cable arrived from the executive branch of the Arya Samaj stating that Swami Dayananda was looking forward to meeting the Alexandrians at the capital of the princely state of Andrapur. Their host there, the Rajah, was a large blustery man with a dyed red beard. He reined over a kingdom not much larger than New York's Central Park, but he did send two elephants to carry his guests through the last part of the journey, and provided comfortable, if threadbare, accommodations. His palace was a centuries-old stone fortress, with a crumbling residence at one end of a courtyard and a domed ruin inhabited by monkeys at the other. Along the inner walls were stalls that had once held royal chargers but were now the home of water buffaloes. The Rajah's elderly wife sometimes had to milk them herself when none of the tottering family retainers could be found to do it. Irena encountered a bat that flew into the bathroom while she was in the tub, but the

host, knowing the habits of these nocturnal creatures (his residence was full of them) had provided an old tennis racket to wal-
lop the visitor with as it fluttered low over the water, and Irena
thoroughly enjoyed her exciting ablutions.

In the palace's *durbar* hall, Ben waited once more for Swami
Dayananda to appear among the guests. But again he failed to
appear. Ben addressed several dozen local officials who eagerly
joined the society and showered him with gifts, including some
gold jewelry and precious stones, to finance the cause. Irena had
disappeared into the palace as he spoke; when she joined him in
the Rajah's sitting room afterwards, she announced that she had
just been in consultation with her mentor, Gulab Singh.

"Did he mention Dayananda?" Davidar asked.

"I can't find out a blessed thing about that man from our
host!" Ben said.

Irena sat back on the enormous pillows on the floor, smoking a
cigarette. "Alas, Dayananda has not been here," she told them.
"Gulab Singh reports that Kut-huri has forbidden him to reveal
the Swami's whereabouts just now. But he did advise me that a
meeting would be likely if we begin travelling into Rajputana, toward the city of Jeypore."

"Good," Ben said. Among his letters was a formal invitation
from the Maharajahh of Jeypore.

"Has Master Kut-huri chosen Gulab Singh to be his medium,
as well as you, Madame?" Davidar asked.

"The Masters have many channels," she said with a gentle
smile. "One day, you may be one of them, yourself."

Davidar tugged at the long strands of hair falling past his face.
"This is my greatest hope."

"And perhaps you will evolve into an actual Master," Irena
went on.

Ben frowned. "Surely that's too high to aspire to."

"Is it possible?" Davidar sat forward.

"I have heard of mortals being called on pilgrimages to the
Himalayas. . . ," Irena exhaled a ribbon of smoke, ". . . of being
swept into secret mountain tunnels, discovering vast under-
ground temples and libraries. . . ."

Davidar's eyes grew damp. He sat still and serene. His gaze was focused inward.

As the Alexandrians traveled on toward Rajputana, Babula made Irena comfortable in the carriage with rugs and pillows. Behind them, imperfectly concealed by clouds of dust, rode the sweaty, miserable-looking Sergeant Bumble. Irena found Davidar an invaluable travelling companion. When Ben barged into village temples and blustered through markets in his impetuous Yankee fashion, Davidar trailed along behind to explain his mission and pick up overturned objects. When Irena offended a local priest with her disapproving views about child marriage, Davidar could smooth over her statements as he translated them. Davidar translated for both her and Ben when they stopped to talk to the holy men they found sitting with their begging bowls outside ancient temples.

In one village, they tried to talk to a nearly naked *sanyasin* who was sitting in the lotus position on a stone platform. "The villagers say this man has not moved from this exact spot for fifty-two years," Davidar told Irena and Ben. The baked, emaciated old man was toothless, with blank white eyes burnt out by the sun. His bones and sinews showed so clearly through his skin that he looked like a three-dimensional anatomical drawing.

On Ben's instructions, Davidar asked him if he would produce some phenomena for his visitors. The holy man spat out a few sentences. "He says foreigners are mad to attempt to call up *bhuta* and *charels*—ghosts and witches," the boy translated, looking embarrassed. "Such beings pollute the countryside and put virtuous people in grave danger."

"Don't worry about the old fellow's rudeness." Ben patted Davidar on the back. "If I'd been sitting in one position for half a century, I might be a little irritable, myself."

The stark, dramatic landscapes of Rajputana began to fire Irena's imagination. Mountains rose abruptly up from the desert, their slopes turning gold and dark pink in the rays of the setting sun. Marble rock-faces gleamed an eerie subterranean pink. This stone was so common here that some of the humblest dwellings had floors constructed of it. Along the mountains' crests, long red-brown walls wound up and up like enormous terra cotta serpents. At the tops, mighty stone fortresses jutted out over cliffsides. Many forts were in ruins, left over from wars in centuries past when the armies of princely states had clashed on the plains below. Irena showed Ben village shrines that honored ancient military heroes who, over time, had been transformed to folk deities and incorporated into the peasantry's pantheons of Hindu gods. She explained how, in return for prayers and gifts, the deities protected the villagers from the wandering spirits of the uncremated dead.

"People whose cycles of reincarnation are interrupted by unnatural deaths—murder, drowning in a well, and so on—roam the valleys in the form of restless spirits. They can cause derangement in living people if not properly placated," she told Ben and Davidar.

And that night, as they camped in their tents on the desert, Irena wrote the story of one such spirit—a lady named Devi—for her Moscow newspaper. When Ben insisted on seeing a translation, she wrote one out for him, and he read it aloud to Davidar and Babula as the four of them sat in the back of their carriage, waiting for the driver to bring up the horses.

The Flying Princess
by
Madame Irena Milanova

In a small village in Rajputana, there lived a beautiful princess whose home, between incarnations, was a clay pot. Because her restless spirit had haunted the countryside so shamelessly after her last death, the villagers had trapped her in the vessel and buried it on a hillside behind a temple. For years she thrashed against her karma in the round clay prison and wept with loneliness. Finally she lay down and, for a decade, slept.

Then one day a priest dug up her pot to make room for some new ones. He set her down on the edge of a low wall in the temple courtyard. The sun's glare soon heated the clay, and the princess-spirit, whose name was Devi, woke up sizzling.

"Release me!" she commanded.

But of course the priest could not hear or see her. Having the power of clairvoyance, she rubbed her huge, almond shaped eyes and peered out through her pot's clay wall and past the stone walls of the temple. Everything out there looked scorched and brown and dry. How would she ever escape this dusty village to find a suitable place for her next birth?

The temple's inner rooms echoed with mournful mantras and the incessant clanging of brass bells. Devi saw throngs of desperate pilgrims climbing over each other to thrust rice balls at the white-robed priests. Dropping the gifts onto braziers, the priests fed the bitter smoke to the monkey-god, Hanuman. His red eyes gleamed out of the altar. When he wished to do so, Hanuman flushed a witch from one of the many supplicants who, hoping to be exorcised, had journeyed here on foot and by bullock cart from the farthest corners of India.

Devi watched a man with withered legs crawl toward the god on his stomach, cricket-like elbows pumping in the air. Two men carried a woman chained to a board, writhing and shrieking. A boy beat his forehead rhythmically against the floor. Priests shook a woman upside down over the blood-blackened rim of a pit to help her vomit a witch.

Strangest of all these sights, at least to Devi, was that of a big, bewhiskered, bespectacled, light-skinned man scribbling in a notebook as he talked with a priest. He wore sandals, a wide-brimmed hat, and an Indian *kurta pyjama* outfit of homespun cotton; a magnificent green canvas bag hung from his shoulder. As far as Devi could see, the foreigner had no affliction. Yet the brain beneath his hat seemed to be as agitated as any of the supplicants'. Devi watched his lips moving in his beard: question! question! His eyes crinkled, his mustache squirmed, his teeth clicked. Suddenly he went silent.

A girl collapsed to her knees before him, twitching with palsy. She wore the long brown skirt of a tribal woman. Her hair, tangled and wild, fell over her caved-in cheeks. She

searched her open blouse for the buttons she'd clawed off and
swallowed, and her little breasts swayed with the motion of
her body. Devi could tell that the stranger found her beautiful,
but the agony in her face made him sad. He didn't see, as Devi
did, that a witch was squatting in the girl's belly, with its teeth
embedded in her liver.

A crowd pushed the stranger into an adjoining room. He
squeezed past hundreds of chanting pilgrims and fled into
Devi's courtyard. Immediately a host of witches swarmed up
his nose to tickle themselves intimately against his nostril
hairs. He sneezed, spraying them across the courtyard. Devi
watched him walk toward her clay pot. His face wasn't hard
like the face of the sultan who had corrupted and murdered
her a century ago. No, this man beamed a restless gaze everywhere; he gathered up pictures and stuffed them into his
mind, never finding enough to fill himself.

But Devi had troubles of her own. Her fists pounded the
clay pot's wall. How she longed to fly again! Just once before
her next birth, she wanted to soar above the treetops. She
wanted to drop from the branches onto handsome young men,
ride them all night, and leave behind a spell to make them
bay in the moonlight whenever they remembered her. Could
she still make a man howl?

Princess Devi watched the distinguished-looking stranger
sit down on the courtyard wall to question a priest about the
pilgrims' beliefs. The priest fed him sugary morsels of karmic
enlightenment. The foreigner swallowed them, his mouth
growing sticky. Devi tried to slip a picture of herself into his
head, but the place was a jumble of flashing images, like a
magic lantern show gone berserk, and if he saw her at all, she
was a mere flicker among many.

His questions stopped. He'd seen the tribal girl again.
Thrashing, her lips foaming with spit, she was carried into the
courtyard by two burly priests. She tried to bite the men as
they pushed her down flat on the ground. A priest set four
suitcase-sized slabs of rock along her back. She gasped for
breath, her face squashed into the hard dirt. Devi's almond
eyes grew damp as she watched. Once she had undergone the

same treatment herself, but her spine had snapped before the cure could work.

The pale-skinned stranger couldn't look at the girl. He couldn't *not* look at her. She began to move her lips. Devi saw prayers fluttering on the girl's lips, and added some long forgotten mantras of her own.

"Leave me!" the girl moaned to the witch inside her, feeling it crawl up her throat.

And now Devi sang her prayers in a high, keening voice, tears streaming down her cheeks.

"Out!" The girl's family shouted from the temple doorway. "Out, filthy demon! Carrion-eater! Sister-fucker!"

"OUT!" the girl shrieked.

And out tumbled the witch from the girl's mouth, a bearded crone who scuttled away like a cockroach, muttering curses.

"Aaaah!" the girl cried.

The sound made the stranger jump to his feet. The canvas bag swung from his shoulder. Clunk! It struck Devi's pot. The princess felt herself tottering, tottering, falling. Sunlight exploded all over her. Shards of pottery lay scattered in the dirt.

Her shell was broken! She could fly again! Expanding to her full size, she rose into the air above the hot, brown earth. Her hair streamed behind her, black and silky. Her purple saree rippled in the wind. She was so graceful, so free!

Her joy lasted only a moment. A careening demon knocked her head over heels into a raucous flock of witches. And now she could see that the air above the temple was as crowded as the rooms inside it. Mantras drifted up from the roof in an enormous net that opened to release thousands of witches into the sky, like ashes swirling through clouds of smoke. Devi watched bald grannies tumble through the air with goats clinging to their withered dugs. Soaring demons gnawed on rotted limbs and sucked the nostrils of skulls. Widows masturbated with their husbands' bones. Old warriors flew by with cats impaled on their swords. A drunken djinn butted Devi to the temple roof, and she rolled off the tiles, groaning. How would she ever escape this fiendish aviary?

As she floated to the ground, she saw priests lifting the

heavy stones from the tribal girl's back. The girl sat up, dazed but no longer twitching. Devi let out a sigh of relief. Now the foreigner knelt beside the girl. What was he doing? He held out a water bottle. He tilted it over her cupped hands. She raised them to her mouth. And Devi knew that she could trust this man.

The girl staggered into the arms of her waiting family. As the stranger watched her go, Devi slid down the strap of his green shoulder bag and dove inside. The bag had become a nest of stray witches. They cackled and clawed at her saree, but she kicked their scaly faces, and they scrambled out, leaving damp putrid trails on the canvas.

Now everything was tinted a lovely green, as if she'd found refuge in a cool oasis. "Take me away!" Devi commanded the stranger.

Why was he so slow to move? He stared down the hillside at the village. Sunlight glowed on the mud brick houses. Bullock carts rested in the dusty streets. From inside the bag, Devi could see dark clouds block his landscape, though the air before him was clear. Now all he could see was his own solitude: himself, standing beside the temple, an alien figure looking down at the dusty desert town.

"If you carry me off," she called, "you'll be rewarded!"

But he still didn't hear. How was she going to get this doleful donkey to move? Passing her gaze down through his body, she saw his heart pulsing against its prison of ribs, and felt a commotion within her own breast. Humming one of her mantras, she focused all her energy between his legs. Poor albino prunes, they hadn't had a release in a long time. Now the little gonads began to simmer happily.

"Good karma!" Devi cried.

Suddenly the man strode away from the temple. She watched an image of the young tribal girl form in his mind. But in his picture, the girl became ageless. Her eyes grew almond-shaped. Now she was wearing a purple saree instead of a ragged skirt and blouse, and her hair, no longer tangled, fell long and black and silky to her shoulders.

Smiling, Devi curled up against the stranger's side and rode back into the world.

"Did you like the story?" Irena asked, as Ben stacked the papers against his knee. The idea of a restless spirit, it occurred to her, might have reminded him of Mary Surratt. But perhaps he had managed to leave her behind in America. Or else he simply didn't think of a young Indian princess in the same way. Davidar and Babula, sitting on the leather carriage seat across from Ben, also watched his face.

He turned slowly toward her, his eyes blazing behind his pince-nez. His cheeks were flushed red, but that could have been because of the hot desert sun. He wore a full beard now, so fuzzy that Irena sometimes couldn't read the expression on the lips concealed within it.

Now they parted. Ben laughed. Irena sat back, fumbling with her tobacco pouch.

"Congratulations, Mulligan," he said. "How did you ever dream it up?"

She pressed her fingertips against her forehead. "It came to me astrally," she said.

"Ah." Ben smiled. "Spiritual and creative forces blend to produce literature. I've always suspected that there's a fine line between them."

"If you are being facetious—"

"Not at all! I've always admired your artistic abilities."

Davidar, however, was still shuddering at the idea of the man in the story being possessed by such a lascivious woman as the Princess Devi. He told Irena about his trepidation.

She gave his knee a motherly pat. "You can be sure Devi didn't stay with her host very long."

"Truly?" he asked.

"Beyond the slightest crepuscular adumbration of a doubt."

"But the princess might visit the man again one day," Ben said, smiling.

"I am quite certain that as soon as Devi was carried out of the village, she flew off in search of a more suitable, *younger* prince." Lighting a cigarette, Irena blew dark smoke out her nostrils. "She was just making temporary use of you, distracting you from your true quest."

"Ah, I see." Ben sat back, stroking his beard. "You know, I do recall a marvelous feeling of fullness," he pressed his hand to his chest, ". . . and then of sudden emptiness. Freedom from possession. Maybe that was when she took flight."

"You're pushing this too far, Ben!"

"I guess I was inspired."

"Flapdoodle!" Irena turned away, her lips pressed tightly together.

Babula and the driver returned, and the carriage lurched forward toward the road to Jeypore. Davidar still looked worried, lines appearing beside his great dark eyes. "Are you vexed with each other?" he asked, turning from Irena to Ben and back again.

Ben squeezed Davidar's shoulder. "Irena can breathe fire like a demoness, but she means well."

"The Captain's true nature will return when we get to Jeypore," Irena said. "You will see."

Davidar stared past the driver at the dusty road ahead and the mountains burning in the distant sunlight. "I will see," he repeated, as much to himself or to unseen others as to Irena.

10

On across Rajputana, Ben journeyed with Irena, Davidar, and Babula toward the capital city of Jeypore. Behind them, Sergeant McGregor doggedly followed. WELCOME BLACKBURN and other variations of this sentiment appeared on banners hung across village streets where enthusiastic crowds awaited the Alexandrianists. They took a river steamer, watching from the deck as fishermen glided along the river bank in boats shaped like new moons. On trains, they insisted on riding in the carriages reserved for Indians—the only white people anyone had ever seen do this. They hated race prejudice, they explained, and preferred not to travel with the colonials in the first-class carriages. Given hospitality and food by Indian travelers, they joined in spirited philosophical discussions and made valuable contacts for the Society. Some Indian men were initially reluctant to speak seriously to a woman, but Irena got their attention by making astral bells tinkle or name-embroidered handkerchiefs appear from the ether. But when she did this several times a day, Ben became uneasy.

"Time was when you could not get enough phenomena out of me, you old fool!" she exploded once in a railway carriage, alarming Davidar and embarrassing Indian passengers who weren't used to hearing a woman talk so freely to a man.

"I don't like to see spiritual energy used for frivolous purposes," Ben replied. Then he noticed Davidar's nervous expression. "A little friction's inevitable between us," he told the boy. "She's Art and I'm Science. Together we create a Alexandrian synthesis."

From Ajmer, they traveled north by bullock cart, tenting on a rise that overlooked the plains. They took their evening meals sitting on *dhurrie* carpets around a campfire. The scene brought back memories of Ben's army days—except now he was surrounded by tranquility rather than war. The scent of fresh-cut grass drifted past on the warm breeze. A silver irrigation canal wound between blue linseed fields. A lone plowman, turbaned and naked to the waist, slowly guided his bullock up and down the furrows. Ben listened to Babula scurry about directing the servants, heard their chatter dissolve in the air like bird-song. He felt Davidar radiating beatitude as he sat nearby reading the *Vedas*. Behind the boy, Irena sat in her American folding chair, scribbling away on a portable lap-desk. Ben lay on his side, his hat shading his face, working on his next lecture. A happy peaceful time, this was.

The next day, the Founders finally arrived in Jeypore: "the pink city," as it was called—for good reason, Ben thought, as he passed wall after turreted wall of reddish terra cotta. "Like Paris done up in raspberry cream," Irena said, sitting back happily in the carriage and twirling her blue umbrella. The streets and avenues were, as in Hausmann's city, laid out in broad straight lines; along them rows of two-story houses were joined at the tile roofs. Many avenues converged on a raised cenotaph under which stood a thrice life-size statue of the present Maharajah, Jai Singh; he was majestic in spreading Rajput mustaches, long robe, and enormous turban. His palace took up almost a third of the city, its outbuildings visible behind low walls. The slit-windowed wall of the *zenana*, or women's quarters, looked like a beautifully filigreed sea shell two stories high. The famous Jeypore Observatory caught Ben's attention: a profusion of enormous painted triangles, rectangles, spheres and other geometric shapes set out in a grassy park.

"The Rajputs consider themselves descendants of Surya, the sun god," he told Davidar, pointing at the shapes. "They've been making solar observations for centuries, and they're far ahead of the astronomers of Europe in their discoveries."

"I hope the Maharajah will explain the structures," Davidar said.

"I'm sure he will. He's invited us for at least two weeks."

"Do you think Swami Dayananda is going to meet us here?"

"I never stop hoping, my boy!"

The carriage came to halt at the palace's main gate. Ben helped Irena step down onto the street. She pressed her face to the wrought iron bars. "Everything I've dreamed of!" she said. "A paradise. Like Xanadu."

Ben gazed at rose gardens laid out between gravel paths that shone in the sun like rivers of gold flakes. A colonnade of tall palms led to a shimmering blue pool. Behind it rose a vast arrangement of striped pink and black and white marble boxes— the Maharajah's famous Rambagh Palace. Cavernous Mogul archways opened to flowering courtyards. Triumphal staircases descended onto wide green lawns. Graceful cenotaphs stood like four-legged birds atop the palace's flat roofs. Ben gripped the gate's bars tight, imagining languid houris reclining on divans, eunuchs salaaming in silken breeches, a potentate puffing perfumed smoke from a hubble-bubble.

The invitation he'd received instructed him to say the password "Alexandrianism" at the gate. This he did when five men in dark pink uniforms blocked his way with leveled muskets. The men's faces remained impassive behind their enormous mustaches.

"Alexandrianism!" Ben repeated, expanding his chest. Several more guards stepped out of the shadows, sabers raised. "Look!" Ben held out the gilt-edged letter.

A turbaned officer speared the paper from his hand on the tip of his sword and let it flutter to the ground.

Davidar stepped down from the carriage. "Maharajah Jai Singh is expecting us!" he pleaded in Hindustani, but his words were met with angry responses.

"What do they say?" Ben asked.

"He orders us to go to another palace," Davidar reported.

Irena leaned forward in her seat. "But why? We are *expected!*"

Ben glared at the soldiers, his heart sinking. "All right—let's go!"

The carriage's driver was instructed to follow a squad of cavalrymen on white chargers, who galloped off, raising thick clouds of dust that left the carriage passengers choking behind them. Beyond the city wall, the road narrowed into a dirt track. The horses stopped, and Ben saw the men point to a low stone structure. Then they were gone in a rumble of hoof beats. Rubbing his eyes, Ben looked back; the road was completely empty except for the faraway silhouette of a lone horseman. Light glinted off the end of a spyglass the man held to his eye. Then he, too, galloped away, and an eerie silence fell over the landscape.

Irena got down from the carriage, squinting at the small, low palace. "This must be a royal cousin's place."

"A poor relation's quarters, I'd say." Ben strode along a dirt walk, up some crumbling steps, and into the foyer. For a moment he felt as if he were stumbling through a bombed-out hospital during the Union army's campaign in Virginia. The halls and rooms were strewn with broken bricks and stone. A long snake lay on the stone floor guarding the doorway to a dining room, a place Ben couldn't have used, even if it had been furnished with chairs and a table, since the party had brought no food. Ben threw a brick at the snake and stomped outside.

"There's been a terrible mistake! I'm going straight back!" he shouted to Irena, and galloped off on one of the exhausted carriage horses. But the sun had set, and he found the massive gates of the city locked for the night.

During Ben's absence, Babula located an outside stairway to the flat roof and set up Irena's folding chair. There was little else to unpack, though. Expecting lavish hospitality, Ben had sent back borrowed tenting equipment—for which Irena berated him when he returned to the derelict palace. He went off like a crate of explosives.

"None of this would have happened if that British spy of yours hadn't scared off the Maharajah!" he shouted. "He probably told Jai Singh you're a Czar's agent, come to capture his city!"

"Do not bellow at me!" Irena screamed. "I did not ask for any *spy!*"

"If you hadn't railed against the British every chance you got—"

"Who do you think has caused the famine in the villages?—"

"Yes, yes!" Ben kicked a broken pot over the wall; he heard it shatter on the stones below. "But it's no good mixing politics with Alexandrianism! I keep telling you that!" He stared out at the horizon spiky with silhouetted trees and roofs. "Besides, the British aren't all our enemies. We need the goodwill of some—"

"*Some*—with round spectacles and musk-melon bosoms!" Irena turned her back on him.

No further discussions took place between the Founders that night. Ben kept to the northern side of the roof. Irena reigned over the southern side from her wood and canvas throne. Babula managed to keep a fire going in the center with sticks of broken furniture he found in the hallways below. Davidar tried to divide his time equally between his two benefactors, wishing that he could stay close to the fire from which Ben and Irena, due to their differences, were forced to distance themselves. Shivering, Ben watched the road from the roof. Surely a servant of the Maharajah's would come to bring them food for the night. After an hour he gave up his vigil. He fetched four carpets from the carriage, gave two to Irena and one to Davidar, and rolled up one around his own body as best he could. As darkness fell over the ruined palace, he and Davidar shuffled closer to the fire. The stars looked like the tips of dangling icicles. His stomach rumbled, and he could hear Irena's belly growling several yards away in the dark, too. Finally he lay down on the hard roof and lay awake until dawn.

"His Majesty is on a religious retreat in Mt. Abu," a clerk told Ben when he inquired about Maharajah Jai Singh at his administrative offices the next morning.

Another functionary stated that the ruler was on urgent business in Jodhpore.

He was playing polo in Udaipore, another said.

Scattering clerks in his wake, Ben barged into an inner office. He emerged half an hour later even redder in the face than when he went in.

"*I was right!*" he shouted at Irena, who was waiting in the office anteroom. "The Maharajah's been advised by the British government not to show us any hospitality. Because our party contains a

Russian spy—of all the preposterous, pernicious absurdities!"

"Wait till I get my hands on that crapulous Limey sergeant!" Irena muttered to Davidar. She was still refusing to speak to Ben.

Irena and Ben didn't have to wait long to encounter Sergeant McGregor. As they walked into the railway station, there the man stood beside a stack of mail sacks at the far end of the platform. He was disguised today as a Lancashire merchant with a canvas hat and cotton jacket, but his drooping mustache and badly sunburnt face gave him away.

Irena didn't break her stride. *"You!"* she shouted at the sergeant. Her voice turned more than a few turbaned heads. "Don't you try to slink away!"

"You scoundrel!" Ben blocked the man's escape, arms folded across his chest. "You've caused us a hell of a lot of trouble!"

McGregor reached up to tip his hat or perhaps just to hold it onto this head. "Sir—Madame—I du' know what you mean—"

"You are spying on us this whole journey!" Irena's purse swung in her hand.

A crowd gathered—travelers and hawkers, railway workers and camel drivers. Grinning, they turned from one pale face to the other as the drama picked up momentum.

"We're American nationals!" Ben declared. "Your government's got no right to harass us!"

The sergeant stepped backwards. "I wouldn't harass nobody, I just—"

"I intend to lodge an official complaint against you with the American consulate!" Ben boomed.

"D'you think I like doing this work? In all the bloody heat and flies and—" Here McGregor backed into a pile of bulging mail sacks. Down he went. His hat rolled onto the train tracks.

By now, Irena's word "spying" had been translated into half a dozen languages. Spectators gathered around the sacks to see the foul villain flailing on his back like an English beetle.

"Listen, you—" Ben leaned over him, tightening his fists at his sides. "This poor lady slept on a freezing palace roof last night!"

"Palace? You lot's been dining with nabobs for weeks! But it's the lonely bleeding tent for me every night!" The sergeant tried to

rise. "Please—give us a hand, gov'nor!"

Ben had to restrain an impulse to reach out to him. Now a burly Rajput scowled down at the sergeant, gripping the handle of a curved dagger at his belt. It wasn't often that Indians got to see their colonial masters in a prone position.

Irena glanced at the dagger. "You will leave this station a soprano if you do not promise to stop following us!" she shouted.

The remark was quickly translated. Peals of laughter rippled along the platform. The sergeant tried to scramble to his feet, but lost his balance and lurched in Irena's direction. Ben jumped forward, knocking him away from her. Irena swung her handbag around in an arc. It clipped McGregor smartly on the side of the head. The Englishman was back in the mail.

"Tell your commanding officers that we have come only to learn spiritual truths from the great Indian people! And not to engage in petty political rivalries!" Irena declared with great dignity, holding her purse against her breast as if to restrain its aggressive instincts.

The remark was instantaneously translated, and a nervous cheer went up. In India, a woman was not supposed to knock a man to the ground; however, a white person calling the Indian people "great" was an event worth shouting about. Fortunately for the sergeant, the hubbub was interrupted by the blast of a train whistle down the track. It sent everyone scurrying back to their luggage. The sergeant scrambled away with them, clutching his hat to his head.

Irena and Ben turned to each other as Davidar, who'd missed the spectacular altercation, came running up.

"You haven't lost your deadly aim, Mulligan." Ben said.

"Nor you your reflexes, Maloney!" Irena took his arm.

Davidar looked at each of them. His face broke out in a smile.

11

I have always known that some people think me devious, Irena wrote in her journal on February 20th of 1880, *But when I am most honest, am I not spurned? The truth is: people love me only when I am exotic!*

The journey to the princely state of Watika had begun auspiciously. First, the British government agreed to stop tailing the Alexandrianists, and Sergeant Bumble was never seen again. Then a cable arrived from Irena's Moscow editor directing her to write her next article about an important meeting that was to take place between a large Sikh anti-colonial organization, the Singh Sabah, and the vast Hindu nationalist movement, Arya Samaj. Until now, the two groups had been rivals, but they were on the brink of joining forces. The Maharajah of Watika, a prominent Alexandrian Society member, was to be host and mediator. The Sikhs were to be represented by a figure Irena had already met in Bombay—the mysterious Gulab Singh. The Arya Samaj, Katkov reported, would be headed up by none other than her old teacher, Swami Dayananda Saraswathi.

"I won't count my swamis till they hatch," Ben said.

"Nor shall I," Irena said. "But think of the opportunity for us—the Society acting as a liaison between the two most powerful patriotic movements in India."

Irena was eager to leave. For some time now, she had been worrying that her life in India had become less an ongoing quest for wisdom than an aimless wandering from place to place. Rent

on the "Crows Nest" in Bombay, the Coulombs's salary, and
travel expenses not covered by donations along the way—all had
been depleting the Alexandrianist treasury. The Maharajah of
Jeypore's refusal to meet her and Ben had been hard on her mo-
rale, too. Now, it seemed, their luck was changing. A carriage
trimmed with gold, driven by four white horses, arrived for them
in the small, dusty Rajputana town where they'd retreated from
Jeypore. Five servants took their luggage and, before starting out,
served them a sumptuous meal warmed on silver braziers. They
arrived in Watika that very afternoon.

The massive palace of the Maharajah appeared to them at the
end of a half-mile driveway. Stone pillars rose from the portico all
along the façade, and in its recesses, turbaned guards in red and
gold uniforms stood motionless like painted ornamental soldiers.
Liveried footmen helped Irena down from the carriage. An oaken
door behind the pillars groaned open, and the Maharajah's *nazir*,
or councilor, greeted the party. Mr. Ayers, as the *nazir* was called,
was a tall, gray-haired Englishman wearing the sort of elegant
frock coat and cream-colored trousers that had gone out of style
decades ago in Europe. He spoke with a clipped accent, and
turned out to have once been the Maharajah's tutor at Cambridge. Irena, Ben, and Davidar entered, and the door shut with a
boom that echoed in the vast corridor before them.

Mr. Ayers showed them around one of the palace's wings. The
rooms were the size of ballrooms. One of them, Irena discovered,
was a ballroom, with parquet floors and half a dozen twinkling
chandeliers overhead. The ceiling was a mirror, a sky with reflected crystal star-clusters rising up and up, fusing into vertical
rivers of light that finally vanished among the highest Heavenly
strata. The *nazir* informed her that Swami Dayananda would
soon set up his camp on the grounds. As a vegetarian, the Swami
didn't like to stay under a roof where meat was served. Irena
didn't care for the way Mr. Ayers's lips grew thin when he smiled;
he reminded her of an over-dressed lizard. "Now these paintings," he went on, "have been bought by his majesty from the finest collections of Europe. This one is a Delacroix. . . ."

She gazed up at a slim young girl in a shepherdess's frock and bonnet. "If Delacroix painted her, then I'm the model!" she laughed.

In the library she was shown worm-tunneled volumes of Shakespeare, and Ben discovered a bag of golf clubs in the fireplace. "Where on this great Indian sand trap could anybody play golf?" he marveled.

The *nazir* reported that from the south lawn the Maharajah often drove hundreds of balls into the desert, where droves of servants waited to retrieve them. "Foolish question," Ben said.

High atop the walls surrounding the great echoing *durbar* hall roosted statues of winged goddesses; they were being cleaned by a servant standing below with a feather duster tied to an amazingly long bamboo pole. He looked as if he were fishing for angels. Naked marble ladies lined a corridor; at the end, a stuffed African lion was frozen in mid-leap. Ben examined a collection of swords and muskets on the walls of a colossal game room. The place smelled like a lawn—for good reason: its billiards table, probably unused for decades, was covered with grass. "Remarkable! Seeds must have blown in—" He pointed to a broken window, "and taken root in the dust on the baize. Look at that—" he touched one of the colored balls half-buried in weeds.

"Like Easter eggs in a child's basket," Irena said.

Mr. Ayers guided her up some stairs to a verandah. There, in front of two doors, turbaned servants stood staring straight ahead. "Your rooms," he said. Then he wandered off.

The suites were connected by an open door. What was that tinkling sound? Irena found a tiny stream that entered the room through a low hole in the wall; water trickled along a stone trough in the floor to an opening in the opposite wall. "An ingenious cooling system!" Ben remarked.

Irena sat on a divan by the window. "Have you ever seen anything like this place?"

"In New York, the firm did business with Cornelius Vanderbilt and some of the other robber barons," he replied. From a table he picked up a heavy gold statuette. "Their houses were nearly as ostentatious."

"In one of my aunt's summer palaces, I was given a herd of

sterling silver sheep to play with. There were silver shepherds and shepherdesses, too. But I had no playmate to help me enjoy them."

"A palace can be a lonely place." Ben said.

"I know. I have never felt comfortable with opulence." She opened a leather-bound book from the divan and inspected a delicately painted Persian miniature of—what was this?—maidens on hands and knees. . . accepting the enormous organs of a lascivious dog, an ape, a bull, a tiger, and even an elephant. She slammed the book shut, revolted. Walking to the window, she looked out on lush green lawns, the desert beyond, and in the distance, the thatched roofs of the village.

"Alas, I see no tents out there," she said.

Ben joined her at the window, draping his arm around her shoulder. "Dayananda will come."

"If we repeat that mantra often enough," she said, "perhaps it will come true. . . ."

The Maharajah of Watika was a small plump man with an enormous black mustache. He wore a turban with a diamond clasp and a suit of pale pink silk. At dinner, he spoke with an Oxbridge accent, often braying at his own jokes. He insisted that his visitors call him "Teddy," as he'd been called at university. Irena's frostiness toward him melted a little as she sank her teeth into real Russian caviar. The pheasant, the fish, the venison, the cheese, the pomegranates, the Turkish coffee—all brought warmer smiles to her face.

After dinner, she reclined on the divan in her room to chat with Ben and Davidar. They left her suite at about ten o'clock and padded off toward their rooms. Ben yawned as he washed, looking forward to a sound sleep in the huge canopied bed. But when he parted its curtains, he found a gift from his host: a naked dark-skinned girl. She looked to be about fourteen. A razor rash made her pubis a nest of tiny red spots: she'd been shaved for the occasion. Her smile was a rictus of terror. Ben wrapped the girl in a sheet and, having noticed her skin sticking to her ribs, ordered the servant posted outside his door to bring a meal for her.

At that moment Davidar burst out of his room, clutching his

shirt over his chest. "A woman—she was lying in wait—" he gasped. In the doorway behind him stood a girl of perhaps thirteen wearing nothing but a string of beads around her waist. Ben gave her a sheet, too. The girls eventually huddled among huge pillows on Ben's carpet to gobble down plates of rice and mutton with their fingers.

The ever-watchful Babula woke Irena with all the details. She lurched out of her bedroom, her dressing gown snapping at her ankles, to find Ben and Davidar seated before the window playing chess. The air smelled of sticky perfume and spiced meat. The *nautch* girls, wrapped from head to toe in sheets, were twittering on the carpet. As soon as they saw Irena's face, they ducked down to hide behind the pillows.

Ben, dressed in a long white nightshirt, puffed on his pipe. "Can't sleep?" he asked Irena.

"With all this commotion?" She glared at the girls.

"Nothing is as it seems!" Davidar reassured her. "We haven't touched them."

"So I have been told." Irena glanced at grinning Babula.

"Checkmate. Pay attention, son!" Ben said to Davidar.

Irena walked to the carpet. The two girls went silent behind the pillows, gazing up at her like plump baby birds in a nest. She reached down and wiped the dampness from the younger one's cheeks. "A little child," she muttered, shaking her head. "A poor, debauched *child!*"

"Evidently a local form of hospitality, sad to say," Ben said. "It seems that not every Eastern custom is spiritually advanced."

Irena suddenly felt faint, and sat down on the nearest pillow. The younger girl snuggled sideways to rest her cheek against her shoulder. Irena's eyes flooded with tears. An image appeared in her mind: silver shepherdesses, blood dripping down their thighs, writhing and sobbing as rams, monkeys, tigers, and elephants mounted them. Then this image was replaced by a wedding portrait of her mother, only fifteen, standing with downcast eyes beside a tall, stern, uniformed man. Then she saw herself as a terrified adolescent bride. . . .

"I have an extra cot in my room," she said, standing. "Davidar, tell these two to come with me. . . ."

The girls slept soundly, but Irena tossed and turned in her four-poster bed, and finally sat up to light an oil lamp and smoke a cigarette. Babula, who'd been snoring like a puppy at the foot of her bed, blinked and gazed up at her. "You should have seen Davidar, Madame. He was terrified of the girls." Grinning, Babula crossed his hands over his groin.

But Irena wouldn't hear criticism of Davidar. "He is becoming the Captain's substitute son," she told Babula in Arabic, their private language. "So you mock him at your peril!"

"You wouldn't let the Captain sack me, would you, Madame? You need your Babula too much!" He crawled up beside her raised knees and laid his head in her lap. At first she tried to push him away, scattering cigarette ashes all over him in the process, but soon she was stroking his cheek as he nuzzled close against her bosom. "And I need my Madame too much," he murmured.

"Stop that, Babula!" Laughing, she pushed him away. "Shall I send you back to your old master?"

"That filthy man, he burned up my bung hole with his battering ram! Don't sent me back!" Babula flung his arms around her neck. Then he rolled off of her and paraded himself before Irena's full-length mirror, admiring his yellow silk *pyjama* suit in the flickery lamplight. "You know, I think Professor Gordon in Bombay likes my pretty arse."

"Don't you start any of that, or your pretty arse will be out on the street." Irena brushed the ashes off her bathrobe.

"I never tell you what Mrs. Gordon and the Captain are doing on the last night in Bombay." Babula curled up beside Irena again.

"I do not want to know those things."

"You ask me to watch the Captain, but you do not want to know those things!" Babula rolled his eyes.

"Oh, all right." She sighed. "An agent cannot be ignorant about the movements of friends or foes."

"This will cheer you up, I know. . . ." Babula sat up against

Irena's knees. "The Captain takes Mrs. Blimpy"—what Babula called Daisy Gordon—"away from the party, into the parlor. It is very dark in there. Many chairs are covered in white sheets. 'Ooh, they look like ghosties,' Mrs. Blimpy says. The Captain says 'Bosh, I know all about *bhuta*—spirits.' This makes Mrs. Blimpy have goose bumples all over. She tells him to feel them on her neck. He feels them there. Then on her shoulders . . . then further down. My, that lady has titties like melons!" Babula giggled.

"If you are going to be crude, you can stop now."

"No! There is no fucking in this story, I promise, Madame!" Babula patted Irena's hand. "So . . . the Captain and Mrs. Blimpy slither their tongues together like mating salamanders." Babula wrinkled his nose. "They fall on the sofa. She has on a purple dress, velvet. The Captain's hand lifts her dress—"

"Babula...."

"Wait! What happens next is very good. Mrs. Blimpy is making moans, Captain is making grunts, I am holding my laughs behind the sideboard." Babula grabbed his mouth. "Suddenly they hear, '*Ooooaah! Ooooaah!*' from behind the sofa. Mrs. Blimpy starts to fall off the sofa, making a high noise in her throat—she's thinking it's ghosties saying '*Ooooaah!*' Captain, he catches her, but his suspenders are dangling down and he trips into the carpet!" Babula giggled again. "But there's no a ghostie at all. It's a drunk English gentleman waking up, crawling out from behind the sofa!"

Irena smiled. "So the two of them fled?"

"Faster than racecourse ponies. No, not so fast. Because Mrs. Blimpy is trying to pull up her purple dress top—doing a juggle like a circus performer—" Babula mimed someone tossing melons in the air, chest-high. "And Captain is tangled in suspenders!" Babula dropped his face into his hands, then raised it. "So, you see, Madame—they are still virgins."

"In a manner of speaking."

"You are not cheered?" Babula rested his chin on her knees and gazed into her face.

"I am very tired," Irena turned away, wiping a tear from her eye. "Please, no more stories for now."

Babula stepped down off the bed and straightened the silk sheets. "Sorry you are sad, Madame. Now you sleep. This will help you..." Pulling a rolled yellow cigarette from his cummerbund, he lit it for her.

The next morning, Irena stayed in her quarters, delighting the *nautch* girls with card tricks. While they napped, she stared out her window at the grounds below. No tents appeared. She saw Ben on the lawn in his Indian clothes, strolling with his hands behind his back. Davidar, dressed in a white *dhoti* and jacket, walked beside him at a sideways tilt, the better to hear his mentor's words. She saw them sit on the rim of a splashing fountain while strutting peacocks made raucous cat-like sounds on the lawn and women in red sarees glided by with jugs on their heads.

In the afternoon, Ben consulted with his host and with the Maharajah Harisinghi, the large jovial ruler of another princely state who was to stay for dinner. Irena, too restless to sit with them, went on an excursion to some local caves, said to be centers of powerful spiritual energy.

The ancient caves were burning with airless heat and nearly dark, but marvelously scented with the smoke left behind by incense-burning holy men, she wrote in her journal. *As I made my way alone along a narrow stone corridor, I felt a hot sensation pass through me, and I swooned to the rock floor. A happy tremor overtook me, followed by a feeling of lethargy. I sensed a sacred Presence in the dark chasm with me. I heard the flutter of mighty wings, felt their hot breeze against my body. They cradled me in a gentle embrace. The Presence was tall, swarthy, inky-black-bearded. He wore a luminescent white robe and turban. And He had the kindest eyes I have ever seen. "Kut-huri!" I gasped. His voice was deep and calm. "You never meant to harm anyone. You are absolved from all blame," He said, just as Moreya used to say when I was a child! Then He melted slowly into the darkness. I sank to the floor of the cave, my head hitting the stone. Yet I was in no pain at all. Quite the opposite. . . .*

On her return to the palace, she was embarrassed about the purplish lump above her right eye, and tied a silk scarf around her head. She wanted to tell Ben what had happened, but kept silent in front of their host at dinner. Ben might have forgiven the man his nocturnal gifts, but she had to struggle to keep her teeth gritted in a smile.

The host summoned a snake charmer to entertain the guests. With many flourishes, the man subdued a swaying cobra, not with a flute but with a curious white stone held in his palm.

"Would you ask this man to sell me his stone?" Ben asked "Teddy," the Maharajah. "I'd like to have it examined by a professor I know."

"Of course—it's yours, old boy! But do you think the stone contains magic vapors repugnant to vipers?" The Maharajah Harisinghi smiled.

"Perhaps." Ben stroked his beard thoughtfully. "But what I suspect is that it contains minerals which are especially good conductors of magnetic currents that repel the snake."

The Maharajah Harisinghi scratched his brow beneath his enormous blue turban. "Then you believe the actual source of energy is not in the stone itself, but the psyche of the person who holds it?"

"It's a hypothesis worth investigating," Ben said, and the men launched into a spirited discussion about the transmission of mesmeric energy through different minerals. The two Maharajahs were quite knowledgeable about animal magnetism, celestial gravity, auras, phrenology, and other scientific subjects. Yawning, Irena decided to retire early.

She slept badly, missing the twittering *nautch* girls, who'd been removed from her room, probably to return to the hareem. Hareems had once seemed like storybook places to her. Now they seemed obscene. Why would an ascetic like Dayananda choose to meet the Alexandrian officers in this corrupt place? She turned over on the mattress, reaching for her tobacco. In the flickery light of her match flame, the walls loomed over her, and again she was a frightened child in a vast, echoing Russian palace. She lit a lamp, and in the mirror on the opposite wall, saw not a child but a shabby-looking woman who was beginning to show wrinkles around the eyes . . . a woman with no home in the world. Some of the beliefs she clung to were getting as threadbare as her night-gown. For instance, the belief that Swami Dayananda intended to meet her—

No! She had to keep up her faith in him and in all Masters, because if Ben saw her beginning to doubt, his own faith would slip. . .soon he might start to think the Swami was a myth. . .that Moreya and Kut-huri were figments of her imagination. . .he might even start to wonder if she herself was genuine! And as other men in her life had done—in Egypt, in Italy, in France—he might begin to hatch plans to abandon her. . . .

As the morning sunlight slanted through her curtains, she was awakened by the happy shouts of servants. She staggered to the window. The air was cool and smelled of flowers. Fountains shot plumes of silver mist over sparkling gardens. And on the wide green lawn Irena saw a dozen or more gaily striped tents with flags flapping from their pointy tops. A long banner strung between two tents proclaimed:

WELCOME • SWAMI DAYANANDA • ALEXANDRISTS • GULAB SINGH

Irena raised her arms to embrace the dawn.

When she'd first met Saraswathi Dayananda fifteen years before, he was wandering the back roads of India preaching to the multitudes. Barefoot, wearing only a simple *dhoti*, he'd railed against the corruption of the Brahman priesthood. It wasn't until he began to present himself as a well-dressed leader of men that he began to attract powerful leaders to his cause. Forming the Arya Samaj, he toned down his criticism of Brahmins and of Hindu customs such as child-marriage.

Now as Irena walked with quick, eager steps toward the tents, she envisaged Dayananda as she'd last seen him, with a turban and black pointed beard. But the man who rose from the carpets in front of his tent to greet her was clean-shaven and bareheaded. He wore a robe of fine white silk with a beige, collarless jacket buttoned over his broad chest. Nearly seven feet tall, he towered among his associates. His eyes were huge and piercing, his lips thick and slightly parted. Slowly they bent into a smile.

"So . . . we finally meet again, Irena Milanova," he said.

His voice was so deep that she felt it resonate against her rib cage. "*Namaste*, my *guru*," she murmured with her hands together.

"*Namaste*." He pressed his own palms together. "And this—" here he turned to Ben, who had come up beside her—"must be the president of your great Society!"

Ben, dressed in his best white *kurta* shirt and loose white trousers, returned the salutations with palms pressed together. "I'm honored to greet you in person, Swami," he said.

"Likewise, my esteemed Captain."

"How elusive you have been, my old friend," Irena said, giving him a smile.

"*Elusive?*" He fixed her with a stare that brought her to the brink of trembling. "You have mystified us, yourself. We hoped you might have reformed in the intervening years."

Irena took a step backwards. "But I have been seeking you since I arrived in India—"

"In a party of two. We were led to expect an entourage of many distinguished American Alexandrianists. And then we heard of the scandals in Philadelphia, the lady medium there, your dubious defense of her. . . ."

"Our society's made great progress since those days," Ben said.

"I know. Madame Milanova has single-handedly gone to war against the British army—at the Jeypore railway station!" The Swami's austere visage relaxed finally, the skin crinkling beside his eyes. "News of your assault has reverberated all the way back to Bombay."

"And here, to you," Ben said.

"Our agents are everywhere, everywhere." The Swami waved his hand toward the expanse of lawn, the desert, and the terra-cotta-tinted mountains in the distance. "But such old matters can be set aside in the light of present circumstances, Captain. We wish to introduce you to our ministers—"

A dozen dignitaries in *dhotis* and robes stood forward one at a time, hands clasped together, and bowed to Ben. The introductions went on with elaborate complements, but none of them—despite Ben's efforts to present her to the men—included Irena. Ben took from his green shoulder bag a sheath of paper—the official stationary of the Alexandrian Society/Arya Samaj.

"Madame Milanova designed it," he said, pointing out the mystical symbols at the top. "Very artistic, don't you think?"

The Swami put on rimless spectacles, studied the paper, and passed some sheets around to his ministers. After checking the expression on their leader's face, they wagged their heads in unison. Dayananda glanced at Irena and then fixed Ben with a beneficent gaze. "Tell Madame she has done admirable service for the society," he said.

Irena, who'd sat on a cushion beside Ben, squirmed with discomfort. "I am right here in front of your face, my respected friend," she said. "You do not need to talk about me as a '*she!*'"

Again the Swami glanced at her and turned to Ben. "It would be against custom for us to address a woman directly, at a meeting of the council of executive officers."

"I, too, am an 'executive officer'!" she snapped. "The Recording Secretary of the International Alexandrian Society. Like the great Arya Samaj, our organization believes in democratic ideals, including the right of women to play important roles in all its activities."

"Ah," Swami Dayananda said, and appeared thoughtful. So did his ministers. Some of them understood English, some didn't; all seemed dismayed by the tone of voice they'd heard from Irena.

Ben plunged into the gap. "It's true. No member would dream of making a decision without her participation."

"We have the greatest respect for your sincerity and zeal, Captain Blackburn, as well as for Madame Milanova's powerful intellect. And we are proud to offer you an affiliation with our organization, as one of our branches—"

"Branches?" Irena scowled.

"The two organizations were to be equally linked," Ben said. "Our correspondence stated it clearly."

Dayananda nodded from his great height. "Well, let us see how the meeting goes today."

"*Branches!*" Irena shook her head, but a glance from Ben kept her silent.

By mid-afternoon, hundreds of delegates from both the Hindu

and the Sikh organizations had convened on the lawn. There were pandits and god-men of all ages, with beards and sweeping Rajput mustaches and a variety of colorful turbans. For an hour Ben spoke to the gathering about the Alexandrian Society's support for Indian culture, leaving his audience full of enthusiasm for the distinguished American visitor and overflowing with the spirit of Universal Brotherhood.

As the sun began to sink over the faraway mountains, Irena tiptoed away from Dayananda's tent to a spot behind some flowering bushes. Her nerves were jangled not only by recent events but also by abstaining from tobacco all afternoon. She rolled several cigarettes and smoked them one after another.

"Gulab Singh is about to approach," she heard the Swami say to Ben in the tent, and she watched a carriage pull up before the palace's columned portico. With the slanting red sunlight in her eyes, all she could make out were two silhouettes, one a tall turbaned figure, the other a short, round one. A second carriage containing a much smaller figure waited behind the first.

"Do you know 'Teddy'?" Ben asked Dayananda as the Maharajah's carriage rolled up.

"An eccentric fellow." The Swami smiled faintly. "But he will be extremely useful to our movement. His network of influence is immense." Dayananda spread his hands in the air.

Irena watched the carriages stop on the drive a short distance from the tents. Gulab Singh, the Maharajah, and three bodyguards began their walk across the grass. A radiance seemed to emanate from the face of Gulab Singh, and his white robe shimmered against the backdrop of the dark, massive palace.

The introductions went smoothly at first. Dayananda and Gulab Singh exchanged greetings and praised each other in English, their common language. When Ben gave the Master a respectfully silent *namaste*, Gulab Singh gently smiled. "I have observed you often, Captain," he said, "and have been well pleased."

"Thank you," Ben said. "I am honored."

"It is good to see you again, Teddy," Swami Dayananda said to the Maharajah.

"I'm most pleased to have you as my guest, old chap." The Maharajah took a step forward. "And now may I present to you—"

At this point, Irena, annoyed at herself for having missed the welcoming reception, hurried around the side of the bushes, a wisp of smoke streaming from her nostrils.

A small girl took her place beside the Maharajah. She looked about eleven. With her head covered by the hood of her saree, little of her face was visible but her nose and mouth. A filigreed silver half-moon perforated her left nostril; her lower lip was quivering.

"May I present—" the Maharajah began again, smiling at Irena, "my newest bride, the Maharanee—"

"Bride—that *child?*" Irena snapped, her eyes narrowing. "Why you royal degenerate!"

Silence fell over the gathering like a collapsed awning. Irena put her hand to her mouth—too late. Ben appeared badly conflicted—one eyebrow arched, the other diving down. Irena wished a cavern would open up in the ground and swallow her up.

The Maharajah stiffened, drawing himself up to his full height—perhaps five feet four. He turned smartly on his heels and strode off toward his carriage. The little Maharanee clinked after him.

At the same time, Gulab Singh turned away. He glided slowly and majestically off across the lawn. With sinking heart, Irena watched him melt into the shadows.

Neither Dayananda nor Ben spoke. Dayananda stormed off into his tent. His council followed without a word.

Irena's face glowed dark red. She turned slowly to Ben, poised to plead her case, or to counter-accuse, or even to apologize— anything to fill the terrible silence swelling around her. But her voice stayed choked in her throat. The expression she saw in Ben's eyes—it was a look of pity—filled her with horror.

12

Beside the Great Hindustan Highway on the slope of Mount Jakko, a cuckoo chirps in a tall deodar pine. Ben wrote in his reporter's notebook on January 3, 1881, resting beside the road. *You listen, and if you're British (as most of the residents of this Himalayan hill station called Simla are) the bird-song will magically transport you to a cool, damp English garden. At the same time, you hear the faint tweeting of a tribesman's wooden flute. It's a sound so Indian, so utterly un-British, so weirdly* other, *that it could be the laughter of pagan demons rising on air currents from the valley below. Such dramatic contrast—West:East—causes a sharp ache deep in your breast. Soon the dissonance becomes intolerable: you'll have to choose to be enchanted either by the cuckoo or the flute.*

And if you're British, the bird will win out. From now on you will embrace everything English with the ardor of someone falling in love with an old flame who after an absence appears even more radiant than she was before. You become much more enthusiastic, more sentimental, more patriotic—more English—than you ever were at home.

And now as you climb toward the town, every Indian you see becomes merely an exotic supporting character in the delightful English drama in which you and your kind are the star performers. Hindu ladies in sarees are playing sweepers and ayahs (nursemaids). The pagan hill tribesmen, with their nose rings and goatskin hair ornaments and woven reed back-packs, act in the roles of bearers; they carry Crosse & Blackwell jam jars, tins

*of Scottish salmon, Fortnum's and Mason's tea cakes, and all the
beloved symbols of home and hearth to be set out as props upon
your stage. The hills on either side become the folds of green velvet curtains that frame Himalayan peaks so high and distant
that they look two-dimensional—as if drawn on a vast canvas
backdrop: a jagged horizon of snowy white, painted below a ceiling of dazzling blue. Superb! you say aloud, feeling the invigorat-
ing cool air rush into your lungs. And you rub your hands together with anticipation of a marvelous English holiday.*

*But if you are an American Alexandrian? You try somehow, as
I have, to synthesize the sounds of cuckoo and flute, of West and
East. It is a challenge my companion and I are looking forward to
eagerly—optimistically—ardently—*

"*Desperately?*" Ben thought, and dropped his pencil like a red-
hot coal from his fingers, refusing to let such an incendiary word
singe itself into his notebook. But he and Irena were, in fact, both
secretly apprehensive about the Society's future and their own
strained partnership. Having burned bridges behind them in New
York and now in India, (sometimes Ben envisaged a series of
charred, smoking riverbanks behind him), and with the rent long
overdue in Bombay, the Founders were forced to turn to the British community for support. (At least until a gift promised by the
Maharajah Harisinghi arrived in the Alexandrian treasury, Ben
explained to Irena, smoothing her Anglophobic feathers. This be-
nevolent Maharajah, too, was to be in Simla.) Daisy had secured
Ben and Irena an introduction to the editor of Anglo-India's most
influential publication, *The Pioneer*, guessing that Irena's reputation as a flamboyant medium would make the more spiritualistic
colonials eager to meet her, despite her professed dislike of the
British. Ben hoped to begin publishing in India's English language press; he and Dayananda had mapped out this strategy to
salvage the Society's reputation and to widen the audience for the
Arya Samaj's message.

The journey resumed. As the Founders bounced along on the
hard seat of a bullock-drawn tonga up Mt. Jakko, the white Himalayan peaks scrutinized their ascent like a race of ice giants
watching the progress of ants. Babula had gone ahead with the

luggage; Davidar had returned to Bombay headquarters to edit *The Alexandrian.* Now Ben rested on a rise just above the town about which he'd just scribbled in his notebook. He draped a shawl over Irena's shoulders against the chill, concerned about her swollen leg and her general moodiness.

At 8,000 feet, the road narrowed and the bullock gave out. Irena covered the next stretch of road in a *jampan*—a wooden sedan chair attached to poles carried on the shoulders of straining coolies. Ben preferred to walk. "Terrific view," he called out. Irena, swaying precariously, moaned as she glanced down sheer precipices. At the outskirts of the town, she was transferred— "like a load of dry goods," she complained—into yet another conveyance, a two-wheeled rickshaw drawn by a pair of uniformed Indians. The rickshaw tilted her backwards, legs rising in the air so that she had to look up the precipice. There, near the peak, English children fed biscuits to the monkeys that frolicked about a little shrine to Hanuman, the Hindu monkey deity.

And finally Simla—"where the little tin English gods come to lark about," as Irena remarked. The town was a jumble of wooden chalets, each with overhanging roofs and verandahs lined with potted geraniums. Signposts announced the places' cozy names: Sunnybank, Woodbine Cottage, Primrose Hill. From the Mall, which was little more than a widened track, Ben looked down on the corrugated metal roofs of several levels of the town. A pink-cheeked English girl, riding sidesaddle with a blanket wrapped around her waist to protect her party dress, was accompanied by a cavalry officer in full regalia. Near a stone church, dark Indian ayahs wheeled pale white children in perambulators. Ben walked beside a lawn where an archery contest was in progress: English ladies stretched back their graceful bows before an audience of gentlemen in long coats. The strains of band music wafted up from the terrace of a lodge, making Ben recall the Music Halls of Union Square where he and Zia had sung along with the gay orchestras. Inhaling the scent of pine and sweet woodsmoke, Ben felt a stirring within: a powerful desire for a lark of his own. He'd been separated from Daisy for much too long.

The coolies let the poles of the rickshaw drop, and he had to

catch Irena as she pitched forward from its seat. They'd arrived at
their destination—Brightlands: the chalet of Percy Sinnett, editor
of *The Pioneer*, and his wife, Patience. According to Daisy, they
were enthusiastic spiritualists. In London, the Sinnetts had regularly attended seances given by the famous Mrs. Guppy, and
they'd read both *The Astral Veil* and *Shadows of the Other World*.

Mr. and Mrs. Sinnett waited on their verandah as Irena limped
up the flagstone walk beside Ben. Percy was a tall, balding man
of thirty-nine with a carefully trimmed mustache; he wore a
cream-colored linen suit and cravat. His wife, Patience, was small
and timid-looking in a gray skirt and pullover. People said she
was brighter than her husband but out of devotion deferred to his
judgment.

The welcomes were effusive. Ben pumped Percy's hand, looking every inch the retired military man in his new khaki suit. Patience Sinnett offered limp, cool fingers to Irena. "Everyone's so
looking forward to seeing you!" she exclaimed, her eyelashes fluttering.

"Indeed. Your reputation has preceded you." Percy smiled at
Irena. "We've never had a genuine medium in Simla before."

Irena groaned, collapsing into a bamboo chair on the verandah. "My tailbone is all aflame from the rickshaw!" she announced.

"We thought you might like to come inside—"

"Too hot."

In fact, the air was cool enough for the Sinnetts to have lit a
fire. "Can we get you a drink after your long journey?" Percy
asked in his reedy voice. "A claret?"

"I never drink the evil stuff. I hope this place is not full of
booze-hounds! Ye gods, my feet hurt!" Leaning over, she eased
off her shoes and her aromatic woolly socks. "Look how swollen
they are! Baby elephants!" She gave out a laugh.

Percy and Patience hadn't been asked to observe the naked feet
of a houseguest before, especially within minutes of meeting one,
but sensing that this was no ordinary guest, they managed to
glance down at Irena's plump toes. Irena's laugh seemed to linger
in the air; they couldn't help smiling.

"I'm so sorry you're in discomfort," Patience said.

Irena heaved a sigh. "Dear Mrs. Sinnett, I would be truly grateful for a pot of cool water. No, two pots—one for each elephant."

Pots were brought, and Irena plunked her feet into them. Then she sat back, smoking. Ben chatted with the Sinnetts. Several times the couple mentioned their hopes of witnessing Madame Milanova's famous phenomena during her visit. Ben, having learned the technique of intensifying people's desires for miracles by evading a promise of satisfying them, kept silent on the topic. Only when Irena heard "tea and cakes" mentioned did she stir in her chair.

"We might go in to the sitting room," Percy said.

He and Ben hefted Irena into an upright position. She lifted one foot from a pot, spilling it, and then the other. A servant rushed to help her on with her shoes, but she padded off barefoot through the open door. Inside, a circle of men and women suddenly hushed to witness the famous guest's entrance. In the dim light, Ben smelled lilac water and hair oil, caught glimpses of long heavy dresses, striped trousers, cravats.

"I feel like a Christian being tossed to the lions," Irena whispered to Ben—not a simile he'd ever expected to hear from her, given her opinion of the religion.

"Welcome to the miraculous Madame Milanova!" Percy exclaimed. His friends rose from their armchairs, smiles gleaming. Ben tried to shield Irena—too late: the British were upon her, their eyes ravenous with fascination.

After months of travel, Irena found the idleness of her life as a pampered house guest at Brightlands oppressive. "You get to run off and amuse yourself all over town," she complained to Ben after a week, entering his room as he prepared another lecture. He kept silent on the subject of amusements. "I have to sit here and be gawked at by an endless procession of nitwits. Every time I try to bring up serious matters, they wander off and start gossiping among themselves."

"You were having a wonderful time with spirit portraits the other day."

"I admit it. But now I am tired. I long for intellectual substance—"

"Talk to our hosts about the Indian cultural revival—"

"They hate Indians! They want a spiritual dog and pony show!" She limped out of Ben's room, slamming the door behind her so that the little vases shook on their shelves like laughing pot-bellied elementals. Ben, sitting at his desk, heard her talking in hushed Arabic with Babula and went back to his lecture notes.

The next evening, Ben convinced his hosts to invite the Maharajah Harisinghi to the evening's gathering, and Irena's mood improved. Dressed in a voluminous skirt and many layers of shawls over a red shirt, she enchanting the Sinnetts and their guests with an impromptu talk on ancient Hindu mysticism. Her glass rings twinkled as she rocked in a bamboo chair before the fireplace. The guests seemed fascinated by the Maharajah, with his splendid sky-blue silk suit, his impeccable manners. Everyone was enchanted by Irena's tales of djinns and demons. Smiling, half-closing her eyes, she spoke longingly of the mountains, where as a child she was taken by her father, the governor of a district in the Caucasus, to meet the Buddhist tribal people, called Kalmuks; the local hill tribes here, she said, reminded her of them. Only the Maharajah seemed interested. The other guests nodded politely and guided the conversation back toward paranormal phenomena.

After dinner, Patience Sinnett lowered the flames of the paraffin lanterns around the room. "Ideal lighting for a spirit visitation, I'd say," Percy exclaimed, his sandy little mustache rising at each tip.

"We could all hold hands around the table!" a spinster suggested, offering her own mottled hand to a handsome cavalry office beside her.

"What if the table levitates?" a portly gentleman guffawed.

"Come, Madame Milanova," Percy insisted. "The bells and handkerchiefs you produce are always appearing when we're preoccupied with something else. But now there are no distractions!"

Irena kept on chewing her Yorkshire pudding.

Daisy Gordon, who'd recently arrived for the season with her children, filled the awkward silence. "The Captain's told me about his early days as a journalist, covering the trial of the abolitionist John Brown. Was he mad, as we heard in England, Captain Blackburn?"

Ben took a sip of water. "John Brown was no madman. He had the sort of zealous dedication every serious social movement requires. . . ." And Ben was off, reproducing colorful American accents in his booming voice. The guests' attention was riveted by his oratory.

Suddenly a triangular-shaped piece of black paper fluttered down from the ceiling and landed like a moth on Percy Sinnett's salad.

"I say!" Percy snatched it out, scattering endives in his excitement. "It's a note!" He squinted at the paper. "What is this language, Madame?"

Irena leaned sideways to look. "The language is Senzar, used by ancient Thibettan sages. I am forbidden to reveal its meaning." The guests groaned in disappointment. "But if you'll unfold it—"

He opened out the note and read aloud the English words written in gold ink. "'The Great Brotherhood of Eastern Masters welcomes you, Percy Sinnett, as a *chela*. You have been chosen to publish our words and prepare mankind for the coming truth,'" Percy beamed. "It's signed—Master . . . uh, 'Koothury.' Who is this chap, Madame?"

"The name is pronounced 'KUTT-hooree,'" she said. "He is one of the Masters, as it says." She closed her eyes for a moment. "To learn more, you would do well, I think, to take a peek into your diary."

"It's in the study!" Patience rushed off with a haste that belied her name. In the diary was another black paper letter from the ubiquitous Kut-huri. It explained what a *chela* was and gave some information about yogic powers, gnostic rituals, and other occult matters. Everyone admired its serpentine sentences and elaborate similes.

"The Masters took on Sinnett very quickly," Ben told Daisy later as the evening wound down. "Irena seems pleased."

"She's a great success here—both of you are!" Daisy smiled. "That letter was a stroke of genius!"

"Yes. . . ." Ben stroked his beard. "Now if only Irena would discipline her astral energy. . . ." But he may as well have hoped for the Ganges to stop overflowing its banks.

In Ben's private journal, where he recorded thoughts and experiences he didn't want to publish, he tried his hand at fiction—or a very slightly fictionalized version of an actual adventure that he normally wouldn't have written about at all.

AN AMOROUS CONSPIRACY

Princess Devi, a wandering spirit who had first possessed Ben in Rajputana, was having too good a time mixing invisibly in the lives of mortals to re-enter the normal death-and-rebirth cycle. As a higher being, Master Moreya—Ben's astral guide—might have condemned her reckless behavior. But the Master occasionally allowed his spirit colleagues and himself lapses from perfection.

Now, as fortune would have it, Devi was in Simla at the same time that Ben and his lady friend Daisy were visiting the hill station. One evening after her arrival, Devi parted the curtains of Daisy's chalet to watch the two mortals approaching along a moonlit path. Moreya joined her at the window. Wrapping her silver saree around her shoulders, she looked out over the Anandale Valley to enjoy the sky's starry serenity.

Ben and Daisy were coming from Simla's little theater where they'd attended a performance of *Walpole*, by Sir Edward Bullwer-Lytton. During the interval, Daisy agreed that it was an uplifting work, but as the second act droned on, Ben heard a faint warbling beside him and had to squeeze Daisy's elbow to awaken her. Suppressing a laugh, she laid a gloved hand over his. The glove became warm, then hot, then damp; at the end of the act, the pair fairly burst out of the theater.

The Simla roadways had been hung with fairy lights that blurred and rippled in the fog. "Like a fête!" Daisy remarked as she swung her arms gaily at her sides. Floating behind, Moreya and Devi saw a picture form in Ben's head—a farm

she could see nothing.

Ben blinked. "If I could just bathe it for a moment—"

"Of course you could—"

And so they proceeded up the flagstone walk toward the verandah. The watchman ran toward them bearing a flaming torch. He escorted them to the door, then slipped off into the shadows, his flambeau leaving a smoking trail in the air. Daisy lit a paraffin lamp, and the foyer flickered into view.

Ben carried the lamp for her through the house to the wash stand in the kitchen yard. Dipping a cloth in a pail of water, she dabbed at his eye. The gnat—Ben later suspected that it was a microscopic elemental spirit—was evicted. He wiped his face on the first towel he found. Then, seeing his reflection in a mirror on the wall, he discovered that he'd been transformed into a Moor.

"Oh, no! I used that towel to clean up some powdered henna I spilled!" Daisy laughed. "Why Ben, you look so . . . so swarthy. . . ."

"So I do. All I need is a turban!" Still chuckling, he smeared the rest of his face with reddish brown color from the towel.

She leaned her forehead against his chest. "My brave rajah," she giggled. "Oh, d'you know what? This house is supposed to be haunted—I just found out!"

"Tell me about this!"

"Well, a beautiful English memsahib was supposed to have fallen in love with an Indian prince here. He was ever so handsome and dashing, but something of a rake, I'm afraid. He went off, and she thought he'd deserted her. She pined away for love!"

"For love. . . ." Ben stood very still. "I think I feel a certain astral energy."

"Do you?" She pressed closer to him. "Oh, so do I!"

He did feel a presence in the air—as well he might, since Princess Devi was hovering nearby. You can guess who it was who'd snatched the powder-dusted towel from the bottom of the laundry hamper and placed it on top of the stack for him to find.

"The energy seems to be coming from the house, from up-stairs," Ben whispered. "I've developed a sensitivity about these things. But I've never been presented with an occasion to test them before."

Daisy smiled. "Shall we go looking for the lovelorn memsahib?"

"We must." Ben wrapped his arm around her waist. Leaving the lantern in the yard, they tiptoed into the parlor. Its furniture was covered in ghostly dust-cloths for the night. They moved stealthily along a hall. Devi flew from gas-jet to gas-jet, blocking each one, but she needn't have bothered. Knowing that astral entities de-materialize upon contact with luminous energy, Ben made no move to light the gas.

The stairs creaked as the two went up. Daisy clung to Ben's arm. They stopped abruptly, seeing a human figure lying on the hall carpet; it was only the children's ayah asleep in front of the nursery door. Daisy checked on the girls, then shut the door softly behind her. Stepping over the supine nursemaid, they tiptoed on. Moonlight streamed through the window at the far end of the hall, making streaks on the walls like splashes of silver.

Ben slowed, half-closing his eyes. "I can feel something . . . very near," he whispered. "Perhaps in here." He opened a door. It made a strange squealing sound, as if unwilling to admit mortal strangers to its depths. He took a deep breath and plunged into the darkness.

He didn't plunge far. It was a linen cupboard. His forehead struck a shelf. His pince-nez fell to the floor. Daisy, sweating in her purple velvet dress, helped him look for it. Since the space was so confined, Moreya and Devi heard a great many grunts and giggles before the spectacles could be found. As they left the cupboard, Devi planted a certain idea in Daisy's mind.

"Take a towel," Daisy whispered to Ben, and he did. She snatched something from a hook before she left.

"What have you got?"

"Won't tell!" Daisy fluttered her hand at her side. "I think I feel the energy. . . ." She opened another door. This one made no squeal at all; it seemed to sway back even before her fingertips touched its surface, as if some force were pulling it open for her—which of course it was. Devi flew off to perch on the bedstead, where Moreya joined her.

Ben examined the maroon towel in his hands. "Ah, a turban," he said, catching on. Daisy helped him wrap it round his head, fastening it with a pin over his forehead. Then she pulled a curtain from its rod, leaving the gauze liner fluttering in the breeze, and wrapped the heavy material around Ben's shoulders.

He pulled her close. "Velvet against velvet," he murmured. "Such magnetic energy."

And they did make sparks as they embraced in the darkness. "Wait—the memsahib would have worn a special costume for her prince," Daisy whispered. She vanished into the dressing room.

Gazing out the window, Ben suddenly heard the faint, haunting notes of a native flute rise from the valley below. Then he turned, hearing the whisper of cloth behind him. Daisy reappeared, looking splendid. She was wearing what she'd snatched from the linen cupboard: the ayah's daytime saree of thin, translucent cotton. The light from the lantern in the yard below flickered in the window like a lovely footlight. Daisy seemed to step out of an oil painting of a Victorian lady in romantic native costume. Her hair rippled to her shoulders. From the saree's bodice her plump white bosom spilled, quivering with each dainty step. Ben could hear her thighs whispering inside the saree.

"The perfect maharanee," he gasped.

"Except for the specs!" She laughed, gazing at the big framed mirror over the bureau. "But I need them to see you, Ben Sahib."

In the mirror, Ben's own glasses made him look, with his new turban, like a distinguished Hindu pandit. A—dare he think it?—a powerful Master!

He took Daisy in his arms. Snatches of music from the rink reached them on the night air. They danced together round and round the room. Dipping, swirling, they glanced over their shoulders at their reflections in the mirror. The light was dim enough to hide their age, kindly revealing them as a young English maharanee and her dashing swarthy prince, reunited at last in the ballroom of the Mogul palace of their dreams.

Now, many have wondered if sensual love occurs between beings in the world of spirits. It does, but it's usually ethereal, like two moonbeams passing through each other, with almost no tactile sensations. Only occasional spiritual shivers ignite the dust motes to remind the astral beings of their former fleshy selves. But when such beings are able to take possession of the bodies of mortals . . . well, then there is physical love between the spirits, indeed.

Moreya, it must be said, had been focusing some powerful energy currents on Princess Devi for some time, noticing her almond eyes, her long black tresses, her slim round hips. Though she was over two hundred years old, she looked not a day older than eighteen, and exceedingly luscious. Of course she had noticed Moreya, as well: his distinguished beard, his burning gaze, his breathtakingly handsome presence undiminished by his own three centuries. As Ben and Daisy danced together, Moreya and Devi gave each other a meaningful glance . . . and dove deep beneath their hosts' costumes.

Perhaps you've read the classic work, the *Kamasutra* (both Daisy and Ben secretly had), and recall the colorful couplings depicted in their pages. Not all of the positions were possible for partners of our lovers' girth and age. But with a certain amount of stretching, grunting, giggling and oofing, an heroic number of exotic postures were enacted in those shafts of moonlight upon the bed. Feet kicked high in the air, arms flailed ecstatically, sarees and robes tangled and rippled and dropped to the floor. Daisy cried out words she never knew were in her vocabulary. Ben chuckled. Spectacles clinked; then they, too, dropped away. The lovers groped blindly. They bounced, they burrowed. They became a single thirsty beast with a head at each end. They became horse and rider (Devi's favorite). They became roaring, mewing jungle cats (Moreya's personal preference). Spotted all over from the damp powder, they purred like leopards rolling in soft, tropical grasses.

Devi and Moreya could have kept them at it all night, but they took pity on their corporeal forms. As Daisy lay panting on Ben's chest, Devi closed her own eyelids, too.

Later, fluttering upwards, Moreya and Devi loosed the bed's mosquito netting from its frame and let it fall in a translucent canopy around Ben and Daisy. Soon the astral lovers were gently rocking together in a wicker chair to the rhythm of their hosts' musical snores.

Did Daisy really need to be prompted that night by the mischievous Rajput princess? Did Ben need any inspiration from Moreya?

Probably not. But astral beings need to have a lark now and then, too.

Asked to amaze the Sinnett's houseguests every afternoon, Irena carefully spaced out her phenomena. Percy Sinnett was kept in a state of perpetual tantalization, never quite seeing how the phenomena occurred, always asking for well-lit "test conditions" for them.

"If I'm a *chela*," he complained, "why won't the Masters give me indisputable proof of their powers?"

"Kut-huri is waiting for you to have more faith before he reveals more of himself," Irena replied.

Kut-huri wasn't stingy with letters, though. He kept Irena up half the night dictating correspondences to Percy. Ten-, fifteen-, twenty-page letters piled up: discussions about everything from ancient Egyptian mysteries to Swedenborgian angels to the Hindu *Vedas*. Many correspondences commented on important issues raised in *The Astral Veil*, which was Kut-huri's favorite book. The letters—said to be apported (transported along astral currents through the ether) to Percy's study—were reprinted in every issue of *The Pioneer*. Many readers wrote to the popular new astral columnist. What were his opinions of Biblical miracles? Did he have a remedy for gout?

Some readers, though, protested that Mr. Sinnett's paper was becoming the mouthpiece for "a cabal of batty occultists" who were spreading "dangerously liberal ideas" among the Indians. *The Bombay Herald* ran a cartoon of Kut-huri as a half-naked buck-toothed fakir. A column, "Hoori the Koot's Diary," appeared in the *Calcutta Times*, with fanciful discourses delivered by an over-dressed witch, a fuzzy-faced soldier who spoke twanging Yankee homilies, and a tall, reedy Englishman wearing a tricorn hat made out of an issue of *The Pioneer*.

"All true visionaries like yourself inevitably suffer indignities from tiny-minded Philistines," Kut-huri wrote to Percy. "Pay the flapdoodle no mind! Keep fearlessly on!"

"I shall indeed! Your faith in me sustains my purpose!" Percy wrote back. He put the note in the sandalwood box in his desk for Kut-huri to find. As a scientific test, Percy always locked the box and the desk in which it was contained, as well as his study door and windows. Each morning, he always discovered in the box a new letter from the Master.

Though Kut-huri found Percy an agreeable target for his occult outpourings, Irena wished the Master had chosen a *chela* with a bit more cerebral dexterity. Surrounded by twittering admirers, she was becoming lonely and bored. Where was Moreya? Every time she contacted the astral plane now, it was Kut-huri's ornate orthography that splashed across the pages of her journal—thrilling stuff, but useless for calming her frazzled emotions.

Irena first met Alan Octavian Hume through his twenty-year old daughter, Minnie, who'd joined the Alexandrian Society in Bombay. Tall and patrician, elegantly handsome, Alan had built an enormous home in Simla, called Rothney Castle. Irena was intrigued by its dark, labyrinthine corridors, though sometimes they gave her the chills, especially when Alan's perpetually drunk wife, Moggie, staggered around the place mumbling to herself. But Alan was always interesting. He'd studied religious texts in the original Sanskrit, as Irena had done years before. When Ben and Irena asked him to invite Indian pandits to his gatherings in the castle's flickery gas-lit parlor, he did so, though the mixing of races was all but unknown in these circles. Among his most prominent guests was the Maharajah Harisinghi, who, it turned

out, had secretly enjoyed Irena's frankness to the Maharajah of
Watika, now a political rival of Harisinghi's. At Alan Hume's
gatherings, he sat calmly beneath his huge blue turban, listening
to Irena's stories, stroking his bushy beard and nodding at her insights. Alan, too, appeared to admire Irena's intellect. Yet when
she spoke of Kut-huri's revelations, he grew sardonic.

"Your Adeptic friend needs to brush up on his English gram-
mar," Alan said after reading aloud from a Kut-huri letter in *The
Pioneer* one evening at a gathering at the castle. The Sinnetts,
other British couples, and Harisinghi were seated on giant striped
cushions. From the walls, stuffed antelope heads stared down
from glass eyes. Babula, who'd helped to arrange the room earlier,
stood motionlessly in a shadowy corner, his eyes never leaving his
mistress. Alan, dressed in a white suit, lit up a cigar. "I suppose
there's a shortage of astral proofreaders in Kut-huri's misty Himalayan abode," he said.

Irena bristled. "The Master's letters are quite eloquent just as
they pour forth."

"And how they do pour forth!" Alan rested his head against
the back of his wicker chair. The firelight flickered on his close-
cropped beard and gave his eyes a demonic glint. "The Master is
fortunate that he has such a brilliant amanuensis."

"He is indeed," The Maharajah Harisinghi said in his deep,
resonant voice.

Irena, feeling disoriented, noticed the guests' expressions
changing from looks of amusement to expressions of respect. The
word "brilliant" from a scholar of Alan's caliber wasn't taken
lightly here, even if it might have been tinged with sarcasm. "We
are all fortunate in knowing Kut-huri," she murmured.

"Ah, your famous modesty." Alan's lip curled up at one corner.
"But see here, when will you satisfy poor Percy with a test of
phenomenonogistic authenticity, you old rogue?"

"Don't you speak to me that way!" Irena snapped. The heavy
curtains seemed to billow out of the shadows as if roiled by the
echo of Alan's mocking intonations.

"My dear Madame, I'm merely recognizing that you've bound
yourself to the precepts of *taqiya*—the code of concealment and

dissimulation practiced by the Isma'ilis since ancient times to protect the true faith from the infidel—"

"Cleverer men than you have tried to persecute me!" Irena turned away from him.

"Did you cast a spell on them?" Alan's teeth showed white as he laughed. "Are they now turned into poison mushrooms, sprouting forlornly on the Russian steppes?"

"Alan's a horse's ass." Moggie Hume muttered. "Don't let 'im get under your skin."

"Fortunately, I've got the skin of a hippopotamus." Irena said.

"Need thick hide around this place!" Moggie's eyes narrowed. Her own once-pretty skin was blotched; her fingers shook when she reached for her brandy glass. Such evidence of alcohol use usually provoked Irena's scorn, but now she had a strong impulse to cheer up this poor woman.

Fortunately, she soon had the opportunity. Professor Gordon, Daisy's husband who had just arrived from Bombay and hadn't witnessed any of Irena's phenomena, made a provocative statement about them that was directed both at Irena and at the Maharajah Harisinghi. The professor's pale, thin face had gone ruddy in the cool climate; he swept the thin wisps of hair from his forehead as he spoke. "In the Golden Age of India, the *Shastras* mentioned yogins who could apport objects and do wonderful miracles," he said. "But nowadays I doubt if anyone—not even you, Madame—can do them."

Ben gritted his teeth. Alan beamed a challenging stare at Irena.

"Oh, they say no one can do it now, do they?" she asked, glaring at Alan. "What do you think, your Excellency?"

Maharajah Harisinghi stroked his white beard. "'They' must be sadly misinformed," he said, smiling.

"Thank you, my friend." Irena raised her arms slowly in the air.

The guests sat back, staring. Crinolined bosoms swelled as ladies held breaths. Gentlemen tilted forward.

Suddenly a cascade of white roses showered down onto the gleaming mahogany piano. They bounced on the sounding board and rolled onto the strings, making faint "pings" in the air. Everyone rushed forward. Alan leapt onto the piano bench to squint up at the ceiling; several other guests examined the piano itself, as if it might have suddenly burst into bloom by some mysterious process. Several ladies picked up the roses and sniffed them.

"Lovely and sweet, they are!" Moggie proclaimed.

"And fresh!" Daisy laughed, pushing a flower behind her ear.

"Bravo Madame Milanova!" the Maharajah Harisinghi boomed, clapping his hands. Several gentleman joined in the applause, looking around for Irena.

But Madame Milanova had swept out of the room.

Irena pleaded illness the next day to avoid a spiritualist tea party. While waiting all afternoon for Ben to return from addressing The Simla Ladies' Book Club, she read a volume on Atlantis she'd brought with her from one of the strange little shops in the Crawford Market in Bombay, her favorite place to hunt for old books and antique jewelry. When Ben finally appeared, he seemed in a hurry to leave again. She sat down in the armchair in his study as he straightened the papers on his desk.

"Have you written to those monks in Ceylon?" she asked. "It's always cold here. I want to go south."

"Never mind the weather—we'll probably need another headquarters, soon. We can't go back to Bombay."

"We can go anywhere!"

Ben glanced at the letter he'd received from Davidar, then dropped it into his drawer. "There's been trouble there from the Arya Samaj, street demonstrations outside the 'Crows Nest.' The alliance has fallen apart once and for all. Some people are saying we're a bunch of meddling foreigners, out to sabotage Indian unity."

"What excremental drivel!"

"Of course, but after what happened in Watika. . . ." Ben looked at his pocket watch and stood up. "Well, let's see how our strategy here works. *The Pioneer* articles are a big hit."

Irena pressed her palm to her chest, smiling. She almost blurted out a "Thank you," so grateful was she for Ben's compliment. "Perhaps I should go to the tea party this afternoon, after all."

Ben locked his desk drawer. "I think you need a rest, old girl. Fewer public appearances."

"Do you think I am overstaying my welcome?"

"I didn't say that—"

"Everyone loved the white roses, don't you think?" She stood, moving toward the doorway to block his exit.

"Many did, yes. But after the flowers, I heard someone remark . . . 'perhaps she'll produce an elephant next!'" Ben sighed. "Possibly there've been enough phenomena. It might be best to hide your lamp under the old bushel for a while." When she gave him a quizzical look, he patted her hand and strode past her out the door.

"What is this 'old bushel?'" she called after him, but he evidently didn't hear her. It was so exasperating, not understanding Ben, after they'd shared so many ideas!

Returning to her own room, she sat at her desk and wiped away some dampness from her eyes. Then she picked up her pen and focused on her journal. Rather, she focused on the shadowy, torch-lit cavern of wisdom whose entrance she hoped would open just below the translucent pages of her journal. Again she heard Kut-huri's voice echo up from the depths; tonight it brought to her mind an image of a certain gold and emerald ring that Minnie, the Humes' daughter, had once given to her ex-fiancé to take to a Bombay jeweler for repair. Minnie, Irena knew, had never seen it again. Irena's pen began moving across the page—it seemed that Kut-huri had a plan for apporting the ring to Simla.

Later Babula tiptoed in and, seeing Irena at work, curled up at the foot of her bed. When she told him about the ring, he jumped up and clapped his hands, delighted with Kut-huri's plan. "I am glad you are cheered! It will help distract you from what I found in the Captain's drawer," he said in Arabic. Babula pulled a notebook from under the hem of his *pyjama* shirt.

"Has Ben tried to get in touch with Moreya again?" Irena asked, taking the book from him.

"I am afraid so." Babula gave her a look, like a puppy who has brought his mistress a prized but gristly object. "And not only with Moreya."

Irena set the journal on her desk, slowly opening it. *"An Amorous Conspiracy,"* she read, and her face leaned back as if singed by a sudden flame. When she'd finished the story, she slammed the book shut and rolled a cigarette with trembling fingers. "Him and his magic turban!" she sputtered. "No wonder he has been so preoccupied."

Babula shook his head sadly. "I will put this back," he said, slipping the journal out from beneath Irena's hand. "But there are more urgent matters."

"What are you talking about?"

"I have heard great treachery!" he exclaimed. "Shatan"—his private name for Alan Hume—"is trying to take the Society away from Madame! He and Tiny Mustache"—Babula's name for Percy Sinnett—"are scheming together!"

Irena turned away from her desk. "What? You'd better not be playing with me!"

"Not playing." Babula sat cross-legged on a chintz pouf. "Those two Englishman say to the Captain, he is too brilliant an Alexandrian organizer to be abused so by you!"

"Abused?" The cigarette she was rolling crumbled in her fingers. "Ben knows my moods—he's never complained of me before!"

"He doesn't complain! But the Englishmen tell him, a distinguished man like him needs to stop putting up with all Madame's tricks. He must take charge of the Society on his own."

"Did he tell those two off, after that?"

"Oh yes, Madame!" Babula's eyebrows rose to the line of his pink turban. "And when they say they want to start an Alexandrian branch with only white people, no Indians, then—" Babula began massaging one of Irena's bare feet. "Then he roars and thunders!"

"Ah, good." Irena nodded.

"They say they are going to write to Kut-huri without showing Madame the letter."

"The devious bastards!"

"Don't weep, Madame!" Babula kneaded Irena's big toe between his fingers.

She pulled a handkerchief from her bosom and blew her nose. "What did the Captain say?"

"He says the Englishmen should never, never contact Kut-huri without Madame."

"That is good, anyway." She shook her head. "Oh, the perfidy of those two traitors! Just wait until till they hear from the Master!"

"Kut-huri is cross?" Babula looked up from her toes, grinning.

"Kut-huri is cross as a butcher's bulldog!" She snatched up her bottle of gold ink. "But he is equal to any challenge those treacherous Brits fling at him!"

In the late afternoon light, the Himalayan peaks shimmered with such whiteness that, seen from the drive, they seemed to hover over the Rothney Castle's nasturtium garden like pointed heaps of whipped cream resting on a fragrant tangerine tart. With the house's French windows open onto the verandah, the sitting room floor extended out onto the sunny flagstones. White petalled ear-trumpets listened from the bushes to the buzz of conversations. A cuckoo chirped among the pine boughs.

The guests sat in wicker chairs, sipping tea, munching cucumber sandwiches, enjoying the view of the valley beyond the garden. Present on this occasion were Ben and Irena; Alan and Moggie Hume; the calm, massive Maharajah Harisinghi; four young Indian scholars; Percy and Patience Sinnett; Professor and Mrs. Gordon and their two little girls. The mood on the terrace was languorous, congenial. Ben relaxed in his loose Indian clothes. Irena's earth-colored skirt swept the flagstones; her red shirt shone splendidly like a tropical orchid. At the piano, she played some gay Russian folk songs for the guests. Seeing that she was chilled, Moggie laid a shawl over her shoulders, and Irena turned to smile at her. Daisy helped her girls paste cut-outs of flowers and angels into a scrapbook. Alan and Percy pushed chess pieces around a board while Ben watched. Irena's fingers slowed on the keyboard. She held a chord until it faded out.

"Ben," she asked. "do you see a certain aura coming from that cigar box?"

The box, a lacquered one from Sikkim, rested on a nearby wicker table. Ben squinted at it through his pince-nez. "I didn't notice."

"I believe an important energy current is emanating from the box." Irena's pale blue eyes widened, their bulge becoming more pronounced.

Nearby conversations died down. "If you want to smoke a cigar, you've only to ask," Alan called to her across the room.

"I'll eat all the cigars in this box if it contains nothing but them!" Irena snorted. "Ben, would you open it?"

"Wait, Irena. Don't you think—"

"Oh, open it, will you, Ben!" Seeing his glare, she softened her voice. "Please, old chum," she added.

He lifted the lid. An aroma of tobacco rose into the air, but several guests remarked later that a gold light also flickered up from the box. "A letter!" Ben said, plucking out a triangular piece of paper. On it was some Senzar script in gold ink, with slanted English letters beneath. Irena asked Percy to read it aloud, since it was addressed to him.

"Oh, I say!" Percy smiled. "'*Chela* Sinnett:'" he read. "'Abandon all nefarious plans to communicate with me without the aid of our sister Irena.'" He looked up, his mustache drooping at the corners. "'Her ways may seem strange, but she is the best emissary we have. Her brilliance has confounded many a cynical defamer. She is not to be trifled with!'" Percy's face flushed pink. "It's signed, 'Master Kut-huri.'"

A buzz rose from the gathering. The letter was passed from hand to hand. The Maharajah Harisinghi frowned as he gave it to Percy Sinnett.

"How did Kut-huri know?" Percy whispered to Alan.

Alan shrugged. "Irena probably has spies."

"That's a mean thing to say," Moggie filled her brandy glass from the decanter on the tea trolley.

A silence fell over the guests. Finally one of Daisy's little girls asked, "Can we paste the squiggly letter in our scrapbook?"

This lightened the mood a little. Irena said she was sure Kut-huri would be honored to have his handwriting in such a fine scrapbook, and Daisy squeezed her arm, smiling at the girls. The party resumed almost as peacefully as before, though Ben noticed that Percy seemed restless at the chess board.

Finally he threw up his hands. "I can't help thinking . . . d'you reckon Kut-huri . . . well, that he might honor us with another phenomena, to show us he's not still cross?"

Patience glanced at Irena. "Percy, Madame Milanova's tired."

But Irena, despite the pain in her leg, stood quickly from her chair. She half-closed her eyes. "I wonder if anyone here is wishing for something—some small thing fondly remembered, perhaps something long ago lost," she said in a quiet, dreamy voice.

The guests glanced at each other. One of the young Indians said, "I am remembering a tennis racket which I left at the Bengal Club—"

"Nothing like that!" the Maharajah Harisinghi scolded him.

"Moggie, perhaps," Irena said, fixing Mrs. Hume with her pale blue stare. "Perhaps something small, precious. . . ."

On the couch Moggie nodded, gazing up. "I think I recall—"

"Don't tell me. Just picture it in your mind." Here Irena pressed her palm to her forehead. "Yes, a picture is coming. . . . I believe it is some kind of family heirloom. . . ."

Now Moggie's eyelashes were blinking hard. She took a gulp from her glass. "An heirloom? Oh, yes, I do remember one—"

"I see it clearly now." Irena spoke in a whispery voice that people had to lean close to hear. "It is gold, with an emerald."

"The emerald ring!" Moggie suddenly sat forward, splashing brandy onto her linen skirt. "Yes, I can visualize it exactly! I gave it to my daughter, Minnie. And she—I think she broke off the stone—" Tears flooded her eyes. "Oh, I'd so love to have it back, Irena!"

Irena nodded slowly. "Now I see . . . *flowers,*" she said. "Do you see them, Moggie?"

She blinked. "Nasturtiums," she said in a small croaking voice.

"The flower beds!" Percy exclaimed. "Would it be there?"

Irena didn't answer for a very long moment. Silence fell over the gathering as everyone waited. A cuckoo chirped from the nearby pines. Finally, Irena raised her face, gazing out past the verandah. "The Master tells me . . . the heirloom is . . . just as Moggie has intuited—*buried among the nasturtiums."*

The chairs emptied instantly. Guests snatched up spoons and butter knives from the tea trolley. They all—except Irena and Alan—scrambled across the grass into the flower beds.

"Which one?" Percy cried out, for there were two beds, and several guests bumped into each other trying to decide which one to attack with their utensils. Irena pointed at the bed to her left. Percy and the Indian scholars, down on all fours in their light summer suits, dug with their bare hands, soon getting their pants and jackets filthy. The Maharajah supervised, tugging at his white beard. Patience received a face-full of soil, but brushed it off as she plunged her spoon into the damp earth. Moggie swayed on her knees and fell sideways, crushing a dozen blooms. Leaves and stalks and petals flew into the air. Laughing, Daisy's little girls shuffled about digging divots with the toes of their shoes. Ben found a trowel and began plowing systematic furrows up the center of the bed.

Then Percy, rooting under some weeds, his nose close to the ground, cried out, "I've *got* it!" As he staggered to his feet, sweat pouring from his dirt-smudged brow, he held up a tiny square box wrapped in black paper.

The guests crowded around. Moggie was helped forward to un-wrap the box, her hair falling over her face. She ripped the paper off. From the box she pulled a gold emerald ring that sparkled in the slanting sunbeams. "That's the one! It's come back to me!" She pressed it to her bosom.

Irena smiled. A cheer went up. Everyone admired the ring. Irena slipped it onto Moggie's finger. The Indian scholars clapped, and Maharajah Harisinghi started a cheer—"For she's a jolly good fellow!"—for Irena, who stood on the edge of the verandah, her face radiant with smiles. At first she was reluctant to accept Moggie's thanks. "I am merely an amanuensis," she protested—but she did agree to pose when Professor Gordon set up his camera and tripod. Percy and Ben suggested writing up an affidavit of authenticity to be signed by all present, and nearly everyone agreed.

"At last, a demonstration in full daylight!" Percy wiped his hands on a napkin. "And with everyone's attention focused!"

"It is indeed remarkable. . . ." Alan Hume lit a long cigar. He was standing away from the crowd beside the decimated tea trolley, his elegant white suit free of any dirt streaks. "The most remarkable thing," he intoned, blowing out a stream of black smoke, "is how Kut-huri knew that this particular ring could be found . . . in Ahmed's Pawn Shop in the Crawford Market in Bombay."

Then the gathering, if noisy before in exultation, was noisier still in consternation: gasps and groans and questions erupted.

"What are you talking about, Alan?" Moggie demanded, the lines in her face hardening.

"I heard the truth from a member of my old regiment. . . ," Alan said, and the crowd hushed to listen. "My friend knew the lieutenant who deserted our dear daughter last year after promising to marry her. She'd given him the ring to take to a jewelers for repair."

Moggie dabbed at her eyes with a handkerchief. "She said she'd lost the ring!"

"But she hadn't," Alan said. "Her fiancé had it. Instead of going to the jewelers to get it mended, the blackguard sold it to the pawnbroker just before he shipped out. Later, my friend recognized it in the shop window. He was going to redeem it for me, but when he returned with some money, he found. . . ." Here Alan turned to Irena. ". . . that someone else had purchased the item."

"Are you saying Irena bought it?" Ben demanded, stepping forward.

"I saw the receipt," Alan said, his voice calm. "The signature was nearly as indecipherable as . . . well, as Senzar!" A smile twisted the corners of his lips. "It was in fact, Arabic. The person who gave the money for the ring—'for his mistress,' the boy said—was an Arabic-speaking Pathan in a pink turban. Resembling Madame Milanova's servant, Babula, I believe—"

"Bombay's full of Pathans in turbans of every color of the rainbow!" Ben pointed his finger at Alan's chest. "You're making a serious accusation—"

"Quite baseless, sir!" the Maharajah thundered.

Others clustered around. The word "fraud," bobbed on the

churning sea of voices. One of the young Indian scholars, defending Irena, waved his fist in Professor Gordon's face and had to be dragged back by his companions. The camera toppled over. Daisy's little girls squealed. Now the grass was looking as trampled and ravaged as the flower beds.

Irena staggered back on the flagstones, her face a dark stormy red. Accusations surged around her. She heard someone laugh. "You traitors!" she suddenly screamed. "For weeks, you have begged me for phenomena like a pack of greedy pigs!" The guests gaped up at the verandah where she stood swaying in place. "You manipulated me! You used me! You called on me to entertain you day after day! And now you *persecute* me!" She glared at Alan Hume. "You especially, you gilded humbug!"

Alan turned his face sideways as if to avoid an unpleasant odor. "Rather bad sportsmanship, old girl, don't you think? You did go a bit far—"

"I helped your poor wife get her ring back, you overblown pumpkin!" Irena sputtered. "You monkey's *bum!*"

"Monkey-bum!" Echoed one of Daisy's girls, clapping her hands.

"I say," Percy said, "That's a bit excessive—"

"Oh, *shut up*," Moggie muttered.

Ben reached Irena's side. "Excessive or not, she's got a right to be furious!" he shouted, his beard glinting in the slanting sunbeams. He turned to Alan. "You pretend to admire her, then you scoff at her—" His fists were clenched, and he might have swung at Alan if Daisy hadn't stepped in front of him. "You owe Madame Milanova an apology!" Ben roared.

"Don't be a fool, Captain!" Alan turned and walked off the verandah. Moggie swayed in place. Then, giving Irena a wretched look, she straggled after her husband.

The guests began to drift uneasily toward the drive. Irena, her swollen leg throbbing, limped back to the sitting room. Ben eased her onto a sofa. Daisy went to fetch her a cup of tea.

"You see how they hate me!" Irena cried in a small voice, staring up into Ben's face. "After all I tried to do to help them. . . ."

"I know." He nodded. "I should have put a stop to it weeks ago."

"But I don't care!" Irena bit her lip. "We don't need these people. We can move on without them, Maloney!"

Ben sat beside her. "Mulligan, the Masters have more important work for us in Asia than anything we can do among these colonials."

Daisy returned with the tea and set the cup down on the table in front of Irena. Then with a sigh she went off to look for her girls. Ben wondered if he'd ever see her again.

The Maharajah Harisinghi lumbered into the room and sat across from Irena and Ben. "That Britisher has wronged you both. But I have resources. . . ." He scratched his beard, his brow furrowed in thought. "You must divert yourself, Madame. Tell another delightful story."

"My friend, you're kind, but she's tired," Ben said.

"I'll wager that she will enjoy entertaining an appreciative audience." The Maharajah 's face broke into a smile. "You see, I understand the temperament of an artist."

"So you do." Irena sank back into the cushions. "What would you like to hear?"

"I enjoyed your telling about the mountain people you met as a child." The Maharajah, too, sat back, glancing at Ben. "Did you enjoy that, sir?"

"I did. It was the old Irena we all knew and loved."

Irena closed her eyes and held out one hand toward the open door to the terrace. "I sense a hush settling over this valley before us like a cloud. The lawn is empty now, strewn with clods of earth and maimed flowers. A native flute tweets far down in the valley. Its notes are spiraling up on the breeze. Do you hear them?"

"I hear them," Ben said, leaning forward, smiling.

"As I listen to its melody, I raise my eyes to the snow-covered mountains as if waking from a bad dream." And here Irena opened her huge blue eyes to stare out the open doors past the terrace. "The flute notes are high and plaintive, like yellow butterflies fluttering in the air."

"I see them," Harisinghi sighed.

"Now a vision forms in my mind: gay pennons rippling from

pointed tents. They belong to the Kalmuk nomads I visited each summer as a child in the Caucasus. I see myself, thirteen years old, trotting up to their mountain encampment on my pony. The music of flutes flutters around me. Dark-skinned children cry out. Women whisper as they rush from their tents in bright skirts and jackets. A chieftain with narrow black eyes and a huge mustache lifts me from the saddle and sets me gently down. Children and adults gather around. Their faces are flushed with delight—the appearance of a pale, wiry-haired Russian child among them breaks the harsh routines of their lives. And too, my presence tells them that the provincial governor—my father—will permit them to camp here for another season." Irena closed her eyes again. "The mustachioed chieftain leads me to the altar at the far end of the tent. There, among chunks of sweet-smoking incense, I see small stone icons. They face a painting of Tara, the female form of the Buddha, seated on her lotus throne. I gaze, transfixed, at the maiden's round Asiatic face, her bulbous eyes. I feel as if I am staring into a kind of spiritual mirror. Suddenly I am sure that the adoring looks the Kalmuks are giving Tara are identical to the looks they are casting at me. I feel the rhythm of their breathing and the warmth of their bodies as they cluster close around me at the altar. Their clothes give off scents of cook-fire smoke, animal fur, mountain meadows. Children gaze up into my face; men and women stroke the lace trim of my blouse's collar. Being engulfed by so much love makes me sway in place. My legs buckle beneath me, and I drop in a swoon to the ground." Irena's head fell back against the cushion. Slowly she opened her eyes again, smiling first at the Maharajah, then at Ben.

"Moments later. . . ." Now she gazed out at the mountains again, "I awake in the arms of the chieftain. Blinking, I gaze up into his black almond eyes. A radiant smile breaks across my face." Her voice sunk to a whisper. "I *recognize* him. . . ."

And now, Irena struggled up from the couch, holding tight to Ben's arm. She seemed drawn by the flute notes rising from the valley beyond the terrace. She took a wobbly step forward. "A fresh breeze is cooling me here," she said, and wiped her brow with the back of her hand. "All of Asia stretches before me." she said. "Harisinghi, I thank you for your faith in me."

The Maharajah gave a little bow.

She stretched her arm out toward the valley. "I feel that our destiny is to the *south*." She walked out onto the terrace, still holding Ben's arm. "What do you think, Ben?" she asked, turning to him.

He stepped down with her from the flagstones. The soft grass was soothing beneath his feet; now he felt a breeze against his face. "The farther south, the better, old girl."

Part Three

Ceylon

13

In October of 1882, Irena sent her condolences to Sarah, now sixteen, on the death of her mother. She also sent a check and a pledge to keep her promise to bring the girl to India as soon as possible to join the Alexandrian entourage. A sympathetic Maharajah named Harisinghi, she wrote, was negotiating with a departing British official to buy the Society an estate in the southern city of Madras. The Founders had abandoned Bombay, where hostile people had sabotaged the Society's work; Davidar and the Coulombs (by now familiar figures to Sarah in Irena's letters) were going ahead to ready the new headquarters in Madras. Meanwhile, she and Ben were on their way to Ceylon. Ben was eager to support the Buddhists' fight against the Christian missionaries there and "establish a beachhead for Alexandrianism." A bright new beginning awaited them—Irena was sure that the island was not called "Serendip" by the ancients for nothing!

Approaching the port of Galle, she stood beside Ben at the rail of the coastal steamer Ellora, scanning the blue horizon for land. She wore a new outfit: a long, tan and white striped dress with a waist-length blue shawl. Glittering on her bosom was an official Alexandrian Society Officer's badge—an image of the sun sprouting golden rays. She'd had a jeweler make it of brass especially for this trip, along with a splendid planet Saturn with silver rings for Ben. It would cheer him up; after the trouble in Simla, he had had several unexpected astral visits from Mary Surratt—who evidently had not stayed put in America after all. Though Ben normally avoided insignia, he agreed to wear the badge for his arrival in

Ceylon—a sign, Irena was hopeful, that their partnership was stronger than ever. He was prepared to blend in with the local population, outfitted in a collarless tunic, long Ceylonese sarong, and sandals. His face and belly had grown rounder, and he looked a little like a wise Buddha, Irena thought, had the Buddha worn a gray beard down to his chest and a pince-nez.

His expression was detached, but Irena noticed a flock of pesky *arupa* hovering around him. These were elemental spirits that one attracted from the astral plane when one thought anxious thoughts. They changed one's aura to a dreary gray, and took on the shapes of one's worries—rather like dust adhering around sticky but invisible barley sugar animals. Several of Ben's *arupa* were shaped like Bombay debts. One was rotund like a lamp (the kerosene bill); one was as skinny as a bedpost, with a bald knob for a head (the bill from the shop where Irena had ordered new beds). She spotted another *arupa* shaped like an elephant—representing, she supposed, the crest of the Maharajah Harisinghi, who had not yet kept his promise to pay the Madras estate's mortgage.

Suddenly she saw Ben's aura turn pale blue—the Buddhist color for confidence. All the gray *arupa* fled, leaving a clear view of the horizon.

"Land ho!" he shouted.

Irena squeezed his arm. As the Ellora puffed into the harbor, she saw three high-masted sailing ships rocking gently on the water. To her left, the surf splashed against a promontory of black rocks, the foam spewing high into the air and collapsing back into the water in silent white explosions. To her right, the old Dutch fort pointed rusty cannons from slits in its high stone walls. And straight ahead lay the town of Galle: jetty, customs buildings, lighthouse, coaling sheds, and thousands of green palms. Among them the tile roofs of scattered white bungalows flashed in the sunlight like semaphore flags.

"Adam's Peak!" Ben pointed to the tallest of a jagged group of mountains where the Buddha had first preached here two thousand years ago.

Irena twirled her blue umbrella over her head. "Magnificent, old chum!"

The splashing surf! The sparkling sunlight! Everything filled the two of them with such wonder that they flung their arms around each other's waists like two children poised at the gate of a miraculous tropical garden. And Irena thought: this may be the highest point in our life together, the moment we will one day recall with the most affection and longing. . . .

"Look!" Ben shouted. Two outrigger canoes were skimming across the water, each garlanded with dazzling white flowers. Banners dipped and rose in unison as the oars churned the water. A pilot boat sailed between the canoes, its gunwales decorated with shaggy green plantain leaves. Irena made out saffron-robed men waving from the boats. She waved back, her long sleeve flapping.

The pilot boat was nudging the coaster's prow. Boatmen shouted up at its deck. "*Sadhoo!* Holy man!" Ben shook his head, but he did raise both arms to acknowledge the cheers. Then, clutching the ropes of the ship's ladder, he climbed down to the little catamaran. Irena wobbled down the side while four sailors kept her from toppling into the sea. As the boat glided off, Ben was garlanded by the crew; wearing a massive collar of white petals, he leaned far out over the prow. Behind him among the sweaty paddlers sat Irena, a single flower-necklace wilting on her bosom.

The sea was too rough for docking at the jetty; the catamaran made for the beach, which was now crowded with dark-skinned men and women. The paddlers' arms rose in unison, paused, then propelled the craft forward over the crest of the last wave. Irena held her stomach as the boat glided down the foam and slid onto the sand with a crunching sound. Ben was over the prow and up to his ankles in the frothing water before anyone in the crowd could assist him. Irena, hampered by her sore leg, wasn't so quick. The boatmen made a hammock of their arms and rolled her into it. She was carried through the surf and set gently down on her behind upon the hot sand.

Roasting like a potato in coals, she could only glimpse Ben through a dancing forest of limbs and torsos. The cries of

"Sadhoo! Sadhoo!" rang in her ears; sarongs swished past her face as people crowded close to the enormous white visitor. Ben was barely recognizable now, so covered was he with garlands. Finally the throng parted before a delegation of monks. Just as they arrived, hands clasped together before their chests, Ben exploded in a mighty sneeze, scattering flower petals everywhere. Far from being offended, the monks roared with mirth; the spectators took up the merriment; several novitiates fell off the nearby jetty and thrashed deliriously in the surf; waves of happy voices rippled along the beach.

Irena saw Ben lean over to touch the monks' feet, a gesture of humility that brought a kind of mass exhalation from the crowd.

"You come to us in our hour of greatest need," a tiny shaven-headed monk said to him.

Irena let out a bellow of misery.

Several young monks clustered around her, but they were forbidden to touch a woman. Finally some boatmen raised her to her feet and helped her across the hot sand. Her skirt was soaked but she limped along with as much dignity as she could muster.

The tiny monk—it was Meggettuwatte, the man Ben had been corresponding with—rushed up to her. Irena didn't care for the sly look in his eyes. "Ah, Madame Milanova!" he cried, clasping his hands together. "The Captain has written us about your books and astral miracles."

If ever there was a moment for a phenomena, it was now. Afterwards, these people would never leave her languishing in the sand again! Sensing that an astrally embroidered handkerchief was about to apport itself from her sleeve to the monk's shoulder bag, Irena swept her arm high in the air. But it progressed no further; Ben's fingers clasped her wrist and lowered it firmly to her side. Irena shook her hand free, but there was no shaking off the glare he'd given her. The handkerchief fluttered to the ground in the commotion, unnoticed. Bare feet trampled it into the sand.

Ben was ushered onto a flower-strewn platform on the jetty. Palm fronds were raised over his head to keep off the broiling sun. Irena saw him take a deep swallow and lift his arms high again. As the crowd hushed before him, she felt like slinking back to the pilot boat and floating off the edge of the world. His speech was translated into Sinhala a sentence at a time by Meggettuwatte. Irena had heard it many times before: the need to save Asian culture from defilement by Western intruders. But today she heard frequent references to the Buddha, each one bringing cheers. When he stopped talking, a hiatus of silence opened around him on the platform. The monks waited, smiling. Barechested, sarong-clad peasants and fishermen gazed at the huge stranger. What, Irena wondered, had Meggettuwatte told these people about him?

"*Pansil!*" Ben said suddenly in a booming voice. "It's time to take our public vows and become Buddhists!"

"Now?" Irena frowned. "The Masters said nothing about this."

Ben ignored her. "Is there a temple handy?" he asked the monk in a voice meant to be overheard by the multitudes. "To show our commitment to the island's great Buddhist revival, we want to officially join the *Sangha!*"

"An excellent idea!" Meggettuwatte replied. "It will be a famous event!"

And it was: the first time in history that any Westerners had publicly proclaimed their conversion to the Buddhist faith. Converts didn't ordinarily take *Pansil*, or vows, in public, but Meggettuwatte understood that the ceremony would attract enormous attention to his revival movement; it would also give a slap in the face to the Christians, who'd been boasting of the conversions they were making among the natives.

News of the event did spread far and wide. Vijayananda temple in Galle, where the *Pansil* ceremony took place on the very day of the Founders' arrival, became a shrine that pilgrims from all over the country were to visit. An artist recorded the historic event. Among the wall panels commemorating the stages in Lord Siddhartha's path to Buddhahood, he painted brightly colored frescos depicting the arrival of the Russian-American mystic and the American Captain at the temple. In the final panel, they were shown kneeling on a woven mat before Meggettuwatte. Irena looked dark and dignified, with flowing black hair as beautiful as any honored Ceylonese matron's. Ben's sarong was painted a rich red (for wisdom), and his beard was shown as bushy and white as that of God as He appeared in Christian missionary pamphlets. The painted scene suggested that the Christian deity himself had bowed his head before the ancient Buddhist wisdom of Asia.

After the public vows, Ben's lecture tours gave the Buddhist revival movement a great impetus among the people. His first speech was at a school in Galle. So many eager Buddhists packed the school assembly hall that Ben had to stand on a desk to be heard. Behind him, the emblem of the Alexandrian Society was drawn in chalk on the blackboard. Students moved the broiling air around with huge woven fans. It was just as well Ben had no notes; his glasses were so fogged he couldn't have read them. But his voice boomed and echoed among the rafters, his hands gestured enthusiastically in the air, his eyes glowed with dedication, and when he finished, the cheers were deafening. He was carried on people's shoulders to a carriage waiting outside.

The American Captain was asked to speak at every stop on the road from Galle to Colombo. He gave lectures in temple courtyards, under palm frond canopies on cocoanut plantations, in roadside tents festooned with swallow-tailed banners. He preached from the back of a cart before the thatched roofs of fishing villages, a crimson sunset for a backdrop, the crash of surf punctuating his exhortations. "A new hope . . . freedom from colonial customs . . . a swelling Buddhist resurgence!" he roared. In even the humblest hamlets he founded branches of the Alexandrian Society and appointed local headmen to take charge of each one.

People brought him pots of steaming curry, fresh fruit and vegetables, much of which he distributed to the poor. He and Irena slept in plush four-poster beds, in hammocks strung between trees, on rough mats on temple floors. Rarely did they have time for more than one meal a day; bathing in the ocean with all their clothes on was a refreshing luxury. They arrived in Colombo to find the city square packed with four thousand chanting Buddhists, the podium lined with the city's most important religious dignitaries.

"I've been asked how the leader of a non-denominational movement like Alexandrianism can announce himself for Buddhism," Ben shouted from the platform. An interpreter cried out his words in Sinhala. "I embrace a noble spiritual philosophy, not a dogma. Alexandrianism has no dogma. It seeks only the appreciation of all great faiths . . . each to reign without persecution in its own land."

The cheers were tumultuous.

Irena wrote a letter to the local newspaper inviting the British community to a public discussion on the topic of religious tolerance. The responses were scathing. "Apostle of Yankee Heathenism," Ben was called. "Advocate of a negativistic, ungodly faith!"

"You see what your overtures to the colonialists result in!" Ben complained.

"Don't scold me when I've created such an opportunity!" Irena said. "Answer the fools *back!* Let them know where you stand!"

"Yes . . . I *will!*" And that afternoon he slammed down his response on the desk of the editor of Colombo's largest newspaper. "If I am a betrayer of my Christian race, so be it!" the next day's issue quoted him. "I shall cease to seek the cooperation of the white community of this island. I throw in my lot with the Ceylonese people!"

Buddhism in Ceylon was divided into sects and even castes; with the publication of Ben's manifesto, each separate group sent delegates to seek the Alexandrian Society's backing.

"I'll meet half of them," Irena said, "You meet the other half."

"Certainly not!" Ben said. He and Meggettuwatte had already mapped out his strategy in an atmosphere of secrecy without consulting her, Irena noted. It was a risky plan: they refused to meet the factions separately; instead, Ben insisted that they sit down together to a communal meal in the huge hall of the building the Society had been given. The monks balked. Ben threatened to return to India. Finally, they sat and ate. Afterwards he berated them for their petty rivalries and adherence to outlawed caste distinctions. "If we want to stop the influence of Christian missionaries, then we must start Buddhist schools from one end of the island to the other!" he exhorted them. "The children of this land

ought to know their religion as well as Sunday school pupils in
America know theirs!" Again, the cheers rocked the hall. Ben
formed task forces and committees; the great educational work
began.

In the few Buddhist schools on the island there were no Buddhist textbooks. So he set about writing one. Consulting with the
monks, he read over a hundred books to prepare himself for the
task. At first Irena helped him take notes, but she wasn't welcome
in the company of holy men—the monks waited until she reluctantly left before getting down to serious discussions. At the end
of his labors, Ben produced the world's first Buddhist Catechism.
It was easily understandable to children and adults alike, and
ready for translation into the languages of all nations where the
Buddha was revered.

Other religions, Ben noted, had their symbols to rally the faithful. Christianity had the cross, Islam the star and crescent. But
what of Buddhism? Ben started sketching.

"Do you really think you are the right one to supply their emblem?" Irena asked.

"Sometimes it's easier for a foreigner to make innovations."

"Like a *deus ex machina*," Irena commented. "But did it ever
occur to you that the monks are inflating you just to use you?"

"Let them—it's for a good cause!" Ben reached for a ruler.

He convened a meeting of scholars and showed them his design
for a Buddhist flag: to the left, a vertical set of blue, yellow, red,
white, and orange stripes, and to the right, a horizontal set of the
same colors. He insisted on a democratic vote to approve it; the
approval was unanimous. When the flag was first unfurled, British detractors commented that with all its stripes it resembled the
American flag. But soon it was much more visible around the
countryside than the Union Jack. It was a bright and cheerful emblem, and the people loved to see it flying.

Irena traveled with Ben from city to town to village on his lecture tours. Though they'd planned a visit of only a few weeks,
they'd stayed in Ceylon for two months already with no end in
sight for the work Ben wanted to do. Irena's brass Alexandrian

badge had faded to a burnished, greenish color, but she continued to display it on her breast. Ben's silver-plated Saturn badge
shone as brightly as ever. In many ways she was glad to let him
shine in this new setting, but having little of her own work to do
was making her restless. Ben finally noticed this, too. Since her
official position in the Society was Recording Secretary, he suggested that she transcribe his addresses. It was a short-lived idea.

"Hire yourself a clerk," she snorted. "I'm no one's amanuensis
but the Masters'!"

She filled some time writing a travel article for her Moscow editor:

Taking the liberating message of Alexandrianism to the fur-
thest corners of Ceylon, I ride an old railway car as it climbs
an escarpment. In the flooded rice paddies below me, wet buffaloes catch the sun and glisten like great silver pods floating
upon the waters. Oh Lovely Lanka!

Sometimes, more prosaically, I bump along a rutted track
in a ramshackle cart drawn by a humpbacked bullock. The
huge wheels creak. Raindrops pelt the leaves beside the trail.
Then I round a bend and—behold!—a band of Devil Dancers
leaps before a bonfire to the thunder of tom-toms! Clouds of
colored smoke fill the air with perfumed scents. Mystical designs painted upon the dancers' chests run with hot rivulets of
sweat. Exorcised demons leap from the dancer's throats and
vanish into the rustling underbrush.

On clear, starry nights, the insect world puts on a scratchy
concert. I hear the flutter of moths whose wings glow gold in
the lantern light. Out of the darkness comes the savage yelp of
jackals, the trumpeting of wild elephants pushing their way
through the cane groves. The fairy moonlight cools the air and
I drift off to sleep on my bed of palm fronds. At dawn, the villagers come out to greet me, bearing coffee, rice cakes—and
radiant smiles. . . .

She reported, too, on another of Ben's famous debates with the
missionaries:

The little hall was packed like a tin of herrings with Buddhists and Christians, smelling nearly as ripe. Ben strode in
waving one of the flysheets the British-paid Ceylonese pup-
pets had been circulating about the Alexandrianists. He

leaped onto a chair and began to read it in a booming voice. It was atrociously written, and the hall rang with laughter. "Is this the best you can do?" he roared at a trembling Presbyterian vicar. He tore the flysheet to strips. Cheers! He stomped on it with his sandals. More cheers! After that, the Christians hadn't a chance. For every Biblical text they quoted, Ben knew a better Buddhist precept. The crowd chanted along with him. The missionaries skulked from the hall with their tails between their legs.

Christians attacked a procession honoring the Buddha's birthday, Irena reported, so the Captain held a public rally, assailing church and state with heroic rhetoric. The monks chose him as their official delegate to approach the British. Approach? He blew into Government House like a thunderstorm in a sarong! Sarong, sandals, tunic, and—not very Ceylonese, but impressive nonetheless—an enormous turban: like a Yankee *Pasha!* Colonial lackeys scattered before him in panic. Irena limped along behind as best she could (her leg had swollen again), but the door slammed in her face as he made his majestic entry into the inner sanctum. Through the door, she heard him shouting at the governor. He pounded the table. He threatened strikes on the rubber plantations. He issued ultimatums. . . . A week later came the government decrees: The Buddha's birthday was declared a public holiday. Those who wished to enter the civil service were no longer required to be Christians. And Buddhist schools were now legalized throughout the colony. The Captain announced the victories at a rally. Never had Irena seen his aura throb with such bold blue confidence. Hosannas and flower petals rained down upon him. He tilted back his head to receive them. His arms rose. His face was aglow. Was it her imagination, or did she see him rising off the platform into the cascades of glory like a hot-air balloon?

It was all rather thrilling, but it was frightening, too—the way his voice resonated, his eyes gleamed. He had let his beard and hair grow so that he seemed to be turning into some sort of white-fringed deity whom she hardly knew. He consulted furtively with the monks, making mysterious plans she knew nothing of, and she felt superfluous and useless. . . .

When Ben returned in triumph to the Vijayananda temple in Galle, Irena was dismayed to find no seat reserved for her on the platform among the dignitaries. Monks rushed up to Ben, forming a saffron wall around him. Crowds pushed Irena this way and that, nearly toppling her in the mud. Flaming torches lit up the night air—normally an exciting sight, but tonight the glare hurt her eyes and the smell of burning pitch made her choke. Fighting her way out of the throng, she made her way toward the town with some novitiates walking behind her at a distance, since a woman did not walk alone at night, lest she be taken for a witch.

That night, she wrote in her journal, *I found myself wandering through the warm, smoke-scented evening in the old Portuguese-Dutch town of Galle. The buildings were of plaster and brick, none taller than two stories, with pretty tiled roofs and wooden shutters. At each corner a lamp glowed faintly from its ornate black stanchion. How I loved the quiet narrow streets, the salt-scented breeze against my face. I stopped to pet a kitten asleep on the warm cobblestones. The only sounds I heard were the exhalations of the surf from beyond the fort's walls, and the low murmur of voices from inside the dwellings.*

As I walked, I caught glimpses of life through the open doorways. Here a Moorman in scull-cap and white robe sat reading his Qu'ran by candlelight. Here some Hindu ladies in sparkling sarees laughed as they combed a daughter's hair. Through another door, I watched a Sinhalese child playing beside a stone Buddha, both his and Gautama's faces illuminated by flames dancing in sea-shells of cocoanut oil laid out on the tile floor.

I thought: here are ordinary people, living their quiet lives with hardly a thought to the mystic forces that have brought them together on this street. Their lives are enough for them; they never need to agonize about the hows and whys of their existence as I do. They do not yearn to make something more out of daily life than they already know. They feel no longing for personal contact with cosmic entities, they have no need to save themselves from the torment of incompleteness. They feel no goadings toward the infinite that would stir them to leave their homes and wander the earth in search of ever-elusive truth. Truth? They have it—they are it! What more do they need? Consider the lilies of the field.

I thought: why can't I be like them? Why can't I just live? Then I considered: if they catch a glimpse of me passing their doors, they must think me an ordinary woman limping along toward home. How wrong they'd be, for what home have I ever known since leaving Russia at seventeen? Home, if I can envision it at all, is a final destination, a sense of completion that I shall probably never find short of the grave, if even then. I can only glimpse it in my imagination—a place of lustrous beings whose voices call me on, then vanish in the whispers of the wind. What a frail refuge is the imagination. . . .

Another thought: in one way, I am an ordinary woman—for I've lost contact with the spirit world. Though I love the island's beauty, I find no yogis or mystics to learn from here. I see no proofs of the Masters' purpose for my life, no miracles to validate Their watch over me. I feel adrift, an empty shell, deprived of my powers to amaze myself or others, unable to bring myself relief from the ever-advancing awareness of my human inadequacy. My mind is dim, an opaque unlit lantern. When I reach Madras I shall erect a shrine to Kut-huri, soak up his radiance, and become my luminous self again, and more so. Here I am nothing but a woman: aging, frightened, homeless.

A paradox: I have dedicated my life to the brotherhood of all mankind, yet here in this quiet old town, I can feel no peaceful kinship with the people whose lives I glimpse from the street. Never have I felt so close to the essence of humanity; never have I felt so alone. . . .

As she traveled with Ben, Irena thought her concerns were going right past him. But he was worried about her aches and pains, and one day he showed her his design for a more comfortable travelling vehicle. A "Buddhist covered wagon," he called it. She had to admit it was a wonderful example of Yankee ingenuity—a bullock cart with compartments that unfolded into bunk beds, folded back into a work table, folded yet again into a speaker's platform. Sliding panels concealed nooks for cooking utensils and provisions. The whole conveyance was covered by a rounded canvas top imprinted with the great seal of the Alexandrian Society. Ben was so pleased with it that he mailed off his design to the Patent Office in Washington, D.C.

In India, rajahs and wealthy merchants had contributed enough to keep the Society afloat and allow the Founders to live modestly. When they traveled, neither Irena nor Ben concerned themselves much with money; karma always brought benefactors to pay for railway tickets, meals, accommodations. The same happened in Ceylon. But once Ben decided to found Buddhist schools, he transformed himself into a fanatical fund-raiser. He collected membership dues; he sold "merit cards"; he handed out little clay banks to children, asking them to get neighbors to fill them with donations. On his next rally in their village, the little ones were invited to climb onto the platform and smash the banks to the ground, causing great cheers with each explosion of coins for the cause.

At one meeting, Irena noticed a ragged woman with silver streaks in her hair place a single rupee into the donations basket. As she trudged away, Ben immediately stopped the proceedings. "My friends, I've seen a wonderful sight!" he announced. "A single rupee has been given by one of the humblest but purest of heart among you. A widow's mite!" He held up the coin for all to see, then asked the woman to tell her story. Despite her poverty, she said in a halting voice, she'd been saving up for weeks in order to make her contribution. Holding her hand, Ben addressed the audience again: "This poor woman has given all she has. I hope that each of you will be moved to match her donation with a single coin of your own. Here—I'll be the first!" And he flung down a rupee into the collection basket. Members of the crowd rushed forward. Coins rained down.

Thereafter, the woman traveled with the caravan, appearing at rallies with her single coin and her tearfully told story of poverty and generosity.

"It's a wonderful trick," Irena commented, lighting a cigarette. "I've seen it at tent shows in Europe."

"It's done by travelling evangelists in America, too," Ben allowed. "But it's no trick—the lady's dedication is utterly genuine!"

Irena eyed him sideways. "How did you know she was a widow?"

"Well, one of the monks did tell me in advance." Ben cleared his throat. "All right, we arranged for her to come forward. Her donation wasn't quite spontaneous."

"Why, you could have knocked me over with a feather!"

"Sometimes it's necessary—if the cause is important enough— to stretch the limits of absolute verisimilitude."

"What big words you use, Ben." Irena blew a smoke ring at him.

From the tropical southern coast the Buddhist covered wagon wended its way north into the highlands, passing vistas where flooded rice fields lay amidst the lush greenery like mirrors on which clouds floated across the land. Elephants carrying huge logs lumbered over red clay fields. More and more people crowded the road; it seemed that everyone was headed for Kandy, capital of the most powerful of the ancient Ceylonese kingdoms and the site of South Asia's most important Buddhist shrine: the Temple of the Tooth.

At Ramapoola, Irena, Ben and a delegation of headmen who'd recently become Alexandrian Society officers boarded a train decked out with American and Buddhist flags. It chug-chugged majestically through fragrant coffee plantations to the Kandy station, where thousands of people stood waiting. As Irena stepped into the carriage doorway in her blue cape, a roar went up and flower petals fluttered in the air. She was tempted to slowly raise her arms the way she'd seen Ben do as he bathed in applause; her heart beat fast. When he appeared beside her, the noise became a typhoon of sound. Looking much like the Ceylonese headmen— only, of course, much taller—he was decked out in blue silken pantaloons, a long red coat with gold frogs across his barrel chest, and a turban as white as the cascading curls of his beard.

"Where's your Saturn badge?" She had to shout in his ear to be heard. She pointed to her own brass sun-badge on her breast.

"Lost it somewhere," he said. "I don't need it."

"Hmph!" Irena said, but he didn't seem to hear.

The Founders were led to a carriage and team. The horses were unhitched, and two dozen cheering students grabbed the harnesses to pull the Founders through the city. From windows and balconies people waved palm fronds at the procession as it swelled into the main square beside the lake. Ladies with parasols watched its progress from white boats that glided like swans on the blue water. On the far shore the green hillsides rippled in the sunlight.

Irena heard rhythmic chanting from a group of buildings that made up the Temple of the Tooth. The tallest, a block of white stone, was capped by a pagoda with its own red-tiled roof. The carriage halted, and a delegation of monks in saffron robes waited for the guests to step down onto a red carpet. The air shimmered with a tintinnabulation of tiny cymbals.

At the tower's doorway, Ben slipped out of his sandals. Irena, who cursed herself for wearing high-button shoes, had to kneel awkwardly to undo them and was nearly left behind. She huffed and puffed up a long staircase, her leg aching with each step. Now only a few of the most important monks accompanied Ben. Among them, Irena recognized Meggettuwatte with his shifty eyes and tight smile. As she entered a room lit by lanterns high on the walls, she felt sparkly things brush against her hair. Rubies, sapphires, and cats-eyes hung on long threads from the ceiling like frozen multicolored raindrops. A bird made entirely of diamonds swung on a gold chain before her eyes.

The delegation stopped before a platform guarded by four silver Buddhas. On it stood what looked to her like an enormous gold wedding cake. A monk removed its outer layer, and another filigreed layer of gold was revealed. It was peeled off, revealing a large ivory box wrapped in red silk. Meggettuwatte slowly unwrapped it.

"Captain Blackburn, the last time the Buddha's tooth was shown, it was to the Prince of Wales."

"I'm greatly honored." Ben glanced at Irena. "Myself and Madame Milanova."

Irena was about to say how honored she was, too, but a hush had fallen over the monks. Breaths were held. The lid of the box slowly rose.

"Behold," Meggettuwatte said in a low, melodious voice.

Inside, lying in a gold cradle, was a large, curved, yellow tooth. The monks stepped back. Ben, then Irena, took a step forward to inspect the holy relic.

"Good heavens!" Irena said. "It's as big as a tiger's tooth!" She started to reach out toward it.

Ben's hand shot out beneath his voluminous tunic, grabbed her wrist, and pushed her arm back down to her side. A silence crystallized around her.

"What she means is," he explained quickly, "it's the tooth the Buddha must have had when he was born in the form of a tiger."

Meggettuwatte smiled. "Ah!" The other monks smiled, too; Irena heard the whispering of their robes as their bodies relaxed.

"This has been offered as one explanation for the tooth's great size," the head monk said. "It has been a wonderful mystery for many centuries."

"Ah," Ben said. He leaned over the tooth again, his palms held above it as if over a heat-radiating fire. "I feel a great force emanating from it—into my hands! It's extraordinary!"

Meggettuwatte nodded. "Many have felt this power."

Ben backed off slowly, his hands still held in the air before his face. "Extraordinary," he repeated, his eyes glazed over with wonder. The party returned to the temple's ground floor.

Irena hardly noticed the paintings on the walls of the reception area: the Buddha tempted by a buxom *houris* draped in silken ribbons, the Buddha assailed by red-eyed demons. When she caught up with Ben and the monks in the courtyard, she found them discussing upcoming debates with the Christians.

"In one parish," Meggettuwatte said, "the missionaries have been attracting huge crowds. Some priests are saying they can cure people by the laying on of hands."

"Magnetism," Ben said. "An ancient principle rediscovered in Germany by Anton Mesmer a hundred years ago. In America, Phineus Parkhust Quimby and others have done some amazing experiments with it." He explained how magnetic currents were projected from the facilitator's mind into the patient's body. "When the hands—" Here Ben raised his own hands, palms down, "—are passed above an afflicted area, a healing force is sent into it."

"We know that there were once powerful mystics in Ceylon who could cure with this method," Meggettuwatte said. "The tradition of the Healing Buddha is very ancient. Many long for its return."

"A lot of people here have told me this," Ben said.

"The tradition has faded as foreign faiths invaded our island. Every day, droves of desperate people come to the temples in hopes of cures." Meggettuwatte said, glancing around at the other monks. "If you could help them, Captain, the benefit to the people—and to our revival movement—would be immense!"

Ben lifted his hands in front of his face and stare at his palms.

"Ben . . . *no!*" Irena whispered, but he seemed deaf to her voice.

"I'd be willing to try," he said.

The monks clustered around him, murmuring excitedly. Irena was pushed to the periphery of the gathering; her lame leg buckled beneath her, and she nearly fell to the ground. The crowd left; she couldn't keep up. And as Ben moved further from her, his white turban glowing above the monks' dark shaven heads, she noticed a floating serenity to his walk, as if he were treading upon a thin layer of clouds.

14

My life, my quest—all has led up to this day, Ben wrote in his journal on March 3, 1882. *Can I finally become worthy of the trust so many have placed in me?*

"We go to the temple now." Mutthu, his assistant, interrupted his thoughts.

Ben had engaged the young Sinhalese man's services at the same time he'd met Sujata, the widow with her one-rupee contribution. He hadn't had time to find out much about Mutthu, but the boy had proved so useful as a translator and general factotum that he now accompanied Ben everywhere. For the day's events, Ben had brought a new sarong, a cotton tunic, and a turban dyed a deep red—the Buddhist color for wisdom. He put the clothes on carefully, and pinned the turban's folds together in front with a clasp made from an oval-shaped yellow stone set in silver. Meggettuwatte had given it to him—a powerful talisman, he said. Ben ran his fingers over its smooth surface, recalling his sister's wooden darning egg—reflector of mysterious images—that had so fascinated him as a child. Finally he took a deep breath and strode outside where the Buddhist covered wagon was waiting, its canvas folded back.

Mutthu, walking ahead with the bullocks, was dressed smartly in a checked sarong and white shirt; his oiled black hair was decorated with a traditional ivory comb usually worn only by noblemen. Irena, looking hot in her long skirt and blue blouse, rode beside Ben; behind them sat several saffron-robed monks from the Temple of the Tooth.

The sun was setting when Ben arrived at Paradeniya, a group of thatch-roofed shops nestled beneath tall palm trees. Men milled about among stalls where the scents of spices mingled with the odor of dried fish. Outside a hut, a village tribunal had just ended; the headmen smoked Jaffna cigars and watched women weave gracefully in and out of the crowd with bundles on their heads. When the wagon appeared, a marvelous cry went up, and the market emptied. Conscious of how eager the people were for his success today, Ben stood and waved, turning slowly to acknowledge the cheers from every side.

The people followed the strange vehicle to a temple whose *dagoba*, or low dome, jutted up like a single whitewashed breast from the grass. Word had gotten out, of course, that something unusual was to happen today. A crowd of at least twice the village's population was waiting for Ben as he stepped down from the wagon. Most of the audience was smiling, but he noticed a number of silent, scowling old men whose sharp eyes followed his every movement.

"Who are they?" he whispered to Mutthu.

"*Vederalas*—traditional herbalists and healers." The young man's eyes narrowed. "They hear a white man comes who can cure the afflicted. They hope you will fail."

"Ah." Ben stroked his beard. "So it isn't only the Christians I'm competing with but the local witch-doctors as well. They're going to be dreadfully sorry today!"

"Be careful what you say," Irena whispered to him.

"We are all having confidence in *Berava* Blackburn," Mutthu said.

Berava was a term for a respected elder; this was the first time Ben had heard it applied to him. Gazing up at the palms strung with the striped Buddhist flags that he, himself, had designed, he straightened his posture. In the temple courtyard he was relieved to see some familiar faces, including that of Sujata, who'd abandoned her ragged costume for a long flowered skirt and orange bodice. The silver steak in her black hair curved along her cheek and sprayed over the soft brown skin of her shoulder. She smiled when he noticed her. Then her dark, almond-shaped eyes continued to scan the edge of the crowd for fanged, blue-faced *yakkhas*, or demons, who (Ben had been told) hover about unhealthy people, ready to jump down their throats and attack their vital organs.

The crowd buzzed. Ben stepped forward. "I am ready! Bring on the patient!" he commanded. He watched in sad silence as a man was carried out into the yard. The man trembled all over; his face was racked by pain. One leg was twisted pitifully beneath him, and he clutched two walking sticks against his chest. The sun burned down into the treetops; shadows fell over the yard. The temple acolytes lit torches. Ben paced around the patient, the stone in his turban flickering. The spectators—perhaps two hundred peasants, village dignitaries, and monks—all went silent to let him work.

He shut his eyes tight, concentrating hard. A picture of suffering souls flooded into his mind. He recalled the crippled beggars in Bombay, the wounded soldiers in a Virginia field hospital, and, most vividly, Mary Surratt gazing in terror at him from the gallows. He stared at the poor man lying on the ground before him. He visualized all his frustrated compassion welling up in his breast like a dammed river. A picture of the Buddha's tooth flashed into his mind. Its point exploded the blockage of the river, setting it free. Ben willed the stream to flow in the form of an electric current from his mind down his arms and into his hands. Leaning over, he passed his palms over the patient's leg an inch from the skin. Was that heat rising from it? It was! It gave his fingers a tug the way water pulls at a diviner's rod. The crowd, the torches, the temple—all receded from his consciousness. Powerful magnetic energy leaped from his hands. He could sense it making contact with the man's muscles. Yes! A circuit was made! Current was flowing, flowing!

The crippled man let out a cry. The crowd gasped. Ben staggered back, his heart pounding. Now the patient was rising shakily. Could he get to his knees? He could! And he continued to rise! To his feet—upright! His walking sticks fell from his hands. Slowly he took one faltering step toward Ben . . . then another . . . and another. A great cheer rose from the crowd. Torches waved, shaking the air. Women wept, children leapt up and down. The patient grabbed Ben's arm, sobbing words of gratitude.

"He says you are as a god!" Mutthu told Ben.

"No, no—" Ben was flushed; his heart kept thudding wildly. The patient finally released him and was escorted away. Monks and townspeople clustered around the bearded American healer. Children reached out to touch the hem of his sarong. He felt a hand grab his own and looked down into the face of Sujata, whose eyes were brimming with feeling. Then he was propelled toward a platform before the temple.

A monk spoke to the crowd: "Now let the Christian priests try to match this feat!" The people applauded; they called for Ben— "*Sadhoo! Sadhoo!*"—until he ascended the platform and calmed them by slowly raising his arms before him, palms out, fingers extended.

"My friends, my friends, the power of the Buddha's precepts allowed me to do this thing," he shouted over the noise, with Mutthu translating into Sinhalese, but the message was lost amid the cheering. "*Sadhoo! Sadhoo!*" rang in his ears until he could no longer think clearly. He stood silently, just letting them gaze at him. And from the corner of his eye, he saw the scowling, defeated *Vederala*s slink off into the underbrush.

Word of the great white *Sadhoo's* miraculous healing spread all over the region. Everywhere Ben was met by the rheumy-eyed gaze of the afflicted and lame. They lay sprawled in the grass at temple doors, they huddled in pouring rain beneath ragged shelters. Ben strode into their midst. Mutthu and Sujata did their best to clean ulcerated sores in preparation for the mesmeric healing. Ben squatted beside streams to wash the pus from the eyes of thrashing children. When he lifted the hot feverish bodies of babies, his hands often dripped with brown fecal fluid. At times he had to rush behind a bush to choke back his nausea or dry his tears. But once he concentrated his mental energy and began to pass his hands above the bodies of his patients, he always felt revived. And when he pulled back his hands, crippled men staggered to their feet, mad women stopped raving, formerly paralyzed children dashed around in circles.

At first, Ben tried to address audiences about setting up Buddhist schools and reviving Ceylonese culture. But his voice faltered, he slumped behind the podium. At the end of a day of summoning all his energy to project it into palsied limbs and bloated stomachs, he had no strength left for oratory. There were so many villages to visit, so many sick people who needed his powers. He collapsed onto the mat in his wagon each night, too drained to swat away the clouds of mosquitoes that rushed to attack him.

He kept up a vigorous itinerary, barely taking time to snatch a few morsels from the meals Sujata cooked for him and Irena on the fire beside the wagon. He washed hastily in rivers and let the sun dry his clothes as he worked. People whispered that he looked like a man possessed—his eyes burning, his jeweled turban gliding majestically above the heads of his patients as if it were guided by heavenly forces. He wore it everywhere now, knowing that people were comforted by the sight of it.

After weeks of healing, he learned to deal with the constant misery by adopting a brisk, jocular manner. He did little tricks with coins to amuse the children. Once, singing "Turkey in the Straw" at the top of his lungs, he danced a jig with an old woman who'd thrown away her crutches. He organized a "cripples' race" for recently cured men. As they lurched across the finish line, exercising their limbs for the first time in years, the spectacle brought great encouragement to the queues of waiting patients. Sujata said that the local demons hated to hear laughter; holding their claws over their ears, they flew from mouths opened in mirth. At night, the underbrush was alive with the *yakkhas'* grumblings, but they kept their distance from the campfire of the powerful white healer.

Ben decided on an experiment to make his work more efficient. He filled bottles with river water onto which he focused his vital energy force. When the patients drank the magnetized water, many of them reported almost the same results as when he had magnetized their bodies. From then on, he arrived at villages with the wagon full of bottles. Several times he was offered money for them, but he always refused it. When a rich merchant tried to buy some water for his pregnant wife with a handful of gold jewelry, Ben lost his temper.

"If I accept payment, the healing won't work!" he shouted.

The merchant gave a confused look at Mutthu, who glanced away. The onlookers murmured about the mystic healers of ancient times who had accepted no money when they banished demons and brought comfort to the afflicted. Only during these modern times, when the people were corrupted by foreign ideas, did healers demand payments.

"Bring your wife to me, my friend," Ben said to the merchant. He fetched her, and Ben passed his hands above her belly. Her whimpering subsided, and in a few days, she gave birth to a healthy baby boy.

Irena's swollen leg kept her from helping with the patients; she grew restless and began grumbling about Ben's "Yankee medicine show," as she called it. Ben bristled. He could tell that her leg hurt her, but to his amazement, she refused to be treated with his mesmeric energy. "Don't try that voodoo with me," she said. "You'll just make a horse's ass of yourself."

Ben was especially exhausted, having worked sixteen hours on only about three hours sleep, and glared at Irena. "If you doubt my powers, then go find some Western quacks!"

"At least they won't give me dirty *river* water to drink!"

"I don't need you constantly sniping at me!" he shouted. "I've got important work to do!"

Fighting back tears, Irena sat up on her pallet in the wagon. "You great humbug! Get me a litter back to Colombo!"

Ben's eyes blazed. "Mutthu! Get this foul-mouthed witch out of here!"

"I'm not going anywhere with your toady!" she screamed. "I wouldn't trust that man to dump my chamber pot!" Swearing like a stevedore, Irena threatened to go back to Russia and leave Ben to stew in his own juices.

"You've been a drain on my confidence long enough!" Ben shouted. "Finally I'm free to do everything I *can* do! *Nothing's* holding me back! You can go solace herself with Kut-huri in the highest Himalayas! I don't need your blasted spirits any more! *I don't need you!* "

Irena gazed up at him. His turban had slipped down his forehead, the jewel staring off sideways; his glasses were fogged. The look on his face was not to be argued with. "All right, Ben," she said, her voice strangely quiet. She touched his arm, then let her fingers fall away.

Ben awoke in the wagon with only the speckled black sky for a canopy. The moon turned the clouds' edges silver. No breeze disturbed the palm trees. Insects whined. Dogs barked. What was he listening for? For the sound of Irena snoring on the other side of the wagon's wooden partition. How many nights had she been gone? He'd lost track. The night was dismal without her. He shut his eyes, but he could feel the partition around him like the walls of a cell, and when he slept, finally, he shared the cell with the silent specter of Mary Surratt. . . . *I promise you,* he told her, and woke shuddering. . . .

Thirty, forty, fifty sick people were waiting at each village. The first several patients, brought in by Mutthu and local monks, were always healed quickly. Afterwards not everyone recovered completely. This is a scientific opportunity, not a setback, Ben told himself; another experiment was called for. He would determine which patients needed individual attention, and which could be treated with galvanic water. He ordered a dozen patients to stand in a line before him and close their eyes. Then he pointed toward each in turn, willing his hand to fill with magnetic force. If the patient leaned toward him, he knew he was dealing with a sensitive who could be treated with doses of water. Less sympathetic subjects he treated personally. Spectators went away whispering excitedly about the *Sadhoo's* wonderful magic.

Now that he was no longer spending evenings talking with Irena, he had a bonfire built to illuminate late healing sessions. Though more exhausted than ever, he often woke to the nocturnal sounds in the underbrush. He knew that Sujata thought demons caused them; he no longer doubted this himself. Late at night, as the moonlight turned the silhouetted palm trees to fantastic shapes, he sometimes felt he was surrounded by contorted elemental figures resembling the bodies of devil-dancers. The demons froze as he focused on them; then as a rustling sound attracted his attention elsewhere, the figures danced again in his peripheral vision.

Often now, Mary visited him on his nocturnal journeys to America. The look in her eyes grew more urgent, more demanding. What did these astral journeys mean? he asked himself . . . and answered: You must penetrate farther into the darkness, deeper into the hinterlands, away from the towns where Western civilization is encroaching until you are indistinguishable from the people around you, taking up their customs, absorbing their faiths into your own the way they blended Buddhism into their own ancient folk beliefs. The darker your surroundings, the more brilliant your flame!

On another night, he awoke to the sound of running footsteps. A form dashed past the huts at the edge of the jungle. Not a demon, a woman. He saw her wrapper flying, her breasts in motion.

"Oh *Sadhoo!*" She collapsed at his feet, her arms outstretched. The moonlight shone on her naked back. She raised her face: Sujata.

"There, there. . . ," he reached out to touch her hand.

She gasped for breath. "A man was . . . chasing me—"

"What?" Ben had thought Sujata was middle-aged because of the silver in her hair, but now he saw that she was not. Her breasts were firm. And only a young woman could have run so fast. "You speak English, Sujata?" he asked her.

"I was forbidden to before." She began to sob. "Now you will send me away!"

"No. You've become . . . well, a dear friend. To us all."

"Mutthu says he will tell you many things about me. So I want to tell first." She covered her breasts with her wrapper. "I am something like a widow, it is true, but I am only thirty-five years old."

"I didn't notice before."

"You have higher things on your mind, *Sadhoo.*" Her eyes shone at him. "I joined your caravan out of piety, yes, but also because I had nowhere to go. Then you gave me true hope." She raised her face. Ben wiped the tears from her cheek. "My husband beat me and chased women. One night, he stood naked outside the hut of one of his whores. A dog came. It leaped and tore his penis with its teeth. He nearly died. The villagers were blaming me!"

"Why you?"

"They said I was a sorceress and sent the demon-dog to bite my husband. They ordered me out of the village." She clutched Ben's hand. "Please—*Sadhoo*—do not make me leave you!"

"Of course you can stay, my dear!" Ben felt the woman's tremors enter his hand.

"Now I love the Buddha!" Her ragged voice fluttered against his face. "I love you!"

"But I'm not the—"

"They say you are as great! I watch you help people. I see your kindness. I feel your miraculous power when I am close to you." She pressed his hand against her shoulder, then down her chest and over her breast. "Feel my heart! It is sick!" she sobbed. "Heal me, my *Sadhoo!*" Ben felt her heart beating in the palm of his hand.

And so another woman came into Ben's life. He'd never been worshipped before. At first, he told Sujata to treat him like an ordinary man, but this caused her to shake her head in fright, so he listened silently as words of adoration gushed from her. With them her terror and trembling flowed away; giving him love brought her strength; what harm could there be in it? He made a pallet for her in the wagon. And when she wept in the night, he removed the partition and lay beside her and kissed her tears away. Her fingers pressed into his back, alive and urgent, and a great force welled up in him that was equal to all her lonely sorrow and longing.

"Oh *Sadhoo!* Oh Master!" she cried out as he entered her, and he felt her arms cling to his neck, her hair swimming against his skin. And when they lay breathing together, spent and peaceful, the moonlight streamed down though the palm fronds onto their damp bodies, and her lips moved against his cheek as if she were whispering prayers. "The night is seething with demons, *Berava*," she said. "Do you hear them? Only your presence is keeping them away."

He listened. "It's only a cock-crow," he said.

"*Yakkhas* have many voices," she whispered. "They can sound like cocks or rustling leaves, they can dance like shadows and moonbeams—look!"

He raised his head, and there, on the thatched roof of a hut, the silhouette of a rooster strutted. Its wings rose and fell to a rhythm that pulsed from the dark forest where the cicadas sent up their noises. The cock crowed again, its beak opening to two points. And high above the trees and the people asleep in their huts, the oblong moon was a great glowing ear that heard the cock's cry, and heard the scrapings and rustlings and cracklings of the forest, too. The louder the bird's cry rose in the air, the brighter the moon glowed, and the more powerful shone the rays that it sent back down.

"Look!" Ben said. "The moon takes its light not only from the day's sun but from the creatures of the night: birds, animals, insects, people, spirits: all are of the same divine substance. All are alive, like us, and not to be feared by each other."

"It is so when you say it," Sujata murmured, pressing her face into his beard.

And Ben slept pescefully.

He journeyed deeper into the countryside, the wagon rolling along dirt tracks into valleys where waterfalls hung like silver ribbons from cliffs and filled the air with billowing mists. When the paths became too narrow for the wagon, he left it with Mutthu and traveled on by riverboat. He was completely surrounded by another world: looming jungle trees and hanging vines, the river rippling below and the sky flickering overhead. The glide of the boat delighted him. Each screeching flame-colored bird, each flower dangling from the tree branches made his spirit leap out toward it. He loved watching the water part before the bow; he loved inhaling the waves of warm air that rushed toward him from the green-scented shadows along the bank. He loved the paddlers' high-pitched songs and the women murmuring beneath the boat's rounded canopy of palm fronds.

Sujata squatted on the deck, cleaning rice; her face was golden in the slanting rays of light. He knelt beside her, taking some rice from her burlap sack and letting the grains run through his fingers.

He could smell the wood smoke in her clothes. Beads of sweat glistened like tiny jewels in the dark hollow below her neck. He raised his arm to point at the stretch of river opening before the boat. *"This,"* he told her, "is where I was always meant to be!"

She smiled. Her dark eyes searched his face. "You are not lonely for your native land?"

"No. I'm freer here than I've ever been!"

"Myself, also," she whispered. "You have freed me."

"I'm glad, Sujata!"

"You have healed the pain in my heart with your warmth. You are the sun." She reached up to stoke the long strands of his hair that fell over his shoulders. "And these are its rays."

Word of the white *Sadhoo's* miraculous powers spread even to this remote region. At each landing, people brought him their sick and lame. At one village, a blind boy was led to him. Ben had never tried to cure blindness, but Sujata squeezed his hand and urged him forward. He suspended his fingers above the boy's eyelids and focused his energy harder and harder until he felt a charged electrical fog settle over his mind and rush down his arm, out his fingers, and into the boy. Finally he staggered back, exhausted, his hands dangling loose at his sides.

The boy's eyelids fluttered. He turned his face up into the light. His lips moved.

"He says he sees you!" Sujata whispered. "Everything is blurred—but he sees!"

The villagers rushed forward to move their hands in front of the boy's face and embrace him. Several of them grasped Ben's feet, murmuring *"Sadhoo! Berava!"* Smiling, Ben gently removed the hands from his sandals. "The boy will need several more treatments," he said. "Bring him back to me tomorrow."

Ben had arranged to meet Mutthu here, and the next evening, the covered wagon clattered into the village. Mutthu, stepping down from the box, handed Ben a packet of mail without a word of greeting. He'd been sullen ever since Sujata had taken over the translator's duties from him, but Ben had been too tired to notice the young man's moods.

In the mail he found a cable with a date that shocked him. How could so many months have gone by? An important convocation of Buddhist leaders was scheduled in Colombo in only ten days, and he was scheduled to be the moderator. He was badly needed, the cable said—Christians had been stepping up their proselytizing, deluding the people with their empty promises of salvation.

"I must go to Colombo. But I don't like leaving that blind boy," Ben said to Mutthu. "I'll have to leave magnetized water for him."

Mutthu nodded, saying nothing.

"Will you take me with you, Master?" Sujata asked, her eyes searching his face.

He gazed at her dark hair flowing to her shoulders, at the soft cotton blouse she wore to conceal the firmness of her breasts. "Of course you must come, my dear" he said.

"Will I contribute the widow's mite again?"

His brows furrowed. "No, we're finished with that kind of thing."

Rains poured down every afternoon. The wagon wheels stuck in the mud. Villagers helped Ben and Mutthu free them, but Ben grew exhausted and lay shivering on his mat at the end of each day. Sujata wrapped him in sheets, massaged his feet and legs until his eyes closed. His grogginess softened the sounds of dripping water, the screech of monkeys in the forest, the roar of cicadas.

A rich merchant had donated one of his mansions in Colombo to the Alexandrian Society, but Ben, not wishing to distance himself from the ordinary people, had Mutthu drive the covered wagon to a humble village on the outskirts of the city. The morning after his arrival, he ignored his fever and took a pony trap to the Society's headquarters in the city. When he walked through the door, he found Irena seated behind a desk in the ground floor office.

"You're here!" he said, stopping short.

"Somebody had to take charge," she said. "Are you at least a little glad to find me?"

He rubbed his eyes and stared at her. She wore her long black skirt and a new blue blouse partially covered with a red cape. She'd managed to shine the brass Alexandrian Officer's badge pinned over her heart. He suddenly smiled. "Yes, I'm glad to see you!"

"You look like a ghost, Maloney!"

Suddenly he felt exhausted. "I'm flesh and blood, I assure you."

"The flesh is hanging off you. Your cheeks are caved in." She pointed to his turban. "Isn't that thing hot?"

The turban was hot suddenly. He took it off and turned away. The office walls leaned toward him; the carriages rolled by outside the window at a strange angle.

"Your hair is so long—you look like a holy hermit." Irena laughed.

"Not a hermit," he mumbled.

She raised one eyebrow. "So I have heard. You have a new woman."

"Yes. Have you had mail from Davidar?" Ben asked. "How is he?"

"Davidar is only twenty-one years old. He is publishing the magazine and holding the Indian branch of the Alexandrian Society on his frail shoulders in a city where he knows no one and the only language he can use among the people is English. We are fortunate he is a genius." Irena sat back in her chair and sighed. "His letters to you are in the President's office upstairs."

"I'd better get them." He left her, finding the stairs to a room where his mail had been piled on an old rolltop desk. Five envelopes from Davidar had been opened. There were three from Daisy Gordon, with its familiar graceful handwriting, still sealed. He went to take a bath. Squatting in the metal tub, he noticed how brown the water turned around him. As he dried himself, he looked in a mirror for the first time in months and saw a strange, gaunt face behind long dripping strands of hair.

When he returned to his office in clean clothes, a young shaven-headed monk was waiting with a portfolio of agendas, lists, manifestos. The delegates were waiting, the monk said. "Yes, yes," Ben muttered, stuffing the papers into his old green canvas kit bag. The letters from Davidar and Daisy remained un-read on the desk.

The city streets looked strange to him. Cabriolets and phaetons rolled by among the bullock carts and pony traps. The stone buildings looked massive and freshly washed. Pale-skinned women in fluffy blouses and long skirts carried parasols; white men wore suits and sun helmets and straw boaters. Palm trees leaned in a row along the Galle Face esplanade, flowers grew in round beds bordered by whitewashed rocks—everything was laid out in orderly shapes and patterns.

In the meeting hall, Ben struggled to remember the names of delegates. Striding to the platform to lay out the conference agenda, he felt as if he were mechanically playing a role which he'd long ago grown out of. The rustle of papers and the buzz of voices seemed to be trapping him; he grew restless, impatient, confused. As others spoke, he left his body and drifted off to a spot slightly above the platform to watch the proceedings. The dreary, methodical tone of his own voice made his detached self want to scream. Then he heard a question raised: how to meet the challenge of medical knowledge the missionaries were bringing to the island. Suddenly he could no longer restrain himself.

"The missionaries know *nothing* of medicine!" he shouted. "They hand out useless nostrums and the people forget all their knowledge of traditional medicine, and abandon their faith in the Buddha's healing powers and—" He wiped the sweat from his face, conscious of the pit of utter silence that had opened before him. He plunged into it. "—and then when the Christians' quackery fails, all they can offer are last rites! *Hollow redemption!*" Ben pounded the podium, the sweat pouring down his face. He heard some applause, but he could feel hesitation clouding the air around him. Ranting and pacing, he quashed conciliatory motions and demanded stronger petitions. He shouted until his voice came out in rasps.

And then the meeting was over. He was walking out of the hall. Someone brought him his canvas bag and hung it over his shoulder for him. He was helped into a carriage and driven down wide, straight streets through sheets of rain. In the dining room of the

Alexandrian Society headquarters, he wolfed down a plate of rice and vegetables, gulped mugs of coffee, and sat back with his pipe. He felt somewhat revived, though still dizzy with fever. Irena and a man in a white suit were holding a discussion about materialist science and Alexandrianism.

"We're on the verge of amazingly important discoveries here in Ceylon," Ben told the visitor, a Dr. Perera, who, despite his Western suit, was Ceylonese—a Burgher of mixed Portuguese, Dutch and Sinhalese descent. He had swarthy skin, neatly combed black hair that gave off a scent of massicar, and large, inquisitive eyes. The doctor listened with interest as Ben described the experiment in mesmeric attraction he'd performed to measure his patients' psychometric receptivity. But the man began to frown as Ben described his treatment of the blind boy.

"The missionaries would say," Dr. Perera said, "that you are attempting to do the sorts of miracles Jesus performed—"

"Those were no miracles Jesus did. Anyone could do them, with the proper knowledge and mental force!" Ben leaned forward in his chair. "There are so many vital experiments that remain to be done! The key ingredient is belief that one can do them! *Science* fueled by *faith!*"

"But doesn't faith slant the hypothesis and prejudice the results?"

"Perhaps to the materialist scientists, this appears to be what happens." Ben's eyes glowed with certainty. "But not to the true spiritual scientist!"

"But how can such faith be generated here from someone who isn't native-born?"

Ben laughed, rifling through his canvas sack. "You want proof? Let me read you—here, these are testimonials I've received—"'O noble philanthropic *Berava* Blackburn—our worst evils and afflictions, our scrofula and boils, were cured by your magnanimous personage.' Here's another: 'In the presence of your lotus-feet, the people's envy and hate and disease have given place to a profound calm, and thanks be to your powers we are plunged into health.'" Ben let the papers flutter down to the floor.

Dr. Perera frowned. "That's interesting, but—"

"These seemingly simple folk know—have always known—
that material and psychic health are the *same!*" Ben said, his
voice rising. "No one who isn't completely at one with the
Ceylonese people could accomplish the healing I've done." He
smiled over the top of his pince-nez at the doctor, who continued
to gaze at him strangely. "The whole of Ceylon is one enormous
laboratory! The discoveries that lie ahead! *Anything* is possible!"

Irena narrowed her eyes. "Should these experiments be tried
first on local people? And not citizens of the West?"

"People in the West don't understand!" Ben tapped out his pipe.
Ashes fell from the edge of the ash pot onto his sarong; he brushed
them off furiously. "Westerners have no natural *receptivity!*"

"Would you perform these experiments on white people?" she
asked.

"What are you suggesting?" Ben leapt to his feet, feeling his
legs wobble beneath him. "I *know* these people! I *love* them!"

Dr. Perera frowned. "But such love, Captain Blackburn, could
it not be dangerous?"

"You *see!*" Ben shook his pipe at Irena. "This man might have
been valuable to my work, but you turned him against me! And
it's from jealousy! *I've* got the psychic power now, and you can't
stand that!" Swaying in place, he heard her voice but he repelled
it with his red-for-wisdom aura. Seen from within its flickering
glow, everything outside became distorted and wobbly. The walls
of the room leaned in on him. The floorboards tilted. His aura exploded in his face.

He woke in a bedroom on the mansion's top floor. His nostrils
twitched—cigarette smoke. Irena was sitting in a chair beside
him. "You had a bad fever, you old fool. Here, drink this." She
held out a glass.

"What is it?" He looked at the glass.

"It's not hemlock. It's water."

Taking the glass, he noticed his hands were trembling, and
waited till the contents stopped sloshing. "You've never fed me
before, Mulligan. I always cooked. . . ."

She smiled. "Extreme circumstances call for extreme measures."

He drank the water slowly. "How things change!" He sat back against the pillow. "Once I was a hack journalist in New York, wondering what to do with the rest of my life. Now I'm. . . ."

She sat forward, touching his hand. "What, Ben? What are you?"

He closed his eyes. The words *berava* and *Sadhoo* came to his mind, but he suspected that she would never understand. "I seem to be two people. One is following his true spiritual calling . . . one is watching the first one . . . impatiently. You know, some artists I've known are like this. When they're too tired to paint or compose, they have to go through the motions of daily living. But they're really just waiting to start up their true life again. Do you know what I mean?"

"Yes." She took the empty glass from him.

He opened his eyes to look at her. The light behind her head made her hair frizzle like tiny tangled wires. Her round face was cast in shadow, yet her eyes had a familiar, penetrating glow. "Of course you know, of course," he said. "When you're not giving seances, doing phenomena, your restlessness eats you up, like an artist's. It festers. . . ."

"I'm glad you understand, old chum," she said, standing up. "But where is *your* true life now, Ben? You used to love organizing things, holding meetings—are they not enough for you now?"

His eyelids fluttered. "Where's my turban?" he asked.

"That thing? It was filthy. I threw it out."

"But the jeweled pin—"

"A piece of glass and tin." Leaning over, she wiped the sweat from his forehead. "You haven't answered—where are you really yourself?"

His eyes closed. "I found myself . . . in those villages. . . ."

"With that woman? Do you love her, Ben?"

He sighed. "I love . . . her *love* for me. And her *people's* love. . . ."

"That's what I thought." Irena's voice sounded weary. "I should never have left you out there in that wild place."

"I heal people—"

"My dear friend, you must heal yourself."

"Healing them is how I can heal myself. . . ."

She pulled the sheet up under his chin and smoothed it gently across his chest. "Sleep, now," she said. "Sleep. . . ."

"Will you be back, Mulligan?" he asked, but he heard no answer.

A few days later, Ben left Colombo and, stronger but still feverish, returned to his camp in an abandoned plantation. Gaping holes let sunlight into the estate house; one collapsed wall was overgrown with vines that framed a view of the bare rooms inside. The goats Sujata milked each day were the house's only inhabitants—the villagers, fearing demons, wouldn't enter it. Ben's Buddhist covered wagon was parked under the house's thatched *porte cochere*. An open yard sloped down from the wagon to the edge of a gully; around the yard's fringes were some huts taken over by Mutthu and by people who'd attached themselves to the Alexandrian caravan.

Ben got little rest at the camp. Moaning patients waited for him to emerge from the wagon in the damp gray light of dawn. Like them, he used the bushes for a toilet, and bathed in the nearby stream. At first, his healing progressed as before. But after a several days, some patients didn't respond to his treatment; they remained squatting on the ground as he moved quickly down the line, their imploring gazes following him. At night, lying feverish beside Sujata, he blamed Irena for stealing his marvelous yellow turban-clasp, the memory of which turned into a golden darning egg as he drifted off to sleep.

He magnetized hundreds of bottles of water and ordered Mutthu to pass them out to the crowds. The yard gradually expanded. Peripheral vegetation was trampled as it accommodated more and more patients. Pilgrims camped in pitiful palm leaf shanties around the covered wagon. Rains poured down. Patients slept rolled in their sarongs like soaked mummies. A child slipped over the edge of the gully and broke his leg. Fights broke out as patients jostled for positions close to the wagon. Ben found Mutthu clubbing them away with a tree branch. He screamed at him to stop. Mutthu threw down the branch and retreated sullenly to his hut.

Moreya, Ben asked under his breath—*what is happening here?*

In the evenings, Sujata massaged Ben's weary legs. He lay back breathing through his mouth. "So many sick patients!" he groaned. "I wonder if my psychic energy's draining away."

"You must not say that, Master! We are depending on your miracles now. Myself, too!" She pressed her hand to her breast, her eyes filling with fear.

He continued to walk among the patients, focusing all his energy into their bodies. The new turban he'd made was already unraveling; his sarong and loose shirt were stained. He was too busy to bathe and had little appetite. His own body began to weaken. When, sleeping off a fever, he failed to appear as soon as the day broke over the settlement, the villagers grumbled and rapped on the panels of the wagon. Sujata had to shout at them to let the *Sadhoo* rest. Some relatives from her village visited her, asking her to return with them—the people no longer suspected her of witchcraft. But she refused to leave Ben. He prayed to Moreya, "Help me! If I can't regain my powers to cure these people—I'm lost—I'm worse than nothing!. . . ."

A village policeman, wearing a cast-off British soldier's uniform, arrived to stop two crippled men from beating a palsied man who'd tried to push ahead of them in the queue. Ben screamed at the assailants. One of them thrust a gnarled hand into his face. Ben had straightened arthritic fingers before, but now when he focused his strength on this man's hand, they remained curled into a claw-like fist. Ben turned away, wiping the matted hair from his brow. Suddenly he knew why he'd failed. His effort had been generated not by love and sympathy but by the need to prove that he could still heal.

"The curing energy's source has always been my great love for the people," he told Sujata that night. "But when brutes beat a fellow sufferer with rocks, how can I love them?"

"Your love is failing?" she asked in a tremulous voice.

"No, Sujata!" he cried, holding her close. "*No!*"

One afternoon, Ben heard a creaking carriage stop out on the road. A swarthy man in a white suit walked into the clearing. He found Ben kneeling before a boy on whose neck bulged a goiter half the size of his head.

Ben staggered to his feet. "You've spoiled my concentration!"

"Sorry to disturb you." Dr. Perera waved his hand through a cloud of mosquitoes. Ben seemed not to notice them, though his face was splotched red with bites. "How are you holding up here?" the doctor asked.

"*She* sent you, didn't she?" Ben wiped his brow with the sleeve of his shirt. Long strands of hair remained stuck with sweat to his forehead below his frayed turban.

"Irena only wanted to know you were all right."

Ben said nothing. It occurred to him to ask for Perera's help, but one glance at the doctor's immaculate trousers and fine boots—as contrasted with his own mud-spattered sarong and bare feet—told him the request would be futile.

"She thought perhaps you'd like to come back to Colombo for a rest," the doctor said.

"Dammit man, can't you see how understaffed I am here? How can I leave? *Look* at them all!"

"Yes, it's a nightmare!" Everywhere the yard was strewn with men, women, children, lying prostrate or sitting against one another in the mud. "Listen , we've a real hospital in Colombo. We'll take you—"

"*Real hospital?*" Ben shouted. "With real missionary *quacks?* You expect me to take all these people to *them?*"

"Well, not all—"

"If you can't be of use here, well, I'm very busy!" Ben walked off down the line of patients.

"We'll come back to check on you again soon," Dr. Perera called out. Getting no response, he shook his head and returned to the road where his horse and carriage were waiting.

Later that week, the rains poured down for four days and nights. Shivering in the wagon, Ben was surrounded by the sounds of coughing, the whine of mosquitoes, and a continual barking noise from the underbrush.

"That barking—the people say *yakkhas* are disguising their voices like hyenas," Sujata whispered in the dark. "They are coming closer to the yard every night."

"Demons, hyenas, what's the difference?" He lit his pipe, feeling its bowl the only warm, dry spot in the wagon. Rain dripped through the canvas, causing the lantern to sputter. The ingenious hinges of the side walls had rusted; one swollen board hung out of the wagon like a long tongue. Ben listened to the barking. "Probably just village pariah dogs," he said.

"Perhaps." Sujata hugged her damp wrapper more tightly around her.

Ben stared out into the dark. "If only those people would stop that pitiful coughing!"

But now Sujata was coughing, too.

On the morning when the skies cleared, Mutthu waited outside the wagon for Ben. "Trouble in the village," he said, pushing the shiny black hair from his forehead. His eyes seemed especially bright today. "*Vederalas*, the traditional healers, they are stirring it up."

"Why?" Ben climbed down from the wagon. No matter how often he wiped his damp lenses, he couldn't see clearly.

"The healers have been having no patients. Because of you, they say." Mutthu frowned at the Ben's muddy feet. "Now they say you disappoint the people."

Sujata's face appeared under the wagon's canvas hood. "Not true!" she said, her face distorting with anger. She placed Ben's turban on his head. It was tied rather than fastened with a pin; a strip of cloth hung down the back like a frayed bandage. "*Sadhoo* can heal! Do not listen to this bad man, Master!"

Mutthu snarled something to her in Sinhala, then turned to Ben. "You must show the *Vederalas*. Or they may bring the village people here with clubs and torches."

"Show them? Of course I'll show them!" Ben clenched his fists.

"We must have a big test, Captain. To prove your powers." He pointed to the edge of the clearing. "That woman lying on the ground—"

Now Ben noticed the body of a woman; two nervous-looking policeman stood nearby. Some patients had gathered around her in a circle. Sujata jumped down from the wagon and ran into the crowd. As Ben came nearer, she rushed out again, her sarong flapping at her ankles. The women from her village tried to lead her away, but she pulled free.

"That woman is dead! Do not go near her . . . do not try—"

"She was breathing," Mutthu protested.

"It is a trick, *Sadhoo!*" Sujata screamed. "This man Mutthu has been tricking you! He was bribed by the *Vederalas* to bring the woman to you. Always he takes bribes! To take rich men to the head of the line; to take headmen's supporters to you—"

"Is that true?" Ben glared at Mutthu.

Sujata flung herself between them, clutching Ben's arm. "Mutthu asks for donations for the Buddhist fund, then he keeps the money!"

Ben gently gripped Sujata's shoulder. "Why . . . why didn't you tell me before?"

Mutthu thrust himself forward, jabbing her in the middle of her chest with his finger. "Because she was my accomplice!" he screamed.

"*No!*" Sujata cried. "Only at the start! Then I told *Sadhoo* about my past because I began to believe in him!" She shrank backwards, her almond eyes flooding. "He was curing all my pain!" She pressed her hand over her heart. "*Sadhoo* is *good!*"

Ben scowled. "Mutthu, you'd better get the hell out of here fast!—"

"Me?" Mutthu sniffed. "Why not her? Because she opens her legs for you?"

"Get away from me—*traitor!*" Ben roared. He strode toward him, his arm raised menacingly. The nearby trees seemed to lean sideways. A wave of dizziness washed over him, and he nearly stumbled.

Mutthu ran off several paces, then whirled around. "Listen, Captain! That man I brought to you the first day of healing—the trembling cripple?" The boy threw back his head and laughed. "The monks bribed him to act sick and recover! I gave him their money afterwards!"

Ben breathed through his teeth. "You lie! What of all the others who were cured?"

"The monks give me money to bribe the first patients of every day," Mutthu spat back. "The monks wanted the people who watched the curing to believe in your powers. It was to help defeat the Christians! Meggettuwatte and the other holy men even got *you* to believe in your powers—"

Ben shook his head hard, his hair flying. *"I do believe!* And there were hundreds and hundreds who also believed—and without any of your treachery! How to you explain that?"

Mutthu scurried off to the edge of the yard. "Perhaps you healed some, perhaps you did not. But you cannot heal any longer—everyone knows that!"

"He can!" Sujata cried.

"Let him try!" Mutthu pointed to the woman on the ground.

The crowd had parted around Ben, but now it began to draw in closer, buzzing, restless. The few people who could understand English were translating what Mutthu had said. Ben saw dark faces clench with worry and anger. A policeman tried to push the people aside, but they refused to move.

"Who is this woman?" Ben asked him.

The policeman frowned, tugging at the bill of his cap. "People say woman a witch. She make plot with bad men. Village people, they hang her for it."

"They *hanged* her?"

"Very bad." The policeman said. "People cut her down from tree. But she still breathing."

Ben moved through the crowd toward the form lying face down on the trampled grass. Her head was turned away from him. Her sarong was torn, her back bare, and around her neck was a swollen, purple bruise made by the rope. Ben shuddered.

"She is not breathing!" Sujata tugged at Ben's arm. Strands of hair stuck to her cheeks and forehead. "I listened to her body."

"She was breathing after men cut the rope," the policeman said.

Ben stared down at the woman. Were her shoulders moving ever so slightly? Was she struggling to breathe? He knelt shakily beside her.

"Listen to her body!" Sujata held his arm with both her hands.

He glanced around at the dark faces of the people. And at that moment he knew that whether the woman was still breathing or not wasn't the important issue to them. They knew what he had to do. And if his will was truly strong, if the power of his belief and of his love was still truly coursing through him, he should be able to heal...anyone!

He shut his eyes tight. *"I must,"* he whispered.

Only Sujata heard him. "Are you sure?"

He nodded, and felt her release his arm. She stepped back and spoke to the crowd. "The great *Sadhoo* can cure the hanged woman!" she announced, her voice quavering with the loving tone Ben had heard so many nights as she'd lain beside him in the dark.

He felt the buzzing of the people's voices recede as if the entire yard were clearing before the waves of galvanic energy that surged within him. His eyelids closed. He saw deep into the darkness, into the source of his faith. A faint glow appeared at the end of a black tunnel. He'd heard of people who'd recovered from near-fatal experiences describe such incandescent astral tunnels—and now he was sure he was seeing one. Yes, his own vision was merging with what the woman must be seeing!

A familiar figure stood at the end of the tunnel, illuminated from above. The woman wore Western clothes—a long woolen dress. A silver cross on her breast caught the light. Her hair was parted in the middle; its two dark wings fell over her cheeks like velvet curtains. And on her neck, Ben saw a monstrous purple bruise. As the woman walked slowly toward him, she lifted a noose of heavy rope in both her hands. A shudder gripped his body . . . but then subsided as he spotted a tall, turbaned figure who walked up behind the woman and rested his hand on her shoulder. The man's gray beard framed a serene, golden-skinned face—*Moreya!* His eyes glowed with a kindly expression.

And now Ben felt more energy surge through him. He knew what he was empowered to do. He called up all his concentration to direct the life-giving current. Slowly he reached out his hand. His fingers hovered above the woman's back, moved up to her bruised neck, and rested upon her skin.

"Arise!" Ben whispered. *"Mary . . . arise!"*

The crowd hushed; only the sound of the dripping leaves disturbed the silence. Then a clip-clopping horse's hooves were heard and the creaking of carriage wheels. Ben, oblivious to the sound, waited for the flesh beneath his palm to turn from clamminess to warmth, from immobility to movement.

But the woman didn't stir. The onlookers began to murmur. They watched Ben's body begin to sway in place. They saw the fingers of his free hand grip the ground to steady him. This they took for a sign of uncertainty; the whispers grew louder.

Ben heard the sound. "Live!" he sobbed to the woman, hunching forward. *"Live!"*

An old *Vederala* carrying a flaming torch pushed his way forward. He leaned over the motionless woman, grasping the back of her head with his gnarled hand. "Cold!" he shouted in a cracked voice. The smoke from his burning stick gave a leap in the air. "This woman is *dead!"*

The crowd surged forward. A policeman pulled Ben upright, standing between him and the villagers. The voices were harsh and loud, but the people were still too awed by this man everyone called *Sadhoo* to strike out at him in anger.

Ben blinked open his eyes to stare into the policeman's face. "You mustn't interfere—" he sputtered. "You must give me more time!"

Then he saw Sujata. Tears streamed down her cheeks. Her mouth was bent down at the corners in a terrible grimace. "Sujata?" he reached out toward her.

She clutched her blouse over her heart. Then the women from her village came up behind her and took her arms to lead her away. She shuffled off toward the trees with them, a high-pitched cry trailing behind her in the air.

Ben slumped to his knees, his hands covering his face.

The policemen escorted him slowly to the road where the carriage had stopped. After the dead woman was carried away, the people jostled each other to get a last glimpse of Ben. A few tried to touch his sarong as if to take away what magic it might still contain. Some children found Ben's turban, partly unraveled and trampled in the wet grass. When they picked it up, their elders made them throw it down the ravine.

The *Vederala*s shouted curses and waved their flaming torches. But most of the villagers stood in silence to watch the stooped, gray-bearded foreigner shamble through the mud toward the road.

"*Sadhoo?*" Some ragged children gazed up at him, searching his face. "*Berava?*"

They were gently pulled away.

The carriage horse whinnied and reared its head. On the box, Dr. Perera yanked back on the reins until the horse stood still. Irena stepped down onto the road and reached out to Ben. She gently placed his hand on the metal rail beside the seat. Gripping it, Ben managed to heave himself up. He dropped heavily onto the wooden plank, and Irena sat beside him. Long gray strands of hair fell over his face, nearly covering his eyes. Leaning close, Irena stroked the hair away with her fingertips.

He stared straight ahead, but what he focused on, no one could tell. As the carriage rolled forward, he slowly lifted his face to wave in the direction of the people. But they had all faded into the underbrush. The roadsides were empty.

Clouds of black smoke billowed above the trees. The covered wagon was in flames.

Part Four

Southern India

15

In Colombo, Irena sat beside Ben's bed, wiping his brow with wet cloths and gently pushing balls of rice between his lips with her fingers; she even cut his hair, she wrote to Sarah—*though I am no Delilah!* Irena never forgot the intimacy they shared during those months, though nursing didn't come easily to her. She'd done it before—for Italian soldiers during Garabaldi's campaigns, and for a Hungarian opera singer with tuberculosis. Unlike many Italian soldiers and the tenor, Ben lived—a great relief to Irena.

In many ways Ben seemed the same man again. He began to rush around the city organizing meetings, starting fund-raising drives, chairing committees. Irena showed him a letter from Moreya that ordered him to stop his magnetic healing. From now on, the Master said, Ben was to concentrate on organizing the Alexandrian Society at the new Headquarters in Madras. "I've already stopped the healing," he told her, and refused to discuss the subject.

His reputation as a spiritual leader of the Ceylonese people rose again, the episode with the dead woman fading from the memories of those who had heard about it. Once a flotilla of catamarans accompanied the Founders from Colombo to Galle where, as their little boat glided into the harbor, they were serenaded by choirs of children from the Buddhist schools Ben had started. People raised a subscription to build a statue of him in the town square. Ben wrote about his work in a series of articles for *The Alexandrianist*, which, like Irena's, began to make converts in Europe and America. Many people wrote that they wanted to make pilgrimages to South Asia, themselves.

Under Davidar's editorship, the magazine was now turning a profit in Madras, and Irena was finally able to pay Sarah's passage from New York to India, as she'd been promising to do since the girl's mother had died. While Ben finished up his activities in Colombo, Irena left for Madras to wait for Sarah—now seventeen years old!—and to see how the Coulombs and Davidar had furnished the new headquarters. She'd signed the papers the Maharajah Harisinghi had sent, transferring the property to the Alexandrian Society free and clear.

Irena's ship steamed into Madras harbor. Along the shore, red- and white-striped IndoSaracenic buildings made a castellated Arabian Nights skyline. She pictured flying carpets soaring from the parapets, wizards guiding her pilot boat in with benign spells. Palm trees along the beach leaned their green feathery heads toward her, and a row of graceful fishing boats nodded in unison on the surf. As her little pilot boat splashed across the waves toward the beach, an Alexandrian delegation waded out to meet her. First was Davidar, who sank to his knees to touch her feet (an Indian gesture of respect) and was nearly sucked away by the undertow. The pink-turbaned Babula jumped up and down in anticipation. Alexis Coulomb broke into a craggy, alcoholic grin as he took Irena's hand. His wife, Emma, her witchy black hair flapping in the breeze, was waiting to greet Irena with stiff formality. She'd resented Irena's sending her ahead to Madras to clean up after the former owners, but Irena was sure her sullenness would disappear now that she was back.

Irena's carriage took her several miles south of the city to a river, which a ferryman poled her across to the two hundred-acre estate that was now the Society's home. *Imagine!*—she mentally composed a letter to Ben—*imagine our carriage rolling down an avenue of tall cocoanut palms, with the river behind us, the blue Bay of Bengal before us, and golden thatch-roofed native huts on either side. We round a curve in the drive, and there before us a long white two-storied mansion rises out of the foliage, its verandahs facing onto a plantation of cashew trees. Alighting, we hear the cries of peacocks that strut like iridescent majordomos among the flowering bushes. The gardens are in a riotous bloom of colors.*

An enormous banyan tree shoots out its boughs like a fountain, branches falling back into the pool of sandy earth at its base. I will rename the estate "Banyan"! (If you agree, of course) I feel I have found a haven from which I will need never to roam again. . . .

In the mansion and the outbuildings, Irena toured the high-ceilinged rooms that Emma had furnished—on her instructions cabled from Ceylon—with solid, impressive furnishings, the sorts of red velvet drapes, heavy chairs, and dignified statuary among which spiritually advanced people, both Indian and Western, would feel at home. Irena avoided the luxury that she knew some gurus in India had acquired with their followers' money. There were no crystal chandeliers or silver centerpieces or gold-speckled tiling. (The Society's dues remained reasonable; it accepted contributions but rarely solicited them.) She recalled the fate of the people of Atlantis whose great utopian cities sank beneath the sea—all because they misused their wealth and powers.

As pilgrims from England and America began to take up residence in the mansion's many rooms, Irena happily resumed her astral activities. Without Ben there to censure her, she caused Masters' letters to drop and astral bells to ring at every gathering of the faithful. Sometimes the guests sighted the spectral figure of Kut-huri walking in the garden by moonlight. Irena again felt the presence of this Master watching over her during the dark hot nights. But she still missed Ben.

Her quarters were on the second floor of the main mansion, two rooms and a verandah reached by an outside staircase. *Standing on my verandah,* she wrote to Ben, *I gaze out at the great marvelous banyan tree! Sarah will love it!—a fountain in the sunlight, a dragon writhing up from the ground in the evenings. From the branches long roots grow back down into the earth . . . and rise again like baby dragon-banyans reaching out toward the radiant moon. The tree is a benign symbol: I have writhed with yearnings to spread my branches out toward mankind, and now my visions have sprouted roots that attach themselves firmly to the Indian soil, planting ideas that shall give birth to more and more great truths long after I have waddled off this mortal coil.*

Sarah arrived in Madras before Ben did. Irena, standing on the beach to meet her pilot boat, saw a slim young woman standing in the bow, her long red hair streaming out behind her like a brightly colored pinion. In her letters, Irena had cautioned her to buy a broad-brimmed straw hat against the sun; she had, and now she put it on, tying its ribbon under her chin with the tails trailing down into the ruffles of her long cotton shirtwaist. When the boat crunched into the sand, she leapt out laughing and splashed through the surf toward Irena. Her skirt frothed at her ankles, the material darkening with water. Her mouth opened in a wide smile as she grasped Irena in an embrace at the water's edge.

"Auntie!" she cried,. This was the name she'd given Irena in her letters. "You're really here—in India!"

"You're a woman!" Irena said, holding her tight around the waist. "I have been writing to a child all these years—and you are taller than I am!"

"And how is the Captain?" Sarah asked breathlessly as she waded with Irena onto the beach.

"Almost as he was when you saw him last."

Sarah paused, kneeling to pick up a handful of warm sand and let it stream through her fingers. "Almost?" she asked, looking up.

"What beautiful eyes you have. I'd forgotten how green they are!" Irena reached out her hand to help Sarah to her feet. "Now come along, my dear! I have so much to show you!"

Sarah's picture of India had been formed by Irena's colorful letters; the real India was even grander and brighter to her, but poorer and dirtier, too. Also, just as enchanting, in ways she couldn't have predicted. Banyan, as the estate of the International Alexandrian Society Headquarters was now called, looked to her like an enormous botanical garden. For days after her arrival, she wandered around in the sunlight fingering the leaves of exotic plants, pushing her nose against silky flower petals, calling out to the green parrots and tiny darting lizards.

Chattering, pink-turbaned Babula, whom she'd read about in Irena's letters, helped her settle in. Emma Coulomb, who was fed up with all the Alexandrianists treating her like a housekeeper, was less helpful. Her piercing stare and long nose frightened Sarah a little. "I can see you're not used to nothing this big," she said when she spotted the girl gazing around her new room. Though she was right, Sarah didn't like her saying so. The resident Alexandrianists—Indians, Britons, Germans, even a few Americans—visited Sarah's room to welcome her. They had dreamy-eyed expressions and moved languorously, as if guided by gentle currents in the air that Sarah hadn't yet learned to sense around her. They praised Irena's extraordinary magical phenomena. The entire estate, they said, was infused with Madame Milanova's radiant "aura."

Irena took Sarah to see the Shrine Room, which was empty except for a kind of dark mahogany cupboard standing on four legs at one end. The thing smelled of varnish. Sarah kept her distance from it. Then Irena took her to a tile-roofed building that housed the offices of *The Alexandrianist*. The editor had just returned from a trip to Bombay. Except for his height, Sarah might have mistaken him for a beautiful dark-skinned girl, his hair was so long and silky black. It streamed down past his cheeks and splashed over his thin shoulders. His lips were full, his cheeks high and delicate. His eyes burned out of deep hollows, masculine, yet gentle, with long curved lashes and nearly black pupils— like someone stepped from the pages of *The Arabian Nights*. His name was Davidar.

"Hello." Sarah's mouth stayed open on the word's last syllable.

"Sarah . . . I'm very happy to meet you at last!" His voice was musical; he seemed to be mentally translating his words from the language of genies or nightingales. "Madame has praised you so."

Sarah's face went crimson. She was conscious of the drabness of her long gray smock, bought for her by matrons in the settlement house where she'd lived in New York after her mother's death. "Are you the editor?" she asked.

"Merely amanuensis to the Captain and to Madame."

"Where *is* the Captain?" Sarah asked. "Auntie won't say a word about him—" She glanced at Irena, who was standing in the office doorway.

"The Captain is in Ceylon. He'll be back soon," she said. "For now, Davidar does everything at the magazine. He will teach you the trade, if you want."

"Oh, yes!" Sarah blurted.

"Do ladies edit in your country, Sarah?" Davidar asked.

"Well, I don't know. I only finished school."

"Of course they do," Irena said. "Have you not seen me working fifteen hours a day, Davidar?"

Davidar continued to gaze directly at Sarah; she felt as if a current of warm air were blowing against her skin. "Then you shall be a co-editor!" he said. "When would you like to start?"

Evidently in India—or at least at this Alexandrian place—a seventeen-year old girl could be anything. "I'll start today," she told Davidar. "Right now."

He was a patient, soft-spoken teacher, and over the weeks, Sarah learned fast; soon she began feeling more like a colleague than an apprentice. She and Davidar designed fliers, wrote letters to authors, answered readers' correspondences, edited essays sent in from all over the world. Taking on the work, Sarah discovered more about science, religion, and philosophy in the short time she'd been at Banyan than she'd learned in all her years of school. She asked Davidar for books to read, and started working her way through translations of the *Ramayana*, the *Mahabharata*, and other classics. Indian and Western scholars held discussion groups on the mansion's verandah; Davidar, though only twenty-two, contributed as much as people much older did. No one put pressure on Sarah to formally join the Society, and so she didn't, since she still wasn't exactly sure what a Alexandrianist was. People assumed that since she liked to read and talk about ideas, she must be one of them.

Four afternoons a week Davidar took her to the Society's primary school that had been founded for the children of local fishermen and sweepers of the Untouchable caste. Along with a Tamil-speaking teacher, she and Davidar kept the students busy with lessons. Davidar squatted in the sand to play a game involving pebbles with them. As he sang *bhajans*—devotional songs—in his deep, quavering voice, they gazed at him wide-eyed. When they saw Sarah coming down the sandy path, they set up a high-pitched cry of welcome that made her run toward them with her arms open.

During those first months at Banyan, she turned almost brown from spending so much time in the sunlight. No one remarked about how dangerously red her hair was becoming, so she stopped pinning it up and let it fall freely around her shoulders as Davidar did when he wasn't wearing his turban. She bought cheap Indian *salwaar kameez* outfits, loose cotton trousers and knee-length shirts in purple, orange, scarlet, green—colors that no one had ever seen in America. Now she hardly ever thought about New York; the city existed on another planet where a drab, awkward schoolgirl had struggled to avoid arousing the scorn of her rich classmates. Here she was someone important—a co-editor, a schoolteacher—with no past to drag around and trip over like a shabby suitcase.

She went for walks with Davidar along the beach, she in her sherbet colors, he in his loose white trousers and dazzling white shirt. They stopped on paths between thatched huts to admire the silvery fish laid out to dry on straw mats. They watched the catamarans gliding through the waves. Sometimes, leaving their maturer selves on the hot sand, they dashed into the surf together, soaking their clothes, laughing, dancing with arms outstretched like sea birds' wings. Then Davidar seemed like the sweet-natured playmate she'd never had: a being with a genius's brain and a child's guileless heart. He confessed that he, too, had been lonely at school, "mocked" by other students for being "scholarly as a holy man." The Alexandrian Society had given him a refuge where his "spirit could soar as high and gracefully as it pleased." Now that Sarah had arrived, he said, Banyan was "Paradise!"

No one had ever spoken to her this way before, much less a beautiful young god with burning eyes. Suddenly she flung her arms around him, pressing her cheek against his chest. His body stiffened. She remembered Irena telling her that Brahmans, fearing pollution, didn't like to be touched by anyone outside their caste. So she quickly stood back, gasping an apology. He seemed to be more out of breath than she was, too choked up to speak.

"I'm not offended," he said finally. "Please don't be sorry."

She wiped her eyes. "It's just that I'm not used to being close to someone so—so good!"

"I'm not accustomed either—to anyone close. . . ." His voice trailed off, and they walked along the sand. Eventually their silence lost its awkwardness. It became as natural as the salty air around them. And soon it was filled again by the cries of sea birds and the splash of the surf and the spontaneous ideas Davidar could never keep to himself when they were together.

Was Banyan Paradise? During those first months Sarah lived there, it was. That was when everything was new—when colors were brighter than they would ever be again, when scents were sweeter, food was spicier, and Davidar's aura was as brilliant as a city of minarets and domes that floated just above the sand on shimmering waves of heat. . . .

One day, Ben returned. Irena hadn't received an advance cable or even a letter from him. Dressed in rumpled cotton trousers, long shirt, and a broad-brimmed canvas hat, he stepped down from a tonga in front of the mansion and walked in. He moved from room to room, staring about as if mentally taking notes. From her second story verandah, Irena spotted him wandering out the mansion's side door. She hobbled down the stairs and called to him from beneath her banyan tree.

He waved. Was he smiling or scowling? She couldn't see in the glare. The sunlight glinted off his lenses, giving him a blank expression. It seemed to her that he walked very slowly over to her; though when he reached her side, he took both her hands in his and smiled down at her through his whiskers.

"Welcome!" She squeezed his hands in hers. "What do you think of the place, Maloney?"

He looked around. "Lavish."

"We'll find uses for everything."

"I'm sure." He turned back to her. "You're limping. Are you feeling all right?"

"Of course. It is just the old—" she waved her hand in the air. "And you. You look about the same. But you seem different somehow."

"Everyone changes," he said, and again his lenses glinted, blocking her view of his eyes.

Ben moved into one of the outbuildings, installing his Spartan army cot and setting up an office from which he could do the Society's administrative work. Irena noticed that soon he began to stride about with his usual vigor, his loose cotton clothing rippling around him. She told herself he was the same old Captain, but in fact he seemed to have little to say to her. He refused to discuss what had happened to him in Ceylon, and when she brought up the Masters, he changed the subject. If she mentioned her success at attracting new members with her astral phenomena, he scowled and looked restlessly away.

Irena's quarters weren't close enough to Ben's to allow for the late-night discussions they'd enjoyed so much in New York and Bombay. In Madras, she found herself alone in her spacious aerie with only the moon, the mosquitoes, and the pulsing of the cicadas for company. One night, seeing a lamp in the window of Ben's bungalow, she went down her stairs to the sandy path that led to his cottage.

"Am I disturbing you?" she asked, poking her head into his doorway.

Ben rose. "No. It's time I stopped work." Ledgers and books filled the shelves of his office; the desk was piled high with documents. Ben helped her to sit in an armchair, then returned to his stool.

"What have you been writing?" she asked.

"Something for the magazine." Ben picked up a page. "'Buddhist Contributions to Alexandrianism: an Examination of Some Pali Texts.'" he read.

Irena nodded. "What are the contributions?"

"Well, Karma, for one. . . ." Ben filled his pipe and lit it. Then, surrounded by heavy smoke, he sat still without finishing his sentence.

Irena hadn't read any Pali texts, and wanted to hear about them. But Ben seemed in no mood to discuss his ideas. She felt strange—nowadays he knew things she didn't, and he was withholding them from her. Why? She occupied herself by picking through some other papers on his desk within her reach. One, she saw, bore the letterhead of the British Society for Psychical Research. "I've heard of this organization—full of atheistic Darwinists. Why are you corresponding with such fools?"

Ben sighed. "They're hardly fools! Sir Ben Sidgwick, Lord Rayleigh—"

"You Yankees!" She rolled her eyes. "So impressed with English titles."

"There are enlightened men in the SPR."

"Flapdoodle."

Ben took the letter from her hand. "Irena, listen—we've attracted so much attention in England with our magazine that the SPR wants to come investigate us."

Irena scowled. "Investigate? Are we criminals, then?"

"No, no! It's what they do. When they finish, they issue a report. It's widely read. This will be terrific exposure for our cause."

Irena cocked her head sideways. "*Exposure?*"

"Publicity." Ben sat behind his desk. "And Irena, we can't refuse to cooperate with them, in case that's what you're thinking. It'd make us look very suspicious—as if we had something to hide." He tapped the letter. "This investigator, Richard Hodgson, is a lecturer at Cambridge University. He wants to visit Madras soon, and we can't stop him from coming here. So I really want you to cut out all the phenomena—the constant bells, falling flowers, buried rings."

"There was only the one ring," Irena muttered.

"You know what I'm talking about." He frowned at her in a way that made her shudder. "It's very important that we avoid any more public embarrassment for the Society in India."

"I notice you don't mention Ceylon!"

"I left Ceylon with the Society's public image intact, enhanced even, despite my personal troubles."

"But it was a close call—"

"I know that very, very well," Ben said, his voice sinking. "All the more reason not to risk our reputation ever again! Don't you see?"

"Yes, yes." Irena glared at the letter from the SPR. "What are you going to tell this Psychical snoop about us, Ben?"

He tucked the paper into his ledger and shut it on his desk, leaving his hand palm-down on the cover. "Nothing you need worry yourself with!"

She'd started rolling a cigarette, but now her fingers froze. Tobacco spilled into her lap. What on earth was the matter with her? There'd been a time she could roll a cigarette one-handed while riding a galloping horse. Here she was fumbling like a palsied crone!

"I don't know why you're speaking to me in this imperious tone," she snapped.

"My voice is the same as always."

"But it is not!" She sighed. "Oh Ben, I did not come here to fight with you."

He neither smiled nor frowned. "Why did you come?"

"To see that you are not working yourself to a frazzle again!" She tried to sound mirthful.

"No more frazzles for me." He smiled faintly, then yawned. "In fact, I'm going to bed."

"Sorry to have intruded," she said, pushing herself up from the chair. She waited for him to say, "Oh, but you didn't. . ." but what she heard was, "Good night, Irena." Despite the heat that made her clothes stick to her skin, she pulled her shawl tightly around her as she hobbled up the path toward her room.

When Alexis Coulomb finished some carpentry work in the back of her closet, Irena had new keys made to her rooms, giving copies only to him and Emma. It wouldn't do to let Ben know about everything that went on in her suite. From her time travelling with an opera company in Europe, she knew that if an audience saw all the ropes and sandbags in the wings, their suspension of disbelief would be destroyed and all appreciation for the spectacle lost. Along the same lines, she told Ben little about her meetings with Indians whom she called Living Masters. These brilliant swamis, priests, and pandits were dedicated to the spread of Indian nationalism as well as to its spiritual revival. Patriotism and religion were, to them, inseparable. She reported these leaders' observations to Mikail Katkov, her Moscow editor, sure they'd

be of use to the Russian Intelligence Service, which would want to
help them. When she wrote about Living Masters in the Moscow
newspaper, *The Alexandrianist* and other publications, she gave
the men coded occult-sounding names, and the public assumed
that they inhabited the astral, not the physical, plane. This was as
Irena wished it. She didn't even mind if her critics believed that
these powerful leaders were figments of her imagination. The
men's true identities had to remain secret to protect them from
persecution by the British colonial government. Though Ben was
against involving the Alexandrian Society in politics, Irena hoped
to make it a haven for nationalists, a place where Hindus, Sikhs,
Moslems, and Jains could make strategic alliances with each other.
Thus when Ben traveled around the country month after month
lecturing about the need for all faiths to join into one great family,
his noble sentiments had more political meaning than he knew.

Irena's spiritual tolerance didn't always extend to the religion
which she believed had hurt her so badly during her childhood.
An article in the *Madras Christian College Gazette* made her
fume: the clergy had gotten Percy Sinnett fired from *The Pioneer*
for publishing "subversive materials"—Kut-huri's marvelous letters! Despite Ben's warnings not to make a public fuss, she fired
off letters to the local papers about the perfidy of Christian missionaries. The letters elicited an angry reply from Dr. Patterson,
rector of the Madras Christian College. Ben insisted again that she
stop writing inflammatory letters. But she published another one
in which she accused Alan Hume—"a snake in sheep's clothing"—of being in collusion with Sinnett's critics. Though she
didn't say so, she suspected that Hume was also behind the nefarious Society for Psychical Research's interest in her activities.

She also wrote to Mikail Katkov: "I shall watch this SPR like a
veritable hawk. Our network of mystical-nationalist forces shall
continue to defy all conspiracies against us of both Church and
State. *"Des boyeaux du dernier pretre / serrez le coup du dernier
roi!"* She quoted an epigraph in *Zanoni*. "With the bowels of the
last priest we shall throttle the neck of the last king!"

One afternoon Irena found a trunk full of bathing costumes left by the estate's previous owners, and organized a gay outing for Sarah, Ben, Babula, Davidar, and the Coulombs on the bank of the river. Like children playing dress-up in adult clothes, they pulled the old swimming suits from the trunk, laughing as they held them against their bodies. Ladies went behind one bush to change, gentlemen behind another. Irena emerged draped in shiny black from shoulders to ankles, looking like "the Empress of Hades," she proclaimed. Babula pranced about in billowing trousers that must have belonged to an Englishman three times his size. Ben looked quite splendid with his gray beard spreading down his blue and white striped jersey, his thigh muscles bulging in tight short trousers. Sarah changed into a jersey, short skirt, and black stockings. She felt quite shy in front of Davidar; though her legs were covered (just), the shape of her small round breasts was visible beneath her costume.

Ben strode into the water and swam out from the shore, his arms spread majestically before him, his wet hair streaming behind him like Poseidon's mane. Irena launched herself into the river with a great splash and did the dog paddle in a circle. The rest of the party waded along the bank. Only Davidar held back. Barefoot in a clean white *dhoti* and singlet, he stood on the water's edge with his arms pressed to his sides like a tall flightless crane.

"You'll never become a Living Master if you can't conquer your fear of water!" Irena laughed as she stood dripping on the bank. "Just watch the way the Captain swims."

Davidar stood motionless. The sun was setting now, filling the sky with a warm purplish haze. Palm fronds swayed in the breeze with a clicking sound. Sarah was about to murmur to Davidar not to pay attention to what anyone said about swimming, but Babula took her arm and pointed to some crabs on the sand. When she turned back, Davidar was in the stream. His head rose just above the water, an expression of terror contorting his features. But he moved his arms in front of him the way Ben did, and was actually splashing out into the current under his own power.

"Bravo!" shouted Irena.

Hearing her voice, Davidar stopped; once he stopped, he must have forgotten how he'd gotten out this far. Down he went, his head vanishing below the surface.

Sarah splashed into the river, churning her arms and kicking hard. She caught sight of Davidar's hand and lunged for it. Ben was there at the same time; together they yanked Davidar to the surface and pulled him back to the bank.

"First aid!" Ben panted, dragging him onto the sand.

Alexis turned Davidar onto his stomach and Ben knelt on the ground applying rhythmic pressure to his back. But Davidar's eyes stayed closed, his wet hair tangled around his face.

"Davidar!" Sinking to her knees, Sarah clutched his hand. "Wake *up*, Davidar!" she pleaded.

"Lift his belly!" Irena screamed.

Babula wrapped his arms around Davidar's waist and squeezed. Water gushed out Davidar's mouth. His thin shoulder blades rose and fell.

Sarah pulled his hand harder, held it against her cheek. "Breathe!" she urged him. *"Breathe!"*

He finally did, coughing up more water. Ben cradled him in his arms. "There, there, my boy. You're all right."

"Very brave, too." Irena stroked the hair from his brow.

Davidar's eyes opened. "I—I failed the Masters!" he blurted.

Emma Coulomb glared at Irena. "The poor daft thing should never've been told to go into the water in the first place!"

"Now look here, Emma!" Irena's face went dark red. "I never dreamed he'd take me literally!"

When Davidar turned toward Sarah, his eyes grew large: she was still holding his hand. Suddenly she was aware that everyone else noticed this, too. She loosened her grip, expecting Davidar's hand to fall like a dead weight. But instead she felt his fingers tighten around hers.

She managed to help him walk on wobbly legs up the bank to level ground. Babula and the Coulombs went indoors. The others all sat down, letting out breaths, laughing with relief. As the darkness fell softly over the bay, they lit a little fire of twigs and branches. Ben sat close to Davidar on one side, Irena on the other, and Sarah lay on her side before him drawing designs in the sand around his bare feet. Ben sang Army campfire songs in his soft, deep baritone. Irena did some card tricks. Sarah glanced from the cards to Davidar's face, enjoying his amazement. Resting her chin on the soft ground, she framed him, Ben, and Irena against the backdrop of palm trees and flowering bushes. How long, she wondered, can we all stay together in this lovely peaceful place?

During the following weeks, the breezes blew hot across the estate, and everyone said an oven-like summer was coming. Irena decided that she'd regained sufficient control over the Society that she could spend a few weeks in the cool climate of the hill station at Ootacamund. When she arrived back at Banyan, she told Emma and Alexis Coulomb that the station had been full of amusing people; she'd hauled some "big fish" into the "Alexandrian net" and they'd be arriving at Banyan very soon.

"We must ready ourselves for them," she said. "How is my dear Christofolo?"

"Christofolo was accidentally burnt up," Emma said. Over-dressed as usual in a gingham frock and yellow bonnet, she stood beside her husband.

"Not an accident!" Alexis muttered from behind his red beard.

Christofolo was the name Irena had given to a life-size doll with a painted cloth face and long robe; Alexis occasionally carried it through the flower gardens in the moonlight when, according to Irena, Kut-huri was unable to make appearances.

Irena was disconsolate, as if she'd lost a member of her own family. "How *dare* you!" she screamed. "You *murderers!*"

"Be careful the way you speak to us!" Alexis said, his eyes burning. The veins in his irises seemed to wriggle like flames; Irena took a step back, clutching her blouse at the neck, "You may break the camel's back with your load of abuse," he warned.

"You think we can't do nothing to defend ourselves, you're bloody mad!" Emma's face was purple with rage.

Irena wiped a tear from her eye. "But why, Emma? What's wrong?"

"What's wrong is the things you make us do," Emma said. "We're fed up with all your secret instructions. It's one thing to 'help out the Masters,' as you say, for Indians, but quite another to perform for white people."

"My dear Marquise—" Irena had taken to calling Emma this as a form of flattery, though Emma bristled when she heard it. "The Society has always treated Indians and Europeans alike. We stand for the brotherhood of all men—"

Here Alexis made a rude noise by blowing through his lips.

"I suppose that's why you put Davidar over us!" Emma said.

"I only meant while I was away—just to help organize practical things."

"You are thinking we will take orders from a native?" Alexis sniffed hard as if some foul smell had just blown past his nostrils. "Such an insult!"

Emma stepped forward, her arms crossed tight across her chest. "Well, we soon put a stop to his telling us to do things, I can tell you. For a nigger, he's not a bad bloke, as long's he's sorted out about who gives orders to who." Her voice was raspy and hard. "But I'm getting too old for all this. It's time we got retirement money so we can leave this filthy climate behind!"

"Emma, I am half-frantic with exhaustion, helping to precipitate miracles for these Alexandrianists," Irena protested. "They are like a housefull of underfed orphans, a nest of twitterous baby birds with open beaks! If you will not help me with them, who will?" Her voice rose to the edge of a sob. "Babula needs direction when I am away. Davidar is too pure and innocent. But you already know all the . . . operational details."

"What about that American girl?"

"Never!" Irena paced in front of the window. "Emma, we should be helping each other . . . just as in England. Do you not remember those wonderful séances we had?"

"I remember a lot of things from England. Including what you did with the Byzantine icons—"

"But you have no proof of anything!" Irena's voice grew sharp. "I have all the letters Jenny Holmes gave me about those things."

Emma narrowed her eyes. "Maybe you do, but what about the notes you've wrote *me*, all the secret instructions—all about Chrisofolo in the moonlit gardens, all the falling envelopes and flowers and whatnot. I've got the letters. . . .!"

"If you tried to use any letters against me, no decent person would believe you!" Irena turned away. "People here are devoted!"

Emma's face glowed splotchy purple again. "You think you're a queen around here, and Alexis and me are couple of serfs, but—"

"I do not think that! I treat you like the dear friends you are!" Irena softened her voice. She pulled open a bureau drawer and lifted out a beautiful teak box inlaid with ivory. "Just look what I brought you from Ooty!" she said. When Emma didn't reach for the gift, she put it in Emma's palm and wrapped her fingers over it. "And for Alexis—" She took from the cupboard a blue matelote's jacket with brass buttons.

"The coat is too hot for zis weather," he muttered, but took it anyway.

"I've decided to ask the board to appoint you Society Librarian, my dear Marquis," Irena said to him. Though Alexis could barely read or write, he was good at putting things away in their proper places, when he was sober. "And I will ask the board for a good increase in the housekeeper's salary for you, Emma."

Emma held the box to her bony chest. "It's a bit late for that—" Alexis shushed her, taking her arm. She allowed him to move her from the room, casting burning glances over her shoulder at Irena.

As soon as the Coulombs had rumbled down the stairs, Babula appeared at Irena's door. "Such ungrateful vipers, those people," he said, lips curling down at the corners.

"Emma gets high-strung sometimes." Irena wiped her eyes with a handkerchief. "But she would never betray me."

Babula opened his mouth to speak, then closed it and stepped into the room, an impish smile transforming his face. "What gift have you got me, beloved mistress?" he asked, standing before her in his orange trousers, yellow silk jacket, and pink turban— like an oriental custard.

Irena settled onto her bed. "Take a look at that package on the sideboard." He tore it open and pulled out a gold chain with a painted pendant. "The naughty child, Krishna—your favorite," she said.

"Mmm, so purple he is!" Babula inspected the god. He looped

the chain around his neck and gazed at his image in her mirror. "I have what you asked for," he said, and handed her a small newspaper-wrapped package.

She sat down at her desk to empty the package into her tobacco pouch, but her fingers went rubbery as she tried to untie the string , and she gave it up. "What news did you bring?" she asked.

Babula sat cross-legged on the carpet at Irena's feet. "The Captain caught me copying from his journal. This is all I have." He thrust out a crumpled paper.

She read it aloud: "*'I understand Irena much better, after what happened to me in Ceylon. I must save her from. . . .*' From whom? From what? What was the next word, Babula?"

He shrugged. "How can I know? I stop copying when I am discovered. The Captain tries to pull off my ear." Babula turned toward her, but she was still squinting at the paper.

"What else did you see on his desk?" she demanded.

"Very charming envelope from Mrs. Daisy. Flowers in the envelope corner, pretty perfume." Babula raised his fingertips to his nostrils, took a deep breath, and sighed. "That lady comes to his bungalow five times while you were away in Ooty."

"More times than he has even spoken to me lately, except in passing—" Irena shut her eyes tight.

Babula rushed to her chair and cradled her face against his chest. He drew out a long silk handkerchief. "Babula's sorry," he murmured, gently wiping her cheeks. He held her nose so that she could blow—an eruption that caused his hand to vibrate. Then he dropped the cloth on the floor and lifted the packet from her desk. "Look, Madame." He untied the newspaper. "Babula will share it with you. . . ."

Mesmerized, she watched his hand flutter over the packet as gracefully as a butterfly.

Finding the editorial offices empty one afternoon, Sarah looked for Davidar in the mansion. She found him with Ben and Irena in the reception room, along with three Indians she'd never seen before.

Babula stepped up beside her. "That is Davidar's father, Mr. Desai," he whispered, pointing to a thin elderly man in a white *dhoti* and long collarless jacket. He gazed at his son as if in mourning. Beside him was a gray-haired woman in a dark saree: Davidar's mother, Sarah guessed. Babula turned to a woman who looked Sarah's age. Her bold dark eyes shone out from beneath the hood of her saree. . . . "and that is Davidar's wife." Babula whispered. "They have come from Bombay. . . ."

Wife? Sarah had had no idea Davidar was married. Leaning against the doorframe, she pressed her hand against her chest. Davidar sat on the sofa between Ben and Irena.

"From the beginning, you know I have supported your Society." Mr. Desai said. "In Bombay, I even donated a fine carriage with horses."

"We're very grateful for your help," Ben said.

"But you have stolen our son!" The old man struck his fist against his knee. "Davidar's brain, his heart—you have ravished completely!"

Mr. Desai's wife dabbed at her eyes with her saree. The daughter-in-law glared at Davidar. She was rather voluptuous, Sarah noticed; her breasts about to explode from her bodice with each breath.

The old man kept his eyes straight ahead, his lips set hard. "My son must hereby choose!" he said. "He can return to his wife and parents. Or he can remain with you and be cut off from us forever—his inheritance will be no more!"

"Sir, surely we can give him time to decide!" Ben said. "There must be some way to compromise."

"Davidar knows the spiritual path he must take." Irena's gaze focused on Davidar, whose eyes were brimming with tears.

"Irena, wait!" Ben said. "We can't cut Davidar off from his entire family!"

But Irena's voice rolled on mellifluously. "Your work has been indispensable to the Masters, Davidar. And it has given your life a new meaning, as you have often said."

Mr. Desai glared at his son. "Choose now!"

All eyes turned to Davidar. He stood up shakily. "My father," he said, "I must follow the Masters!"

In a shuddery voice, Mr. Desai translated for the women. His wife's face dropped into her hands. His daughter-in-law heaved a dangerous sigh in her husband's direction. Slowly the three members of the family rose and, with great sorrow and dignity, left the office.

Ben lay his hand on Davidar's shoulder. Irena gave his arm a squeeze. Wiping his eyes, Davidar gazed gratefully at them both. But when he saw Sarah in the doorway, he turned his face away.

Davidar told her about his marriage the day after his family left. They were sitting side by side in the magazine office. Etchings from previous issues were tacked to the wall. He drew a cover; she stenciled in lettering. The room smelled of India ink and fresh paper.

"Why didn't you tell me about your wife?" she blurted out, letting her pen slip from her fingers.

"I was ashamed," he said.

She turned slowly to him. The white turban he wore looked heavy as a boulder. "Ashamed?"

"I couldn't do my procreative duties." He squinted down at the magazine cover on his drawing board. It was seething with swirls and plumes, twining round and round the lettering and forming layers of darkening clouds for the words to rest on. He explained that his family had arranged for him to be married at thirteen, when his bride was eleven. He hardly knew her. She'd come to live with him and his family three years after the wedding. Though he and his wife had been left alone for several nights in their bedroom, both had remained "pure." She had refused to give up, causing him to flee from his house to the Bombay Alexandrian Society headquarters.

"Oh Davidar, you're much too kind to hurt a child that way!"

"Perhaps that's why I couldn't. . . ." His great dark eyes brimmed over. "Yes, you understand! You know, it was not only because of Madame and the Captain I decided to stay here at Banyan."

Sarah felt her breath catch in her throat.

"It was you, Sarah." His voice was soft, faint. "I know that you will never mock my—my pure spirituality."

"No, it's—wonderful!" And she believed this while she said it. She believed it as she looked up into his face, where a smile was starting to appear. Now she reached to take his hand. His fingers were warm, strong, alive, and she couldn't bear to let go of them.

Many readers' letters arrived at *The Alexandrianist* addressed to Irena, but one in particular caught her attention: it was thirty-three pages long. The author was a young Scotsman named William T. Brown. He'd read about Kut-huri in a book that Percy Sinnett had published, and wrote to inform Irena that he was coming to Banyan to meet the Master in hopes of being cured of a nervous disorder. Irena wrote back that few people ever saw Masters, who in any case didn't work cures. But he'd already set sail for Cochin. A week later, a letter arrived from his father thanking Irena for taking William off his hands. Enclosed was a check for a sum that, she calculated, would pay for hundreds of books for the Society's new library.

It happened that Ben was in a town near Cochin on one of his lecture tours, and so Irena cabled him to meet Mr. Brown there. She also dispatched Babula to meet the two of them and make sure Mr. Brown's journey to Madras was as interesting as possible. To welcome him to Banyan, she assembled a stellar array of guests. Many moved into rooms at the mansion.

This annoyed Emma Coulomb, who'd have to house and feed them. "A mob of lunatics!" she complained.

Irena shushed her. "Surely you remember, from our British circle, that highly strung people are often the most—"

"Malleable," Emma snorted.

"*Sensitive*," Irena corrected her.

Among the guests were the Reverend Moncure Daniel Conway, a Unitarian minister from Virginia who was writing a book proving that Old Testament patriarchs were reincarnations of the *Mahabharata's* heroic gods.

Another guest was a pale Anglo-Irish girl named Eliza Flynn, who'd repeatedly threatened suicide in order to win her parents' permission to move herself and all her possessions, five trunks worth, to Banyan.

Dr. Frantz Hartmann, a mustachioed German entrepreneur who'd recently made a fortune in Turkey and always wore a fez, was trying to convince Irena to invest some Alexandrian Society funds in an African gold mine he owned.

St. George Lane Fox, a British engineer, had befriended Irena's old colleague Lady Marie Caithness, and was taking notes for a book he planned to write about Lady Marie's spirit communications with Mary, Queen of Scots.

A former Anglican vicar named Charles W. Leadbeater arrived with plans to found a breakaway church. He wore a purple bishop's robe he'd designed for himself, and rented a thatched hut from a local fisherman, whose delicate bronze-skinned son became his constant companion.

A ruddy-faced middle-aged medium, Sally Parker, who had first introduced William T. Brown to spiritualism in Edinburgh, arrived a day before he did and commandeered the room adjacent to his.

Professor Gordon, arriving without his wife Daisy, brought with him the bearded young investigator from the Society for Psychical Research, Richard Hodgson. Mr. Hodgson hoped to get a chance to talk with Captain Blackburn after the gathering. Irena told him she doubted that there would be time.

More than half the guests were Indians. There were Hindu men in *dhotis*, turbaned Sikhs, Moslems in robes and skull-caps, several shorn Buddhist monks visiting from Ceylon, and a Jain priest wearing—as was the custom—nothing at all but a cloth covering his mouth to prevent him from killing helpless tiny insects with his inhalations.

Among the Hindus was S. Ramabadra Ramaswamier, a clerk who had once set out to seek the masters in Thibet wearing a yellow pilgrim's robe and carrying an umbrella, but had turned back when he reached the snowy Himalayan foothills.

T. Subbha Row, a brilliant young Madras attorney, was appointed by Irena to keep his eye on Richard Hodgson at all times. When he reported to her that Hodgson was whispering with Emma Coulomb, Irena grew furious and dispatched several ladies to surround Hodgson; she was pleased to see Emma beating a retreat back to her quarters.

A place of honor was reserved for the Maharajah Harisinghi and his entourage, which, numbering ninety-five, set up carpeted tents all along the river. The ruler, his mustaches bushier than ever, wore a chest-full of medals on his orange silk suit for the occasion of William T. Brown's arrival.

Sarah was there, dressed in her best sea-green *salwaar kameez*, trying to brush the humidity out of her long thick hair. She looked worriedly at the darkening sky and searched the verandahs for Davidar. She found him discussing the *Kalpa-sutra* with the "sky-clad" Jain monk. She'd never discussed religion, or anything else, with a naked man before, but managed to make a few polite comments before the man padded off.

Rumors were circulating that something extraordinary had happened to William T. Brown on his way to Madras, but no one knew what. When Mr. Brown stepped out of his carriage in front of the Banyan mansion, he had a somewhat enraptured expression on his face. Ben, getting out behind him, looked tired and annoyed, as if he'd much rather have retired to his room with his pipe than attend a meeting. He didn't change out of his rumpled cotton traveling clothes.

Irena helped Davidar and Sarah find seats near the east door of the mansion's big marble-floored reception hall. The place was packed with visitors, despite the storms blowing about the estate. Servants set out lanterns on the floor and arranged the chairs in several concentric circles. Woven cocoanut-frond mats were hung over the two doors. The wind caused them to billow into the room at intervals. Jagged strokes of lightning flashed above the roiling palms outside. Irena couldn't have asked for a more exciting backdrop for Mr. Brown's revelations; in fact, several guests whispered that her psychic powers were actually causing the dramatic weather.

Irena looked splendid in a long black skirt, blue blouse sparkling with glass brooches, and several colorful silk scarves. She seated herself beside the Maharajah Harisinghi in a fan-backed wicker chair in the first circle, facing the guest of honor. Ben didn't sit beside her but across the inner circle from her with Mr. Brown. Seated on Mr. Brown's other side, Sally Parker looked exotic in a gold saree, her curls shimmering like a headdress of glossy black feathers.

William T. Brown was a rather concave young man, with sunken chest and cheeks, a pale complexion, and locks of blond hair that fell over his forehead. His Edinburgh tailor had outfitted him for his Asian adventure in tall boots, jodhpurs, and a khaki shirt with a great many pockets, just the sort of costume a lion hunter would find useful on a jungle expedition. In Scotland, he wrote romantic adventure novels; tonight he talked as if he were reading one of them aloud.

"We traveled by rail to Batalore," he said in a reedy tenor, "and set up camp several miles outside the city. That night, the cookfire sank low. Just the Captain and I and his servant Babula remained 'tenting it' beside a gentle steam. No moonbeams—" He blinked hard. "No moonbeams rippled the surface of the clouds. The night was of an immense, cloak-like darkness. The landscape was eerie and portentous."

Several ladies leaned closer as his voice sunk almost to a whisper. Ben shifted sideways in his chair, staring at the roof beams.

"I slept—then awoke," Mr. Brown continued. "I thought myself at first in the midst of a dream. Suddenly, feeling a pressure on my shoulder, I sat straight up—straight up—straight *up*—" His hard blinks kept time with his stammer. Mrs. Parker laid her hand on his wrist, and he continued. "Yes . . . I sat up, thinking perhaps I was being set upon by—by one of the notorious Kali-worshiping thuggers I'd read about!" He chuckled, looking around like someone who's just tossed out breadcrumbs in hopes of attracting doves. His eyes grew fervent again. "But the touch of my awakener was . . . gentle. An uncanny *warmth* was spreading down my arm!"

A mat flapped in the wind over the south doorway; he waited for it to subside.

"For the first time," he whispered, "I beheld . . . my visitor's face. His black beard took on a silvery glow in the moonlight. 'Do you not know me?' The stranger asked. I could only nod in response. I'd often pictured his radiant visage as I'd read his letters in Mr. Sinnett's book—"

"It was Kut-huri!" Sally Parker gasped.

"Yes, my visitor was . . . none other than . . . the *Master!*" Mr. Brown concluded, and sat back to take in the excited whispers that rippled around him. "We spoke of things which, I'm sorry to tell you, he forbade me to disclose. But before he left, he slipped something into my hand—"

Here a loud rumble of thunder interrupted Mr. Brown. A flash of lightning turned faces ghostly white for an instant. Lanterns flickered wildly in the wind.

"Then the Master majestically glided away through the moon-light." Mr. Brown's voice became high-pitched and quavery. He pushed his knuckles against his lips to calm himself. "The moon plunged behind the clouds. When it broke free, I saw the Adaptec silhouette a hundred yards away. And it seemed to me that the moon was . . . resting on his very shoulder like . . . ." Mr. Brown took a deep breath. "like a great luminous . . . silver . . . *turnip!*"

Sally Parker sighed.

Mr. Brown sat back, letting out a long breath. "Then the Master vanished—utterly," he said. "And the plain was as flat and empty . . . as if no footsteps had ever crossed it."

The room went silent. Outside, the wind rattled the palm fronds.

"What was it he gave you?" Mrs. Parker asked.

"Tell us!" urged Mr. S. Ramabadra Ramaswamier.

Mr. Brown slowly undid the straps of a leather bag beside his chair. He reached into it. With a sweep of his hand, he drew forth a large, black envelope. Just at that moment the eastern doorway's mat snapped high into the air like a carpet being violently shaken out. A blast of wind blew sheets of rain into the room. A dozen people, including Davidar and Sarah, were instantly soaked. Women shrieked. Chairs toppled as men ducked away. In the flashes of incandescence that followed, Irena's face lit up with a bright smile. Several wet guests moved off from the doorway, yet none wanted to leave. Sarah could feel Davidar shivering in the darkness beside her, whether from cold or spiritual agitation she couldn't tell.

"A letter!" exclaimed the Reverend Monclure Daniel Conway.

Eliza Flynn, her wet dress stuck tight to her skin, clung to his arm.

"Correct!—in this very envelope. . . ." Mr. Brown pulled forth a square of black paper with gold lettering. "Shall I read it?" he asked—as if anyone would have denied him! He fixed round spectacles over his nose and around both ears. Then he read: "'Brother Brown . . . I welcome you to the ancient land of Hindustan . . . heed the wisdom of our loyal sister Irena—' That is Madame Milanova, I presume."

Here Irena puffed on a cigarette. "Go on," she directed him.

"'Serve her well. Keep faith in the brotherhood of all mankind . . .' and it's signed . . . 'Kut-huri.'"

"Ah!" Sally Parker clasped her hands at her bosom.

Then Professor Gordon sat up straight in his chair. "Captain, did the, um, Master speak to you?"

Ben frowned. "I was addressed by . . . a certain Indian gentle-man near my tent."

The professor glanced at his companion, Mr. Hodgson, then back at Ben. "And this was Kut-huri?"

"He didn't tell me his name!" Ben snapped.

Mr. Hodgson's eyes narrowed. "But Captain—"

Now the thunder cracked open the sky just above the roof. Silver light flashed all about the building and reflected on the wet, shiny floor. Guests stood up and huddled together around the few lanterns that remained lit. In the near-darkness, people bumped into each other as they moved, laughing, clutching at sleeves. Sarah held tight to Davidar's arm.

Eliza Flynn stood in a doorway, her arms raised to the sky, her head thrown back; a flash of light illuminated the graceful outline of her body beneath her thin cotton dress. Reverend Monclure Daniel Conway gently covered her with his jacket.

In another flash of light, Lady Caithness, her gray hair blowing around her face, pressed herself flat against St. George Lane Fox.

Charles W. Leadbeater's burly chest shielded the face of his young Indian companion.

Now a lightning bolt revealed William T. Brown and Mrs. Parker standing hand in hand on the lawn as hailstones bounced on the flooded grass.

On the verandah, Irena and Ben gazed out into the yard, talking. Sarah and Davidar were too far away to hear what Ben was saying to Irena, but he seemed to be shouting at her over the crashing hail. His face was red with exasperation. She clutched the scarves at her throat, her eyes bulging at him; her mouth opened and shut as if she were taking great bites of air.

Then, strangely, Ben and Irena walked down into the garden arm in arm! Irena was gaily twirling her blue umbrella over her head.

"They're together again," Davidar said, smiling at Sarah.

"I wonder," Sarah whispered, as much to herself as to Davidar.

The hail stopped. The noisy wind died down as if its motor had been turned off. The thunder rolled off to the west where it rumbled faintly over the rooftops of the city. The guests ventured out onto the garden paths, turning their faces up to the silvery clouds. A gauzy moon glided free, and everyone sighed. From the bushes white night-blooming trumpets blew scents into the air.

Sarah and Davidar joined the guests strolling about on the lawn. They stepped around puddles, gazing at the hailstones that shimmered strangely like snow among the palm trees.

Irena picked up one and fed it to Ben. He swallowed it with a gulp.

And as the moonlight streamed down, there was not a man or woman present who did not peer into the garden hoping for a glimpse of a Master's face among the shadows.

16

The first newspaper to print the story of William T. Brown's sighting of a Master was the *Madras Christian College Courier*, which had surreptitiously sent a reporter to Banyan. Ben considered its editor, the Reverend Nigel Patterson, a pompous but clever man, and wished that Irena hadn't criticized him so often in her own articles in the Madras papers. Once she'd described him as "a clerical lapdog of the British Viceroy." As Ben would have expected, the *Courier*'s piece about Mr. Brown was scathing. Accompanying it was a cartoon that showed a wide-eyed little man in a safari suit being terrified by an Indian fakir holding up a huge hairy "Master" mask. Other publications in India reprinted the story and its cartoon. From his bungalow, Ben watched Irena set fire to several newspapers on her verandah. Strips of blazing paper rose like red-eyed demons into the black air.

As the hot season approached, Ben had noticed Irena's moods beginning to darken. Her swollen leg was diagnosed as a symptom of Bright's disease, a painful liver ailment. The doctor recommended diet and rest—a regimen Ben knew she was incapable of following. One afternoon, he heard her screaming at Davidar—"Keep him out of there!" "Him" was Richard Hodgson, Ben learned; "there" was the mansion's Shrine Room. Ben had to intervene. Irena was right to keep Hodgson out of the mansion's inner rooms, he conceded, but she was wrong to lose her temper with Davidar. She said she was sorry to Davidar, who tearfully accepted the apology. Later, Ben took him aside. "Listen, my boy— she only flies off the handle at people she truly cares about—I've got personal experience of that!" He laughed and slapped Davidar gently on the back. Davidar's shoulders collapsed forward, but he managed a smile.

Originally Ben had liked Richard Hodgson. He recognized something of his own past self in the ambitious young attorney who'd cultivated influential friends and was now anxious to shine among them. Hodgson seemed able both to appreciate spiritual science and to detect excesses among its practitioners. Yet his preliminary report was strangely tentative. He described Irena's phenomena in meticulous detail, but left his own opinions of them unstated. *The housekeeper, Mrs. Coulomb, has complained that Madame Milanova used her, her husband, and the servant boy, Babula, as accomplices in staging 'astral' communications and sightings of masters. Mrs. Coulomb has so far offered no proof of these alleged transgressions*, the report stated. But its author made no further comments. If a clerk in Ben's New York law office had presented such a brief to him, he'd have immediately sent him packing! And Hodgson called himself an investigator!

When he came to Ben's office for a response to the report, Ben found his fastidiousness annoying. Even in the heat of the approaching summer, he wore a brown suit and brown Oxford shoes. He had brushed his beard forward from his chin to give his face a sharp, forceful aspect, and his hair was trimmed back from the ears, making them stand out like powerful listening devices.

"Hello, Richard," Ben said, showing him to a chair and sitting behind his desk. "Are you finished with the investigation?"

"Just about. Of course I haven't been able to have a look at your Holiest of Holies—" Hodgson meant the Shrine Room, Ben supposed— "but I understand it's for members only. Other than that. . . ."

Ben waited for him to finish his sentence, but it hung in the air. "Do you want to interview more members?" Ben asked finally.

"No, no. They seem to be unanimous in their praise for you, old chap. 'An able administrator,' 'an inspiring orator'—as you must have read."

"I did."

Hodgson sat forward, smiling. "D'you think there's anything I haven't included—some things you'd like to add?"

"No. You're the one conducting this investigation."

Hodgson watched Ben's face. "You seem somewhat, shall I say?—unsatisfied with the report."

Ben leafed through its pages. "I did find it vague in its conclusions, Richard." Why did Hodgson keep smiling like that? His swept-forward beard seemed to prod Ben. "The part about Mrs. Coulomb's charges against Irena, for instance—they're completely unsubstantiated."

"You think I should follow them up, do you?"

"I never said that!"

Hodgson nodded. "Well, Ben . . . I've a decision to make. Confidentially, I must agree with you that the report doesn't present as watertight a case as it might—either way. But the SPR officers in London are clamoring to have something. And it does seem to present favorable conclusions about your work here."

"Seem?" Ben frowned. "That's the point. It ought to either make accusations and back them up with evidence, or else declare our work utterly genuine."

"Hm." Hodgson raised his eyebrows. "I suppose I could stay on here a few more weeks. . . ."

Ben watched Hodgson stroke his beard. And at that moment he had the feeling that a word from him could stop the investigation and send Hodgson away for good. Yet he said nothing.

"Very well." Hodgson stood up. "I'll keep at it then."

Ben stood, too, aware of a sharp pain fluttering in his gut. "The Society's purpose has always been a search for truth," he said. "We've got nothing to fear and everything to gain from it."

The Shrine Room, one of Irena's most notable creations, was on the mansion's second floor, adjacent to her suite. She'd had its walls hung with vertical swaths of gold and crimson silk to give it the atmosphere of a royal reception hall. The Shrine at the far end was a tall varnished cabinet with a protruding shelf, or altar, behind which a wooden window could be raised to present written requests and receive Kut-huri's replies. Irena had described it as a kind of astral postal counter.

According to her (Ben wasn't so sure), the Shrine had helped to dramatically increase the fortunes of the Society. Many wealthy Indians had come to receive messages from the Master. Some visitors took to kneeling before the cabinet, even touching their forehead to the carpet. This sort of salaaming made Ben reluctant to even enter the room. But he did relent once when she invited Professor Gordon to "meet" the Master. The professor had acquired several hundred rare Tamil manuscripts that Irena hoped he would contribute to the new Alexandrian library. The donation would make Ben so much more appreciative of her than he had been lately.

Also there, besides herself, Ben and Professor Gordon, were Emma Coulomb and Davidar. Irena later reported to the Society that the occasion had been a complete success. After addressing Kut-huri aloud, she said, she'd raised the Shrine's window, and there on the shelf inside was a lovely Wedgewood plate the Master had left as a gift for the Professor. On it was a picture of milkmaids seated charmingly beside a lake, with swans. Emma reached to take the plate, but it slipped from her fingers to the floor, where it broke into two pieces. But this was no disaster—far from it! Irena lay the two pieces of the plate back on the altar and closed the window. When she raised it again, the same plate was there, miraculously whole—repaired by Kut-huri! The milkmaids' complexions were unscratched, their smiles as radiant as before.

This wasn't the way Ben recalled the scene. Later that day, he wrote in his journal that Professor Gordon, wearing his customary rumpled suit, his thin gray hair stuck to his perspiring forehead, looked bemusedly at the red- and gold-striped drapery as he entered the room. The Shrine's square mouth was shut but looked ready to release a colossal sneeze in response to all the itchy incense smoke floating in the air. The cabinet was supported not by its spindly legs but by two stout wires attached to the ceiling—"a god on a trapeze," Ben described it.

Irena stood beside Professor Gordon, dressed in a long gold blouse and a floor-length blue skirt that matched her rolled blue umbrella and her eyes. She pressed her fingertips to her forehead.

"The Master has a gift for his learnéd visitor," she intoned. "Yes . . . I see it arriving. . . ."

The plate appeared in the window. Emma made a lunge for it, one step ahead of Irena. Her eyes narrowing, Emma held it up to the light to examine it. Limping off-balance, Irena knocked it from her hand. It rolled off along the floor with the two ladies in hot pursuit, and smashed against the wall.

"Davidar!" Irena placed the pieces in the cabinet's mouth. "Tell Kut-huri we've had an accident!" Davidar stood swaying in the doorway. His face went ashen. He stepped out of sight. Emma followed him, whispering. Ben paced back and forth. Irena smoked three cigarettes. The professor shuffled his feet, tugged at his wispy mustache. Finally, Davidar was back, looking confused, his huge dark eyes puffy with suppressed tears. The Shrine's window clattered up and down, then stuck open in a state of rictus. The plate—or a plate—appeared. Ben examined it. He thought he recalled two swans on the original instead of the one he saw now. How many damned milkmaids had there been?

At any rate, Professor Burtron accepted his gift, announced his donation of manuscripts to the library, and hurried away.

Later that evening, Irena appeared not to notice Ben's black mood as he helped her climb the steps to her verandah. "Aren't you pleased with Professor Gordon's gift?" she asked. "I invited him especially for your sake, you know."

"I know. And I thank you." Ben took a deep breath as Irena settled herself in her wicker chair. "But dammit, Irena, I never intended anything like this! And how could you have involved Davidar in it? You've gone too far!"

"What on earth do you mean, Maloney? The boy loves visits from Kut-huri."

"It was dreadfully wrong, whatever you did with that plate!" Ben paced on the balcony. "I've told you and told you—all these manifestations of yours have got to stop!" The twilight cicadas roared in his ears like an approaching mob.

"If Kut-huri wants to visit us, how can I prevent him?" She glared up at him, her eyes bulging. "I must obey my Masters! I am *nothing* if I can't act in their behalf!"

Ben shook his head. "This Kut-huri's dangerous to you—and to the Society!"

"Flapdoodle!" Irena rose from her chair, her face contorted with pain as she put down her weight on her swollen leg. "You have changed very much, Ben. I do not know why you are persecuting me this way—" She wiped her eyes—"but I cannot listen to any more from you today!"

Ben watched her limp off into her suite and shut the door behind her.

Whatever else was happening at the Society's Banyan headquarters, Ben noted, Sarah was thriving. Her skin was dark and healthy-looking; her eyes always looked bright with some new discovery. Her sadness about her mother's death returned only occasionally; most of the time she was happily preoccupied by the magazine or the school or, of course, Davidar, who seemed to glow in her company. And it was good for Irena to have the girl there—someone to fuss over, compliment, give little presents to, to mother in a way Irena herself had obviously never been mothered, herself. Ben, who'd begun to take dawn walks away from the estate, was glad to see Sarah standing outside her room one morning in a loose *salwaar kameez* outfit. As she watched the sun rise over the bay, she brushed out her long red hair.

"Good morning, Captain." She waived gaily at him. "Look!" She pointed at the clouds, whose edges were tinted pink by the first rays of the sun.

"I see." Ben smiled. These days, he sometimes forgot to notice the beauty of his surroundings. "Do you want to walk to the village?"

She did, and they walked along a sandy path past the flowering bushes and spiky palmettoes. Raucous Indian crows walked among the palm fronds overhead, and a flock of green parrots circled in the dawn sky like beads being swirled around a pale open seashell. Ben and Sarah waved to Mr. Lane Fox, who was doing calisthenics beside the river. Mr. S. Ramabadra Ramaswamier and Franz Hartmann were meditating in the lotus position. Leaving the estate, Ben strolled with Sarah through the fishermen's village of thatch roofed huts beside the water. Somewhere a baby cried, a cock crowed. Women in faded sarees sat in doorways combing out their daughters' hair. Men sat against earthen walls repairing nets in their laps. In the shade of an awning, Ben squatted to buy a *bidi*, a tiny cigar. But when he put an anna on the vendor's mat, the man pushed the coin away, smiling. These people knew him—they tended the estate's gardens and took care of the buildings. They were grateful for the school his society had founded for their children.

"So many Indians have come to know and trust us," Ben said to Sarah. "I can't bear the thought that we might let them down."

"Why should we?" she asked, cocking her head curiously.

He gazed at her, then was suddenly distracted. They'd come to a spreading neem tree, and from beneath it came the throbbing of a *damaru* drum. A *gilli-gilli* man was setting up a magic show. The audience made room for the tall, bearded white man and the young woman. Ben and Sarah sat cross-legged on the sand. The turbaned performer gave them a toothy grin, waving his hands in the air over the props arrayed on his mat. He was singing a song that mentioned Indra many times. Then, sitting back on his haunches, he placed a seed in the sand beneath an overturned basket.

"I marveled, the first time I saw this trick," Ben whispered to Sarah. After more incantations, the man raised the basket to reveal a tiny mango tree growing from the sand. Sarah clapped her hands.

Ben watched the faces of the spectators; their gazes were rapt with pleasure. "What audiences witness," he told Sarah, "— whether Ceylonese villagers, Alexandrian devotees, or Indian fishermen—it's all part of the natural order of things. It's marvelous and magical, to be sure, but it's well within the bounds of reality, just as statues of Kishna and his bull, Nandi, are said to take on life when worshipers offer hymns to them at the local temple. So once people step willingly into the net of Indra—he's the god of magic—they're seeing affirmations of their faith in the divine presence in everyday life."

"Oh." Sarah smiled.

"In the *Upanishads*," Ben continued, "Shvetashvatara spoke

about this to ascetics in his forest retreat. He said—approximately—a Magician created this world by magic. Nature is *maya*, the first illusion, and the Lord is the illusionist. The things of this world are but elements of Him.'"

"So nature's *maya*—an illusion?" Sarah asked, looking a little confused. "I'll see if I can really understand it, before I decide if I believe it."

"Good plan." That morning, Ben was having trouble, himself, believing in the wonder that should have been radiating from the work of this illusionist. In fact, he was filled with horror as he watched the magician's assistant, a thin, delicate teenaged boy, sit trembling before his black-bearded master. Suddenly knowing what would happen, he stood up and pulled Sarah to her feet.

"Let's go, Sarah," he whispered, still gripping her wrist. She walked backwards, watching the magician, as Ben hurried off toward the huts.

"*Gilli!*" the illusionist intoned. Leaping to his feet, he threw a filthy blanket over the head of the boy—probably his son, Ben thought. From the shade of a hut, he heard the crowd gasp, then saw the magician's sword plunge into the quivering mound beneath the blanket. In a few moments, he heard more mystical spells shouted—*Yantra-mantra-tantra!*—and saw the blanket whipped away to reveal the boy lying on the ground with a bloody death-wound in his neck.

"It's only illusion," Ben told Sarah.

"I know," she said, but she peeked through her fingers as the boy was covered again with the blanket. Another roar rose from the crowd. The boy threw off the blanket and stood with his arm raised in the air, smiling—miraculously restored to life. Ben let out a deep breath. Sarah applauded.

Some village children followed Ben and Sarah as they wandered on along the path. Recognizing Sarah—"Teacher!"—they all wanted to hold her hand.

Did the villagers know, Ben wondered, that the murder and revival of the magician's boy was *maya?* Or did they—like Ben when he'd first arrived in India—believe literally in the magician's apparent power? Ben recalled that he'd once considered such magic the expression of lost scientific knowledge of ancient Eastern masters. In Ceylon, he'd even allowed himself to believe that he could tap into this power, himself. Now what did he believe?

Arriving at the beach, he and Sarah sat on the sand, leaning back against a wooden fishing boat. Several children rushed under the sloping prow to join them in the shade. In hushed silence they watched Ben take out his pipe, tobacco, and matches. "Do they think that matches are a form of Western magic," he wondered aloud, "just as I once thought mango trees growing beneath baskets were Eastern magic?"

"I think they've seen matches before," Sarah said.

"Of course," he said, and lit his pipe. But he was still thinking. Once he'd encouraged Davidar's belief in Irena's amazing phenomena: her magic would inspire people, he'd said, making them passionate to search for spiritual wisdom. But how could her phenomena be justified if she risked hurting Davidar and others?

The villagers must have seen *gilli-gilli* men perform many times, he considered. For them, the question of whether the boy was actually killed and revived evidently wasn't relevant to their understanding of what they saw. The magician's performance with his son—the primal sacrificial act—horrified and then delighted the people because it reinforced their faith in the inevitability of death and rebirth. The villagers were glad to be dramatically reminded that more lives awaited those who, like them, kept the faith by participating in sacrificial rituals.

"So, it's a mysterious paradox—this *gilli gilli* performance," Ben said, turning to Sarah. "a great truth gets illustrated—by an illusion!" He got to his feet and brushed the sand from his palms. "The fatal sword-wound was *maya*. But the magician's plunging his sword into the burlap mound again and again—that was no illusion."

"But it was dramatic," Sarah said, standing up.

"The conjuror used a real sword," Ben went on. "If he'd guided it carelessly, the boy might have truly been killed."

She shuddered. "That's true." Then Sarah took his arm in both her hands. "Oh Captain, look!"

Along the sand a tiny child was leading a massive black water buffalo along by a rope attached to a ring in its nose. The animal moved with a plodding grace, its head bobbing slowly, its curled horns feinting harmlessly in the air a few inches from the boy's shoulders. Silvery sunlight glistened on its smooth black back. The beast's huge eyes were calm but watchful, as if defying anyone to challenge either it or its small master. The boy wore rags; his legs were caked with dirt, his arms spindly and sun-burnt, but on his face was a radiant smile; he seemed to love leading the huge beast past all the people on the beach. The two of them walked silently by Ben and Sarah, leaving small foot- and huge hoof-prints behind in the damp sand. An after-image of the boy and beast remained in Ben's mind, a profound visual resonance.

"They looked like Krishna and his bull, Nandi—don't you think?" Sarah asked.

Ben smiled. "Maybe that's who they were!"

On Ben's journey to this great land, he'd seen holy men produce evidence of powerful cosmic magic. But even more importantly, he'd learned to discover extraordinary magic in the ordinary life of India. By magic, he meant an intimation of a spiritual presence that flooded over him, leaving him breathless—perpetually amazed that he was fortunate enough just to be alive among children and water buffaloes and other miracles! He looked around. Sarah was running through the surf, the water soaking her trousers up to her knees, her feet kicked up behind her. Ben watched her throw up both her hands as if to catch the drops of water—or of sunlight—in her hands. Then he felt the surf splash against his own ankles. He waded in, letting the waves rise around him and fall away along the cool, wet sand.

Davidar lived in a small two-roomed bungalow near the fishing village. The main room was lit by a flickering oil lamp. Ben found him standing beside his desk. Slowly the boy turned to stare at his visitor. The skin around his sunken eyes appeared darkly bruised. "Captain—" He swallowed hard. "I think Madame has been lying to me!"

"Madame loves you like a son." Ben rested his hand on Davidar's shoulder. "As I do, Davidar."

Did the Captain recall, Davidar asked, the scene in the Shrine Room, the problem about the broken plate? Ben said he remembered it. "Well, after Madame spoke to Mrs. Coulomb," Davidar said, "Mrs. Coulomb whispered to me to return to my room to fetch a plate Madame gave me last month. I did this. Mrs. Coulomb took it from me and rushed off. After that, I don't know what happened! The cabinet's window rose—and there was my plate!" Davidar leaned forward, his long black hair falling over his face. "Did Kut-huri make the plate appear? Or did someone else? I hope you can tell me the truth, for just now my heart is feeling shattered."

"The truth. . . ."

"I've striven to be like the Masters. I gave up my life to their service—and yours, and Madame's!" He pressed his fists to his flooding eyes. "What have I done?"

"Madame would never intend to hurt you, my boy." Ben sighed. "But she's got a mind so sensitive that she can't always control it. And lately, I'm afraid, Kut-huri has clouded her judgment."

"Why is he doing this? Who is he?" Davidar's voice rose high and quavery. *"Where is he?"*

"I used to believe the Masters lived in the Himalayas. And perhaps they do. But my ideas have . . . evolved." Ben began to pace the room, his boots making hollow thuds against the floor. "I do know that the Masters stand for all wisdom that is hidden from us," he said. "They represent all that's spiritual and creative that we can strive toward—"

"Stand for! Represent!" Davidar collapsed into his desk chair.

"They're in *us*, Davidar!" Ben blurted, smacking his chest with his fist. "Moreya and the Masters embody the cause we've dedicated our lives to." He stared into the lamp's shrinking flame; it quivered behind the dark, clouded globe. "But the terrible truth is . . . Kut-huri may no longer be our best guide."

"Then . . . who is?" Davidar's face turned slowly toward him. *"Who is?"*

Ben had no answer.

The next day, when Daisy found Ben stomping about his office, she could see that he needed a change of scene. She'd squeezed her ripe figure into a cheerful yellow dress with a purple jacket, and carried a handful of chrysanthemums she'd picked on her way to his bungalow. One of them in Ben's boutonniere might make him at least look a little more cheerful, she thought. But since he was wearing a long *kurta* shirt with no buttonholes, she pushed a flower into the thicket of his beard and kissed him on the nose. A smile emerged from among the whiskers. She took his arm and guided him toward her carriage.

Once across the ferry, they turned up the high road, the horse clip-clopping quietly on the packed sand. Ben began noticing how pretty Daisy looked as the sunlight flickered down through the palm fronds into her thick curls. She rested her head against Ben's shoulder. They caught glimpses of high white mansions rising from the tropical foliage—estates erected by East India Company magnates of the previous century. Farther up the coast, the old Portuguese Basilica of San Thomé, with its simple lines and high spire, towered over the roadside Hindu shrines. Having recently heard a lot from Ben about the Christians who were attacking his Society, Daisy refrained from remarking about the cathedral's graceful architecture.

Soon the carriage was rolling along the new Madras Marina, a promenade that skirted the long harbor beach. Ben directed the driver to pull into a grove of palms across from the Chepauk Palace and gave him a few annas to go buy himself some tea. Sheltered beneath the trees, the carriage rested in a quiet spot equidistant from the roar of the surf and the cheers from the cricket grounds behind the palace's red brick walls.

"After Ceylon, I thought Banyan would be a haven. Little did I know. . . ." Ben pressed his hand to his belly. A bat with razor-tipped wings seemed to have recently taken up residence there; now it fluttered painfully to life. The bat was his image of his dilemma. "Irena's doing more damned phenomena—astral letters dropping, flowers falling, all of it," he said. "Even when that investigator, Hodgson, is around taking notes." Ben sighed. "I tell her to stop, but it's almost as if she wants some sort of cataclysm to erupt—I don't know."

"I remember you used to defend her tricks when I questioned them."

"It's like I told you—I found out how dangerous that sort of thing can be." He recalled his magnetic healing in Ceylon, and the intoxicated feeling that came over him as he used psychic energies (or believed he did) in ways everyone considered miraculous. How quickly he'd become addicted to power and gratitude; how much he'd loved those sensations of intimate connection to the cosmic forces. "I can't stand the thought of hurting Irena—yet I have to find a way to stop her from destroying the Society. That's the dilemma." Ben said, and on cue, the bat flapped its sharp wings deep inside him. "You know, Ceylon was a revelation. I don't just mean my breakdown. The more I preached about the Buddha, the more I got to like him. He says we're supposed to avoid attachment. I can't do that completely—"

"Well, I hope not!" Daisy's eyes twinkled.

"No. But I have to detach myself in some ways from Irena. To save Irena from herself—whether she can ever forgive me or not." Ben sat back, his arm around Daisy's shoulder. She was the only one he could confide in now. He'd even told her about Mary Surratt's recent nocturnal visits and how the poor woman's gaze still burned into his dreams.

"You know, I've always wondered about something." Daisy said. "You never told me why you were annoyed with Mr. Brown, after the account he gave of your trip together on the way to Madras. Do you think he didn't truly meet Kut-huri?"

"Well, the Indian that Brown met outside our tents may have called himself Kut-huri," Ben said. "But I recognized him from one of our gatherings in the Punjab."

Daisy raised her eyes to see past the swirls of Ben's beard. "Did he arrive . . . astrally?"

"More likely, he arrived by rail from Rampur. Between you and me, Daisy, I think Irena cabled him to come and present himself to Brown as Kut-huri, so that later Brown would amaze her Banyan friends by telling about the meeting. And I told her this that night—after Brown's story."

"My husband said you seemed furious with her on the verandah."

"I did lose my temper, but the hail was coming down so hard I don't think many people noticed. She called me some choice names, too." Ben smiled. "Then we both realized we had to put up a show of solidarity—for the members' sake."

Daisy sat up and turned toward him. "I've never heard you speak this way about Irena. D'you think Hodgson's suspicions about her are true?"

Ben shifted uncomfortably. "I have to admit, most of them sound plausible."

"Tell me, do you ever think that Kut-huri's a . . . a figment of her imagination?"

"I've got no doubt that Irena believes in him devoutly."

"What about you?"

"Kut-huri seems too erratic, almost deranged sometimes." Ben sighed. "But if I can't believe in him—how can I believe in any of the others? In Moreya?"

"I don't know, Ben. How can you?" When he said nothing, she stroked his cheek and lightened her voice. "Well, we all need some mystery in our lives. It's the source of hope and inspiration, isn't it?"

"Yes," he said. "Also the source of a lot of damned aggravation!"

"Maybe it's time to forget all that for awhile." Snuggling closer, she pressed his hand to her bodice. "Unless you want to go back to Banyan—"

"I don't. Hodgson'll be snooping around. Your husband, too. Sometimes I think those two are in collusion."

"So do I." Daisy pressed his hand tighter. Ben felt her breast swell beneath the purple gingham. "Meanwhile," she said, "there's a delightful new hotel—its called the Connamarra, and I hear they've some lovely rooms."

He kissed her eyebrow. "Connamarra it is. I know some Irish songs I'll sing to you. I hope I can remember the words."

"I hope you can, too, my darling," she said.

Once Hodgson resumed his investigation, he must have gone straight to Emma Coulomb, Ben noted. It didn't take her long to find her way to Ben's office with a stack of letters she said Irena had written to her.

"I want three thousand rupees for these!" she said, narrowing her eyes.

Ben frowned. The woman's pale face and greasy black hair always put him off, and today her breath smelled of garlic. "What on earth are you talking about, Mrs. Coulomb?"

"If you don't want these letters, I'll sell them to someone who will!" She thrust one of the papers at Ben.

Ben blinked the sweat from his eyes. The letter was dated almost a year previously; it had been sent from Colombo:

> My Dear Marquise
>
> A grave crisis is approaching, but we can turn it to a miraculous OPPORTUNITY. The Maharajah Harisinghi writes me that he is on his way to Banyan and he expects to meet none other than Kut-huri! I cannot be there, but you must see to it that a KH message arrives to welcome the Maharajah. Let this message be delivered through the holy window of the Shrine. Christopholo might also need an outing in the garden—to show to Harisinghi, who is about to pay off the Banyan mortgage for the Society. The poor Captain in his current mental state has great need of a sanctuary there. I know I can count on your aid and discresssion, as always.
>
> Your loving friend — Irena

Ben ground his teeth but managed to keep his face immobile. "This letter's worthless." He drew himself taller, assuming his best courtroom demeanor. "It's a damned forgery!"

"It's not! You know her handwriting as good as I do."

"I've edited her work. Her writing can change—" Ben cleared his throat. He'd had no idea such documents existed. Could Irena really have written them? "You're a cynical and greedy woman!" Ben said. "If these letters were genuine, they'd indict you as an accomplice!"

"I don't rightly care any more. Alexis and me're going to America. Nobody there'll know nothing about us—from so far away as India."

Ben's eyes burned; his beard rose and fell on his chest. "Keep your letters!" he thundered. "The Alexandrian Society has too much to offer the world to be brought down by people like you!

Its true message does not depend on miracles—and it cannot be destroyed by blackmailers!"

Passing the ferry landing, Ben paused to watch the long flat boat approach. When Richard Hodgson stepped ashore, the two men stepped in to a nearby grove of trees.

"Let's not waste time," Ben said. "I'm willing to help you prepare a report that will do a great deal for your reputation with your friends in London. But you'll have to agree to certain conditions."

Hodgson nodded. "You've new information, then?"

"First the conditions." Ben gazed at the long white bungalow beyond the grove. "One—you must agree not to question our assistant, Davidar, about anything I tell you. He's been under a lot of pressure, and I don't want him hurt. Two—any documents you receive from anyone must not be published. They may well be forgeries."

"What documents are you talking about?"

Ben took a deep breath. "Emma Coulomb's got letters she says Irena wrote. I expect she'll want to sell them to you."

"She's been hinting about them to me, but I suppose she thought she'd get more from you," Hodgson said. "The SPR hasn't got that kind of budget. But I wonder, why don't you buy them from her yourself, Ben?"

Ben sighed. How had this man ever passed a bar examination? "It would look as if the Society was suppressing potentially damaging evidence."

"Ah," Hodgson said. "Yes."

"Condition Three—" Ben frowned. "Whatever you write about Irena, the report mustn't implicate anyone else in the Society."

"Such as yourself?" Hodgson asked, and took a nod for an answer. "Well, I can understand your concern for your reputation, Ben, but I don't see how I can leave out any mention of you."

"I'm willing to be seen as . . . overly incredulous, if it comes to that. But never as an active accomplice."

"Have you ever been one?" Hodgson stroked his beard.

"Things have gone on that I probably should have investigated more closely. I should have stopped certain things from happening. That much I'll acknowledge." Ben pushed the toe of his sandal into the sandy ground. "Like any organization that investigates hidden knowledge, the Alexandrian Society has made use of certain miraculous events to attract followers. Whatever Irena's done, it's been for the sake of the Society." And for the sake of my health, when I needed a sanctuary from my troubles in Ceylon, Ben recalled, fighting off a twinge of wretchedness. "The point is," Ben went on, "I intend to see to it that the Society survives any report you make. But it can only do so if my own reputation for integrity remains intact. I'm a kind of symbol of the organization, like it or not, to thousands of people. The Alexandrian Society's my life, and I mean to continue its work until I die—no matter what Irena may do."

"She's indubitably a remarkable lady." Hodgson said. "D'you think she'll cooperate?"

"Dammit, I don't speak for her! I offer you my own cooperation under the conditions I've laid out. If you don't agree to them, you'll get nothing at all!" Ben glared at him.

"My good man, I'm grateful for everything you've offered." He smiled. "I'll certainly do my best to meet your conditions. You have my word as a gentleman." Hodgson put out his hand.

Ben shook it. Hodgson's grip was firm, his palm slippery.

When Ben complained of the bat-pain in his stomach the following week, Daisy ordered a glass of milk brought to their room at the Connamorra; she said it was soothing for ulcers. Their room was a pretty one, with emerald-tinted watercolors of Ireland on the walls, a canopied bed, and a sitting area with a table and chairs. Outside the gauzily curtained window, the colonial officials' white mansions, or "garden houses," stood on the plain like a row of huge vanilla cakes. Ben, barefoot in a pair of loose-fitting Indian trousers, carried his milk glass to the window, then set it down on the sill. In the street below a bullock cart rumbled by. Dust rose like a beige fog, dulling the green of the palmettos in the hotel garden.

"The investigation rolls on," he said with a sigh. "I'm worried, Daisy."

"I know you are." She walked to the window to stand beside him, pulling her peignoir closed at the throat. "Why did you let Hodgson get so far with it, Ben?"

"I hoped that having him around would keep Irena from setting up another Simla fiasco. It didn't. Then I hoped the preliminary report would deter her—but it didn't, either. The next thing I knew, she was involving Davidar with that plate-switching in the Shrine Room—"

"So the plates were switched!"

"I'm afraid so." Ben sighed.

"And now you want a more damning report from the SPR—to stop her once and for all."

"If it comes to that." Ben paced to the bed with Daisy holding his arm. He sat down hard. "But I'd much rather that Irena leave before the report comes out—to spare her, to spare Davidar, to spare us all."

"Poor Irena." Daisy shook her head. "Do you think she'll really go?"

"She's resisting like hell. I've written the Alexandrianists in London to invite her there. I should get a reply, soon."

"Meanwhile. . . ." Daisy picked up the glass of milk. "You haven't drunk this."

He took the glass from her. "You're a thoughtful woman, Daisy."

She watched him drink the milk, then stepped closer to him so that their knees were touching. "It's only enlightened self-interest, you understand."

"I do understand." Smiling, he drew her closer to him.

With his gray-white beard and dignified bearing, Ben was aware that he may have looked like a holy man to the villagers of Ceylon and India, but he never thought of himself as an ascetic. He had as much vital energy as ever. At fifty, he was in his prime, and Daisy noticed this with pleasure each time they frolicked beneath the bed's canopy at the Connamarra Hotel. Ben still knew how to be playful as he nuzzled her soft breasts with his whiskers, or brushed his lips against even tenderer parts of her, eliciting moans, cries, and wild musical notes. He didn't need the theatrics that had once impressed Zia, or the charisma that had first overwhelmed Sujata in Ceylon. As he tenderly caressed Daisy's body, his hands were infused with the power of his own warm feelings, not with any astral force, and this affection was quite sufficient to arouse her passion and gratitude.

At thirty-six, Daisy had once thought she was past her prime, but she discovered that until Ben appeared in her life, she'd never even reached one. Never before had she let herself thrash and squeak with such girlish abandon as she did with him. She wasn't ashamed of her figure; she had as good a time cradling his head against her generous bosom as she did tickling his whiskers like a coy ingénue. And when, passion spent, she lay quietly among the disheveled sheets with him, they could murmur together like the intimate friends they were.

Ben lay back on the pillow, his arms folded behind his head. "I sometimes wished I'd met you years ago. We might have run off together."

Daisy rested her cheek on the lace-edged pillow. "No, my darling, you met the lady you needed to run off with. You enjoy sensual affection, but you save your truest love for the unattainable woman."

He gazed into the sunbeams streaming through the curtains. "Meeting Irena changed my life, it's true. But I know now that she only woke up something in my nature that'd always been there. Whatever it is, it took me to India, and it's what keeps me going now, not her."

Daisy nodded. "Perhaps you no longer need her, but you can't stop loving her, in your way."

"We'll see," he said. "We'll see."

As much as Sarah enjoyed the tranquility of Banyan, she sometimes grew restless to explore the world beyond its boundaries. So when she heard of a religious festival behind held in Mylapore, a temple village on the outskirts of Madras, she begged to go. Davidar agreed to accompany her. As night fell, they hired a tonga and driver, and set out for the temple complex. The dark roadsides were lit only by little oil lanterns in the windows of straw-roofed mud huts. Davidar and Sarah squeezed together on the seat in back. They heard murmurings, occasional snatches of song, a stray rooster crowing from the black-fringed foliage; people appeared as moving silhouettes in doorways and yards. Sarah though she'd felt Davidar's mood lighten as they left Banyan behind; now she got up the courage to ask him what had been making him so tense and withdrawn lately.

He leaned forward in the seat as if he didn't want the driver to hear what he had to say. "I'm struggling to hold onto my faith in the Masters," he whispered, his eyelids quivering. "If I can't dedicate my life to them, I don't know what can I do with it!"

She gazed up into his face. "Can't you just live it?"

"I don't know." His shoulders slumped forward.

"There's so many wonderful things to do here!" she went on. "The magazine work, the school, our walks along the beach. . . ." Her cheer didn't rub off on him; his face kept its brooding expression, but she wouldn't give up. "I've never been so happy anywhere before," she said.

"I'm glad for you," Davidar said. "I've been happy, too, in the Alexandrian life. But if it ends, can I go back to my old faith—all those gods and rituals? A strange thing, Sarah—" His forehead was nearly touching hers; a vein was throbbing in his temples below his turban. "Alexandrianism preaches the revival of Indian culture, yet I've grown so close to the Society, I'm cut off from the Indian life I knew before."

"But you can find it again." she said, and immediately felt a rush of sorrow: if he did find it, he'd leave her far behind. "I mean, if you really want to."

"I'm going to the festival tonight to see if I can still belong. . . ."

More and more figures appeared along the roadsides. Men ran by holding blazing torches in the air. Sarah saw the great Mylapore temple, its walls and tall painted roofs lit up against the night by thousands of lamp-flames that burned like glowing eyes. Before the wall, a great dry pool a hundred yards long was packed with white-clad figures. They moved in a continual procession like phosphorescent water flowing through holes in a dam—into the wall's gates to the temple courtyard. Sarah felt the pull of the crowd tugging her forward. When the tonga stopped, she gave a little cry and jumped out onto the road, her feet already in motion. Holding Davidar's arm, she joined the river of people that flowed toward the dazzling lights. The main temple's roof was covered with freshly painted life-sized plaster gods and goddesses who reclined on its steep slope like mountain-climbers resting along a cliff face.

Sarah covered her head with her cotton shawl; many women were dressed in *salwaar kameez* outfits like hers, and with her sun-darkened complexions, no one took any particular notice of her. She passed a cluster of bare-chested priests sitting on the temple floor and chanting. A bell clanged from a recessed altar-room; clouds of sweet-smelling smoke drifted past. She moved with the crowd through another door into a street and became part of a vast procession circling the temple. Finally she and Davidar made their way up some steps to a terrace where they could watch the people pass before them.

A group of men came by carrying a palanquin on which rested a gigantic red god's head wearing a crown of blazing candles. Behind them more men in white marched with slender squawking trumpets held to their mouths. A litter followed: a huge wooden frame from which a swing was suspended. A woman swooped out over the heads of the crowd, her bright saree billowing—or was she a costumed plaster goddess? Sarah heard a deep rumbling sound: dozens upon dozens of stooped, turbaned men pulled taut ropes along the street like the pyramid-builders of Egypt. Out of the smoky darkness rolled a massive carved wagon. Its wooden wheels—the source of the thunderous rumbling—were taller than the men who walked beside them pushing on the thick spokes to help roll the vehicle forward.

"Davidar, what's that?" Sarah shouted at him over the squawking and rumbling and chanting.

"The temple car," he said. "Transporting the deities."

And then she saw them, wooden gods and goddesses in brilliant green, gold, red, and yellow clothing, all riding majestically along, gazing down at the crowd like dignitaries in a parade. Each time they jerked to a halt, the people shouted up to them, and Sarah could almost hear the replies of the giant figures: the roar of a mustachioed god brandishing a silver sword, the plinking notes from a lyre a goddess cradled in her four arms, and the mirthful trumpeting of an elephant-headed deity sitting cross-legged on the car's front seat.

"Let's join the procession!" Sarah said to Davidar.

His eyes burned, as if he wanted nothing more than to plunge into the throng, but his lips were pressed together in a kind of grimace.

"What is it?" she asked him.

"This is a beautiful spectacle," he said, "but now it seems very pagan to me. I long for the serenity—the contemplative life that I've found studying the Masters."

Sarah hadn't given much thought to the spiritual meaning of the festival; when she tried, she could only view it as an acting-out of the fantastic folk stories she'd read. She loved being in that heroic world, feeling the soft flower petals underfoot as if they were magical lotuses, smelling the plumed sweet smoke rising from braziers, hearing the rhythmic shouts that sounded as if throngs were welcoming back heroes from great celestial battle-grounds. She exchanged long looks with statues of sacred be-ings—this was called *darshan* in the Hindu faith, she knew: be-ing blessed by being in the presence of holy personages. Wasn't this a spiritual experience? She wasn't a Hindu, of course, but sharing the street with these adventurous gods and their beautiful consorts was certainly more inspiring than following any of the sober Christian rituals she'd observed in America.

"Isn't Alexandrianism about soaking up all beliefs? About looking for your own meanings in them?" she asked Davidar. They'd started walking along the terrace.

"I think you're finding in it only reflections of your own inner yearnings and fears," Davidar said.

"But isn't that the point?" She walked faster to keep pace with him.

"There must be more to it than that. External presences are necessary. Spiritual ones—not fanciful painted idols."

"But. . . ." she looked around, as if hoping all the gods might see her and help her know what to say. But their eyes continued to stare out over the crowd, and their lips didn't move. She took Davidar's hand, slowing his pace.

"I just love all the colors and the excitement. I love feeling the way people are all so happy and fervent!" she blurted. "Isn't that all right?"

"Of course." Davidar stopped. "If it all makes you love something—"

"It does!" Sarah squeezed his hand.

"Then there must be great good in it." He smiled, and they walked on more slowly through the smoky streets as the deities watched them from their carts and rooftops.

On the night Sarah and Davidar visited the Mylapore festival, Ben and Irena nearly come to blows. Irena saw some of the letters with which Emma Coulomb was trying to blackmail her, and summoned Ben to her room. To him, the evening sky seemed raucous with black witches. As he walked up the steps to Irena's verandah—it felt like the longest staircase he'd ever climbed—the winged demons drew jagged lines overhead as if crossing out a painting with strokes of charcoal. The deadliest of the witches—Ben's bat—dove deep into his guts, its razor-sharp wings whirring and slashing.

Irena's door was open. She rose from her wicker chair and blocked his entry, her face puffy and dangerously red in the lamp-light.

"What treachery!" she screamed, waving one of Emma's letters in front of his eyes. "These are vile forgeries!"

He stopped before her on the verandah. "Are they, Irena?"

"You doubt me? You would betray me to the British dogs?" Her eyes filled with tears. "I trusted you, Ben! How could you do this?"

"You're making no sense—I didn't give Emma those damn letters!"

She flung the papers to the floor. "But you refuse to keep Hodgson from using them against me! Are you betraying me, Ben? Do you want to take over the whole Society yourself?"

"No! I'm trying to save you from the worst scandal ever. I don't want you hurt."

"Then why won't you stop the investigation?"

"I can't. It's gone too far to stop!" Ben reached out to touch her arm, but she took a step back. He saw that her lower lip was trembling. "Please listen, damn it! If you want to avoid a truly damaging verdict, you've got to leave India!"

"Quit India? Retreat? *Never!*" Back-lit by the doorway, her wiry hair shook as if charged with electric currents. He wanted to smooth it down beneath his palm, hold her steady as he spoke to her, but her eyes—he recalled how radiantly blue, how hypnotic they'd once seemed—were bulging with hurt and rage. "I have never backed away from my persecutors! Including you!" She folded her arms tight over her bosom. "Banyan is my home now. I have nowhere else—"

"You've moved many times."

"Too many! Why do you want to be rid of me, Ben?"

"I don't! It's not personal!"

"Not personal. . . ." She shut her eyes tight. He heard her breathing through her teeth. Then she glared at him, her fists pressed to her temples. "It's treachery!" She shouted. "Get away from my door, traitor!"

He stood his ground. "Think about what I've said, before it's too late, Irena!"

"Go!" Her arm shot out; she pointed to the staircase with a trembling finger. "Begone!"

Ben's demon thrashed in his raw stomach. "We will speak about this again," he said, and turned to walk down the steps. At the bottom, he stared one more time up at the verandah.

A moving shadow blocked the lamp-light. Irena lumbered to the top of the stairs. "The Masters will always protect me!" she screamed. *"But who will save you, Captain Ben Blackburn?"*

17

In the final months of 1884, Madras became an oven. Irena remembered the way priests had tried to terrify her as a child about Hell, making her picture hairy devils flinging shovels-full of red embers all over her body. India seemed like that at times. The temperature reached 115 degrees, and rarely dipped below 100, even at night. Everyone longed for the cooling monsoon rains to come. On the Banyan grounds, Irena saw tamarind pods hanging like strips of charred skin from the branches; the palm trees were so dry they made death-rattles in the breeze at night. The servants pulled woven straw blinds over the windows and doors and sprinkled them with water, but the dust blew in everywhere under her dress, up her nose, into her eyes. A cobra got into the main hall seeking some cool stone; the Alexandrian Society members, wilting on the verandah nearby, could barely rouse themselves to scream. Ben, the only one there not overcome by heat, finally swept the serpent away with a broom, unwilling to kill a sacred creature.

Some nights, as Irena tossed and turned on her tangled sheets, needle-nosed Russian fairies rushed into her bedroom to prod her swollen leg with burning spears. Her bed was surrounded by an enchanted river where *roussalkas* sang eerily, their green tresses swirling in the current. The corpse of a child she'd frightened nearly forty years ago lay tangled in wet green tendrils; his drowned eyes stared at her from their sockets. "Forgive me!" she whimpered, writhing on her mattress.

Babula told her that *raksasas*, Indian demons, had gotten into her body. She could feel them sliding just under her skin in the heat. And they seemed to be outside it, as well—taking the forms of the Society for Psychical Research members. Hodgson continued to snoop, snoop, snoop. Alfred Hume, a probabable SPR confederate, arrived in Madras from Simla with vile, execrable lies about her. And she discovered that Emma Coulomb, after all the kindness she'd shown the woman, was in collusion with her persecutors, too.

When she caught Emma and Alexis whispering with Hume outside the Shrine Room one night, she gave the couple their walking papers. They refused to leave the estate. Some loyal Alexandrian Society members clanged pots and pans outside Emma's quarters to drive her out. She sent a servant to fetch the local constable, and the poor old man arrived dressed up in a *dhoti* and wool military jacket that looked left over from the Battle of Waterloo. He waved his swagger stick at the members, ordering them to decease and desist and begone. Lane Fox, addled with tropical heat, punched the unfortunate policeman in the nose. Barefoot officers in ill-fitting dragoon caps were called in as reinforcements, and they hauled Lane Fox off in a bullock-drawn paddy-wagon. It was a rather splendid pandemonium, Irena thought, watching it by moonlight from her verandah. But when the Coulombs left—no doubt to go conspire against her with the Christians—the night was twice as black and silent around her, like hot poured tar rising to her nostrils.

The worst of all her torments was Ben: she suspected that he was turning against her. Hadn't he been urging her to flee to London because of the SPR investigation? He had. And hadn't he actually considered letting Hodgson inspect the Shrine? Irena would *never* allow that!

One night, taking her portable writing desk out on her verandah, she sat smoking a Moroccan cigarette and scribbling in her journal in hopes of contacting one of the Masters. Finally, Moreya's words began streaming out of the end of her pen. First, he cautioned her about reckless Kut-huri's influence. Who *was* Kut-huri, truly? Irena asked. The answer appeared in spidery script beneath her moving hand.

I recall him as a youth who, aeons ago, I trained in Our adeptic ways in one of the hidden cities in the mountains of Thibet. Kut-huri was a spirited young apprentice: brilliant, impatient, irrepressible with his audacious jokes. I taught him all I knew which, as you can imagine, took several centuries. He modelled his appearance after Mine in many ways, though he wore his turban at a rakish angle and trimmed his beard to a devilish point. He reminded Me at times of young Lucifer about to tumble from Heaven's grace. And tumble he did. He strayed out of Our subterranean caves and lost himself among the snowy Himalayan peaks.

I heard that he fought in a war in China during the Pang Dynasty, inadvertently blowing up the palace of his emperor with gunpowder intended for a victory celebration. During the Albagensian Heresy in France, he nearly got burnt at the stake. In Peru, he supplied the Inca kings with potions that rendered their warriors invulnerable to every conceivable weapon except— tragically, as it turned out—Spanish harquebuses. It was not long after this adventure when he turned brigand, and a century later entered your life, Irena, as the materialized spirit of John King rescuing you from a shipwreck near Alexandria, then accompanying you to Naples, Paris, and hence to New York.

But sometimes I think that it was you who rescued him, Irena. If you had not repeated his story so dramatically in the salons of Europe, America, and Asia, he might have faded like an errant shadow from human consciousness. Adepts of his low rank depend on their hosts' memory and imagination to sustain their life force.

Why did I ever allow him to attach himself to you? Was I not your principal guardian? Indeed I was, and will always be. But I was forbidden, barring dire emergencies, such as your fiery baptism, to intervene directly in your life. Besides, when like a defiant schoolgirl you first ran off with Kut-huri, I had the wisdom to recognize that he was to play a vital role in your karmic destiny. I have faith that he will eventually lead you back to My guidance.

Irena's hand rested on the paper; Moreya was gone again. Now her consciousness rose with his into the clouds like the virgin of

Gurov's famous painting, *The Ascension*, which she had so loved as a child. And into her mind came a vision of graceful wisdom-bearing calligraphy unwinding from her pen. Above her verandah, she saw the resplendent design of a new book fanning out like silver threads through a great tapestry and filling the moon-tinted sky with the secrets of the ages revealed, all their strands harmoniously connected into a pattern such as the world has never before beheld! And when she drifted back down to her old wicker chair on the verandah, she saw the palms and other trees take on fantastic shapes: hump-backed hippogryphs, dancing serpents, a burning phoenix with iridescent wings raised as if about to take flight. The moon's throbbing silver eye watched her expectantly.

Once again, Moreya descended; his warm hand guided hers across the paper in an ornate, slanted script. Something new, something wondrous began to appear on the paper. An hour, two hours went by. Only once did the pen fall from her fingers when she was interrupted by Ben. She was in such an exalted mood she forgot their recent quarrels; they talked as they had in olden times.

"It's good to see you inspired again," he said, sitting beside her.

"Moreya has visited," she said. "He appeared like a transparent fish swimming through the air. He left behind a shimmer, such as hot air makes when rising from a stove."

Ben nodded. "And what did he tell you?"

A smile spread across her face. "He showed me . . . well, I have sketched out a new book, Ben."

"Good for you! Have you got a title?"

She hadn't. But suddenly it arrived as if on moonbeams: "*The Hidden Wisdom*," she said. "It will be marvelous! There will be new insights—"

"Like *The Astral Veil?*"

"Yes, but even greater! Moreya as enriched by the Hindu *Vedas*, the Moslem *Qa'ran*, the Sikh *Granth*, the Zoroastrian *Gathas*, the Jain *Kalpa-sutra*, the Buddhist *Dhammapada*."

"You know, Mulligan, your news makes me happier than I've been in months!"

"I too am happy, Maloney. But now I feel Moreya nudging my elbow. . . ."

Ben left her then, and she resumed writing. Moreya stayed with her deep into the night.

But all evening she felt the presence of Kut-huri, too hovering about her verandah like a jealous lover. Was he hoping to precipitate a clash with Moreya? Could she withstand such a cataclysm?

Sometimes Davidar seemed to be a canary in the Alexandrian coal mineshaft, Irena thought. He was coughing a lot, looking limp and distressed as he dragged himself around the grounds. He rarely spoke to her; he couldn't even raise his eyes from the ground to meet hers. Sarah said that he was working eighteen hours a day on the magazine; sometimes she found him leaning over manuscripts with tears dripping from his eyes. She begged Irena to give him time off. Irena offered him as much leave as he wanted, but he refused to stop working. Only when Ben ordered him to take a trip to the hill station of Ootacamond did he reluctantly agree to go. Sarah was to accompany him, along with several Indian chaparones.

For the trip, Sarah wore the straw hat with ribbons she'd brought to India with her, along with a long cotton dress and some wool pullovers for chilly evenings. Davidar took his usual white *dhoti*s and white pyjama outfits, and packed a lot of scholarly books. He did take a warm white sweater at the last minute on Sarah's insistence.

She was happy to see him resting in the chaise lounge on the deck of the cottage they shared with several other Alexandianists. She loved taking walks along the roadways with him, past the cricket fields and polo stables and the little stone church in the town square. They gave a wide berth to the chalets where British matrons sat lumpily in lawn chairs scowling at them—an Indian man and a white girl arm and arm on a public thoroughfare. As the week went on, Sarah waved to the ladies; a few of the most elderly of them broke into smiles and waved back. As long as he was with her, Davidar seemed healthy and, for him, relaxed. When she found him alone on the deck, he was often staring longingly out at the snow covered mountain peaks beyond the pines. His lips moved as he as he gazed.

"What do you see?" she asked once, leaning against the wooden rail beside him.

"See? The holy mountains."

"You look as if you're hearing something," she said.

"Sometimes voices. But not ordinary hearing. Words in reverberation." He pressed his fist to his chest.

She took hold of his hand. A chill passed over her—she could feel a trembling in his fingers. "What words?" she asked. "Who says them?"

"The Himalayas are the ancestral home of the Masters," he said.

Sarah sighed. "Masters. Madame and the Captain are always fighting about them!"

Davidar stared at her. His turban was slightly askew on his head; strands of long silky hair fell over his cheeks, past his jaw, dangling almost to his thin chest. "Those fights are *agony* for me!"

"I can see that." She gazed up into his eyes. They'd never been darker, more bruised-looking.

"But the acrimony at the estate isn't the Masters' fault." Davidar said, gazing back at the mountains. Sunlight glinted off the bare rocks on the snowy peaks as if floodlighting veins of gold. "The Masters have been here for thousands of years."

Sarah sighed. "Do you really—well, believe in all that?"

Davidar took a step back. "Sarah!"

"All right—I know you believe. I shouldn't have asked, but you spend so much time reading and thinking about the Masters here. So I sort of miss you." She looked up, her eyes blinking hard to keep from leaking. "Can we go for a walk—someplace different, where nobody's watching us?"

"Of course!" A gentle smile broke out on Davidar's face, the first she'd seen in weeks. "Where?"

Sarah had scouted out a path that led to a stream on the mountainside below the cottage. The trail led through some tall deodar pines, where she and Davidar stopped to listen to the stream splashing against the rocks below; the sound made the cool air even cooler, and the spiced scent of the pine needles seemed to spray up around them.

"If you lick your lips, you can taste the water," Sarah said, striding along over the spongy ground.

Now they were within sight of the stream; just beyond some bushes the sunlight's reflections on the water danced as if patches of the water were covered in tiny flames.

"We've never been so far—" Stopping on the path, Davidar glanced up at the cottages, which looked small as toys. He took a deep breath. "This altitude, it's like inhaling toddy!"

"Oh, Davidar are you drunk?"

"In a way." He smiled. "I've never been to a place like this. Are there many like it in America?"

"I think so. But I've never seen them." She picked a flower and pushed the stem through the top buttonhole of her dress. She was conscious of Davidar watching her curiously. "Purple on green. Is that pretty?" she asked, looking up.

He turned away, pressing his lips together.

"Why won't you tell me?" she asked. "You can say what you like out here, you know."

"You are beautiful," he whispered.

He was in profile to her; his long lashes moved fast against his cheek like the wings of butterflies about to take flight. She had to kiss them. Leaning forward, she wrapped her arms around his neck and pressed her lips against one eye and then the other. He turned toward her. She felt his palm softly collide with her breast, and stayed very still, eyes closed. They stood together under the trees, motionless, her hand cupped over his. Finally she felt a shiver pass through him, as if he'd just woken from a dream, and they were standing apart again.

She ran off along the footpath. Gravity carried her down in a headlong rush as the slope grew steeper. Hearing him behind her, she turned to see where he was. Suddenly a pain shot through her ankle. Tumbling sideways, she rolled down the slope. Clawing at the ground to stop herself, she only tore up handfuls of pine needles. Finally she felt something so cold against her leg that she

cried out. She'd came to rest, lying half in the steam in a grove of
pines.

Davidar knelt beside her, out of breath. "Sarah! Are you all
right?"

Her ankle hurt and she felt foolish, covered in brown needles
like a clumsy porcupine, but otherwise she wasn't injured. She
decided to remain supine, though; the cold water felt good against
her leg.

"Speak to me, Sarah!"

"*Oohhh!*" She turned slowly toward him. "Is that you,
Davidar?"

"Yes!" He stroked her hair away from her face. "Are you in
pain? Where does it hurt?"

"All over," she groaned, and reached out to him.

Holding her under the arms, he pulled her out of the water until she was lying in a bed of pine needles. He used his shirt to
wash the dirt off her face and neck. His touch was gentle. She
loved the way his chest shone in the sunlight; she wanted badly to
touch the silky hair there.

"Your teeth are chattering," he said.

"I'm so chilled!" Sarah whimpered. "It may be terminal."

He cocked his head. "Sarah!"

She broke out giggling. Her arms went around his back, her
fingers gripping his bare skin. He was slippery with sweat; she
was mad to hold him. He embraced her awkwardly; she heard his
sobbing breath, and held on tighter to keep him from flying away.
The soft ground gave way beneath her—they were rolling toward
the stream. As he dug his hands into the soft earth, she rolled
against him.

"You're chilly. Let me warm you!" Sarah whispered, and
moved closer, her long skirt covering his bare legs.

Then her own legs were cool and bare as his hands stroked
them; he kissed her like someone mad with thirst. Reaching her
arms around his neck, she arched her back, whimpering as his
cool, wet fingers peeled away her clothes.

Long after they'd stopped moving together, they clung to each
other, cheeks pressed close, fingers stroking hair. Davidar's turban

lay partially unraveled on the riverbank. Sarah's dress was so soaked and needled that she took it off, along with her petticoat.

Davidar gazed at her. "Have I hurt you?"

She looked down. A streak of blood had dried along the inside of her leg. "Not much. I'm happy now."

He let out a long breath. "I never thought I could do what we did. . . ."

She rinsed out her clothes on some flat rocks and she sat beside him. "We're not the first to ever discover this," she said, resting her head against his chest. "I'll bet even the—" She'd been going to say something light-hearted about the Masters, but the look in his eyes stopped her. He glanced up the hill in the direction of the snowy peaks, which had never been out of their sight here. Now they were invisible behind the pines. Had the mountains heard? Had they seen? Sarah glanced at Davidar and, shivering, reached for his hand.

The rivalry between Pachiappah's College, a school for high-caste Hindu boys, and the Madras Christian College, where places were reserved for the sons of wealthy Christian merchants, had been intensifying in recent years. The tension even broke out in brawls when students of one school were caught scrawling slogans on the walls of the other. The Reverend Patterson, rector of the MCC, had recently hosted a reception for the British governor, Mountstuart Elphinstone Grant-Duff. In retaliation, Pachiappah's students invited Madame Milanova to their school. What better way for them to cock a snoot at their MCC rivals than to honor a woman who publicly attacked the pro-British Christian newspapers. The invitation came at just the right moment for Irena, when news of the SPR's investigation was beginning to leak out. She decided to break her rule against speaking before large audiences. It was time for some good press, for a change.

Davidar and Sarah, just back from Ooty, decided to stay at Bayan, so Irena and Ben left without them. The Pachiappah students arrived in a carriage, joyfully making room for the distinguished guests behind the driver. The vehicle rolled along the Marina with boys hanging off it, waving, spooking horses and annoying passers-by. At the school Irena was loaded into a wicker armchair and hoisted on the shoulders of the students. Cheering and shouting slogans, they carried her triumphantly toward the great lecture hall. Several eggs flew past her, launched by hidden MCC students who were quickly routed. The chair picked up speed, with Irena rocking and rolling on it like a passenger on a storm-tossed raft. "Help me catch some eggs!" she cried to the boys, waving her hat in the air. "We shall make an omelet of them!" Amid much mirth, she was deposited on the platform inside the auditorium. Several journalists slipped in through the back door.

Lately Irena had received letters from some distinguished people in London with whom Ben had started a correspondence, and she'd decided to make them the subject of today's talk. "I am happy to report to you that not all the citizens of Britain have a colonial mentality," she announced. "An important *opposition movement* is developing among those who have been drawn to Moreya." The boys let up a roar of applause. Irena beamed. Sitting in the wicker armchair at center stage, she looked splendid with her sky blue cape pulled around her shoulders, her glass pendants twinkling in a shaft of sunlight that slanted down from the window. She waved a peacock feather like a wand as she spoke. "I have heard from a young London Alexandrianist named Annie Besant," she continued. "This brilliant woman wants me to join in her struggles for justice. You may have read that she has been a protegée of George Bernard Shaw, the radical playwright. She is also a women's-rights champion. And she has actually been arrested for openly advocating *birth control.*" Irena paused for some loud gasps. This was the sort of outrageousness the boys had been hoping for. "Mrs. Besant wrote me that, one day, she would come to India to help Indians organize against colonial op-pression. She described to me a small, intense Indian law student recently arrived in England from South Africa." Here Irena pressed her fingertips to her forehead "And I had a vision of him bald as an egg, wearing only a *dhoti* and spectacles rousing mil-lions of Indians to action and *routing* the British!"

A great cheer rocked the auditorium. The journalists' pencils flew over their pages.

"Meanwhile, our craven enemy, the Christian missionary conspiracy—oh noxious *basalisk-breath!* Oh lethal *cockatrice-glance!*—how they continue to persecute those of us who love the glorious traditions of India!" Irena's voice rose. "The hottest parts of Hell are reserved for them! I picture the MCC's Reverend Patterson writhing like an impaled lizard on the end of a demon's pitchfork, forced to recant his scrofulous accusations against me."

Another cheer rattled the windows. Ben, worrying about a libel suit, strode up beside Irena. The schoolmasters sitting behind her on the stage let out a collective sigh of relief. She was so overcome by the roar of applause that she didn't object when Ben finished the talk himself. Ending on a quieter note about a revival of the Golden Age of India, he managed to keep the boys' attention while preventing them from rioting. A reception, with tea and biscuits, followed. Stories of the Madame's ability to clear a plateful of biscuits in seconds were circulated among the student body as enthusiastically as reports of her scandalous utterances about birth control and anti-colonialism.

While Irena was at her triumphant speaking engagement, three officers of the Shrine Committee, instructed by her to "make an inspection" and "take appropriate action," made their way to the Shrine Room with the keys Irena had provided them.

Mr. St. George Lane Fox was the first to approach the cabinet. "Looks quite solid to me," he said, patting its side.

Mr. Frantz Hartmann, the engineer, slid open the wooden window above the shelf. "Well constructed," he pronounced.

Mr. S. Ramabadra Ramaswamier contemplated the Shrine. "I am appalled that anyone could be accusing Madame of treachery about this. Look here." He reached through the open window, moving his hands along the back of the cabinet. "It is absolutely *solid!*"

At just this moment, however, his knuckles brushed against a wire spring. With a clatter, a concealed panel in the back of the cabinet flew up. Mr. Ramaswamier reached further inside through the just-opened back window and into an opening in the wall behind the cabinet. His hand plunged into a hanging cotton dress. His fingers groped about in the cloth in such a way that had the dress been occupied, its wearer would have screamed. All three gentlemen now crowded their heads together to peer into the Shrine's astral window system. Through it, they observed a closet full of Madame Milanova's brightly colored dresses, skirts, and blouses.

The committee retired to the opposite end of the room to hold an emergency session. Several explanations were proposed. All officers agreed that while constructing the cabinet, Alexis Coulomb, always a suspicious character, must have installed the secret panel and wall-hole in order to incriminate Madame Milanova when Richard Hodgson would investigate. A question was called: should the Society, during this difficult period in its history, take action to prevent the sort of biased scrutiny the Shrine's construction was likely to attract? The vote was three "yea's," no "nays."

At this point in the proceedings, Davidar entered the Shrine Room, extremely agitated that members had walked in without (as far as he knew) proper authorization. "This is sacred ground!" he shouted. "You gentleman must not poke about in the *Shrine!*" Here he was overcome with coughing, his throat clogged with dust and rage.

"Look here, my good man, perhaps you'd like to go lie down," Mr. St. George Lane Fox suggested, gently taking Davidar's arm.

Davidar pulled away as if stung by a scorpion. "You're tampering with the Masters' property!"

"Surely they would be wanting you to care for your health," Mr. Ramaswamier urged.

"This heat is oppressing everyone," Mr. Hartmann agreed.

But Davidar broke free and rushed up to the Shrine. It was still swaying on its wire supports. "Why is the window open like this? Why? " Here he stopped, gaping into the maw of the cabinet. When he saw the hidden wires and springs and hole in the wall, his face went suddenly ashen. He turned to stare at the committee, his deep-set eyes burning with tears.

The members decided to make Davidar an ad-hoc officer of their Committee. He stood dazed, unsteady on his feet, as the gentleman administered the oath of secrecy. Then a motion was put on the floor. After some discussion about its wording, Mr. Ramaswamier wished to insert the phrase "cleansing ritual," but Mr. Hartmann's phrase, "de-construction," was favored. A vote was called. The four men huddled together, the Shrine watching them with an expression of open-mouthed terror on its varnished wooden face.

The motion was carried, with a final tally of three in favor, one opposed. The committee solemnly exited the Shrine Room and headed for the caretaker's shed to fetch an axe.

Irena postponed Richard Hodgson's inspection of the Shrine Room indefinitely, while Hartmann plastered up the hole in the wall. But Ben wasn't reassured about the cabinet's sudden disappearance.

"Hodgson's damned suspicious about it!" he roared, standing in the doorway of Irena's room.

Irena, seated at her desk, glared up at him. "It was stolen. A tragedy, but temples are robbed every day in India."

Ben, looking exhausted in sweat-stained *kurta* and trousers, glowered at her. "You've involved Davidar again. He's been wandering the paths in a state of torment. He shuffles around with his face in his hands, muttering. He won't talk to me."

"I am very sorry he is upset. But if he was a party to the robbery, I know he was just doing it to protect me from persecution."

"*You deceived him!*" Ben thundered.

"You, too, influenced him!" she snapped.

"I never asked him to commit deceptions."

"You know that at times I *have* to produce miracles!" Irena glared at him, her eyes bulging. "Without them, would anyone pay attention to a frowzy, foreign woman."

"Attention, that's what you wanted! And power!" Ben collapsed into an armchair.

"For a great *cause*, Ben!" Irena intoned. "Listen—you have read in the *Janakas* that the Buddha attracted followers by preaching while sitting in the air. You know that he cut off his limbs with a sabre and reassembled them for the crowds. He dove into the earth as if it were water, he walked on the water as if it were land." She lit a cigarette, a flame shooting up before her face. "*All* great astral messengers have done these things! Jesus walked on water, too. The loaves and fishes phenomenon—surely he learned it from Hebrew conjurors."

"You're mad—comparing yourself to Buddha and Jesus!" Ben mopped his brow. "Did they smoke hashish, too?"

"Who knows? Throughout history, mystics have always known of its powers to enhance visionary experiences." Irena took a puff. "But this is just tobacco, a rather good Turkish blend." She held the pouch out to Ben. Despite her smile, her hand was still shaking. "Peace pipe, old chum?"

Ben took out his own tobacco. "I'll stay with the Virginia," he murmured.

"Ah, Stars and Stripes Forever."

"It's a hollow sound, that laugh of yours." Ben's own voice sounded as if it were rising from the bottom of a dark well. "I fear for you, Irena."

She tried to laugh again, but her throat was too dry for any forced mirth. The high-pitched pulsing of cicadas outside sounded louder than before. She steeled herself against more of Ben's abuse. But the next voice she heard was not Ben's, but Sarah's.

"Madame! Captain!" The girl burst into the room. The door, swinging wide, cracked against the wall. Sarah's face was violently flushed, her hair wild. A steak of red was smeared across the bodice of her pale cotton dress. "*Davidar's gone!*" she cried.

Irena reached her before Ben did. "Sarah what do you mean, gone?"

"Davidar's left Banyan forever!" She raised her face to Irena, tears streaming down her cheeks. "He was going to kill himself. But he ran off to the Masters instead!"

18

Parts of the Banyan estate had reverted to jungle over the years, never tamed by the former owners or, later, by the Alexandrians. In the northern corner was a particularly overgrown area, where vines dangled from tree branches like pythons exhausted by the buzzing heat. Along the ground grew plants with leaves the size of elephants' ears. A sandy path still wound through the jungle to a small clearing that the villagers said was populated by *bhutna*— witches. The stagnant air broiled with the almost tasteable odors of decomposing vegetation.

Today, as Sarah, Ben, and Irena made their way into the clearing, the place smelled not only deep rank green but acrid black— wisps of smoke rose from a crude pit that had been hacked into the sand. Around its edges lay two axes and a machete. In its center jagged bits of charred wood poked out of the earth like dragons' teeth; coiled metal viscera were half buried in ash. This was all that remained of the once-sacred Alexandrian Shrine.

Standing beside the pit, Sarah began weeping silently. Irena, still panting from the walk, could only gape in silence at the smoldering ruins before her. Ben stood ramrod straight, his face dark red, his whiskers glittering with beads of perspiration.

"Damnable!" he muttered.

Irena found a handkerchief and mopped her dripping face. "How did you ever find this place?" she asked Sarah.

"We'd come here before, Davidar and I—" Sarah glanced down at the ground. "Today, I was in my room when I heard a chopping sound. I smelled smoke and rushed out here."

"You say Lane Fox, Hartmann, and Ramaswamier were with Davidar?" Ben asked.

"Yes, they ran off when they saw me. They left Davidar with the machete. He was leaning against that tree—" she pointed at a thick gnarled trunk rising from the sand. "The blade was against his neck. He was going to slit his throat with it! He said he had to—he couldn't stand to live any more!"

"He always was high-strung," Irena said. "You mustn't believe he meant it."

Sarah clenched her fists at her sides. "He told me *everything!* The switching of the plates, the concealed windows in the shrine, the way he'd been ordered to help destroy the thing. He said he burnt it to protect you. Even though he knew that you'd lied to him about it!" Sarah glared at Irena, her knuckles pressed against her lips. "It's true—you *lied!*"

Ben felt Irena fall against him. Too late, he clutched at her arm; she dropped to the sand. Now she sat in a heap, looking around dazed. He started to reach for her, then stood up again; the sand was soft, she wasn't hurt, and he wanted to hear Sarah.

"Irena's all right," he said to Sarah. "Go on, dear—what did you say to Davidar?"

Her face was still flushed, but her voice sounded clearer now. "I told him the Society, the school children—everybody needed him. But he wouldn't put down the machete. Then I told him *I* needed him to live, and—oh, I shouldn't have said this—" She shook her head hard, her hair flying. "I told him the *Masters* needed him."

"And that stopped him?" Ben asked.

"He lowered the blade a little." Sarah wiped her eyes. "That's when I grabbed for it. We both tugged. I got cut—" She showed Ben her hand. A long red line ran from her palm down the inside of her wrist; her skin was streaked with nearly-dried blood. Irena gasped. "It bled a lot at first," Sarah said, glancing down at the red stain on the front of her dress. "But I think it scared him more than me. He said he'd turn *bad* if he stayed here—he had to leave forever!"

Irena raised her head. "Back to Bombay?"

"No. To the Masters, he said," Sarah stared off at the entrance to the path where Davidar had left. "He kept saying 'I have to go to them!' His eyes were wild and strange!"

"Did he tell you *where* he was going?" Ben asked.

"Thibet. He said he'd walk there. Many pilgrims had gone— he'd start today."

"No one *walks* to Thibet!" Irena said. "Almost nobody has ever gone there even with expeditions."

Sarah looked from Irena to Ben. "Do you think he'll come back?"

"We have to hope," Ben said. "Right now, we have to take care of your hand."

Irena hunched forward, her fingers gripping the sand. "You must hate me, Sarah!"

"You brought me here to India. You were kind to me. If it hadn't been for you—" She gazed down. "But why did you let Davidar destroy the Shrine? Why did you hurt him? *He trusted you!*"

Irena took a deep breath. "And he will again, Sarah, I know. He'll come back, and we'll talk, and things will be as they always were with us—" She looked up at Ben. "With all of us."

He let out a breath through his teeth. "We have to get Sarah out of this infernal jungle now," he said. "Do you need a litter, Irena, or can you walk?"

She narrowed her eyes. "I can walk!" She lurched to her feet and limped off toward the mansion.

Sarah, bandaged and recovered, insisted on going with Ben to Davidar's house in the village. The door was unlocked, and almost nothing except a few books and a pair of boots were missing from his room. But the air in the little house felt still, uninhabited, as if the place expected no one to disturb it ever again.

"Look!" Sarah pointed at a small white envelope on the desk in Davidar's study.

Ben tore open the envelope. There was only one sentence. The words were scrawled across a piece of Alexandrian Society stationary: "*Sarah—Captain—Madame,*" Ben read aloud "*—I must find the Masters in Thibet to seek Their help for my mental torment.— Your loving Davidar.*"

"It's nothing he didn't tell you," Ben said, sighing.

"*I* want to leave, too!" Sarah cried. "I can't stay here any more with you, you—" She took a step backward, her hair wild around her face, her eyes wide open, "—you *frauds!*" she screamed.

That night, Irena rose from her tangled sheets and, wrapped in a dressing gown, went out to the verandah to sit in her wicker chair. Her portable writing desk was on her knees, pad, pen and inkpot ready. To help her find the Masters, she smoked her Moroccan cigarettes. Finally, she felt her fingers twitch with life. She recognized the presence of Moreya. Taking up her pen, she gave him voice.

My darling Irena, he wrote in his graceful hand. *You know that I vowed never to interfere with your destiny. Yet at this time of your worst crisis, I can see clearly that your karma has already been interfered with by a force (Kut-huri's!) that has diverted it from its natural course like a river raging madly out of control. I cannot let you be swept away! I have had to act!*

Tonight I found Kut-huri riding his horse beside a waterfall high in the Himalayas. Striding across the mountains, I shouted words of warning at him. He merely flung rude epithets back at Me. This interchange felt strange to Me. Kut-huri resembled Me so closely, in his flowing robe, his beard and enormous turban, that as I assailed him about his reckless treatment of you, Irena, I seemed to be screaming into a mirror. My voice clouded its surface until all I could hear was a fuzzy echo. Suddenly I pulled back from the glass. I recognized an old trick: Kut-huri sought to draw Me closer and closer to him until he might suck Me into the dark miasma of his consciousness.

Now he rode into a forest of burning trees and reappeared with a cavalry of raksasas. These demons were hideous to behold, with their pointed tusks and red, bulging eyes. I called upon a nearby choir of celestial nymphs, whose high keening hymns burst the eardrums of the raksasas and sent them tumbling down the mountainside.

Kut-huri shot a hundred arrows at Me. Quickly turning Myself into a hailstorm, I knocked them all harmlessly to the ground.

Kut-huri then took the form of a dragon with blood spraying from its eyes. On its back rode the goddess Kali, her necklace of skulls bouncing on her breasts, her six arms whirling like windmills to send axes and spears flying at My head.

I ducked into a cavern. Kut-huri entered in the shape of a demon whose penis was coated with red chalk, its glowing red tip bobbing in the air before him like a lantern. I hurled a discus and castrated him with it. He whirled, howling, his wound dripping gore. He tore the testicles from a passing ram and attached them to his loins. Panting and roaring, he charged into the darkness.

I eluded him, taking refuge in a subterranean chamber, and when I came out, I saw him in the form of a buffalo grazing on a mountain meadow. I rode toward him in a chariot drawn by white horses. Hurling thunderbolts at his head, I decapitated him cleanly.

But from his neck-hole leapt a pack of snarling jackals. Kut-huri took on the form of a hulking, hairy, jackal-headed giant. He swallowed My horses with his hideous laughing mouth. But one of the horses kicked its way out of his belly and carried me back toward my rival.

Now Kut-huri vomited forth a wave of black foam that enveloped Me like a foul-smelling cloud. My horse shriveled beneath Me. I staggered back, gasping for breath, inhaling soot and noxious fumes. My limbs grew heavy, as if coated with tar. My eyelids were weighted down with gloom. I beheld a landscape of jagged pain and smoky confusion. Conspiracies careened through the sky like drunken red-eyed ravens. Needles of cruel laughter rained down. Fires of madness burst out of the soil's crust. Explosions of words erupted everywhere—ponderous nouns, jagged verbs, sticky adjectives and adverbs. I stumbled into the craters they made; I lurched into heaps of them piled on all sides like dark snowdrifts.

Now I understood that Kut-huri had enveloped Me in his consciousness. There seemed no escape! Then, on the verge of suffocation, I heard a small, urgent cry. And through the storm I glimpsed the radiant face of a plump little girl huddled in the library of her grandfather's palace. She opened a big book, revealing a woodcut of My radiant face! Her eyes streaming with tears, she held the page up to her lips . . . and kissed it! And in that moment I found the strength to claw My way out of the terrible cloud of woe.

I alighted on the crest of the waterfall where I had first spotted Kut-huri. There I took gulps of clear sunlit air, feeling my life force return. Below Me I saw the dark cloud writhing and squirming. It had become Kut-huri's own prison. I heard pitiful choking sounds. I watched arms and legs thrash out of the black effluvia. Trailing loops of filthy mucus, the cloud slid down the mountainside, turning to a raging stream. Like burning lava, it cut a swathe through the rocks and snow; it parted forests; it flooded the valley and rolled on toward the Bay of Bengal. As it poured into the surf, a great hiss went up. I saw a dark stain spread through the water all the way to the horizon.

The air around Me was clear and warm. The grass rippled in the breeze. Flowers raised their heads and whispered their fragrant thanks to Me. I walked across the meadow, Irena, and in several strides returned to your verandah at Banyan. From now on, I alone shall guide your steps with all the brilliance that you first, as a beautiful child, came to expect from Me.

Sitting in her wicker chair, Irena opened her eyes to see the sun rising above the bay, singeing the dark sky with its long pink flames. Doves began their cool, cooing murmurs. Never in her life had the air seemed so crystalline; never had her mind been so clear. "Moreya!" she whispered.

Hearing his breath in the morning breeze, she knew that her karma was back on course.

But what of Davidar? He neither returned nor sent word about where he was. Sarah decided to stay at Banyan for a while longer lest he find her gone if he came back. She threw herself into her school teaching. While she played with the children, listened to their happy singsong recitations, read them fables, she was distracted and content. But as soon as she left the schoolyard, a heavy sadness fell over her and she began to look for Davidar along the beach where they'd walked together so often.

Every day she went with Ben to the little tiled-roof telegraph office in the village. She helped him write cables to monks and officials he knew along the roads north that led in the direction of Thibet. Davidar would have to stop at monasteries to eat and rest, Ben said. Someone would surely recognize him from Ben's descriptions and telegraph back the news.

But weeks went by and there were no responses to their inquiries. 1884 finished without celebrations and 1885 began without Davidar. Sarah started working at the magazine office again as well as the school. At the long desk where she and Davidar had edited articles together, she read over his essays, hoping to hear his voice in the sentences. But his thoughts were so spiritual that she detected only a kind of hum in the air—his presence lingering around her, she told herself. Was this what was meant by an astral body? Or did you have to be dead to have one? She wept silently. Her memories of his face, his voice, his touch—all were still with her. Could she bear to stay here without him?

The Connamarra Hotel was Ben's refuge from Banyan, but it was also, he discovered, where Alan Hume had checked in for a long visit. He encountered Hume one afternoon as he cut through the bar on the way to the stairs.

"Ah, Captain Blackburn!" The man rose from his table. "Join me for a drink, won't you?"

Ben drew back his shoulders. "No thanks."

"There's some important business we ought to discuss, Ben." Alan pulled a chair out and stood behind it, looking trim and elegant in a light tropical suit and shining boots.

Ben made no move toward the chair. "I can't think of any business."

"I can. . . ." Alan thrust a newspaper at Ben—the *Madras Christian College Courier*. Its headline screamed: KUT-HURI UNVEILED: HOUSEKEEPER'S REPORTS

Ben's kept his shoulders firmly back. "I've heard those stories."

"You've read the letters from Irena to Emma Coulomb?" Alan stood beside Ben to look down at the paper. "Hard to believe the old *babushka* would be so witless as to write down things like that!"

"They're forgeries!" Ben snapped. He wanted to wring Hodgson's treacherous neck for letting the letters be published. But a tiny, rational voice told him that of course Hodgson hadn't done that. He'd simply refused to buy the letters, knowing that Emma would take them next to Reverend Patterson at the *Christian College Courier.* Then Hodgson got to read them for nothing.

"It's a shame," Alan said. Ben saw beads of sweat sparkling on the man's bald dome. "The SPR's final report is due out soon. I'm afraid Emma's made statements in it, besides providing the letters."

"I heard you and Hodgson interviewed her together—correct?" Ben asked.

"Look here, why don't you sit down," Hume said. Seeing Ben remain at attention, he went on. "All right, our interview will be in the report. Emma gave us a demonstration at her new quarters—all about how astral letters got delivered. Rather ingenious, I must say. A long thread is looped through a concealed hook-and-eye in the ceiling. On one end of the thread is attached a letter—black, blending with the dark rafter. On the other end of the thread—in the next room, out of sight—is Emma or Babula." Alan held a napkin in the air. "At a word-signal from Madame, the thread is yanked, and—" He opened his fingers; the napkin fluttered down. "—the letter drops!"

Ben frowned. "That may explain one phenomena—not all of them," he said.

"Perhaps, but there are so many accusations of trickery that our dear Irena is going to wind up looking like a music hall conjuror—and you the conjuror's assistant." Alan stepped close enough to him that Ben could smell the whiskey on his breath. "I was thinking, it might be a good time for you to take a trip back to New York to check on things."

"You were thinking that, were you?" Ben felt the blood rush to his face.

"Yes. Meanwhile—well, I've gotten to know Hodgson, and I believe we could work out an arrangement to tone down the report significantly. If I were to take over the Society—"

"Never!"

"Look here, old man—it's all up with Irena! The old girl's completely gaga—"

Ben's arm shot out. His fist cracked against Alan's jaw and sent him toppling backwards into the table. Glasses crashed to the floor. The table collapsed, and with it, Alan Hume, his arms flailing in the air. Ben stood straight again, trembling with rage. Alan made no move to get to his feet. Turning on his heels, Ben strode from the room.

In the estate gardens, the villagers stopped work to gaze up at the broiling sky. Flat gray clouds floated slowly across it from the Bay of Bengal, but without releasing a single raindrop. Crows scolded the heat, demanding the arrival of the monsoon. The Alexandrian Society members sat about in wicker chairs on the verandahs, motionless, sweat-drenched. All had seen the *Christian College Courier*. They'd also read newspapers from Calcutta and Bombay where the article was reprinted beneath lurid headlines: RUSSIAN MEDIUM EXPOSED and KUT-HURI: MASTER OF DECEPTION. Several "Coulomb Letters" were on the front page. They described the moonlight visits of Christofolo, the human-sized turbaned doll. They quoted orders Irena had allegedly given Emma and Babula to embroider personalized astral handkerchiefs. They detailed instructions Alexis said he had received to construct a secret opening in the Shrine Room wall behind the now-vanished cabinet.

As Ben read the newspaper, the members simmered around him, giving off a low bubbling sound. Irena, he was told, refused to come downstairs. He agreed to convene a meeting without her. He urged Sarah to come. "I hope what I'll say will affect you, too," he told her.

"I don't see how it could," she said stiffly, but she followed him to the mansion and quietly found a seat in the back of the Great Hall.

Ben stood before an audience of dripping faces, white and dark, arranged in circles beneath the high ceiling. Ladies fanned themselves rapidly; gentlemen squirmed in their chairs. "Members and colleagues," he began. "As you know, Madame Milanova, our guiding light, has been accused of misusing her powers. You have asked me—how should we respond to this assault on her?" Ben stood tall in a shaft of sunlight. "Well, I know what I, for one, will say. I will tell the world that I have been privileged to know a woman of monumental brilliance whose every action was made in the interest of spreading truth—by whatever means she could muster." Ben paced down an aisle to the doorway from which he could gaze up the stairs to Irena's suite. His loose white trousers and long shirt rippled as he moved. "I will say that I am certain that this woman has never deceived anyone about the genuineness of her ideals. I will tell her accusers: read her book, her scholarly works—hear her championing the brotherhood of man and the ancient wisdoms of Europe and Asia!"

Ben walked to a spot from which his lowered voice resonated. "I acknowledge that, because of her sensitive nature, Irena Milanova has at times been difficult," he said. "Geniuses cannot always control the manner in which they express themselves. But I insist that her manner in no way invalidates her dedication to the cause that has changed the lives of all who have been touched by her message."

Some members started to applaud. Then Mrs. Parker spoke up: "But Captain, the newspapers say she used magic tricks."

"Magic?" Ben stepped forward, his voice deepening. "*Certainly*—magic! In magic is contained the hidden wisdom that has attracted us all to the cause!" Ben began to pace again, drawing all eyes with him. "Let me tell you about my own discovery of magic in its truest sense. I was an attorney in New York. I went to my club, I plotted strategies for enriching myself. And I was a hollow man. I saw no further than the materialism of our gilded age. My life was bereft of magic—no creativity, no art, no spirituality—no belief in anything greater than pallid Christianity and shaky scientific rationalism." Ben sighed. "After our terrible American civil war, I saw a poor woman hanged because she believed her Christian religion had told her to commit treason. I learned what that kind of religion was worth. I myself had collected testimony from her, evidence that should have convinced rational men that she had been disoriented by her beliefs and did not deserve to climb the gallows. I learned what scientific ratio-nality was worth—not enough to win mercy for her in the highest courts of the land!" Ben wiped the sweat from his face. "But I dis-covered, through knowing Irena Milanova, that there were far truer faiths to explore than those offered by any church . . . far loftier ideas to investigate than those hypothesized by materialist science. I discovered, as you have, that there is no greater purpose in life than to freely explore the new, the ancient, the scientific, the spiritual—and to seek the powerful synthesizing principles that unite them all in harmonies most people have only dreamed of." Ben turned slowly to gaze up the stairs to Irena's verandah again. Sarah did, too. Irena stood at the rail in her bedraggled dressing gown, her damp cheeks shining in the sunlight. Ben smiled and turned back to his audience. "I was invited to dream such dreams," he said. "And I have no intention of condemning the woman who gave them to me!"

Here more applause broke out. Ben raised his hand to quiet it.

"Irena is, at present, under siege. She, too, faces a kind of pub-lic hanging. Her tribulations have badly sapped her physical strength. She is in a condition in which her sensitive nature may cause her to behave in ways that could invite further persecution of us." Ben shook his head. "However—I do not intend to allow her to risk this. I say this out of respect and love for her and all she has done for us. But I also say it out of concern for the Society she helped to found." Ben strode to the center of the room again like the courtroom attorney that he had been; he stopped abruptly and whirled around to face his audience. "Irena Milanova must survive to become a powerful symbol of the Alexandrian quest—the quest to discover the creative powers of men and women, the secrets of their true nature, the potentialities of their art. Yes—art, with all its profound magic. Madame Milanova's life has been a great artistic creation—a strange, fasci-nating masterpiece of theater, if you will. . . ." Ben slowly sur-veyed the faces of the members. "Every great spiritual movement in history has needed its ascendant virgins and guiding angels, its founding saints and ancestor-prophets. Madame Milanova must be regarded by future generations as *our* founding light! My role in this crisis is to safeguard our future history. Therefore I intend to do everything in my power to remove Irena from any further assaults on her character—not only for her own good, but for the good of our Society in years to come." He looked about slowly. "All I ask of you now . . . is your continued support, patience . . . and faith. . . ."

He fixed the audience with a calm, deep stare. He didn't appear to want applause so much as for his words to reverberate in the listeners' memories. Finally he walked slowly across the floor and out the main door of the hall. Sarah stared after him. To her and to the rest of the audience, this lone figure, moving with such conviction, now represented—even more than Irena did, for all her brilliance—everything that had ever drawn them to the seeker's life.

Sarah was silent as she and Ben took their afternoon walk to the telegraph office in the village. He stepped behind her through office door. She rushed to the table beside the machine. Today, finally, after all these months, a cable was waiting for them.

"You read it—I can't!" Sarah said.

He did, his voice sunk to a whisper.

> Plukru, Kingdom of Sikkim—20 January 1885
> Dear Captain Benjamin Blackburn:
>
> I am writing on behalf of one Davidar Desai. He is studying to take vows at our monastery. Lamas of this order are not permitted to communicate with the outside world except through myself. News reached us here that you are concerned about Davidar. We, too, are concerned about him, though he has made good recovery since he first sought refuge with us. Sometimes he still speaks of returning to you. We shall see how he progresses. Meanwhile he wishes everyone at Banyan to know that he is well in body and mind and spirit.
>
> Sincerely—Khenpo Situ Rinpoche, Abbot

Sarah sat down hard in the chair beside the telegraph machine. She stared at the black words each in its own patch of gray on the telegram form. "He's all right," she said finally, looking up at Ben.

Ben leaned against the table. "I'm more relieved than I know how to say."

"I wish Davidar could have heard your speech today."

"I do, too." Ben gazed out the door at the sandy path between the thatch-roofed houses. "But I think he's come to some under-standing with us, on his own." He turned back to Sarah. She looked much older, especially around the eyes, than she had when she'd arrived in India over a year ago. As she rose to her feet to walk to the doorway, her movements in her loose flowing *salwaar kameez* were relaxed, confident. And when she looked out at the village children playing in front of the huts, she no longer played with her hair as she used to; she'd pinned it back now as the local Tamil women did.

"I miss Davidar terribly," Sarah said, "and if he comes back, I'll be happy to see him. But if he doesn't . . . then he must be in the right place for him."

Ben stood away from the table so he could look out the door with her. "And you?"

"When you finished speaking about why you'd come to India, well, I finally decided," she said. "This is the right place for me, with or without Davidar. I like the school and the magazine. I want to start training some local people to learn the things Davidar showed me how to do."

"I'm glad to hear this." Ben smiled back. "We're going to need you here—especially now."

She cocked her head. "Why now?"

"I think," he said, "a small apocalypse is about to occur."

Despite his sense of foreboding, Ben felt calmer that night when he went to sleep than he had in a long time. Just before dawn, he was taken on an astral journey to the dark, brick-walled cell where he'd spoken so often to Mary Surratt. She stood slowly rocking back and forth in the deep shadows; her wool dress fastened tightly at her neck to partially cover the rope burn. She was holding something against her chest with both hands. He couldn't see her face.

"I had to do what I did, Mary," he said. "With you, with Irena."

"I heard your speech," she whispered. "I understand."

"I hope you'll be able to rest now."

Slowly she raised her cupped hands before her. A glow came from them, as if she were holding a tiny lantern. Her eyes shone in its reflection. He saw her nod, smiling faintly at him.

Then she blew out the light in her hands and was gone.

Irena often said that she expected Davidar back soon, and Ben, who'd never shown her Davidar's farewell note, had found no reason to dampen her hopes. Her swollen leg hadn't recovered, but she seemed markedly less panicky and irascible these days. Not that she couldn't still be stubborn, as Ben discovered when he came to see her in her room on the evening after his speech.

She was pasting clippings into her scrapbook when he arrived. Closing it, she looked up at him from her desk. "I suppose you think that your bombast will help manipulate me into leaving India," she said.

"Every good general knows when the time is right for a strategic withdrawal," Ben said.

"You're still only a Captain." She pushed the top down onto her glue pot. "And I will not be ordered to retreat, just because of unsubstantiated accusations in some newspaper article."

"What *do* you want to do?"

"Well, I can sue for libel!"

"I'm afraid you can't. I won't represent you, and neither will anyone else."

"Then I'll represent myself!" She struck the table with her fist, making the glue pot jump. "I will sue not only Emma Coulomb but Reverend Patterson. And I will stay in India for as many years as it takes to see the case through. And then some!"

Ben reached slowly into the inside pocket of his jacket and took out two pieces of paper. "I hoped I wouldn't have to show you this."

Unfolding a worn sheet of Alexandrian Society stationary, he set it down before her on the desk. Then he took a step back as she read it, his fingers opening as if to catch her if she fell out of her chair.

She nearly did. *"Davidar!"* she screamed, her hands flying to her face. The glue pot skidded across the desk and crashed to the floor. "Oh—oh, that poor boy!"

Standing beside her now, Ben rested a hand on her shoulder. Until this moment, he realized, he hadn't felt the full impact of Davidar's anguished farewell. Now he felt his knees trying to buckle beneath him.

Irena raised her face. "But he is too frail to go all that way!"

"I know." Ben's fingers sank into her shoulder; he couldn't get a grip on her soft flesh. Her whole body seemed to shift precariously as she turned to stare up at him. Never had her great bulging eyes so unnerved him as they did now, filled with a fright as great as his own.

"Do you remember when he first came to us in Bombay, Maloney?"

Ben shut his eyes tight. "He was all soaked with rain. . . ."

"That intense, musical voice!" Irena's voice sank to a tearful whisper. She clutched Ben's arm. "I—I let him down!"

"We both did, Mulligan."

"I should never have encouraged him to leave his family," she said. "He might have had them to go back to now."

"He wanted you and me to be his family. Us and Sarah."

"We were a good family, for a time—weren't we, Ben?"

"For a time. . . ." His hand still on her shoulder, he lay the cable from Sikkim in front of her. "But Davidar's all right, now. Look, Irena."

She leaned forward, reading the words. She let out a long breath. "Oh—what a relief!"

"I know."

"But will he be—a *monk?*"

"Perhaps he will."

"In any case, he's lost to us, isn't he?"

Ben felt a tremor rise up Irena's back. Then he could stand alone no longer. Wrapping his arms around her neck, he dropped his face to her shoulder and sobbed.

That night, Ben wrote a journal entry directly to Moreya:
Ever since I came to know you in New York, I have believed that

you read what I write in my journals, as Irena told me you did. I'm not so certain of this now. In any case, I realize that I no longer need to share my thoughts with a Master. I used to picture you, in turban and robe, as an exotic, beneficent opposite of all I found wanting in myself. You were an image in a magic mirror, with the power to transform me into a person with greater power than I possessed over myself and—yes, I admit it—over others, as well.

I wanted to play Prospero again as I had as a boy—wrapping myself in a wizard's garments, commanding the spirits of the ether. I wanted the power of the artist to paint pictures in air, to make verses of the bird-songs, to call forth music from the wind. With your help, I believed I could create a life around me more marvelous than any I had dared to imagine before.

It was maya, *illusion. And not-*maya.

Maya: *because I believed you were outside me, leaning down from the Himalayas to put words into my mouth and visions into my mind.*

*Not-*maya: *because you were alive within me—a spirit that inspired me to explore strange worlds in order to discover truths in familiar scenes. Is there magic in this? Yes! I have felt it in my new power to change and seek and create and to trust in what I can only begin to understand.*

For this I thank you, and for this I must continue to live.

And now, I'll no longer write to you, but to myself, and to readers of history. . . .

With Daisy, Ben had finally discovered how to enjoy the companionship of an attainable woman. As he now knew from the Buddha's teachings, one can expect no more from love than what the present moment offers, but he'd learned how to live a lifetime in such a moment.

All Madras was waiting miserably for the heat to be broken by the impending monsoon. Ben saw no reason to wait for love, though. With temperatures soaring above 110 degrees, he postulated that the heat generated by the friction of his and Daisy's bodies—at 98.6 degrees—would actually cool them down. Daisy agreed that it was a scientific experiment worth conducting.

Was there ever an aphrodisiac as potent as human perspiration? Or a sight so enchanting as golden beads of sweat that glow along the lip of a loved one, or shiny wet jewels that rest among the tendrils curling up from adored loins? Did ever a taste so intoxicate lovers as madly as the salty drops that hide in creases of flesh or drip down a nose to mingle with a kiss? Did a perfume ever smell so sweet as the scent of two gleaming, slippery bodies rubbing softly together? As Ben and Daisy frolicked inside the mist of mosquito netting that surrounded their bed, they knew of no happier sights, tastes, smells, sensations.

Later, they drank as much of a pitcher of water as they could hold and Daisy dozed off. Ben strolled to the window where he saw a newspaper-seller on the pavement below. He beckoned to the man to bring up a copy of the evening edition. A half-hour later, Daisy woke to see Ben slumped in a chair, a sheet wrapped around his waist.

"It's over," he said in a ragged whisper.

Daisy rubbed her eyes. "What's over, dear?"

"The wondering what will happen." Walking to the bed, he opened the *Madras Express* to the front page. There it was—the final report from the Society for Psychic Research.

Daisy put on her spectacles. She read down the first page—column after column of detailed descriptions of how Madame Milanova had supposedly deceived Alexandrians with "bogus astral phenomena and other marvels." Finally she looked up. "It couldn't be much worse, Ben."

He sat beside her on the bed. "Yes, it could. As you see, I'm still alive and kicking."

Daisy managed a smile. Then she read aloud: "'As for Madame Milanova's motives, we can only postulate, though this is beyond the scope of our investigation, that she has been working for the secret intelligence service of the government of her native Russia.'" Daisy turned to Ben. "They think she's a spy! Isn't that a bit far-fetched?"

"Well, she's been publishing articles in Moscow newspaper since she arrived in India," he said. "And cabling coded messages to her editor—all very cloak and dagger. She loves that sort of thing."

"Is there anything to it?"

Ben shrugged. "She's made contacts in the Indian nationalist movements. They're probably of some interest to Moscow. But I would think the Russians have better ways to conduct top-secret operations than by depending on a woman who's always getting herself into the papers."

"Still, the British government must be nervous about her being here. D'you think they encouraged the SPR to go after her? That's what my husband thinks—though of course he's all in favor of it."

"It's possible."

Daisy turned to the report's last page. From the street outside came the rumble of a bullock cart. The window curtain swelled, more from waves of heat than any breeze. "'In conclusion,'" she read, "'We regard Madame Milanova as neither the mouthpiece of hidden seers, nor as a mere vulgar adventuress; we think that she has achieved title to permanent remembrance as one of the most accomplished, ingenious, and interesting impostors in history.'" Daisy dropped the paper to her lap. "What a statement! D'you think it will finally force her to leave?"

"I hope so." Ben wiped his face with a handkerchief.

"Poor old girl!" Daisy picked up the paper again. "But at least there's not much in this about you."

"That's because I cooperated with Hodgson. If I hadn't, the report could have wiped out the Society."

"Here's something—'We find that Captain Blackburn, though acting with credulity and inaccuracy of observation, is innocent of any willful deception.'" Daisy sighed. "That's pretty dreadful!"

"It's the best I could get. But it leaves me enough to keep going."

"You don't care if the SPR thinks those things about you?"

"History will judge me by my accomplishments. I know what I am and what I stand for."

"Many others do, too—like me." Daisy rested her hand on his arm. "Everyone who really knows you has great respect and admiration for you."

He kissed her forehead, tasting the saltiness of her skin.

"Thank you, my darling."

For a while, they discussed the future. She was to go on home leave with her family to England. He would be leaving soon on a lecture tour to Burma and Japan. They'd meet again in Madras in two month's time. Now they washed and dressed quietly. After covering herself with talcum powder, Daisy put on her white blouse and maroon skirt and brushed her damp curls in the mirror. She looked like a pretty, plump matron again. Ben wore a dignified Western suit and heavy boots today, looking formidably military to face the worried Alexandrians he knew he'd find back at Banyan. He and Daisy embraced beside the window.

"We won't say good-bye," Daisy whispered in his ear.

"Only *au-revoir*," he said, his lips moving in her hair.

Daisy waved to him from the verandah as he walked out of the hotel into the blazing sunlight. The next time he'd see Daisy, he reflected, many troubles would surely be behind him. Meanwhile, as everyone in Madras had been doing for weeks, he gazed at the sky in search of the monsoon. A few rain clouds seemed to graze the tops of the palm trees at the end of the avenue. Would they ever douse the broiling earth below?

At Banyan, the sunlight fell in slanted rays between the clouds. Occasional murmurings of thunder brought children running out of their huts and tempted Alexandrians to the edge of their verandah to squint up through the trees. The air, shifting in hot waves, was maddeningly empty of the scent of rain.

Arriving in Irena's room, Ben found her pacing and muttering. She'd read the SPR report. Seeing Ben, she collapsed on her bed with a long groan. Her threadbare dressing gown billowed and sank over her. Pulling a chair up to her bedside, Ben rested his palm on her forehead. "Mulligan, you've got a fever."

She raised her head. Her eyes were damp and unfocused. "So, have you been celebrating with Hodgson and your other fellow-conspirators?" she asked in a quavery voice.

"Nonsense—and you know it!"

"Or have you been lapping up your British tart? Does she give jam when you squeeze her?"

"Don't talk like that."

"Yes . . . sorry." She sat up and rubbed her eyes. "You have a right to some fun."

"Damn right I do."

"I suppose she is a very nice woman."

"I like only very nice women." Ben went to the sideboard and poured a glass of water. He put it carefully into her hands and sat down. "I'm sorry about the report. But you must have known what was coming."

She sipped the water and looked at him over the top of the glass. "You warned me. But now you really must represent me in a libel suit."

"You're in no condition to give testimony in a court of law."

"Do you think I would rant and rave and be an embarrassment to the Society?"

Ben watched her face; her resistance was not only weakening, it was little more than a token show of defiance now. "You've read what the report said about your being in collusion with the Russian intelligent service," he said. "At a trial, your enemies would ask you to respond to this accusation, under oath."

"What of it?" Her voice was ragged.

"You'd be required to name names—all your friends, your Indian contacts. They've trusted you to keep their identities secret. Do you want to endanger them?"

Her face fell. She fumbled with her dressing gown, drawing it closer to the folds of flesh beneath her chin. "No," she whispered, wiping her eyes. "I only want to help our Society."

"I know that. . . ." All Ben needed now, he sensed, was to find a way for her to change her position without losing her pride. He leaned forward, taking her face gently in both his hands, and gazed deeply at her. "Look at me now. Look into my eyes. . . ." His voice grew quieter, deeper. "You remember the letters you read from Mrs. Besant and the Alexandrians in London. They invited you there, didn't they?"

"Yes. . . ." Her voice was whispery. Her eyelids began to droop.

"You can picture London, Mulligan. You can see the Alexandrians seated around a parlor there. Brilliant people—poets, professors, and that Indian law student. . . ." He leaned closer to her. Not since Ceylon had such energy stirred in him. He could tell that Irena felt it, too. An expression of calm spread over her face. "You can help them in England," he continued in his soft voice. Overhead, he heard a faint rumble of thunder; the window curtain began to stir. "I see you seated in the center of a circle of important people. You feel everyone watching you, listening to your every word. Journalists are taking notes, publishing respectful articles about you."

"Respectful. . . ."

"Yes. And I see you writing in a quiet room." Ben relaxed his hands on her face. Her chin now rested easily in his palm. "No fevers or enemies distract you from your brilliant new book."

"My book. . . ."

"*The Hidden Wisdom*. You can finish it," Ben said. "It will be an extraordinary accomplishment. Your reputation will ascend again. I see thousands of people reading the book all over Europe. Do you see them, Mulligan?" She nodded slowly. "Generation after generation will read it," he went on. "Into the Twentieth Century and beyond."

"Beyond. . . ." Irena's eyelids fluttered.

"You have a new territory to conquer. Soon you'll begin packing for your great journey to Europe. . . ." Ben removed his hands slowly from Irena's face and sat back in his chair. From outside, he heard the sound of birds flapping expectantly in the nearby palm trees.

Irena sat up, blinking. She looked all over the room—at her desk and books and writing instruments—and finally, at Ben. "I have come to a conclusion," she said, a faint smile appearing on her lips. "I have decided—for the good of the Society—to accept the invitation to go to London."

Ben nodded. "A wise decision."

"Indeed." She wiped her eyes with her bed sheet. It occurred to Ben that she'd left her hypnotic state rather abruptly. Had she truly been in one? He'd never know. "And what," she continued, "do you see in your own future, Maloney?"

Ben pressed his fingertips to his forehead. "I see ships, high seas . . . lectures all over the world."

Irena laughed, a suddenly girlish sound. "Do you remember that opera we saw in New York—*Il Vascello Fantasma?*"

"Yes." Ben smiled. "I remember imagining myself as the Flying Dutchman."

"And I, the woman who redeemed him." Irena rolled her eyes. "Have you been redeemed?"

"Somehow . . . it happened."

"Then you did it yourself." She leaned closer to him, whispering. "You thought I did it. Or the Masters did. But it was always you."

"I know," he whispered back. "Still, I had help."

"Well, of *course* you did—I admit it!"

He moved from the chair and sat beside her on the bed. She relaxed into the pillows behind her. Sunlight from the window ignited the curls at her temples. Her face looked flushed, radiant.

"Europe could be my Alexandrian territory," she said. "Asia could be yours."

"That sounds like a good plan," he said.

"And what about America?"

"They'll know about us there, too. Everyone in America will read your new book."

She smiled at him. "Asia, Europe, and America—" she said, "they will never be the same again!"

Some people believed that the Masters caused the thunderclaps to explode over Madras on the very evening when Irena made her decision to leave India. But whatever precipitated the cloudburst, the rains did suddenly roar down out of the sky, engulfing the city in torrents of cooling water. Sarah was at the school when it started; like her pupils, she stepped outdoors to stand with her arms stretched up to the teeming sky. All over Madras, children dashed out of their huts to stand in the vertical river, soaking it up with shrieks of laughter. Their parents watched from doorways, smiling as the windblown raindrops drenched them, too. In the European quarters, ladies and gentlemen went for carriage rides with canvas tops raised. The cows that roamed the streets lowed and lifted their heads to take in moisture. Everywhere the air smelled fresh, clean, wet. Curtains flapped, tile roofs clicked. Puddles turned to ponds and flowed into wide streams.

The next morning, water covered the roadways. Palm fronds floated down the streets along with the ingeniously constructed toy boats of children. The continual gushing noise of the rain caused people to raise their voices. Everyone sounded as if they were happily trying to sing above an orchestra of instruments that plucked a single note thousands of times each second.

On the following day, the water had risen to the knees of sloshing pedestrians and covered the wheels of bullock carts up to their hubs. Riding with Sarah in a tonga to the steamship office, Ben held tight to his seat as the wheels dipped into hidden ruts. Like everyone else, he was smiling at the weather—feeling completely different than he had during his first monsoon in Bombay. Through the curtain of rain he could barely make out the shapes of the buildings he passed. At the ticket office, some Englishmen regarded him curiously in his drenched Indian shirt, trousers, and broad-brimmed American hat. He presented to the clerk a stack of rupee notes that the members had given him—a hastily raised subscription that was to pay Irena's and Babula's fares to London.

On the morning of Irena's departure, the gardens at Banyan were completely under water, and the paths formed a delta of muddy rivers speckled with floating white petals. Unable to walk with her swollen leg, Irena was carried down her stairs to await transport to the docks. The horses were too skittish in the downpour to pull the closed carriage, so the driver hitched a humpbacked bullock into harness. It waded stolidly through the water, pulling the vehicle over the flooded lawn to the edge of the verandah. There Sarah and several members lifted Irena onto the seat. She was dressed in all her splendor today, with a dazzling red cape over one of her sky-blue blouses, and a long, dark gypsy skirt tucked around her ankles. She carried her blue umbrella.

Babula, too, was dressed in his finest outfit—tight trousers, pink jacket and matching turban. He leapt into the carriage beside her. Sarah's green dress was already drenched, but the air was warm and she didn't mind. Ben helped her into the carriage, then ducked under the canvas top to take a seat facing Irena. The

Society members lined the mansion's lower verandah, waving and shouting their farewells. Many kisses were thrown; much luck and good fortune were wished. Bouquets were passed into the carriage until the floor and everyone's knees were covered with bright flowers. The driver shouted and snapped the reins, and the carriage lurched forward into the deluge.

"We should have engaged a boat, Mulligan," Ben shouted.

Irena gazed at the bullock. "I hope that beast can swim!"

Babula helped her open her umbrella. "Is there a monsoon in Europe?" he asked.

"There are wonders there beyond imagining." She took the umbrella, but a gust of wind nearly snatched it away and she had to fold it in her lap.

In the city, Sarah watched shapes of trees and buildings loom out of the rain and vanish again. Occasionally a figure dashed through the storm, clutching a panicked chicken or a laughing child. At the harbor, the surf pounded the docks, sending up explosions of spray. Water sloshed from the pilings all the way into the steamship office, and the rain clattered on the tin roof overhead. Ben, looking somewhat military in a new cotton jacket and loose white trousers, smoked his pipe. Finally the storm subsided a little. Sitting by the window, Ben and Irena, Babula and Sarah watched the steamer approach like a great looming shadow riding the water. Its smokestacks belched white clouds that immediately were scattered by needles of rain. Breakers slid away from its hull to crash against the sand.

The clerk gave the signal to get ready to board the pilot boat.

"Good-bye, my dear." Irena, still seated, turned to Sarah, her arms going around her neck.

Sarah hugged her back "Good-bye, Madame. . . ."

"If Davidar comes back, give him my love," Irena said to her.

"I will." Sarah blinked hard.

Irena and Ben rose together.

"When—" Ben cleared his throat "—when you finish your new book. . . ."

"I will mail you a copy," Irena said, holding his arm, "wherever you are."

"I'll always come back to Banyan. It's my home now."

"It is the best home we ever had," Irena said, and wiped her eyes.

Three burly dockhands in *dhotis* and turbans were waiting for her just outside on the wharf. Ben had ordered an invalid's chair, and now a man rolled it up—a heavy contraption of metal and wicker with spoked wheels. The dockhands lifted Irena into it. Ben wheeled her toward the doorway. Sarah walked beside him while Babula ran ahead. Outside, Irena adjusted her scarlet cape around her shoulders. The palm trees along the beach somehow kept their ragged heads up through the heavy mist. Sea gulls glided over the waves, their squawks careening through the roar of the surf.

"Do you remember when we arrived from America?" Ben leaned close to Irena's ear.

Irena nodded, her hair brushing his nose. "I remember everything." She raised her face to him. "But now I am looking ahead, not back."

"So am I." Leaning down, Ben wrapped his arm around her shoulders. Touching her cheek with his lips, he tasted the salt of her tears.

"Give me a real kiss, old chum!" Irena said.

And he did, his lips pressed to hers as the raindrops streamed down their faces.

It was time, Ben thought, for Moreya to leave Madras as well. To the Himalayas? Europe? America? Wherever he was needed—to prepare the way for future generations of enlightenment-seekers, many of them inspired by the books of Irena Milanova.

A crowd gathered to watch Irena's ascension; such a feat of engineering hadn't been seen here before. Many of the onlookers were children attracted by the sight of the steamer's tall steel crane whose arm was poised to reach out over the waves. As Ben wheeled Irena onto the deck of a small pilot boat, she waved at the crowd, her heart gladdened that a farewell party had appeared for the historic occasion.

Leaving Irena on the pilot boat, Ben returned to the wharf to stand beside Sarah in the office doorway. Irena's little boat splashed through the waves to the steamer. Babula clambered up a rope ladder that was lowered down the ship's hull.

From the steamship's top deck the crane's long arm swung out over the boat and dropped a chain and hook. Additional hemp ropes were lowered to the waiting sailors, who tied Irena's chair so elaborately that it looked like a makeshift cage for transporting a circus animal. Irena parted the ropes so that she could see out. There was room inside for her to open her umbrella, which she did, though it scarcely deflected the ocean spray.

The crane's engine gave out a fast trembling sound like the flutter of gigantic angels' wings. The chain rattled and went taut. Slowly Irena rose above the waves. Up and up she soared. Her cape made a spot of bright red against the misty silver backdrop of clouds. Now, swinging majestically in the air, seemingly about to enter the clouds themselves, she ascended high above the steamship's deck.

Her face was turned away from him now. Ben whispered, "Turn around!" And he believed that she must have made the same plea, hoping to influence the movement of the wind—for just as her chair paused to descend to the top deck, she was twirled around to face the wharf, her cape flapping in the wind.

She leaned out through the ropes toward him, holding her umbrella over her. Suddenly it flew from her hand. Was it snatched by the wind, or purposely released? Ben would never know. Caught by an updraft, the blue umbrella was swept high into the air above the ship's smokestacks. Up and up it rose—and perhaps Moreya with it, pitching and bobbing as he directed its flight above the city's rooftops and out over the bay.

Ben could see Irena laughing as she pointed at it. They waved to each other one last time. Then, raising their faces to the sky, they searched the clouds for the elusive speck of blue.

Afterword

Spiritualism, the conviction that that the dead are able to contact living people from an afterworld, is an ancient belief found all over the world. In the United States, it gained popularity in the 1840s, when a pair of young sisters in the Fox family of Hydesville, New York, attracted attention to their séances, where they reportedly summoned invisible beings who communicated to them via coded rappings on a table in their darkened parlor. Soon séances were being held all over the country. Some became theatrical, a form of popular entertainment, but most were small, somber affairs in which spirit guests were said to speak to their living relatives in soft voices or leave messages scribbled on slates in the dark. Séances always involved mediums, men or—more often—women who reputedly had special powers to communicate with the next world. Often the mediums entered trance states and afterwards had only blurry memories of what had occurred. Some, like the famous Poughkeepsie seer Andrew Jackson Davis, wrote volumes of erudite philosophy, reportedly dictated to him from beings in the Other World while he was in trance states.

As soon as Spiritualism became a popular belief, it became controversial, and after nearly every "miracle" reported in the press an investigation would follow during which some expert would report that the medium was grossly fraudulent and another pundit would announce that she or he was utterly genuine. Photographs were taken of spirit visitors, who appeared as white, vaguely human shaped blobs of "ectoplasm" or as disembodied faces floating among images of living people. (Photography was a new invention, and few knew how easy it was to doctor prints in a darkroom.) A group of learned men in England, to which the movement had spread, formed the Society for Psychical Research, which used the latest scientific methods to test the practices of mediums.

Spiritualism gained more popularity after the American Civil War, when survivors tried desperately to contact family members who had been taken from them. The mid and late Nineteenth Century was an era of breakaway churches and utopian communes. People wanted to find their own ways of communicating with the supernatural without the rituals of old established churches, which many thought no longer served their needs. The theories of Charles Darwin threatened religious beliefs, postulating that God did not create human life in seven days, as the Bible said. New scientific discoveries and technological advances, it seemed, were draining life of its spiritual meaning. The Spiritualist Movement offered ordinary people an opportunity to prove to themselves that men and women possessed immortal souls. It also offered women a chance to become community leaders, attracting the citizenry with their spiritual powers and organizational skills.

One such woman was Madame Helena Petrovna Blavatsky, a Russian-born mystic and scholar who debunked other mediums as she used her considerable intellectual gifts to rise to the top of the Spiritualist hierarchy. In 1874, together with her partner, Colonel Henry Steel Olcott, an attorney and a popular journalist, she founded the American Theosophical Society in New York, which attracted many of the leading thinkers and celebrities of the age. When scandals cast doubts about the couple's activities, Madame Blavatsky and Colonel Olcott reestablished the Society in India and Ceylon, where they had considerable success spreading its ideas. They continued to absorb into its doctrines the ancient wisdom of Sufiism, Buddhism, and Hinduism. Both Madame Blavatsky and Colonel Olcott wrote popular magazine articles and books, which helped spread the word to Europe and America, while they sought confirmation of occult beliefs in the East. In 1886, when the partners parted ways, Mme. Blavatsky returned to Europe, again under a cloud of scandal, but regained her reputation in London, where she attracted such luminaries as Annie Besant, W.B. Yates, and the young Mohandas P. Gandhi to her Theosophical gatherings. Colonel Olcott spent the next two decades lecturing all over the world. The Society today has branches in over fifty countries; the books written by its founders have outlasted the hundreds of "exposés" written about them over the past 130 years. Spiritualism has survived as well, reshaped in eclectic New Age beliefs and in widespread Christian assemblies that still offer opportunities to contact the souls of the deceased and learn from their wisdom.

Though *Shadows and Elephants* is a work of fiction, parts of it are loosely based on some of the events that occurred in the lives of Colonel Olcott and Madame Blavatsky. With the exception of people whose names are well known, such as Thomas Edison, Abner Doubleday, and a few other others, I have changed the names of historical figures and invented several characters of my own. I have made up a great many events, as well. As the novel progressed through drafts, its two central characters became fictional inventions, and neither of them are intended in any way to represent actual historical figures. In other respects, I have attempted to portray the locales and the times as accurately as possible.

Acknowledgments

Some published information about the Theosophical Society's history was useful to me as background material. I thank the officers, staff, and members at the Theosophical Society Headquarters in Colombo, Sri Lanka, and in Adyar, Madras, India, for access to their materials. During my month in residence at Adyar, I was permitted use of the society's library and part of the society's archives, including the thirty-three volumes of Mme. Blavatsky's scrapbooks, which she compiled from contemporary newspaper and magazine clippings. I was not given access to the journals of Colonel Olcott or any unpublished materials; all journal entries and articles ostensibly written by the novel's characters have been wholly invented by me. Two sentences from reviews of my character's book are closely paraphrased from contemporary newspaper sources, as are three sentences in my account of Baron Von Palme's funerary rites. None of the material in the novel has been vetted or approved by the Thesophical Society.

Madame Blavatsky's two philosophical texts, *Isis Unveiled* and *The Secret Doctrine*, provided some ideas, as did her travel journalism collected in *From the Caves and Jungles of Hindostan: 1883-86.* Some of her letters (two sentences of which I paraphrased in the novel) are published in *H.P.B. Speaks*, edited by C. Jinarajadasa. The first three volumes of *Old Diary Leaves*, an autobiography-cum-history written by Henry S. Olcott, were useful. Two of the many biographies of Mme. Blavatsky I found helpful were *HPB: The Extraordinary Life and Influence of Helena*

Blavatsky, Founder of the Modern Theosophical Movement, by Sylvia Cranston (a text highly favored by the Theosophical Society today), and *Madame Blavatsky*, by Marion Meade (a book not in favor with the Society). I paraphrased two sentences from the still-controversial report on Mme. Blavatsky by the British Society for Psychical Research. Two biographies of Colonel Olcott provided some ideas for the novel: *Yankee Beacon of Buddhist Light: Life of Col. Henry S. Olcott*, by Howard Murphet, and *The White Buddhist: The Asian Odyssey of Henry Steel Olcott*, by Stephen Prothero. *Net of Magic: Wonders and Deceptions in India*, by Lee Siegel, was a source of information on magicians. K. Paul Johnson's history, *The Masters Revealed: Madame Blavatsky and the Myth of the Great White Lodge*, also provided background material. The best material of all, of course, came from getting to know the people of India and Sri Lanka during my stays there over a period of twelve years.

I wish to thank the Virginia Center for the Creative Arts for two residencies that allowed me to work on this book. The Fulbright program, which offered me teaching and academic research positions for two years in India, was also an invaluable sponsor. Organizations like these, public and private, merit the support of all who care about the arts and humanities.

For their generous hospitality in India and Sri Lanka, I thank Tim and Maureen Murari, Anuj and Jane Millicans, Keith and Pauline Gomez and all the family, Jim Moore and Richard Reedy, Mrs. M. K. Mukerjee, A. Deveraj, C. Elongo, Michael Joseph, Daya and Francine Krishna, Vivian and Coral and Maya de Thabrew, Arun Joshi and Dr. O.P. Joshi, and all my colleagues and students at the University of Rajasthan and at Loyola College, Madras.

My thanks also to Ira Wood and Marge Piercy of Leapfrog Press, for their invaluable editorial work and encouragement.

I'm grateful to Wesley Gibson and K. Paul Johnson for their useful suggestions about my manuscript.

And I'm especially thankful to my wife, Alison Lurie, for her insightful, sensitive readings of the novel and for her patience with its author.

About the Author

EDWARD HOWER is the author of four previous novels as well as a book of folk tales, *The Pomegranate Princess*, which he collected while on two Fulbright grants in India. His writing has appeared in *The New York Times*, *Atlantic Monthly*, *Southern Review*, *Epoch*, *Transatlantic Review*, *Smithsonian*, and elsewhere. He has been been awarded creative writing grants from the New York State Council on the Arts, The Ingram Merrill Foundation, and the National Endowment for the Arts.